HANGMAN'S
GAME

HANGMAN'S GAME

BILL SYKEN

MINOTAUR BOOKS

A Thomas Dunne Book

New York

A THOMAS DUNNE BOOK FOR MINOTAUR BOOKS.
An imprint of St. Martin's Publishing Group.

HANGMAN'S GAME. Copyright © 2015 by Bill Syken. All rights reserved. Printed in the United States of America. For information, address St. Martin's Press, 175 Fifth Avenue, New York, N.Y. 10010.

www.thomasdunnebooks.com
www.minotaurbooks.com

Designed by Steven Seighman

The Library of Congress Cataloging-in-Publication Data.

Syken, Bill.
    Hangman's game : a Nick Gallow mystery / Bill Syken. — First edition.
        p. cm.
    ISBN 978-1-250-06715-9 (hardcover)
    ISBN 978-1-4668-7511-1 (e-book)
  1. Football players—Fiction. 2. Murder—Investigation—Fiction.
3. Sports stories. I. Title.
    PS3619.Y52H36 2015
    813'.6—dc23

                                                          2015017159

Minotaur books may be purchased for educational, business, or promotional use. For information on bulk purchases, please contact the Macmillan Corporate and Premium Sales Department at 1-800-221-7945, extension 5442, or write to specialmarkets@macmillan.com.

First Edition: August 2015

10 9 8 7 6 5 4 3 2 1

To my parents and my brother, for their constant support and also for their reading recommendations

How often have miscarriages of justice been overturned because some punter wouldn't stop digging?

—VAL MCDERMID, *THE DISTANT ECHO*

HANGMAN'S
GAME

CHAPTER 1

I FIGURED IT OUT ONCE. I calculated the time I spend actually performing the task that gives my job its title, and it came out to fifty-one minutes per year. Not even an hour. And that calculation is generous, believe me. The total grows if I include practices, but still, that leaves me with a lot of anticipation to chew through.

Tonight—it is early June, and warm—I am wearing my one and only suit, which is black and made to measure, and I stand outside of the Jefferson, a short-term residential apartment building that's been my home for the last five years. My dinner companions are running a couple of minutes late, but I am handling the wait like the pro that I am.

Soon enough, the Jefferson's doors hiss open, and out shuffles a towering black man in a red clinging workout shirt, baggy jeans, and sneakers. Though we have never met, I have seen enough news footage to recognize him as one of the men I am dining with tonight, Samuel Sault. The newest, richest member of my team, the Philadelphia Sentinels, has short-cropped hair and a neatly trimmed goatee, a wide mouth that is slightly downturned, and eyes set far enough apart that I wonder if he has more peripheral vision than your average human. He is as tall as advertised, at six foot seven, though he looks so thin that I immediately assume his listed weight of 301 pounds is a media-guide fiction. I wonder if this skinny pass rusher isn't a waste of the second-overall pick, the latest mistake of our foundering franchise.

Samuel is also staying at the Jefferson, directed here by our mutual agent and the third member of our dinner party, Cecil Wilson. Although I imagine Samuel's tenancy will end as soon as he finds a mansion that he deems worthy of slicing off a chunk of his $12 million signing bonus. I've stayed at the Jefferson entirely out of superstition—I took a fully furnished room here when I surprised everyone, including myself, by making the Sentinels as a rookie free agent, and I continue to stay here because I am absolutely sure that the moment I buy a home or sign a long-term lease, the Sentinels will cut me.

I raise a hand, which Samuel ignores as he goes to a spot a few yards down from me on the Jefferson's semicircle drive-way and stands, eyes down and arms folded. I study him for a moment and see that he's more sleek than skinny, really. Most players his weight have a certain puff to their muscula-ture, but Samuel's torso is flat as a fashion model's. He is broad in the upper body, with bulk packed into his shoulders and upper arms—it looks like he has ham hocks stuffed into his sleeves. Maybe that listed weight of 301 is more honest than I thought. The jeans he is wearing are of a loose cut, and could be concealing a disproportionately large butt and thighs. In football, it's all about the butt. I have never once looked around the locker room and seen a narrow ass.

"Samuel?" I say, walking over to him. He looks up and briefly meets my eyes and then looks down again, without answering. Perhaps he is assuming that I am an autograph seeker.

"I'm Nick Gallow," I say. "We're having dinner together." He turns toward me, surprised. "I'm a client of Cecil's, too," I add. "I'm the Sentinels' punter."

"Hey," he says, with a slim smile and brief raise of the eyebrows. He then goes back to staring at the ground, except now he is bobbing his head nervously.

From news stories I know the basics of Samuel's background: that he grew up in rural Alabama and lived with his parents through college, shunning offers from bigger schools to live at home and attend the nearby Western Alabama A&M, which is a historically black college. In these stories, all encomiums to country humility, Samuel's quotes had been sparing and few.

Samuel's head-bobbing is so odd that I wonder for a moment if he is not just shy, but autistic. Or maybe he has Asperger's. Or something. It is all too easy to imagine how a "slow learner" with Samuel's physical gifts might glide through college, especially at a small school that would have believed itself blessed to host such a rare talent.

Or it may just be that Samuel is feeling overwhelmed. Yesterday he signed his contract, and this morning he was hailed as a team savior on the front pages of both the *Inquirer* and *Daily News*. And he would have seen the *Inquirer*, at least, because the Jefferson slides the paper under the door of its guests every morning.

"I'm glad you're here," I say to Samuel. "I'm looking forward to playing with you."

Samuel nods, eyes still trained on the pavement, showing no interest in grabbing on to the simplest of conversational lifelines. He looks so cowered that it is hard to believe that he is the same person the press has dubbed "Samuel Assault" for his ability to inflict pain. During his three years in college, he injured eleven quarterbacks, knocking them out of games with broken arms and collarbones, torn knee ligaments, ruptured spleens, and concussions.

As the two of us stand there waiting, residents flow into

the Jefferson, almost all of them turning to gawk at this colossal young man as they pass.

At last, Cecil pulls into the driveway, driving a rented black Escalade. Usually I see him in a Ford Focus.

A portly man with shaggy black hair, moony dark eyes, and a not-quite-walrus mustache, Cecil managed a hardware store before switching careers and becoming a football agent six years ago. I was his first client, and for a few years his only one.

Cecil shakes hands with Samuel—which I note because Cecil and I have always hugged. "How you doing, buddy?" he says to Samuel. "Have you met Nick?"

"Yeah," says Samuel quietly. Even in familiar company, Samuel shows an unusual amount of diffidence, especially considering he is a twenty-one-year-old multimillionaire.

Cecil shakes my hand, too. "Love the suit, Nick!" he says.

"Love the car," I answer. "What are you listening to in there? 50 Cent? Cee Lo?"

"Trisha Yearwood," he says, scratching the back of his neck. As he scratches, the sleeve of his suit jacket pulls back to reveal a gold watch with a black leather band. That is new.

"So how obsessed are you with Woodward Tolley right now?" Cecil asks me with a grin. Woodward Tolley is a rookie free agent punter that the Sentinels signed last week to compete with me for a roster spot. Cecil's smile is meant to show he's not concerned with this threat to my job. Of course now that he has Samuel, my revenue stream is something he can afford to joke about.

"Trying not to think about him too much," I say.

"And how's that going?" Cecil laughs. When I don't join in, he pats me on the elbow and adds "C'mon, you can handle that kid in your sleep." Cecil then turns to Samuel and asks, "So where would you guys like to eat?"

Samuel shrugs with indifference.

"Nick, you choose," Cecil says. "You're the local."

"Let me think," I say. Rittenhouse Square, on which the Jefferson stands, has a high-end restaurant that serves hundred-dollar Kobe beef cheesesteaks, but I don't want to endorse that sort of absurdity. We could head toward Northern Liberties, a neighborhood where new and interesting restaurants are popping up all the time. But then Cecil isn't a guy who likes his food interesting, and Samuel probably isn't, either. We also need a place where my suit and Samuel's workout shirt will be equally appropriate.

"Let's go to Stark's," I say. Stark's feels like a safe choice for an evening that already seems like it could use some help. Stark's is a steakhouse, and a popular players' hangout. I almost never go there, but it is staffed by young and agreeable waitresses who reportedly do everything they can to make Sentinel players feel welcome.

I am riding in the backseat when an e-mail pops up on my phone. It is from someone I've never met, and whose acquaintance I have no interest in making. It is my girlfriend Jessica's husband.

Hello, Nick. This is Dan Steagall, Jessica's husband. I would like to invite you to our house for dinner. Jessica has told me wonderful things about you, and I would appreciate the chance to get to know you. I am away this week and part of next, but just name a date after that, and we'll make it happen. Do you like lamb? I cook a mean lamb. Thanks.

I feel caught. The e-mail's benign language suggests that he believes Jessica and I are merely friends, but I can't help but be concerned. Dan works at the Philadelphia branch of the Federal Reserve, and he has a hand in the managing of our nation's economy. I have seen photos of him, and he is physically slight, certainly not the sort to challenge me to a duel. But I imagine he would seek revenge in some form if he learned exactly how Jessica and I spend our time together. Yesterday afternoon, for instance, she and I had engaged in yet another one of our role-playing games. These games had many variations, except that my character was always named Troy. Yesterday I was Troy the organic turnip farmer, who valiantly peddled his produce door-to-door because Big Grocery wouldn't give him a break. Troy was so weary, so misunderstood, and so in need of love . . .

"Hey, Samuel," says Cecil. "Did you have a chance to get to the Franklin Institute and walk through their big human heart?"

"Nah," Samuel says. "Didn't feel like it."

Dan's invitation has come at a time when I really don't need the distraction. The Sentinels have a minicamp in a few days, and I will be going against my new competition, this Woodward Tolley. I need to focus on him, not Jessica's husband.

Without replying, I forward Dan's message to Jessica with the comment *WTF?*

Jessica must have slipped up somehow, is all I can figure. Jessica is intelligent, but also restless. She is a painter, but not the kind that tries to sell her work. I have always seen her ennui as our primary vulnerability to being caught. The third or fourth time we were together I actually said to her, as we lay in bed, "You should try to keep yourself a little more busy.

I don't want you to let your husband catch us just because it's Wednesday and you're bored."

"But if I weren't so bored, my darling," she answered me, stroking my neck, "what would I be doing with you?"

Stark's Steakhouse is situated not far from the Delaware River, in an area where the urban grid opens up. The building is a low-slung gray rectangle with the restaurant's name written on its upper left corner in neon red script. Stark's is upscale, but it is not intimate. They do a volume business. The place has an expansive parking lot, which is nearly full when we arrive. We park off to the left, and we have a good forty-yard walk to the entrance.

The Stark's lobby is defined by its wall of fame, featuring autographed eight-by-tens of the players who have eaten here over the decades. The photos tilt heavily toward stars of the sixties and seventies, and many of the photos are in the goofy style of the old football publicity stills—men in buzz cuts leaping or charging in front of empty bleachers. The pictures aren't just of Sentinels, either; the wall features players from around the league who visited when they were in town for a road game.

The restaurant is busy, with the tables full in the lower tier and many well-dressed men, mostly in their thirties and forties, hovering near the bar.

It is then that I notice Jai Carson, the Sentinels' star linebacker, in the restaurant's upper tier, which is reserved for VIPs—which, here, usually means athletes. Jai is wearing an electric-blue tracksuit, and he seems to be in typically high spirits. He is on his feet with a cocktail in his hand, entertaining friends with a bawdy story. Though I can't actually hear what he is saying, I feel confident that Jai's story is bawdy because he appears to be pantomiming a sex act, thrusting his crotch as he holds on to an imaginary pair of hips.

Perhaps anticipating such antics, the maître d' has seated Jai and his crew in a deep corner of the upper tier.

Jai's dining companions include only one Sentinel that I can see—his best friend on the team, Orlando Byrd, the 342-pound defensive tackle who goes by the nickname Too Big to Fail. The other guys at the table come from Jai's private stock of friends, buddies from his hometown of Memphis that I have often seen milling around the locker room.

Jai concludes his story with a broad slapping gesture that is greeted with whoops of laughter—the loudest being his own. He spins in a 360, a giddy pirouette, and as he settles down, he notices us. And by us, I mean Samuel. His eyes light up, and his arms open wide.

"Fuck me!" Jai shouts across the dining room. "There's a beast in the house!"

Jai hops down the couple of steps and charges across the main dining floor and throws his arms around Samuel, who has watched Jai's approach with something other than anticipation. On contact with Jai, he flinches.

"Shit, rookie," Jai says, stepping back, taking in Samuel's size. "You stacked up!"

Samuel does loom over Jai, his chin level with the linebacker's tapered eyebrows. Even though Samuel is maybe fifty pounds heavier than Jai, he is the leaner of the two. Throw in a couple other physical details—like Samuel's straight and firm hairline compared to Jai's shiny dome, shaved to mask male pattern baldness—and it is hard not to look at the two defensive players and see Jai as the old model and Samuel as the new and improved version.

"Hi, I'm Cecil Wilson, Samuel's agent," Cecil says, hand extended to Jai.

"Cecil Wilson, congratulations!" says Jai, shaking his hand energetically. "You got your boy signed quick, didn't you? I bet the bosses love you."

The last line, though delivered in a friendly enough tone, is not a compliment. Cecil has in fact been getting ripped on football message boards for having Samuel agree to a contract in June, at least a month earlier than is typical for top rookies. The critics argue that Samuel could have received more money if he waited until August, when full training camps convene. The agent for the player chosen third overall publicly proclaimed that he was going to be seeking more money for his client than Samuel received, because "he was not going to let the market be set by a neophyte."

If Cecil notices the backhandedness of Jai's compliment, he betrays no sign of offense, and Jai now turns to me with blank expectation. He seems to be waiting for an introduction.

He doesn't know who I am.

Unbelievable. As a punter, I am used to slights to my ego— casual insinuations that I am not a real player, not actually part of the team. But if Jai doesn't recognize me, after five years in the same locker room, this will top them all. Times ten.

"Hello, Jai," I say evenly.

"Hey, man," he says, extending his hand to me as if he is doing a corporate appearance, and I am the salesman of the month. "Good to see you." With no indication whatsoever that he knows we are teammates, Jai turns his attention back to silent Samuel, who still has not said a word.

"I can't wait to see you and Samuel on the field together,"

Cecil says, rubbing his hands together with pronounced eagerness. "Who are they going to double-team? They won't know what to do!"

"You know it," Jai says. "Samuel and JC are going to fuck some major ass together. I bet there's quarterbacks at home right now clinching their buttholes up tight just thinking about it!"

This is Jai as he ever is, continuously and joyously profane. Samuel's jaw clenches and his posture rises—I am guessing this is different from the dinnertime chatter back home with his parents—and his eyes zero in on Jai's necklace, which asks in shimmering rhinestone lettering: WANT TO?

Samuel's silence is making Jai uneasy. His eyes dart, searching for signs of appreciation. No showman likes a mute audience.

Jai then asks Samuel a question he shouldn't ask, one that a more cautious person might have swallowed, understanding that the wrong answer would create unspeakable discomfort:

"You do know who JC is, right?"

Jai Carson's personal mission over the last decade has been to get his face on as many television programs, talk shows, magazine covers, video game boxes, and roadside billboards as he could. He recorded his own CD, *Sack Dance*, starred in a reality dating show, and he also has a line of JC earrings. Hell, he has even been on *The View*. There could be no bigger insult for Jai from anyone, let alone a rookie on his own defense, than to say: I don't recognize you.

In response to Jai's question, Samuel scans the dining room, as if he is looking for the "JC" that this boorish and insistent stranger is talking about. For all the awkwardness of

the moment, I smile inwardly. Jai is paying the price for referring to himself in the third person.

"Samuel comes from a poor family," Cecil says, placing
his hand on Samuel's shoulder. "Very poor. They don't have
television. And he lived at home all through college. So he's
kind of a TV illiterate." Given Samuel's muteness, the word
illiterate lingers uncomfortably in the air. "At the draft, Samuel didn't know who Chris Berman is," he adds with a nervous chuckle.

Jai considers this explanation, and though I am sure he
believes himself to be a bigger deal than any ESPN broad-
caster, he makes an effort to appear placated by Cecil's words.

"That's cool, that's cool," Jai says. "I know about being
poor. When I was growing up, all I could afford to eat was
pussy."

Jai laughs at his joke, as do Cecil and I. Samuel's nervous
smile could, I suppose, pass for an appreciative response.

At this point, the Stark's hostess inserts herself into our
group. She looks to be in her mid-thirties, which is old enough
to qualify her as the den mother of the restaurant's young
female staff.

"Good evening," she says. "Are you all joining Mr. Carson's
party? We can pull up another table."

"Let's do it," Jai says. "I know there's a lot of ugly motherfuckers in my group, but these are quality people." He shouts
across the restaurant, "Hey, Cheat Sheet. Stand up!"

The man who rises from Jai's table is maybe five foot six,
skinny, and wearing a bright purple jacket with an orange
shirt and pants. He smiles, flashing a full grille of gleaming
gold.

"He's my pastor," Jai says.

Somehow I don't think the presence of that particular pastor will appeal to Samuel's country values. But still, we need to accept this invitation, before this potential rift between the defense's veteran leader and its high-priced rookie opens any wider.

"Let's . . ." I start.

"No."

Samuel says this quietly and firmly while looking at Cecil.

"I see a table over there," Samuel mutters, and begins walking into the dining area—not toward the players' section but to an empty table on the far side of the regular dining room. The hostess grabs three menus and runs out in front of Samuel, attempting to gain control of the expedition.

Up to this point, I have been feeling sorry for shy, sheltered Samuel, but his refusal is unmistakably rude.

"Well, fuck me," Jai says, mystified. Then, angrier: "Fuck me!" For Jai, the phrase is like "Aloha" or "Shalom," in that it carries many different meanings, dependent on situation and inflection.

I wish I could tell you that I have never seen anything like this, a simple disagreement that quickly escalates into high-grade hostility, but football is populated by thin-skinned competitors who see every conflict as an urgent test of their manhood. That's great when it's fourth-and-goal on the one; less so when you want a peaceable dinner.

"Later, buddy," I say to Jai with a shrug, and I hold out my fist for a bump. He looks at me dubiously before returning my bump with a shot that bears an uncomfortable resemblance to a punch.

At our table, the three of us study our menus quietly. "Porterhouse or rib eye, the eternal question," Cecil says with forced jollity. I wonder if Cecil is thinking about what a disaster that was. I certainly am. Just as a nation divided against itself cannot stand, a locker room divided against itself cannot win. Between Jai's ego and Samuel's reticence, it is not clear who will initiate peace talks.

Soon we are greeted by our waitress, who is quite a sight. I would guess that she is in her early 20s. Like all the waitstaff, she wears a pale pink dress shirt and a short black skirt. She has blond hair that she wears tied up on top, feline green eyes, and round, freckled cheeks. She is the shortest girl on the floor, which accentuates that she is also the most buxom, the lone girl here whose curves dominate her straightaways.

"Howdy," she says with a broad grin. "I'm Melody."

"Howdy," I say. "I'm Nick." And then I introduce Cecil and Samuel.

"Are you Samuel Sault?" Melody asks Samuel, eyes wide.

"Yes," Samuel says quietly. And that is all he says. Though he is making strong eye contact with her breasts.

After a decent interval of silence, Melody taps pen on pad and asks for our order.

"I'll have the rib eye," Cecil says. "Medium rare. With creamed spinach and mashed potatoes."

"Excellent," she says, and turns to Samuel. "How about you, big fella?"

"Same," Samuel says.

"Very well. And you, sir?"

"I'll have the broiled salmon," I say. "And for side dishes—the broccoli, can they steam that?" I ask.

"I think so, but I'll check. You get a second side as well."

"Just the steamed broccoli will be fine."

"And what if they can't steam the broccoli?"

"Then no sides for me."

"Really?" She eyes me curiously. "You have a beauty pageant coming up or something?"

Cecil snickers. "Every day, miss. Every day."

"For your drink, let me guess . . . club soda with lemon," Melody says. "Am I right?"

That is exactly what I was going to order, but I suddenly don't want to admit that.

"Lime, actually."

"You really wanted lemon, right?" she says with a grin. "You're saying 'lime' to fuck with me?"

"Fine," I say. "Lemon." Maybe it's because I'm in need of a distraction, but this waitress's sauciness feels entirely welcome. I check her left hand to make sure this one doesn't have a husband. The ring finger is clean.

"Anyone ever call you Mel?" I ask her. '

"Not if they want me to answer," she says with a chuckle. "Mel-o-dee. Three syllables. Trust me, I'm worth the effort." She winks and walks away.

Samuel unabashedly eyes Melody as she goes. He smiles boyishly, his eyes relax, and I see that he is handsome when he's happy. His teeth are a little here and there, but in a sweet sort of way. I can picture that smile in an aftershave commercial, or on the cover of *GQ*, if he wants to make that happen.

Samuel excuses himself to go to the bathroom. When he is out of earshot, I say to Cecil,, "He's not the most loquacious fellow, is he?"

"He's a good kid," Cecil snaps. "He's just out of his element. You should see where he grew up. It's like they got indoor plumbing a few weeks ago. He's in shock just being here."

"If you say so," I say. I grew up in a small town, too, though I only came to Philadelphia from Upstate New York, and I had always wanted to live in a city, whereas Samuel seems to have been forcibly relocated here by the magnitude of his talent. And when I arrived in Philadelphia, none of the locals knew who I was, and none of them were counting on me to make their Sundays happier ones.

"Samuel is going to need help," Cecil says. "I need you to look out for him in the locker room, and keep him on the right track. Can you do that for me?"

I don't really think I can help much—Cecil may be overrating my influence—but I owe Cecil my best effort, seeing as I wouldn't be a Sentinel without him. I came from a small school and had only punted for one season in college, and I wouldn't have drawn a single invitation to a training camp without his aggressive campaigning on my behalf. He was the only agent who even thought I was worth representing. We made it here together. "Mr. Wilson," I say. "I'll do everything I can."

Samuel is now walking back from the men's room, moving quietly but more erect, without the diminishing shoulder slouch from earlier in the evening. I look across the restaurant and see that Jai is staring at Samuel predatorily, tracking his movements. All the guys at Jai's table are doing the same. Even from this distance I see a distinct malice in their gaze.

Samuel, oblivious to the eyes upon him, arrives at the table with an amused smile. "They have a picture of me in the john," he says. Stark's posts the sports page on a tack board stationed above the urinal, so guys can read while they pee. Today's headline, if I recall correctly, is "Can Sault Save the Sentinels' Defense?"

Jai has no doubt read that story as well—and given that he considers himself the soul of our defense, he surely did not care for the implication that it needs to be saved.

I know how on edge I have been the last few days, simply because the team signed Woodward Tolley to compete for my job. While Jai's job is not threatened by Samuel's arrival, his status as alpha dog certainly is.

"Maybe we should order a bottle for Jai's table," I say.

"Good idea," Cecil says. "I'll take care of it when the waitress returns with our food."

A few minutes later Melody is back with their steaks and my salmon.

"Hi, sweet thing."

This is Samuel, greeting Melody as she places food in front of him. Great.

"Where are you from, Samuel?" Melody asks eagerly. If she can recognize Samuel, the details of his contract—$64 million with a $12 million bonus and $30 million guaranteed— are likely embedded in her frontal lobe.

"Alabama, ma'am," Samuel says. "Vickers, Alabama."

"Really," she says. "Welcome to the big city. And just to let you know, those red and green things you see hanging in the middle of the street? They're traffic lights."

Samuel titters and then goes silent. Melody waits with professional patience for the next beat in the conversation. Meanwhile, steaks in the kitchen go from medium to well.

"Miss, I have a request," Cecil interposes. "Please send a bottle of champagne to Jai Carson's table. Cristal if you have it." Look at Cecil, name-checking champagne brands. "Tell them it's from Samuel."

"I'll get on it right away," Melody says, placing her hand on Samuel's shoulder. "They'll be very impressed."

She walks to the back, without having looked at me once.

As I fork my way through my salmon and steamed broccoli, I glance back and forth between the kitchen and Jai's

table, hoping to see Melody return with the champagne before Jai and his friends leave. I can see Jai studying the bill,
unsheathing his wallet and dropping a pile of cash on the
table. Then he and his guys all stand up and begin to move
out. The path of their exit steers them closer to us.

"Bye-bye, motherfuckers," Jai shouts as he passes the nearest point to our table. "Don't nobody take my shine. You
don't know who JC is, you going to find out real soon."

Sigh.

Back in college, I had majored in anthropology, and last
season I could have written a master's thesis entitled "Constant Defeat and its Effects on Inhabitants of a Closed Society." As the losses accumulated, I could see players blaming
one another, tuning out coaches they no longer respected, con-
cluding that fate was against them, and anesthetizing themselves to the weekly ritual of failure by deciding that all that
mattered was finishing the season without getting hurt. If
Samuel and Jai's first meeting is any indication, this year
promises to be yet another chapter in an ongoing study in the
behavior of losers.

And of course, now that Jai has left the restaurant, Melody emerges from the back, bottle in hand, only to discover
that there is no one to whom she can deliver our conciliatory
gesture.

She heads our way, grimacing and shaking her head.

"I'm so sorry," Melody pleads. "I had a big order that was
running late, and then it turns out I had to go back to our
storeroom to get your Cristal. And the storeroom was locked,
and I had to find the manager, and then he had to find the
key, which wasn't where it is supposed to be . . ."

"Don't worry about it," Cecil says politely. "It happens."

"Do you still want the bottle?" Melody says.

Cecil considers the question. Did the former hardware store manager, however newly enriched, want to blow five hundred dollars on booze he never wanted in the first place?

"Keep it for yourself," I say to Melody. "My treat. I'll even autograph it for you." I take the bottle from her hand and write my name and my phone number, on the label. There is another player at the table, even if he doesn't have a $64 million contract with $30 million guaranteed.

"Give me a call sometime," I say as I hand the bottle back to Melody.

"Nick Gallow," Cecil says, amused. "Going for it on fourth and long."

Melody's cheeks flush—in excitement, I hope.

"Well, thank you," she says, sounding confused but also pleased. "I have always appreciated the kindness of strangers."

"You're welcome," I say. "But isn't the line, 'I have always depended on the kindness of strangers'?"

"I don't depend on it, I'm not that dumb," Melody says, cradling the champagne affectionately. "But I do appreciate it when it comes along."

Afterward, I assure Cecil that I will reimburse him for the champagne—and then to shut him up I pull out my wallet and hand him $500.

We carve through the rest of our meal with quiet efficiency. The conversational highlight is when I ask Samuel about his training regimen.

"Cars," he says, not looking up from his plate. Samuel has cut his steak into tiny pieces. Before he picks up a bite he drags it around in a pool of steak sauce on his plate. With this latest piece he appears to be tracing the letter K.

"Cars?" I ask, confused. "You race them?"

"No," he says tersely, as if my remark was made out of con-descension, not confusion. "I push 'em."

"I've seen him do this," Cecil says, wiping his mouth with his napkin. "I keep telling Samuel it could be a great ESPN feature, it's very visual. He pushes a car from one side of a field to another. It's a perfect workout for a lineman. He stays low, it builds leg drive, and it's all short bursts, just like he's in a game."

"How'd you come up with that?" I ask Samuel.

"I dunno," he mumbles. "Just did."

"C'mon, Samuel," Cecil says. "Tell him the story."

Samuel takes a bite of steak and doesn't say anything. So Cecil begins.

"One day, Samuel's mother is out at the Walmart down the road and her car breaks down," Cecil says. "A Chevy Mal-ibu, I believe. So she calls a tow truck. But then it turns out the tow truck costs like a hundred dollars . . ."

"One-fifteen," Samuel mutters.

". . . a hundred and fifteen," Cecil continues, his thick fin-gers interlaced on the table. "Which is more money than she has to spare. So Samuel pushes the car to the repair place himself. And remember, this is in August, in Alabama. It's sweltering. Samuel's father—he's a long-haul trucker—is away on a job. And the repair place is five miles down the road. . . ."

"Four," Samuel says. He has a new piece of steak on his fork and he is tracing the numeral "4" in the sauce.

"Four miles," Cecil says. "That's still a lot. And how many days does it take you to push it down the highway, all by your-self?"

"Two," Samuel says, changing his drawing pattern to a "2."

"After two days he gets it to the shop, and they get the es-timate, and they can't afford that either. So Samuel pushes the car back home. Then football season starts, and Samuel is tossing aside offensive lineman like they are cardboard cutouts."

"I'll have to try it sometime," I say, genuinely impressed. I wonder why Samuel wouldn't want that story told. Maybe he thinks it makes him sound poor and backwoods. Or perhaps he has an instinctive resistance to his uncalculated actions being transformed into myth.

We clear our plates within minutes. At one point I look up from my food and catch Samuel staring at me, and his eyes quickly return to his steak.

I had woken up this morning thinking that I would spend the evening with Jessica, whose husband left tonight for a business trip to Switzerland. But I canceled out on her when I received Cecil's invitation. If I could go back in time, I would stick to my plans and send Cecil a particularly thoughtful e-card.

After dinner Cecil suggests that we drive to the Sentinels' stadium, operating on the logic that this shitpile of an evening might look more like a sundae if he can somehow place a cherry on top.

"We'll be quick," Cecil assures me when I object. "Just a few minutes at the stadium, then it's back home. Samuel likes to get to bed early."

"As do I, Cecil," I say. "As do I."

I am tucked into the backseat of Cecil's Escalade like a child. Samuel sits mutely in the front passenger seat, staring straight ahead. A smaller man might disappear in his silence, but Samuel looms.

We arrive at the stadium and the parking-lot gates are

closed, and there is no guard to whom we can flaunt our insider status. We circumnavigate the dark metal hulk—opened for business in 2002, capacity 74,000—but we can't find a way in.

Cecil pulls over to the curb, quiets the engine, and opens his door. Apparently we are to stand on the sidewalk and genuflect as if we are superfans who have come to the stadium on a pilgrimage. All we needed to complete the picture are some Sentinels banners to wave forlornly in the night.

We disembark from the Escalade and stand three abreast by the chain-link fence, looking up at the stadium, its halves curving inward like the mouth of a Venus flytrap.

"Kind of ugly, isn't it?" Samuel says.

I laugh. "It sure is."

My phone buzzes. I have a text from Jessica, who, after my cancellation, apparently hasn't made any other plans for the evening.

> I'm feeling tightness in my upper thighs. I think I need my trainer friend Troy to come by and loosen me up.

Her note is a reference to our first meeting, which took place three years ago at the Jefferson gym. Jessica and her husband stayed there for a month when they were relocating to Philadelphia for his job with the Federal Reserve. She and I were in a spin class together, facing each other on opposite bicycles. After the class we were stretching and she suggested that if we went up to her apartment we would have much more room to splay out. She didn't call me Troy that day, but she has in subsequent reenactments.

"Darn it, I left my phone in the car," Cecil says. "I should get a picture of Samuel at the stadium. Maybe I can send it out on Twitter."

"You tweet now?" I ask.

"I'm managing an account for Samuel," Cecil says. "He needs one. It is 2009, after all." He dashes back to the car for the phone.

As Cecil disappears Samuel kicks at the chain-link fence with his high-tops, setting off a metallic rattle. I am guessing Twitter was not his idea. I am also guessing that this photo op is the reason Cecil, that budding media impresario, wanted to come to the stadium. If only he could find his phone. He searches under the car seats with one loafered foot on the sidewalk and the other in the air.

Samuel stands by the fence, chin jutting out, eyes closed, fingers curled around the links, looking imprisoned.

"Hey, Samuel," I say. "Just take care of your job, you'll be fine. Better than fine. You'll own this city."

Samuel opens his eyes and studies me.

"I know," Samuel says softly. "I will." Whether he means that he would do his job or own Philadelphia, I am not really sure.

Cecil comes back, grinning, holding his phone up like a trophy. I am thinking that I don't need to be in these pictures; Cecil seems to have the same idea. He leads Samuel a few steps up the sidewalk, positioning him to get a better angle of the stadium in the background.

"How about a smile?" Cecil says. And after that request is not immediately granted, Cecil adds, "Think of something happy. Your parents and your sister will be up from Alabama in a couple of days to help you look for a home. That's going to be fun, right?"

Right. While Cecil continues to try to coax joy from his model, I respond to Jessica's earlier text message.

If your thighs are tight, I think Troy has a tool that might come in handy.

I don't like a single one of the words I've just typed, but I don't want to improve the message either. Maybe my half-hearted effort will tamp Jessica's enthusiasm and bring this riff to an early end. Not that I don't enjoy silly double entendres every now and then. It's just that ironically cheesy, two-bit innuendo, when you're not really in the spirit of it, can feel incriminatingly like plain old two-bit innuendo. I am thinking that Troy needs to meet an unhappy accident, and soon.

I hit the Send button.

Then, as if timed to the depression of my finger, I hear a thunderous crack, which is accompanied by a flash. The crack rattles from my ears down to my feet. I drop instinctively into a crouch.

Then another crack, and I hear the screech of a car racing down the street.

I look up and see Cecil stumbling toward me. "Drop, drop!" he shouts to me as he falls against the fence. I lower myself to the ground as a burning smell penetrates my nostrils. I see a car's red taillights already fifty yards gone and speeding away. The car has a bumper sticker with a quarter moon. The moon seemed to be grinning.

My hearing is muffled by the blasts, but I can make out a guttural groan from Cecil, who is on the ground, propped up against the chain-link fence. He is holding his wrist and his yellow shirt is darkening across the bottom. Samuel lays motionless on his back with his head turned to the side and a puddle expanding rapidly around his body. A gush of blood seeps down the sidewalk, over the curb and into the street. The flow is torrential; it is like a main has broken. Samuel's broad mouth is open, as are his eyes, as if he can't believe it either.

I step close, into the river of blood. The warm liquid soaks through my shoes. "Samuel?" I say. His head is tilted more over to the side than it should be, with his cheek resting flush against the sidewalk.

He doesn't answer, and he won't. Samuel's head seems unnaturally angled, I now realize, because it is no longer completely attached to his neck.

I have spent so much of my life training; for this I am completely unprepared.

CHAPTER 2

"So what happened here?"

The police officer has a pudgy face and a buzz cut, and he is a good six inches shorter than me. We are twenty yards down the block from the crime scene, where other officers are at work. This guy has a pad out and is ready to write.

The real answer to his question is that I have no idea at all what happened here. I am completely disoriented, and I keep forgetting to breathe. I feel like I have been simultaneously sat on and flung through the air.

But I need to be helpful, so I begin to put words together, enumerating what facts I can: a driver came out of nowhere and fired at us, twice. My name is Nick Gallow, and I live here in Philadelphia. The man who was taken away in the ambulance just a few moments ago is Cecil Wilson of Massillon, Ohio, and the person being zipped into a body bag is Samuel Sault. . . .

"Samuel Sault the football player?" the officer asks, his voice squeaking high for a moment. I would bet this nightshifter is not even twenty-five years old. "He just signed his contract, right?"

"Yes."

"Damn," the officer says. "We can't catch a break."

It takes me a moment to comprehend that the "we" he is referring to is the Sentinels.

"How many people were in the shooter's car?" he asks.

"I didn't really see."

"How about the car? Can you tell me anything about that?"

"It was a four-door, dark-colored," I say. "Black, I think."

"You think?" the officer asks, concerned.

"Could have been dark blue," I say. "Or maybe even dark green."

The officer sighs. "So all you know is it's dark. Did you get the make?"

I search my memory for any kind of brand emblem or signature. "No."

The officer's brown eyes flare with exasperation. "Anything distinguishing about the car? Anything at all? Please. This is important."

"There was a bumper sticker with a quarter moon on it," I say. "The moon looked like it was grinning."

"Grinning?" the officer asks dubiously. "How can a moon grin?"

"I don't know, but that's what it looked like." I feel like I am failing, useless. I inhale deeply, hoping to steady my nerves.

"How about the license plate? Did you get a look at that?"

"No," I say, cringing inwardly. "No license plate." How is it that I noticed the bumper sticker but not the license plate right next to it? It is an obvious mistake. The killer is going to get away, all because of me.

The officer flips a page on his book. "Okay, let's move on. Where were you guys before you came here?"

"Dinner," I say. "At Stark's."

"Anything happen there that was out of the ordinary?"

I hesitate, thinking about Jai. However angry he was at Samuel, I can't believe that had anything to do with the shooting, and I don't want to point the police toward a teammate simply for the sake of full disclosure.

"Nothing that would lead to murder," I say.

The officer narrows his eyes. He says nothing, probably hoping that I will rush to fill the empty air, and blurt out whatever I am holding back. But I maintain my silence.

"You'll have to go to the station," he says finally. "I'm sure the chief detective will want to do a more formal interview."

Soon another officer drives me to a district police station ten minutes away. In my twenty-eight years, I have never been inside one of these places. As I am led inside, I know that I will have to do a better job of explaining what has happened—to this chief detective, and also to myself.

The district police station in South Philadelphia is depressingly municipal. Men sit too close to one another, behind low cubicle walls that offer only the illusion of personal space. Old metal desks squeak with each opened drawer. From the pantry comes the smell of burnt coffee. These people have such important work to do, and such an awful place to do it in. I can't help but compare it to my workplace, where I stride on plush carpet, fresh towels are always at the ready, and I can drink complimentary protein shakes from an always-stocked refrigerator.

I sit at an unoccupied desk, on a square-backed wooden chair, where I have been told to wait. After a couple of minutes a detective, a tired-looking older man with thin brown hair and a gray front tooth, walks over to me.

"I'm Detective Senecker," he says. "Can I get you anything?"

"Have you heard anything about how Cecil Wilson is doing?" I say. "Any update from the hospital?"

"Let me see what I can find out," Senecker says, removing his phone from a holder on his belt. He turns his back and steps away from me as he dials.

Cecil cannot die on me. Three years ago I lost my father, who had been my high school coach. My dad and Cecil are the two people who both understood what I do and looked after my interests as if they were their own. The two of them would sit next to each other at games, and my dad made a point of paying for the peanuts and the beers. He'd tell Cecil, "After what you've done for my son, your money's no good with me." Whenever the two of them got together they referred to it as a meeting of the Board of Directors. It used to be one of my routines that before I would leave the house or hotel for a game, I would speak to my dad on the phone, and he would talk me through various coaching points. I didn't really need the instruction, but I found reassurance in the ritual. After my dad died, it was Cecil who took on those Sunday morning phone calls. Cecil didn't bother to talk to me about my drops or my kicking motion, just general chatter about the game plan and the mood of the team and so forth. But he was always ready when I needed him. I think of Cecil dropping to his knees on the sidewalk, one hand on his perforated stomach, yelling at me to get down, still trying to protect me.

"He's being operated on. That's all they're saying," says Senecker, turning back to me. He asks if I want some coffee, or a Coke.

"Water would be fine," I say. He brings me a bottle of water from a vending machine, and then he starts talking to me about the shooting and our conversation veers between an interview and an informal talk. He is no more impressed with my level of detail about the shooter and his car than the young officer on the scene.

"So the bumper sticker had a quarter moon on it, huh?" Senecker says, underwhelmed. "What do you think that might mean—maybe the shooter's in an astronomer's club? Maybe he eats at a restaurant called the Moonbeam Diner."

"I wish I knew," I say.

He looks at me blankly, and I feel even more useless.

The conversation soon peters out, and Senecker returns to his desk. I drink my water and close my eyes. I keep seeing the shooting, and the bodies on the ground, all that blood pouring out of Samuel. I wish I had seen that license plate. I wish I hadn't been texting Jessica. Then maybe I would have noticed the car coming, and had a better look at everything. Maybe I would have been aware enough to run after the car, sprinting as hard as I could. I could have been hit, too, but maybe I would have been able to catch up with the shooter. Then I would have reached into the car and wrestled the rifle away. I would have grabbed him by the collar and dragged him out through the open window and onto the street, threw him to the ground and climbed on top of him. I would have punched him hard in the bridge of the nose. And then I would have punched him again, and again, and again. He would have been the one spurting blood. . . .

"Mr. Gallow?"

"Yes?" I open my eyes and see Senecker standing over me, and he looks taken aback. I don't think I barked my answer, but perhaps the anger of my fantasy seeped into my voice.

"Ah, just a couple things," says Senecker. "First, Detective Rizotti—he's the lead investigator on this case—is on his way in, and he's going to want to talk to you."

"Okay."

"Also, I need your suit jacket, if you don't mind," he says. "We have to test it for gunshot residue. Just so we can rule out that you didn't fire the gun."

I am surprised—don't they believe my story? But I understand the need to be thorough in one's work. I stand up, slip off my jacket, and hand it to him.

"When will I get it back?" I ask. I have the disconcerting thought that if Cecil dies and I need to attend a funeral, this is my only suit.

"Tomorrow," Senecker says. "Or the next day, at the latest. I'm sure with a Sentinel involved, you'll go to the front of the line."

The detective's comments jolt me to another reality—how huge a news story these shootings will be.

I look at my phone and see dozens of texts and e-mails piled up. Teammates, friends, and my brother, Doug, have all tried to reach me. I quickly reply to Doug, telling him where I am and that I'm okay, and that Cecil is being worked on. I also sent a note to Freddie Gladstone, who is a team vice president and my best friend, telling him that I am okay and that I am at the police station awaiting questioning.

I look for, but do not see, a message from my mother. I suppose I should not be surprised. Her longtime boyfriend, Aaron Handley, the man she left my father for years ago, owns a cabin in the northern Pennsylvania woods, about a half hour south of Elmira, and the two of them retreat there whenever they can. The cabin has no television or Internet service, and cell phones are all but useless.

I send my mother a text message telling her I am doing fine, so that she will see it when she reconnects to the outside world.

It is nearly 4:00 A.M. when Detective Rizotti finally arrives. It may be a further indication of my tiredness and my mood that upon meeting him, I cannot get past how physically repellant he is.

He is short, in his mid-forties, with wiry black hair and an aquiline nose that dives low on his face, as if it is taking a peek at his nicotine-stained teeth. All this perched atop a body that resembles a bag of garbage sagging on the curb. I cannot believe a person so little in command of his appearance is directing a major murder investigation.

Rizotti asks me to come with him into a small conference room. There, we sit on the opposite sides of a plain green table. He rests his hands on the table, looks directly at me, and makes an obvious effort to smile.

"Nick Gallow, age twenty-eight, born in Waverly, New York, and a resident of Philadelphia for the past five years," he says. "Is that correct?"

"Yes."

"I understand that you're the punter for the Sentinels?" he says, sounding skeptical.

"That's right," I say.

"Funny," he says. "I usually go to one or two Sentinels games a year, and I catch the rest on TV. Your name doesn't ring a bell with me." He says this as if it is my fault.

"I suppose that's good, in a way," I answer, straining to be polite. "It means I didn't screw anything up too memorably."

Rizotti nods in appreciation. "It's the same with cops, they always remember your mistakes. Name me a police officer from the last twenty-five years more well-known to the man on the street than Mark Fuhrman."

"Yes," I say. "He lives in infamy."

"The thing is, Mark got a bum deal," Rizotti says. "I know him a little bit. Good guy, good cop. Great cop, actually. And that O.J. is guilty as sin. Don't you think? You guys must know. Even a punter must hear stuff."

Even a punter.

"I don't have any good O.J. gossip," I say patiently. I have a hard time believing this is what he has kept me around to ask me.

"What's it like being a punter, Mr. Gallow?" he says. "Is it like you're part of the regular team? Do you get to talk to the other players much?"

These are the kinds of questions I get from the most ignorant fans. Rizotti's little nudges feel intentional, like he is trying to rile me up.

"We players all talk to each other," I say. "Some more than others, of course."

"How about Jai Carson?" Rizotti says. "You talk to JC much? You guys pals?"

Rizotti has only one reason to bring up Jai. He has heard

about the Stark's incident. Which is natural enough, given that it took place in full view of the hostess as well as the bar patrons. And everyone in the place had to have heard Jai's parting shouts.

I realize I have to choose my words precisely. Anything I say about our team's biggest star could end up on the ESPN news crawl. I consider whether I should ask for a lawyer, but I decide that I can handle myself for now.

"Jai and I have been teammates for five years," I say.

Rizotti pulls his seat in closer to the table. I feel this room getting smaller.

"The two of you buddies?"

"We know each other professionally."

"I understand that Sault and your agent were together at Stark's restaurant earlier tonight," Rizotti says. "Were you there as well, Mr. Gallow?"

"I was." If he knew about the fight, how would he not know I was there? Also, I told the other officers I had been at Stark's, and Rizotti has clearly been briefed.

"See, this is helpful already," Rizotti say. "The hostess said Sault was there with two guys she didn't recognize. She had Cecil Wilson's name from the credit card receipt, but she had no idea who the third man was. Now we know it is you."

He smiles smugly. It feels like Rizotti's only point in asking me these questions is to tell me that I can pass through a football haven like Stark's unrecognized.

"Mr. Gallow, I understand that Carson and Sault got into a disagreement before dinner," Rizotti says. "Carson wanted Sault to eat at his table, and Mr. Sault refused."

"Yes," I say. "That's right."

"Why didn't you tell that to anyone earlier?"

"Because I can't imagine it has anything to do with the

shooting," I say firmly. "If Jai felt like he needed to put Samuel in his place, he would have rubbed Bengay in his jockstrap, or taken a dump in his cleats. That's how you teach a rookie a lesson. You don't kill someone because they don't sit at your table."

"You wouldn't do that, and neither would I," Rizotti says, scratching his nostril. "But we're not talking about you and me here, are we? We're talking about Jai Carson. A world-class piece of shit."

Not that Rizotti is rushing to judgment or anything. Although of course, Jai did have a colorful history with Philadelphia law enforcement.

Once Jai was arrested late at night for DWI, and explained to the officer that he needed to be written up quickly because his favorite strip club was about to close. Another time he had been cited for public indecency after attempting to stage an X-rated photo shoot on the *LOVE* statue near City Hall. Most incriminatingly, there was the time Jai was arrested outside a man's apartment, wearing only sweatpants and threatening him with a pistol. It was all about a woman Jai had been feeling proprietary about at that moment. To Jai's credit, the gun turned out to be a water pistol—which, strangely enough, was loaded—but it took the police who arrived at the scene awhile to figure that out. Jai was lucky he hadn't been shot.

"I understand that at the end of this argument Carson yelled 'Fuck you' at Samuel," Rizotti says.

"He yelled 'Fuck me,' actually," I say.

Rizotti is about to write this down but then he looks up at me. "That an important difference to you?"

"Jai says 'Fuck me' all the time," I continue. "It's not a big deal."

"It is a big deal, and this is part of my point, Gallow,"

Rizotti says, pointing his pen at me. "If people like you and I yelled curses in a crowded restaurant, it would be an exceptional event. We're civilized. But not this piece-of-shit teammate of yours."

I wonder if Rizotti isn't giving himself a little too much credit. For being civilized, I mean.

"And I've watched JC, whatever he calls himself, for ten years now, and you can see it on the field. The guy's the most overrated linebacker in the league. He's more interested in playing to the cameras than doing what it takes to win. He's poison on that team. He's the reason we can't make the playoffs anymore."

So somewhere along the line we have slipped into sports talk radio. I want to thank Rizotti for calling and tell him I will get to his question after the commercial break.

"I really don't think Jai did this," I say.

"Do you think that, or do you know it?" Rizotti asks.

"It's what I believe," I say.

"It's not what I believe," he says.

He lets the room go quiet. I maintain my stillness, hands folded beneath the table, waiting him out.

"I understand you saw a bumper sticker on the shooter's car," Rizotti says. "It had a quarter moon on it."

"That's correct," I say, and I brace myself, because I can feel a hit coming.

"You know what would have really helped us?" Rizotti sneers. "A license plate number. I thought you athletes are supposed to have great reflexes. How could you see the bumper sticker but not the license plate?"

"I wish I had seen that plate, believe me," I say. "No one wishes it more than me."

"Oh, someone wishes it more than you," Rizotti sneers. "Me. Let's face it, punter. You made my job a lot harder. You fucked up."

I search for a response, a way to be helpful.

"What if you had me hypnotized?" I ask. "Maybe we could recover the memory that way."

"Please," Rizotti says, pulling back. "Where did you get that bullshit idea, from some TV show?"

I did, actually.

"I'll need to look at your phone," Rizotti says. "The time stamps on your texts will help us nail down the details of your story."

I want to help, but I am not going to let this oaf thumb through my phone. First, if he really wanted the time of the shooting, he has my 911 call. Second, if my salacious messages to Jessica become part of the police record, they will inevitably go public—if not for the pure gossip value, then so I can become the scapegoat for an investigation going nowhere. I can hear it now: we don't know anything about the killer because the punter was too busy sexting another man's wife.

"I'd prefer to keep the contents of my phone private," I say. "What's on it is personal and has nothing to do with the case."

"I'd like to judge for myself what is relevant to the case," Rizotti says. "You'd be surprised what possibilities people leave unconsidered."

"I've been answering your questions because I want to help," I say firmly. "But if I need to get a lawyer now, I will."

"Anytime anyone holds something back from me," Rizotti says, cocking his head back and smacking his lips, "I assume the worst. You're climbing right up my list of suspects, punter."

"What?" I say. "I couldn't have been the shooter. I was standing right there on the sidewalk with Cecil when he was shot. Just ask him."

"If Cecil Wilson dies," says Rizotti, "I won't be able to ask him anything, will I?"

He somehow manages to look as if he has said something savvy and wise, rather than callous and hateful. I ball my fists.

"Let's assume you're right about Jai Carson," Rizotti continues, with revolting casualness. "That raises one big question: how did this shooter know you were going to be at the stadium? At least Carson would have been able to follow you from the restaurant."

It is a fair question.

"Maybe the shooter was already in that area, for some reason that has nothing to do with us," I say. "Aren't there random killings in this city every day?" The crime news in Philadelphia can be astoundingly bleak—perhaps because the city's economy has been trending downward for a good century or two.

"A random shooting?" Rizotti says disbelievingly. "Is that the best you can do? Come on, punter. You're my lone eyewitness. Give me something better than that."

I feel a deep despair—that I don't know more, and that I now must depend on this cretin to find justice for Cecil and Samuel. I have long held that one of the chief problems in this universe is that there are more positions of responsibility than there are people equipped to fill them. This detective seems to be a particularly painful example.

I push back my chair and rise from the table.

"If you want to ask me any more questions," I say, "I'm going to need a lawyer. If not, I'm going home. It's been a long night."

I move toward the door. Rizotti stands, but he doesn't try to stop me.

"One last question, Gallow, if you don't mind," he says before I can turn the knob. "Ever consider the possibility that this shooter was after you? It's night, it is dark, you guys aren't that far apart. All three of you are big. And Sault is light-skinned for a black guy. From a distance someone could easily mistake Sault for you. Or your agent. Maybe they just shot the wrong guy and didn't even know it."

I had not considered the possibility. But it couldn't be, could it? I am taller and leaner than Cecil. And Samuel, streamlined as his body was, still had eighty pounds on me. Even at night, you'd have to be blind . . .

"Nah, probably not," Rizotti says, waving his hand dismissively. "After all, you are just the punter."

CHAPTER 3

THERE ARE MOMENTS when, if you are in the mood, you can look at the people around you and view them as a judgment on the state of your life at that point. It might be at a birthday dinner, or a New Year's Eve get-together, or finally, I suppose, your funeral, though I do not believe the dead can see such things. I am having that kind of moment now, as I emerge into the police station lobby and see my one-person welcoming party: Freddie Gladstone.

My friend looks sharp, at least. His long brown hair is styled and wavy, and he is wearing an apricot-colored designer T-shirt and beige linen pants. He looks as if he might have come from some all-night party. Five in the morning is often the shank of his evening.

Freddie is seated under the WANTED posters and has his body tilted at a forty-five-degree angle, studying the screen of his iPhone. He doesn't notice my approach.

"Hey, pal, what's going on?" I ask casually, standing on top of him.

"Oh, hey, Hangman," Freddie says, not looking up. He calls me Hangman because my last name is Gallow and punts are measured by hang time, and why let an obvious pun sit on the shelf? "Check this out," he says. He turns his iPhone toward me. It has a black-and-white image of a nude woman looking over her shoulder with an embarrassed grin on her face. "It's one of these deals where ordinary girls pose for a calendar to raise money for some charity."

"What's the cause?" I ask. We should be talking about me, but at this point I welcome a distraction.

"Um . . . anal cancer, I'm pretty sure," Freddie says. "That's why the girls are all photographed from behind. It's pretty good. Sometimes I like that whole amateur thing better. It's more transgressive in a way. But hey, how are you doing?"

Thanks for asking. I catch Freddie up on my evening. He listens in a rapt but calm way, and he is never more stoic than when I describe the shooting itself. It is only when I get to the police interrogation and mention that Rizotti implied that I might have been the shooter that he shows emotion.

"What a dick," Freddie says, scowling

"It's understandable," I demur. "He is trying to get me off balance. Just doing his job."

"It still sucks," Freddie says. "I should have been in there with you."

"What would you have done?"

"A lawyer might have helped."

"Right," I say. "I forgot."

"Fuck you." Freddie has a law degree, but it is easy to lose sight of that fact, given that he has never put it to any use. Nominally he is a vice president of the Sentinels, but he was given that job because his dad, real-estate billionaire Arthur Gladstone, owns the team. Freddie attends front-office meetings at his pleasure, and it's not like when he goes off to Ibiza or Bali or Costa Rica on a vacation of undetermined length, anyone scrambles to cover for him.

In fact, the team employs two in-house lawyers, and Freddie is not one of them.

"Have you heard anything about Cecil?" I ask.

"He is still being operated on, is the last I heard from O'Dwyer," Freddie says. Jim O'Dwyer is the team's longtime public relations chief. "That was about an hour ago, but he sounded positive."

"A PR guy sounding positive," I say. "Why am I not reassured?"

Freddie shrugs. "That's all I got."

"Let's go to the hospital," I say.

"O'Dwyer's information is pretty recent," Freddie says. "He would let me know if . . . anything changed."

"I should go anyway," I say. "Even if it's a one-percent chance I get in, I want to try."

"I'll give you a ride, Hangman," Freddie says. "But I may leave you at the doorstep. Me and hospitals, you know."

"That's fine. No worries."

When Freddie was fourteen years old he watched his mother slowly die from something called Creutzfeldt-Jakob disease, which attacks the brain, causing dementia, hallucinations, and loss of body control, before death. Freddie doesn't speak about the experience often, and when he does it is quickly and without detail, always cutting himself off with the refrain that it was "a long eight months."

"When you go outside, be careful," Freddie warns. "The vultures are in heavy swarm."

I walk toward the door and see that predators have assembled in the predawn darkness: news vans, cameramen, and reporters, in a needy search for quotes and pictures and video.

"At least you look nice," Freddie says, straightening my shirt collar. If only he had seen me in the jacket. "Follow my blocking. And remember, don't give them anything to work with. Don't look anyone in the eye, don't say anything. Just keep moving forward."

With Freddie leading the way, we exit the police station. We keep our heads low and our eyes ahead toward Freddie's black BMW. Still, the crush comes, the scuffling for position, the thrusting of arms—the reporters exhibit the body language of a mob.

"Nick, what happened?"

"Are you okay?"

"Hey, Nick, look here!"

"Are you a suspect?"

"Who did it?" The last question comes from a particularly aggressive blond woman who steps in our path and momentarily blocks our movement.

"Your mom did it," Freddie snaps at her. "They're looking at her pimp as an accomplice."

Who wouldn't want this man as their legal counsel?

We squeeze through to Freddie's car, shutters clicking all the while. I feel a momentary sense of relief when the doors shut, but then I see the cameramen fan out in front of us, forming a barrier as they aim their lenses through the windshield.

"C'mon!" Freddie screams, honking the horn before we have even moved. Freddie is generally an easygoing guy, but he is prone to bursts of temper when he doesn't get his way—simply because, unlike most people, he has little practice at it. He can be particularly prone to road rage, and I have seen him lose it in a ten-second traffic jam.

He begins inching the car forward, his knuckles whitening as his grip on the wheel tightens, but the camera guys remain rooted to the ground. Samuel's killing is going to be a huge story. They must come home with footage.

"Easy, Freddie," I say. "It's been a rough night already."

He slaps the leather steering wheel in disgust. "Look at them! They're just standing there!"

"Easy, pal . . ."

Then, as if by magic, the flock disperses on its own. Or rather, it flies off and reconstitutes by the station house door.

And I see what has caused the cameramen to reorder their priorities. The star attraction has arrived.

Jai Carson, wearing the same blue tracksuit he had on at Stark's, is being escorted into the station by four uniformed officers. Bingo. This is the shot the camera guys needed, the one that will lead the morning newscast, and *SportsCenter*, and maybe even CNN. Hell, one day they might be able to license this footage to documentary filmmakers.

Freddie and I have been cleared to go.

CHAPTER 4

FREDDIE DROPS ME off at the hospital, where they tell me that Cecil is out of surgery and in serious but stable condition; I can't see him, but he is now sedated and asleep. Which sounds like a great way to be; I have been up for nearly twenty-four hours. I text Cecil's wife, Vicki, but I receive no response. I hope she is in transit from Ohio.

Feeling like last night has finally stopped happening, I take a taxi home.

I arrive at the Jefferson at 6:50 in the morning. I plop on my sofa—the Jefferson's sofa, technically, since all the furniture has come with the place. I look at my texts. No answer yet from Vicki. Nothing from my mother, still. She must be squirreled away with Aaron at his cabin. Perhaps they are awake but still in bed, listening to the birds chirp. I have only met Aaron maybe a dozen times, at breakfasts or lunches, so I can't claim to be an expert on the man. But what little I know about his biography explains why he clings to his cabin and its remove from civilization. Aaron was once a police officer but he quit the force after suffering some kind of breakdown. Now he teaches criminal justice courses. My dad, when he was alive, liked to trumpet Aaron's career change as proof of his essential weakness. "Those who can't do, teach," said my dad, who coached high school football and taught gym during the school day.

I scroll back through my texts and come to an unread series of messages from Jessica, sent just after the shooting. She

was describing for me, in barely veiled innuendo, the progress of her masturbation, until at long last she noticed I wasn't
responding. After I failed to acknowledge her *Where are you?*
she sent a final note that read, *I'll assume you're in post-ejaculatory
slumber. 'Night.* She has no idea about the shooting. Typical of
Jessica—she is quick to notice any ripple in her pond, but she
can be oblivious to the broader tides.

The morning is bringing a fresh rush of text messages.
Among the most recent is one from the Sentinels coach, Jerry
Tanner. It is rare that he communicates with me directly; usually if I receive a text from him it is part of a blast to all the
players about a change in practice schedule, or some hoary
coaching aphorism he feels impelled to share.

Here's what my head coach has to say to me on this morning of tragedy:

> If you are going to be at the facility today, stop in
> and see me. I'll be here all day.

I would have preferred inspirational blather. Or at least
semantic honesty. *If you are going to be at the facility today.* I know
an order when I see it.

I nap for three hours, on purpose. I've read that the most ef-
fective sleep comes in three-hour blocks because that interval
matches a cycle of our brain rhythms. I shower, consider my
breakfast options, and realize that I am in no mood to eat
anything, and drive to the Sentinels' practice facility, telling
myself it will be good to see people. I arrive a little after 11:00
A.M. The facility is near the stadium, just a couple of minutes
down the street from it. The stadium looms tall as I approach

from the highway; it is unsettling to return to this area so soon. As I pass I see two police cars still at the crime scene. But I cruise on, following the route to the Sentinels facility no differently than I have a hundred times before. Consider it a testament to the power of muscle memory.

The main doorway of our training complex is twenty feet high and shaped like a football. The players do not walk through the football; that honor goes to visitors and business employees. Players park in a private, fenced-off lot to the side and enter through a nondescript metal door we open with a key card. TV crews are set up along the border of the player's lot, and my arrival inspires a stirring of activity. *Man walks from car to building: film to play every ten minutes, until something better comes along.*

Before going up to see Tanner, I first visit Eleanor Cordero, the team's assistant public relations director. Tanner has apparently spread word that I will be coming in; Eleanor sent me a message asking that I stop by her office as soon as possible.

It is an easy choice as to which person to visit first. Cordero is a sprightly woman in her mid-twenties, with wide, gentle eyes and wavy brown hair that flies back as if she has just had a door opened in her face. She giggles easily and carries herself with an air of coy haplessness that allows her skill and efficiency to sneak up on people. I know Cordero just a little bit; she often accompanies groups of players on visits to children's wards and such places that make for positive news stories. I volunteer for these trips, even though they can be deflating for me. One of the great joys of being a football player is seeing bedridden children light up simply because we walk into the room. But then when we fan out to talk with the children one-on-one, I often see my specific kid sag at the shoulders when he learns he is stuck with the punter, and he scans the room looking for players he has actually heard of. This is when Eleanor swoops to the rescue. "Nick is one of the best punters in the game," she will say. "He's the reason the other team has to go so far to score. We'd be in big trouble without him." A few admiring words from her is usually enough to get the kid excited again.

This morning Cordero wears a crisp black business suit and has a tall cup of Wawa coffee on her desk. Her workspace is decorated with framed pictures of her curly-haired daughter, Ana, who Eleanor must have had when she was in college. She also has, hanging on the wall behind her, a crucifix that depicts Jesus as contorted and in violent pain; it is as if, when crucifix shopping, she asked the clerk for the one that showed Jesus in the greatest agony. Cordero is such a chipper and efficient young woman that the extreme and tortured icon leaves me wondering what lurks behind her ever-present smile. I had always liked her, but I also sensed that hers was not a territory to be entered lightly. She did not do much just for the fun of it.

"I am so amazed that you are even here," Cordero says as I take a seat across from her desk. "If I was in your place I would be running home to my mother."

Her comment reminds me that I don't know for sure where my mother is.

"Any news on Cecil?" I ask.

"Serious but stable," she says, and then adds, pained, "I'm so sorry, Nick. Cecil is the sweetest man. I remember the first time I met him, he was with your dad at a game. Those two just cared about you so much."

I muster up a smile. "Thank you, Eleanor. What can I do for you?"

"You have about a thousand interview requests," she says, with a look that is both apologetic and pleading.

"The answer to all of them," I say, "is no."

"I figured," she says. "But I just wanted to let you know."

"Now I know." I understand that players are required by contract to talk to the media and thus promote the league, but what happened last night doesn't seem like it belongs in the sales brochure.

"How about a statement for the cameras?" she asks, as if I might find this a reasonable compromise. "It could be short, I could even write it for you. You wouldn't have to take any questions. Just a few quick words, to give them a little something and make them go away?"

"I have a plan for making them go away," I say. "Tell them to fuck off."

Cordero's head pulls back as if she is dodging a face slap. I normally wouldn't use such harsh language around her.

"We should at least issue a written statement," Cordero says cautiously. "You won't have to do anything or talk to anyone except me. I'll write it up and distribute it."

"Okay, let's do that."

"Thank you so much, Nick," she says, relieved. "I know this is the last thing you want to be dealing with now."

She clicks a few keys on her desktop computer and then signals to me that she is ready to take dictation.

"What kind of statement does one make in a situation like this?" I ask.

"How about I throw out some questions to get you started?"

"Please."

"Are you sad?"

"Sure." And getting sadder. Three seconds in, and this process is as empty as I feared it might be.

She begins typing, her long fingernails clacking at the keyboard.

"Shocked?"

"Definitely."

"Condolences to the families of all involved?"

"Of course."

"Prayers?"

"Not really." I didn't think false piety would help anyone right now.

She paused.

"Did Samuel say anything about how he is looking forward to being a Sentinel?"

Lest we forget to push the product at a time like this. "Honestly, no."

Eleanor looks up, flummoxed.

"Can we say that you were looking forward to having him on the Sentinels?"

"Sure," I allow. Especially since our defense could very well be fucked without him. Although perhaps that part is not for the release.

"Do you have a sense of what sort of person he was? Kind, decent . . . ?"

"Both of those."

"Anything else?"

"Honest. Actually, put honest first. And get rid of 'kind.' I don't know about that, really."

Cordero checks my eyes as if to debate the matter, but then she lets it go. It's not as if reporters will notice that the word "kind" is absent from the boilerplate.

"Anything else you'd like to add?"

I think for a moment. "Should I be saying anything about Jai?"

Eleanor shakes her head. "Not now. We're going to wait a little bit on him. Jai Carson is usually handled exclusively by Jim O'Dwyer, but this morning we put a crisis consultant on retainer, so I imagine anything we have to say about Jai will come from them."

"A crisis consultant? Whose idea was that?"

"Arthur Gladstone himself," Eleanor says, and that is interesting. Mr. Gladstone is notoriously hands-off with his Sentinels, but then he might be more comfortable managing a business problem than making a draft pick. "We all had a conference call at eight thirty, and their emissaries should be arriving from New York by one or so."

"Wow." If they've brought in these consultants, they are expecting Jai to be arrested.

"Yes. I have a couple very competent"—she holds up her crossed fingers as she says this—"junior staffers converting Conference Room B into an office for the consultants. I'll be checking up on them after we're done."

I nod as if I've ever been in Conference Room B. It must be the province of the team's ever-growing business staff.

"In that case," I say, "I think we've pretty well said it all."

"Great, I'll have a draft to show you in a half hour." She quickly types a few words and then studies them on the screen. "Maybe sooner."

"No need, Ms. Cordero," I say. "Just type it up and get it out there. It's news. A nation awaits."

I walk up to the second floor, where the coaches have their offices. I don't use these stairs often. I have never been up to visit Tanner, who defers heavily on special teams to our unit coach, Perry Huff, the one holdover from the previous coaching administration. Huff has an office up here, too, but he rarely calls me in. "My favorite thing about you, Gallow," he once told me, "is that you don't require too much attention. You're like a cactus."

I approach the reception desk, where a heavyset woman about my mother's age, with short dark hair and librarian glasses, sits focused on her computer screen, not looking up, even though the building is nearly empty.

"Is Coach in?" I ask.

"Since six A.M.," she sighs.

The poor woman. I don't know her name, but I have heard the story—the first week Tanner was on the job, she complimented him on his haircut as he walked by her desk. Tanner paused, confused, before continuing to his office. A few moments later Tanner's staff assistant came out and told the secretary, "Coach prefers that you not speak to him unless he speaks to you first. It breaks his train of thought."

Have I mentioned that I really don't care for our coach?

Tanner was a quarterback in his playing days. A backup quarterback, actually, for his entire eleven-year career. He spent two decades as an assistant before being hired here as head man. He is conventionally handsome, and he keeps himself meticulously arranged—clear blue eyes, brown hair always in place—and he spends an hour in the gym every day, making sure that when he is seen in side profile, his chest protrudes further than his belly. No love handles allowed. His physical appearance mirrors what he likes to project as a coach: a man in total control.

Tanner is reading a printed report. His head snaps up when I knock on the door.

"I really appreciate you coming in today, Nick," he says. "Have a seat."

I settle into the chair across from him. He is wearing a gray Sentinels polo shirt, tight enough to show off his musculature. Tanner's office also has a long black sofa, on which he reportedly sleeps at least a couple of nights a week during the season, rather than waste time traveling home to his wife and three daughters in the suburbs. On the left side of his desk is a monitor that is wired into all the coaching rooms and allows him to look in on meetings.

But the ultimate reminder of Tanner's authority is a tackboard on the side wall of his office, blanketed with eighty index cards. Each of those cards has on it a player's name and uniform number. Over the summer he will cut the roster down to fifty-three, and twenty-seven of those cards will land in the circular metal trash can by his desk.

He slides the report he was reading into a yellow folder and focuses his blue eyes on me. "You've had a hell of a night. How are you holding up?"

"As best I can, Coach." And my eyes fill with tears. All from a mundane expression of concern from an authority figure I don't respect. I drag my hand across my cheek, trying to look like I am rubbing my eye out of exhaustion.

"That's all you can do at a time like this," Tanner says, not seeming to notice. He rests his toned forearms on his desk. "It's such a fucking shame about Samuel. I've never seen anyone like him. Great athlete. Great kid, too."

Tanner spent much of the spring studying Samuel in advance of the draft—interviewing not just him but his coaches and family members, and watching film of every snap Samuel played in college. And I'm sure the digging didn't stop there. If you're going to invest $64 million in a post-adolescent, you have investigators look into what coaches refer to as "character questions"—such as whether a prospect might have ever cheated on a test, or gone on a coke binge and strangled a hooker.

"Do you have any idea why anyone would have wanted to kill Samuel?" I ask.

"No idea," Tanner says. "Samuel had the cleanest sheet I've ever seen. Lived with his parents. He dated only one girl, a friend of his sister's. He was a nice, quiet kid, simple as that. He's the last one of you guys I would expect to get a call about in the middle of the night."

There is a pause, as we both think of the player who is surely the first guy Tanner would expect to be woken up for.

"Do you think Jai did this?" Tanner asks. I am guessing this question is the reason he called me in here.

"I don't think so," I say. "Do you?"

He leans back in his chair and sighs. Behind Tanner, outside the window, I see a young man I don't recognize jogging from the practice fields into the building.

"Who the hell knows with that dick-for-brains?" Tanner says, massaging his wrist. "I sure hope not, but I wouldn't put anything past that guy. If we lose him too, we're . . ."

And then Tanner cuts himself off. The last thing he would do is allow himself to admit in front of a player that he thinks the team is screwed.

I look at the yellow folder on the desk. It has the letters DEs written on it in black marker—DE as in defensive end, which is Samuel's position. Tanner is looking at scouting reports, already evaluating potential replacements, less than twelve hours after the twenty-one-year-old's body was zipped into a bag.

"Why don't you go home and rest," Tanner says.

My eyes drift over to the tackboard with the index cards and seek the one marked 11 GALLOW. My card is toward the bottom. Immediately underneath it is a fresh card marked 10 TOLLEY. My newly signed camp competition.

"I'm going to go downstairs and get some work in," I blurt out, though this had not been my plan at all. "Since I'm here, you know." And now that I have said it, I have to do it. I like to keep my word that way.

"Good for you," Tanner says slowly, eyebrows raised. "Good for you. Keep your mind on the business at hand. That's the message we're going to need to send to everyone. That would be a great example."

And he picks up the folder and goes back to reading his scouting reports.

I leave Tanner's office and pause halfway down the hallway. Just thinking about how I teared up in Tanner's office, I begin to do so again. I blame it on the sleep deprivation. It's all of a piece with my cursing at Cordero. I've read that even one restless night causes a noticeable degradation in brain functions.

I collect myself in the empty hallway, dry my eyes, and then I go around the bend and peek into Huff's office, hoping to find my unit coach. He isn't there, but I see that his computer is on and his knapsack is in the corner, so he has to be around somewhere.

I head downstairs to the locker room to change into my gear. As I go, I talk myself into being okay with practicing now. I did need to kick at least a couple of more times between now and my minicamp face-off with Woodward Tolley. I suspect I won't feel like driving back here tomorrow, so I might as well go ahead and knock out a session now.

I enter our capacious locker room, with its lush gray carpet and wide wooden stalls for each player. In the middle of the carpet is the team logo of a vigilant-looking man in a colonial tricorner hat. I see Huff in the far corner, near my stall, talking to the same young man I saw running in from the practice fields.

"Hey, Gallow, how you doing, buddy?" This is Jacque Newton, the team's fullback, calling at me from his stall to the left of the locker room entrance. Jacque, along with Huff and the young man, are the only people here on what is scheduled as off-time for players. Jacque is wearing on his knee a heavy black brace—he is still healing after tearing his ACL last October. I imagine he is here for a rehab session with a team trainer.

"How is your agent?" Jacque asks.

"Out of surgery, I'm told."

He shakes his head sympathetically. "He's going to make it, I know he is."

"I hope you're right," I say, though of course Jacque couldn't know anything.

"Do they have any idea who did it?" he asks. "Did you see anything?"

"It all happened very fast," I say, shrugging. "I wasn't much help to the police, I'm afraid." In short, I didn't rat anyone out.

"This team is cursed, man," Jacque says, shaking his head. "After a while it's like, what's the next thing that's going to happen around here?"

I shake my head, too.

"How's your knee doing?" I ask. "You going to be ready for next week?" I steal a glance toward Huff, who I don't want to miss, but he is still in the corner, talking to that young man.

"I hope so," Jacque says. "I've been targeting this minicamp as my comeback date." As well he should have. The Sentinels drafted a fullback in the seventh round, and teams rarely keep two of at that position.

"Good luck," I say.

"Good luck to you, too."

Huff is now limping across the locker room to greet me. He is African American, in his late fifties, with short salt-and-pepper hair. He is a former linebacker, and his souvenirs from his playing days include an artificial hip, false front teeth, and two crooked fingers. He wears these disfigurements as proud signifiers of a kamikaze abandon, the kind he wants to instill in his players.

"You should be at home, Nick," he says. Then he hugs me. In five years together we have never hugged. "How are you doing?"

"I've been better," I say.

I hang my head, fighting to stay composed. Huff looks away.

"Stay strong, Gallow," Huff says, squeezing my shoulder. "You'll get through this, I know it."

And then Huff leaves. His abruptness is surprising, and bracing. I turn and watch him limp off.

When I reach my stall, still dazed by this brush-off, the young man to whom Huff had been talking is staring up at me. He sits on a stool a couple of stalls down, in an unmarked space traditionally used by the most transient players. He is wearing only gray underpants and one sock that he has just pulled on, and his dark hair is still damp from the shower. He looks as if he wants to speak to me.

I glance at his leg muscles, and I know right away. Huff only had a few seconds for me, but he had plenty of time for this young man who has come to take my job.

For here is Woodward Tolley. Hunter, meet hunted.

"Hello," I say evenly. "I'm Nick Gallow."

"Hi, I'm Woodward Tolley," he says, standing up quickly. His brown eyes are aglow, but he strains to maintain a respectful somberness, as befitting the morning news. His lean and gangly frame carries some muscle, but he still has plenty of filling out to do; I would guess that he only began working out with professional seriousness in the past year.

But even in his immature state, Woodward has a competitive advantage over me. Woodward will play for the rookie minimum, which is about a third of my $970,000 salary. Plus, I'll be due a roster bonus of $350,000 if I am with the Sentinels for the first day of full training camp in late July. I thought the idea of the bonus sounded cool when I signed my contract, but as its date of payment approaches, I now see it as a reason for the team to get rid of me. I suspect the front-office folks see it that way, too.

"Welcome to the Sentinels, Woodward," I say. We shake hands, firmly. Very firmly.

"Thank you, Mr. Gallow," he says. "How are you doing? How is your agent?"

"I'm okay," I say. "Cecil made it out of surgery. And please, call me Nick."

"That's great, Nick," he says, hands on his hips. "I'll be praying for the best."

"Thank you."

"I know it's a strange time, but I just have to say, ever since they signed me, I've been looking forward to meeting you. I am such a big fan of yours. I mean, that hit on Dez Wheeler last year, that is just about the coolest thing I've ever seen a punter do."

If Woodward is going to attempt to curry favor with

compliments, at least he is choosing his wisely. The Dez Wheeler play happened last year, against Atlanta. Wheeler is their speedy return man, and among the most feared in the league. I hit a strong punt, about fifty-one yards with decent hang time, and he fielded it, sidestepped our first man down-field and shot forward, picking up speed with each tackler he passed. He was about to hit full sprint—that is, until I charged, planted my feet, and drove my shoulder into his midsection. Wheeler went horizontal, and the ball popped skyward.

We didn't recover Wheeler's fumble, of course, and the Sentinels were already trailing by two touchdowns, on our way to yet another loss, so it wasn't much to celebrate in the moment. But on the next morning's *SportsCenter*, my hit made their countdown of the top ten plays of the day—coming in at number four. I have the countdown saved on my DVR, and on a slow Tuesday I've been known to watch it a time or ten.

"Thanks, Woodward," I say. "And please, go ahead and finish dressing."

Woodward dutifully reaches for his other sock and pulls it on, and then grabs a shirt.

"You know, my folks actually saw you the other day over at—what's that place called, the Jackson Suites."

"You mean Jefferson?"

"Yeah, Jefferson, that's right." He pulls a gray Sentinels T-shirt over his head. "The team told me about it." Which is exactly how I found the Jefferson years ago, after I won my job. "What a neat place. My family's all staying there in one big setup. The team's giving me a room when camp's on, but I'm staying with my folks for now. My dad, my mom, two un-cles, an aunt, and a couple of my cousins are all there. The Jefferson only rents by the week, so they came early and made a vacation out of it."

"Do they know the minicamp isn't open to the public?" I ask.

"Oh, they know." Woodward smiles, pulling on a pair of tight-fitting jeans. "But when the Sentinels signed me, they were all so excited. They just had to come. I guess they figure that these three days might be my whole professional career."

He's right, the camp's three days might be his whole career. They could also be the end of mine.

Woodward is on his way home. I have the entire outdoor practice area to myself, and my choice of the three fields behind the facility. I go to my regular spot, Field Three, which is in the back and where the kickers traditionally work.

I begin my standard practice routine, one I have repeated hundreds of times over the years, unvaryingly, in the quest to stamp perfect form into my muscle memory. I go to the jugs machine and set the timer to shoot a ball to me every forty-five seconds. Then I set up fifteen yards away and field balls and send them flying. It is only in my most active spurts—when I am catching the snap, and doing my step-step-step-kick—that the shootings leave my mind. Over the session a scenario develops in my mind. I imagine that I am in a game, getting ready to kick, and the guys on defense are distracting me by pantomiming reenactments of the shootings. I will be counting off the players in front of me to make sure we have eleven men on the field, and a guy on the defense will pretend to shoot two of his teammates; one will stagger and clutch his stomach, while the other falls lifeless and flat, and then bites down on a blood pellet. And with this distraction, the play clock runs out on me. After which the defense high-fives, and

Tanner whispers about how sad it is, that I am psychologically ruined and he will have to get rid of me.

Despite this fantasy, I work my way through thirty-five punts, my standard number, and I manage to hit every kick solid. I hope Tanner is watching from his window; my proficiency is a little inhuman, given the circumstances, and he would no doubt see that as a plus.

During my post-kick stretching, lying on my back, the memories of last night flood in uncensored. As the side of my face touches the turf, while my arms are wide and one leg is crossed over the other, I think about the gruesome sight of Samuel's head resting on the ground, halfway blown off. Then there is Cecil, a bullet taking up residence in his digestive system.

I wonder if there is there any chance, as Rizotti speculated, that the shooter was actually after Cecil. Samuel, it seems, didn't have an enemy in the world. But I can't think of anyone who would be after Cecil, either.

Or perhaps I was the target. Rizotti had raised that possibility, too, albeit primarily to set up an insult. But who would want to shoot at me? The only candidate that comes to mind is Jessica's husband, Dan, assuming he's found out about my three-year relationship with his wife. But Jessica assured me he hasn't, and besides, Dan is supposed to be out of the country. And if he is planning to kill me, why e-mail me a couple of hours beforehand, for the first time ever? Plus, he is a rising star at the Federal Reserve. If he wanted to mess with me, he would be more likely to have me audited than to engage in a poorly executed drive-by shooting that hits everyone but its intended target.

Is the popular theory the right one—that Jai Carson was the shooter after all?

As I sort through the possibilities, I feel like I am drowning in ignorance. There is too much I don't know. I tell myself I need to worry about my job, while I still have it, and let others do theirs.

I wish my meeting with Rizotti had inspired more confidence. He seemed more interested in nailing Jai than in conducting an open-minded search for the truth. I imagine myself pressing Rizotti to do his job better, and his response to me comes automatically. *You're the one who didn't get the license plate.*

CHAPTER 5

I NEED A FRESH IMAGE of Cecil to erase the one that keeps coming back to me from last night. So after I shower and down a mango-flavored protein shake from the team pantry, I return to the hospital. And I am able to see Cecil this time, luckily slipping into a brief window of visitation, though I don't find the new image all that comforting.

Cecil has been moved into a small private room. He is covered with a pale green blanket, and he has an intravenous tube in his forearm. His body is sunk limply into the mattress, and his eyes are half open.

And he has visitors. His wife, Vicki, has made it in from Ohio, along with daughters Rose, nine, and Violet, six. Rose, a chunky blond girl, is wearing a sweatshirt from the Quad Cities Twisters, while Violet, a chunkier brunette, sports a shirt from Springfield State University. The shirts are a reminder of Daddy's travels; he always brings home souvenirs from his trips to the small colleges and minor-league football franchises that he visits on scouting and recruitment missions. Rose and Violet are seated on the long gray sofa by the window having a pinch fight, which I take as an encouraging sign about Cecil's prognosis. The kids, at least, have been assured they don't need to worry.

I am surprised to see DaFrank Burns here. DaFrank is Cecil's other active client, and the reason Cecil was able to land Samuel in the first place. DaFrank, like Samuel, went to Western Alabama, and his strong personal recommendation meant more to Samuel than any multimedia presentation from the big-boy agents.

DaFrank, a former college safety, is a special teams gunner down in Washington, and an intense young man. He makes his living running headlong into others with little regard for his own body.

"Hello, DaFrank," I say, shaking his hand. "Good to see you."

DaFrank shakes my hand and then pulls me in for a hug. Something between a bump and a hug, actually.

I go to Cecil's bedside. "How you feeling?" I ask, placing a hand on his upper arm, above his IVs. He has a tube coming from his stomach area that I can't look too closely at.

"I'm okay," he says, though his muddled whisper suggests otherwise.

I turn to Vicki, who shrugs. "He's going to be here a couple more days, at least," she says. "The bullet hit the small intestine. They had to resect it. The doctors say his wound is amazingly clean, as these things go." She smiles wanly at what now passes for good news, and adds, "We still have to worry about infections though."

"Samuel's funeral is in two days," Cecil whispers, eyelids half closed. "I'm going."

"You can't go anywhere," Vicki says, "until your bowels are working again."

So he's here until he proves he can take a shit.

"I'll be at the funeral, Cecil," DaFrank says. "I'll be your ambassador."

I put my hands on DaFrank's shoulders.

"See, Cecil," I say. "You'll be well represented." I wait a moment and then add, "It's about time one of us is." Cecil normally rolls along with my jibes, but with this one he just closes his eyes, seeking out dreamland.

In the dark of the hospital parking structure I sit in my Audi, titled on the downslope, and check my messages. My mother, at last, has been clued in.

> Nick, where are you??? Are you OK?

I have missed a couple calls from her as well.
I send her a note:

> At hospital, visiting Cecil. The prognosis is positive. I'm fine. I'll talk to you later.

That is as much of a rehash as I am up for right now.

Jessica has been writing me, too—she has, at long last, gotten the news. In her first text, she asks how I am doing. In the second, she asks if I still want to come over tonight, referencing a date that feels like it was made in another lifetime. In the third, sent a half hour later, she says that she understands if I can't make it, but she wants to see me soon, and she is worried about me. The messages reek of an earnestness that, coming from her, underline how wrong the last twenty-four hours have gone.

Not that Jessica and I don't share intimacies with each other. Many times has she bemoaned to me the big lie of her marriage—her husband, Dan, son of a workaholic father, pledged to Jessica he wouldn't live at the office, but now he puts in seventy-hour workweeks under the justification of "I could be Treasury Secretary someday. My name could be on money!" Jessica, meanwhile, has heard plenty from me about the stress and the boredom of my lucrative but low-security job. But mostly our time together is an escape from all that. She regards polite conversation to be an abomination; she prefers to keep people off balance. Once she told me this story about her husband, Dan. "Last year for my birthday, he took me the U.S. Mint," Jessica said. "It was around one A.M., the building was empty. We went to the printing presses, and he turned on the computer guide and adjusted the setting to one-thousand-dollar bills. Then he hit a button and the presses whirred to life and sheets of money started flying off the rollers, and Dan spread his arms wide and said, 'All for you, my dear. All for you.' The catch was that I couldn't spend any of the money. So I now have sheets of thousand-dollar bills lining my underwear drawer." I was naive enough to ask: "Really?" She gazed at me pityingly. "If my husband were capable of such bold and romantic gestures, do you think I'd be here with you?"

That is the standard with us, all goofs and grab-assing. I write Jessica, tapping out the polite letters in a lifeless dirge:

Thank you, I'm holding up fine. I just need to be alone now.

After hitting Send, I see that a new text message has arrived, from a number not programmed into my phone.

Are you OK? I would really like to see you. Melody from Stark's.

I remember how I gave her my number on that champagne bottle, and my need to upstage a twenty-one-year-old in front of a waitress on what turned out to be his last night on earth. I feel guilty, and small.

I am about to tell Melody, as I told Jessica, that I need to be alone. But of course that's not what I need at all.

I call her from the parking lot.

"Please tell me this isn't all my fault," Melody says, her voice less assured than it was last night. "If I had been quicker with the Cristal . . ."

"That has nothing to do with it," I say. "I guarantee it."

Is Melody assuming Jai is guilty, too? I wonder if she or one of the other waitresses heard Jai say anything absolutely damning.

"I hope you're right," Melody says, not sounding all that assured. "Do you think JC did it, though? I saw the police had him in for questioning."

"I don't think he did it," I say. "I don't think so at all."

"I hope not," Melody says. "But who do you think did it then?"

"No idea," I say, already weary of the topic. I had hoped that she would be an escape. "Probably some crackhead."

"Hmm," Melody says. I have left her nowhere to go with that. "Anyway, I'm calling because I am wondering if you wanted to get together. Drink that champagne you gave me."

"Champagne?" I rarely drink, almost never during the day, and I try to keep my systems especially clean before I have to perform. Minicamp is five days off. "What are we celebrating?"

"I don't know," she says. "Being alive. Another glorious day on God's cement-covered earth. Come on. I feel like I need to be with someone right now, and I was just Samuel's waitress. I can only imagine what it's like on your end."

"Fine," I say. "Let's do it." Sitting in my car, in the dank gray of the parking lot, I feel like I need to do something.

Melody asks me to meet at Thirteenth and Locust, near a club called Voyeur—which won't be open, she says, but it doesn't matter because that's not where we're going. "There's this place that I know how to get to from there," she says, "but I don't know the address."

Melody arrives wearing big movie-star sunglasses, jean shorts, and a curve-accentuating tight black T-shirt with the words BUSTIN' LOOSE written across her bountiful chest in fluorescent green script. She is fully clothed, and yet mildly obscene. She grips the bottle of Cristal by the neck.

"We're going this way," she says, pointing south. "And then that way." Pointing east.

We walk south on Thirteenth Street for a couple of blocks, and then we stop at a corner and she points her finger around as if it is a divining rod. "This is it," she says, and we turn east, down Pine Street.

"Where are we headed exactly?" I ask.

"Oh, you'll see," Melody says. "It's a neat spot."

We walk on until Melody slows and then stops in front of a coffee shop whose front window is papered with reviews from newspapers and Web sites.

"Is this the where we're going?" I ask dubiously. This coffee shop is more crowded than I would prefer.

"Actually . . . no," Melody says, distracted. "I'm just remembering something. Let me pop in here for a second." She opens the door and I move to follow but she places her hand on my wrist, stopping me. "Better if you wait outside," she says. I release an involuntarily sigh of impatience. "I'm getting you a little treat," she says, with a reassuring smile. "I'll just be a second."

I wonder if she is in fact lost and is going inside to ask for directions. I watch through the openings between the taped-up reviews as she goes to the counter. A woman attempts to wait on Melody, but Melody waves her off. She then walks over to a young man operating a cappuccino machine and pulls something out of her bag—not all the way, just an inch—and the young man fetches a pastry, wraps it in paper, slides it into a bag and hands it to her. No cash is exchanged. She grabs a couple coffee cups on the way out.

Melody pops out of the store. "We're moving again," she says. "We should be there in a minute."

We continue our trek east. "Did you know that guy in there?" I asked.

She looks at me askance. "Were you watching me?" she asks, with one eyebrow cocked.

"Yes," I say. "What did I see, exactly?"

Melody taps my arm. Now we are turning right, headed south again.

"That guy is part of a little collective I've set up," she says.

"It all started when this guy at Stark's left to work at one of those Garces restaurants, Chifa. He'd drop by Stark's and want free drinks, so I thought, hey, what can he do for me in return? Long story short, we ended up starting this network of people who work in the food service industry. We give each other free stuff. Just little things. All we have to do is flash this card."

She pulls a card out of her handbag. Its only marking is the "no" symbol—a red circle with a line through it. But there is nothing behind the line. Nothing is forbidden.

"So you're an organized crime boss," I say.

She snickers. "I'm an organized misdemeanor boss at best. The stuff we scam costs five, ten bucks at most. And we all work at places that are very successful. We're not ripping off any struggling mom-and-pops. The group has forty-four members in thirty-nine shops. I've said from the beginning, the key to making our thing sustainable is to keep the ratio of businesses and members as level as we can. That way no one is hit too hard. Keep it a mile wide and an inch deep."

She taps my arm again and we turn east again. We are now walking down Addison Street, a narrow residential avenue with little foot traffic. We stop at a small park, maybe ten yards square. It is well maintained, planted with fresh flowers, and it has three benches—each tucked into a corner, and unoccupied.

"Here we are," Melody says. "Pick your spot."

I choose the bench in the far corner, and when I sit I notice that the planters are arranged so that each bench is in its own green enclave. For being in the middle of a city of two million people, the seclusion here is magical. I wonder why I have never heard about this park before.

"Pretty cool spot, right!"

"Very cool," I say. "How'd you find it?"

"It was last fall, my first week working at Stark's," she says. "I went out with some of the busboys and we all got totally smashed. None of us could remember where the car was parked. So we wandered around this neighborhood for two hours looking for it. We kept passing this place and I filed it away for future reference."

"So you've been coming here ever since?"

"Nope," she said, shaking her head. "This is actually my first time back. But I figured after last night, you might prefer someplace a little out of the way."

She unloads her pastry bag, which has the coffee cups and her pastry—a large whoopie pie. "Mind if I do the honors?" she asks, holding up the champagne bottle.

"Please."

She loosens the wire cage of the cork and then covers the top of the bottle with the empty pastry bag. She manipulates the cork underneath the bag until it pops loudly but harmlessly into the paper. With a turn of her wrist she pours the champagne into the cups, and there we are, bubbles rising.

We clink paper cups, as best we can.

"It's nice to be here with you," she says.

"Yes," I say. "It is nice." I drink. My early review: if you ever buy a $500 bottle of champagne, don't drink it out of a paper cup, because you will taste the paper in every sip.

"Is this what good champagne is supposed to taste like?" she asks.

"Not quite," I say, setting the cup down on the ground beneath the bench.

"Seems okay to me," she says, and she tosses the rest of her drink back like it's water and pours herself some more. "But then again I almost never drink champagne. On New Year's Eve, I usually end up working."

"Here's a question for you," I say. "If you're not much of a champagne drinker, how'd you get so good at opening the bottles?"

She pauses, as if caught. "I served a lot of champagne at the last place I worked," she says. She pulls her knees up to her chest and cradles them in her arms.

"Oh, yeah? Where is that?"

"This place in Providence. It is called—brace yourself— the Winking Oyster."

"The Winking Oyster?" I laugh.

"It's a funny name, right?"

"Exactly what kind of establishment is the Winking Oyster?"

"It's a strip club," Melody says, and a sly smile tugs up the corner of her lips.

"So you were a . . . dancer?"

"Bartender," she says. "I'd bring bottles back to the champagne room, that's all. Don't tell me you're going to get all judgmental on me now." She says this with a trace of sternness, as if she has been judged before and it has not gone well.

"I'm not judging," I say. "Not much, anyway."

She takes another drink. "Think whatever you want. I loved it there. We were like a family, all on each other's side, no questions asked. I felt at home there."

I rest my hand between Melody's shoulders, and with my index finger I traced small circles on her neck. She barely seems to notice my touch.

I gaze around the park, which is still empty. In the time we've been sitting on this bench, I have seen only a couple of people walk by. The quiet is beautiful. After a few lazy minutes she pokes me in the ribs and picks up the whoopie pie. "Want some?" she asks, holding it up to my face.

"No thanks."

"Sure?" She waves it suggestively in front of my mouth. The pastry is all airy chocolate cake and shimmering cream.

"I'm sure."

"Whatever," she says, pulling it back and taking a big bite. "One taste won't kill you."

"You never know," I say.

"C'mon, Nick," she says, wheedling. "Just one bite."

"I don't eat sweets," I say. "In my whole life I've never eaten an Oreo, drank a Coke, anything like that."

"Never?" she says, incredulous. "Not even when you were, like, five?"

"No processed foods when I was growing up, no candy, no sugary snacks. My dad had lots of rules."

"Sounds tough," she says softly.

I shrug. "He just wanted me to be the best. He'd always say, 'Victory has a price.'"

She returns my shrug. "Sometimes you can overpay." She finishes off the rest of the whoopie pie with a big bite, stuffing it into her mouth in an intentionally theatrical display of gluttony. "Enchanting, aren't I?" She smiles, teeth full of chocolate, and pours herself another cup of champagne. "I used to be an athlete myself, you know," she says, after she has taken a drink and licked her teeth clean. "High school soccer. I was my team's co-captain."

"Excellent," I say. "What was your career highlight?"

"New Hampshire Class A state semifinals, my senior year," she says, her face lighting up. "Score tied, less than two minutes left, I nailed one into the upper left corner. Game winner. It was awesome. We all went nuts. I did the whole Brandi Chastain thing, I ripped my shirt off and ran around in my sports bra."

"Is there video of that by any chance?" I ask dryly. I am imagining a lot of bouncing.

"You wish," she says. "So do I, now that you mention it. And of course we ended up getting clobbered in the finals. But still, that moment was pretty cool."

"It's great, isn't it?" I say. "When I was in high school, we won districts my senior year. The fans stormed the field. Everyone was hugging and hollering. My teammates carried me off on their shoulders. . . ."

"They carried off the punter?" she asks.

"I was a quarterback in high school, actually."

"Really?" she says. "What happened to the quarter-backing?"

"Things changed," I say, with a sigh. I pick the wrapper from her whoopie pie off the ground and place it in the plastic bag. "So I have a question about this Winking Oyster place."

"Shoot."

"If it was so great there," I ask, "why'd you ever leave it?"

She shifts, pushing herself around to face forward. "Oh, you know how it is. You don't leave the old behind, you never get anyplace new."

"Really?" I say. "You were just restless?"

"Pretty much," she says unconvincingly, and then adds, "I think I'm the kind of girl who likes to go from place to place. My dream is to live on a boat one day. Just sail from harbor to harbor. If I ever get enough money."

I have the money to buy her a boat today. A nice one, too, I'd bet.

"I know how to fish," I say.

"I fish, too. What's your point?"

"If two people were on that boat and knew how to fish, they might not have to come into harbor for a long time." I imagine myself sitting on the boat's rear deck, rod in its holder, my shirt open, sunglasses on, eyes on the line.

"Two people, eh?" Melody says with a chuckle. "So now we're sailing away together?"

She's right to laugh. I was exhausted and beginning to lose my form.

"I should go," I say.

"Already?" she says.

"Yes," I say, standing up. "But thanks for bringing me here. It helped."

"My pleasure," she says, disappointed. "Can you give me a ride home? The bus can be a pain in the ass."

We walk to the street meter where I parked my Audi, our arms occasionally brushing against each other. On the drive Melody directs me up onto the Interstate, and then to a low-rent section of North Philadelphia that I have never been anywhere near before. The surroundings look more industrial than residential, and we are not talking about a thriving industry, either—more like one whose jobs migrated to the South decades ago in search of weaker unions, before realizing they could save even more money by just taking the whole operation overseas.

Melody's house is a narrow two-story structure, adjacent to elevated train tracks, standing alone on a block curiously absent of other homes. A poor little row house that has lost its row. It seems like a miserable place to live. I would have figured a waitress at Stark's might have settled into one of Philadelphia's burgeoning hipster neighborhoods.

There is only one vehicle parked on the street, a shiny red F-150 pickup truck in front of Melody's house. I would appraise the truck as having a greater value than the residence.

"So you really don't think Jai Carson is the one who shot

at you guys?" Melody asks after I put the car in park. "If he didn't do it, who do you think did?"

"I'm sure the police will figure it out," I say without conviction. "They have their top guy on it."

"Really?"

"No," I say.

"Who's the top suspect, do you think?"

"O.J."

"No, seriously, did they give you any idea . . ."

I place a knuckle under her chin and raise her head up and kiss her on the mouth. She doesn't seem to mind being shut up this way. Her return kiss is confident and aggressive. She places a hand on my chest and claws in. We are off to the races.

But it is suddenly all too much. I push her gently away. It is wrong to forget so soon. "I should really go home," I say.

"I'm sorry," she says, looking embarrassed.

"I'll call you after minicamp," I say.

"Promise?"

"If I say I'm going to do something," I assure her, "I do it."

She gets out of the car and, as she walks the uneven cement path to her house, the door opens for her. I see a male figure standing behind the screen door.

Strange. Melody hadn't mentioned a roommate. In fact, when she called me, proposing our rendezvous, she had declared that she didn't want to be alone.

CHAPTER 6

BACK AT THE Jefferson, I check my messages. My mother has called again. It sounds like she is on the way to Philadelphia, though her phrasing is imprecise. She says in her message, "I'm going to come down there," but it isn't clear if she is stating an intent of future action, or if she is already in her car, driving. I call to seek clarification, but her phone is off, as usual. She only turns it on to talk.

I need to sleep, but I suspect she is in fact on her way, so I resist the urge to go to bed. The champagne I drank has left me with a mild headache. I put Irma Thomas's *Straight from the Soul*, which I have been listening to a bunch lately. Her lyrics can be childish, but her voice conveys heartache with a deep clarity.

As the music kicks in I sit on the sofa and pick up an issue of *Esquire*. Some actress I've never heard of is the sexiest woman alive, apparently. I turn my body lengthwise, with my feet up and my head on a pillow and I close my eyes and lay the magazine down as Irma wails for me.

I am roused by the tinny chime of the Jefferson doorbell. "Coming," I shout. My body feels dead. I stumble to the door, and there is my mother. She's made it here. So has her boyfriend, Aaron, standing back a couple of judicious steps in the hallway. It is a jolt to see him outside my door, as he has never been down here before. Our previous encounters have been up in Elmira, where they now live.

It has been a couple of months since I last saw my mother. She is wearing a denim shirt and jeans, a combo unfamiliar to me; she has let her hair grow longer than its normal shoulder length, and she is more tanned than I am accustomed to her being.

Aaron has a deep tan, too. He is tall and reedy, with longish hair and an overgrown and silver-streaked goatee. He is wearing khaki shorts and an olive-green T-shirt.

It may be my imagination, but I feel like the two of them are starting to look alike. Aaron and my mother have been together since the divorce seven years ago—if not longer than that. She would never tell me how or when their relationship began. She announced that she was divorcing my dad and taking up with Aaron just after my brother, Doug, two years younger than me, left for college, and the timing made it seem as if she had been waiting for the kids to clear out. She refused to answer our questions, declaring them "inappropriate," so Doug and I were left to guess the circumstances. Perhaps she and Aaron met during my junior year in high school, when she suddenly started experimenting with her hairstyles, claiming that she wanted to inspire customers at the hair salon where she worked. Perhaps it had something to do with her book group, which sometimes took overnight trips related to that month's selection. After reading *World's End* by T. C. Boyle, they visited Peekskill, New York; for *Ironweed*, they were off to Albany. I remember asking my mother who else was in her book group, and she answered curtly, "No one you know." When she left, I wondered if there ever was a book group—and if so, did it have just one other member?

One side effect of this mystery of their origins was that I

regarded Aaron with suspicion, a man with a secret. It had taken me a good couple of years to see him as just another guy trying to get through life.

My mother once made an attempt to explain what she saw in Aaron. "I matter to him," she said to me, sitting across from each other in a diner booth up in Elmira. "Your dad, he could make me feel as if he didn't need me at all, like I was this inconsequential nuisance." And then she added, meekly, "I have a soul, you know."

I felt bad for my mother, that she imagined the existence of her soul was in doubt. But I also questioned the acuity of her perception. Of course she mattered to my dad, as the aftermath of their divorce proved all too violently.

"Oh, Nicky," my mother says, throwing herself upon me urgently, as if she is somehow shielding me from last night's bullets.

"It's okay, Mom," I say, stepping back after a moment. "They didn't get me." I hold my arms out. "See, no holes." She tries to smile, though I can see tears well in her eyes. "Hello, Aaron," I say as he sidles forward to stand beside my mother.

"That has to have been a horrible thing to witness," Aaron says. He has a black roller bag at his side.

"It was." Even after all this time, and in these strange circumstances, I do not find it natural to make chitchat with this man. I can't help but wonder what my dad would say if he saw us talking like family.

"Come on in," I say.

"Apologies for our appearance," Aaron says as they enter. He deposits his roller bag by the door. "We're still in our country outfits."

"No worries," I say.

"How is Cecil doing?" my mother asks as she takes a seat in the armchair, while Aaron goes to the sofa.

"Could be worse," I say.

"Is Vicki with Cecil?"

"She's here," I say. "The girls, too. They flew in from Ohio this morning."

My mother smiles stiffly. I can see she feels guilty. Vicki was at Cecil's side before my mother even knew what was going on.

"How have the police been with you?" asks Aaron.

"About what I'd expect. Just doing their job."

"If anything is going on that you think isn't right, let me know," he says. "I used to be on the force. . . ."

"Yes, I know," I say. "You used to be on the force."

I avoided any obvious disdain, but Aaron catches it anyway, this reference to his having quit his policeman's job.

"Yes, I used to be on the force," Aaron says patiently. "And I've been training officers for more than a decade now, and I know men and women in just about every department in the Northeast. If you feel like something's going on that isn't right, just give me a call."

"He wants to help, Nicky," my mother says.

"I appreciate that," I say. "I really do."

"This has to have been a great mental strain on you," Aaron says. "Your mother and I wondered if you might want to come to our cabin for a few days. You'd have your own bedroom. There are hiking trails nearby. Couldn't be more peaceful. We could leave now if you wanted, you could sleep in the back of the car. . . ."

"I can't go anywhere right now," I say.

"How come?" Aaron says, concerned. "Did the police tell you not to leave town?"

"No, it's not that. I have minicamp in a few days. Not a good time for me to go away."

"Oh," my mother sighs, as for the thousandth time, football takes priority.

"Surely with all that's happened," says Aaron, "the team will understand if you ask for some time off. . . ."

"Surely they won't," I say flatly.

"But . . ." my mother begins.

"The beat goes on," I say, rubbing my eyes and leaning against a wall. "And on and on and on. It's been a long day, Mom."

"I know it has," my mother says.

It is then that I think of Aaron's black roller bag by the door. "Where are you guys staying?" I ask. My apartment has one bedroom.

My mother and Aaron look at each other. I sense they haven't planned out their lodgings for the night.

"You guys are welcome to crash here," I say, but with something less than pure enthusiasm. "I'll be fine on the sofa."

There is an awkward pause.

"Let's find a hotel," Aaron says to my mother.

"There's plenty of good ones nearby," I say.

While Aaron steps to the kitchen and punches around on his phone to see what's available, my mother and I talk some more, though she shifts the topic of conversation to my furnishings, and how they might be rearranged. Soon Aaron reports that he has made a reservation at a Sheraton a few blocks north, near the city's museum row.

"That's perfect," I say. "There's a good breakfast spot around the corner. Let's meet there tomorrow. Nine thirty." That is later than I normally eat breakfast, but it will give some time for the business crowd to clear out.

After I close the door behind them, I lie back down on the sofa. I wish my dad were alive. I wonder what advice he would have for me. Probably that he is sorry that I had witnessed a tragedy, but we all experience awful things if we live long enough. The only thing we can do is to keep fighting. Keep fighting—that was always his message.

Right until he drove himself into a tree.

CHAPTER 7

I PLAY THE rest of the Irma Thomas record and I end up falling asleep on the sofa. At five in the morning I wake from a nightmare. The details evaporate immediately, but I know I had been talking to my dad. In the weeks after his crash he visited my dreams nightly, to the point to where I considered believing in ghosts. Now he rarely comes by. In this dream he and I were on a boat, and he was wearing a plaid bathing suit, like the kind he used to wear on our annual family vacation at Cayuga Lake. He was fishing, and he caught a big one. He always said that he would be embarrassed to come home from a fishing trip without having caught anything. Everything else I forget.

For breakfast I meet my mom and Aaron at Sabrina's, a funky spot with a goth waitstaff and a menu where even the standard breakfast dishes are tricked out—blue cheese where you might expect cheddar, challah in place of white bread. "I didn't know Philadelphia had places like this!" my mother says excitedly, after a man with tattooed forearms and six earrings brings our menus. It does. More every week, it seems.

"Did you have a chance to read that story I sent you the other day?" she asks.

I think back to what story she is referring to, and then I remember: she e-mailed me an article about a new study detailing the long-term health effects of head injuries on football players. The headline claimed signs of brain trauma were being found in living players in their forties and fifties. I deleted the e-mail without reading it. Studies like this seem to come out weekly now, and my mother forwards me every one she sees. I feel like I can skip reading these stories because I've seen plenty of them and I grasped their point a long time ago. Football is bad for you. I know, I get it. But football is my job, and worrying about what damage might be done to my brain—and what damage might have happened already—isn't going to help me get through my workday. I once saw a study claiming that concussions are more likely to cause long-term brain damage if you have two of them close together, and I choose to keep that factoid at the top of my thoughts, because I've only had one serious concussion, and that was back when I was a college quarterback. I haven't had one since.

"I don't want to talk about it right now, if you don't mind," I say.

"I understand," my mother says softly. She has been on this campaign for a year now, trying to get me to quit football, suggesting one day that I could go to law school, another day into real estate, throwing out career possibilities as if I were an unfocused wastrel.

In search of a more pleasant topic, I ask my mom what is going on around my hometown of Waverly—she still works at her old salon there, though she lives in Elmira. She begins by reporting that Charlie Wentz, my dad's old offensive coordinator, is doing well in his recovery from prostate cancer. Grace Albini, a girl from across the street who is a few years younger than me, just moved to Namibia to work for a nonprofit group treating women with HIV—despite her parents' best efforts to talk her out of it. The big scandal in town: my old high school teammate Robby Polchuk, who I will always remember as the guy who caught my first touchdown pass, was just arrested and charged with seventeen counts of insurance fraud.

"Really?" I say. Robby has always been a knucklehead, but not a particularly malevolent one, and he never struck me as the criminal type.

"It's the craziest thing," she says. "Robby would stop short so drivers would crash into him. He did it a couple of times a month. He had claims going against all these different insurance companies. It's a wonder he didn't get himself killed."

"What an idiot," I say. The funny thing is that Polchuk always avoided contact when he was running routes over the middle. I guess you can become pretty desperate in ten years.

"Scams like that are more common than you'd think," chips in Aaron, turning toward me.

"And this you won't believe," my mom says, cradling an oversized coffee mug in both hands, her eyes lighting up. "Anna is getting married."

This is Anna Vilius, the woman who, my mother once believed, should have been my bride. Anna was my girlfriend for my junior and senior years of high school, and my mother to this day keeps our prom photo on her mantel. The one time I asked her to remove it she declined, saying, "It's one of the few pictures I have of you smiling." The photo shows Anna in a strapless white gown, with long blond hair and tan shoulders gleaming, and me in a complementary white tuxedo she had picked out. We looked completely goofy, which was the idea at the time. After high school Anna went off to Michigan— her dad's school—while I stayed in New York for college, going to Hudson Valley State. She and I made what was in retrospect an obviously doomed run at staying together despite the distance, and that lasted only to Thanksgiving break, when she informed me that she had met another guy in Ann Arbor. (That relationship did not even last to winter break, by which time I had taken up with a girl from the Hudson State volleyball team.) Even though it was Anna who had left me, my mother would often look at our prom photo and murmur the same wistful sentiment. *In the olden days, she would have worn your ring.*

"She's not marrying that same guy, is she?" I speak with forced disinterest, because I can feel my mother studying my face for signs of disappointment.

"No, thank God," my mother says. "She finally wised up on the rock star." The guy we are talking about is a musician Anna had begun dating after she returned home from college with a sociology degree. He and Anna broke up and got back together again several times—even after she had, unbelievably, born this bum a son, whom she ended up raising on her own.

"Who is it, then?" I ask.

"Richard Wibb," she says, giddy with her surprise.

"Wibb? Really?"

"Yes. Isn't it amazing?"

Richard Wibb was in my high school class, but I barely knew him. I remember him taking all the top-track classes, and also being very skinny and intensely shy. I never saw him out anywhere, at the diner or a football game or even the prom. I couldn't remember seeing he and Anna talk to each other, though I think they both took French.

"Apparently he wrote Anna a note on that Facebook site," my mother says. "They started seeing each other, now she and her boy are moving to New York City to live with him. Isn't that something?"

"What's he do in New York?"

"He's a lawyer," my mother says. "A very successful one, from what I hear. And I'm told that Richard just dotes on the boy. Would you have ever guessed back in high school that those two would end up together? How many times have I said it to you, Nicky—there's a lid for every a pot."

As she says this last part she casts a warm glance at Aaron and takes his hand underneath the table.

Poor Dad.

"Tell me, Aaron," I say. "Any thoughts about the murder?"

Aaron, after pulling his hand back from my mother's, offers a long series of qualifications, which establish that he is only engaging in speculation based on second-hand information. But then he says that he understands why the police are looking hard at Jai Carson. If this were his case, Jai would be his prime target.

"This crime feels like an angry one," Aaron says. "A drive-by shooting, with two other people around—it's just not smart. Wouldn't it be better to go after your victim when he's alone? And why leave a witness?"

"So if the killer knew what he was doing, I'd be dead?" I say.

"Well," says Aaron, blinking a couple of times. "Yes."

I am being a smart-ass, and I take no actual offense at Aaron's analysis. His point is a good one. But still, I let my question hang there until it becomes uncomfortable.

I plow through my breakfast, a spinach-and-egg-white omelet, and before too long I have Aaron and my mother on the road back upstate with a pledge that I will visit them some time after minicamp.

Soon after I am back at the Jefferson, I receive a text from an unexpected correspondent:

> Some guys are working out at my house today. Come on by!—JC

My first question: how did Jai get my number? Then I remember the team distributes a contact list. I imagine Jai sitting with a newspaper in one hand, the phone list in the other, matching up my name and dialing the number.

I guess he knows who I am now. And I can imagine why he wants me to come on by.

According to the news, Jai was interviewed by police for five hours yesterday, then released without being charged. In the worlds of talk radio and online message boards, however, Jai has been all but convicted. The argument between Jai and Samuel is now public knowledge; today's *Inquirer* re-creates the scene in startling detail, in a story that carried the bylines of five reporters.

Jai's alibi for the time of the murder is that he lingered with his friends in the Stark's parking lot, drinking out of his car's built-in cooler, and then they went to a club for several hours and then out to eat again, and then home, where Jai was collected by police. Jai, however, arrived at the club a decent interval after the shooting, and particularly damning is the fact that the crew traveled in two cars—with Jai and his pastor Cheat Sheet (real name, Lewis Whicks, juvenile arrest record for auto theft) showing up to the club much later than the other guys, and in a sedan. The sedan was black, which means it could have been the one I saw speeding away after Cecil and Samuel were shot.

Jai's explanation for his delayed arrival at the club was that after leaving Stark's he was seized by an irresistible craving for a Four-Dollar Feedbag, a fast-food product of which he is a proud endorser. The Four-Dollar Feedbag consists of two small cheeseburgers, a small fries, and a chocolate-chip-and-peanut-butter cookie. "I'll be honest with ya," Jai says in his commercials, with a wink at the camera. "I'm in it for the cookies." When police raised the point that on the night of the shooting Jai was coming from just having eaten a steak dinner, he responded by saying, "When I'm hungry, I eat!" It is an alibi designed both to account for his time and to please a sponsor.

Seeing the details of Jai's police interview in these news stories, sourced to anonymous figures close to the investigation, makes me feel justified in being circumspect with Rizotti during our questioning. But Jai has to know that I talked to the police, and that I am the only eyewitness. He is asking me over to his house for that one reason—to find out if I am for him, or against him. He wants to look me in the eye.

I accept his invitation because I want to look back.

CHAPTER 8

JAI LIVES IN a gated residential neighborhood in Haddonfield, New Jersey. He resides outside the city for tax reasons. I might be doing that, too, if my superstitions didn't lash me to the Jefferson.

Jai's home is an Etruscan-style mansion on what has to be at least four acres. The house has an electronic gate that opens for me when I arrive; I pull up into a large semicircular drive and park next to a black Mercedes, a white Bentley, a black Cadillac Escalade, a black Range Rover, a dark-green Prius, and, at the end, a true junker—an old boat of a car that looks to be at least fifteen years old and in horrible shape, with one panel of dark maroon, while the rest of the body is baby blue.

The black Mercedes looks more like the shooter's car than the Prius, though I find the precise memory of the car is fading quickly. But I look at both cars' back bumpers, and they are clean. If anyone scraped a sticker off last night, they did a thorough job.

Jai emerges from the front of his house to greet me. He is shirtless, wearing only black compression pants, casually displaying his broad chest and shoulders. A peacock trails listlessly by his feet.

"Nick Gallow," he says with a broad smile. "Welcome, my brother."

"So you do know my name," I say. "The other night at Stark's I could have sworn you had no idea who I was."

"I had no fucking clue," Jai says, shaking his head and

laughing. "But believe me, I know now. I done talked about that bullshit in the restaurant like you wouldn't believe."

Jai says this as if it is amusing—as if one of our teammates isn't dead, as if he isn't at the center of a murder investigation, and certainly as if I have no right to be offended at not being recognized by a teammate of five years.

After a pause I change the subject. "So you have a peacock."

"This is Peayoncé," he says, giving the birds a gentle pat on the head. The bird bobs back and wanly ruffles her tail feathers.

"She looks a little sad," I say.

"Yeah, she's a smart gal," Jai says, looking down at her admiringly. "She knows there's some shit going down."

At least someone in the household is concerned.

"Whose car is that?" I ask, pointing at the older one with the rust spots.

"That's mine, man," Jai says. "One of mine, anyway. I call it my crunk-mobile. You recognize it?"

"Should I?"

"You ever see the movie *Hustle & Flow*?"

"Yes," I say. "It was great." The movie is best known for the Oscar-winning rap "It's Hard Out Here for a Pimp." And now that Jai mentions it, the car is beginning to look familiar.

"That's from the movie," Jai says. "This is the car the pimp and his girl worked out of."

"How'd you get it?" It is an odd piece of film memorabilia—not exactly an Aston Martin from a James Bond movie.

"They were selling it at auction," Jai says. "Pretty sure it was a benefit or something."

"How much did it run you?" Without the movie association, the beater wouldn't have been worth $300.

"I don't know," he says. "I just told my guy, get me that car, and here it is." Jai then starts singing a song about popping his collar, and he mimes popping his collar, even though he is shirtless. He waves for me to follow him and we walk inside, him beat-boxing the instrumental notes along the way.

We walk through the columns of the front porch, past the tall white doors and inside into a wide circular atrium with a high domed ceiling and a marble-tile floor. Inlaid in the floor, in gold script, are the words SWAGGA LIFE.

That inscription will do wonders for the home's resale value, no doubt.

"I hired the same architects who worked on the Bellagio," Jai says.

"It shows."

"Here, let's go this way," he says, pointing through a doorway. "You got to get the tour of the house. Everyone gets the tour."

We walk back and to the left, and into a room filled with candy. The shelves hold large glass jars filled with Gummi worms, Tootsie Pops, gumdrops, butterscotches, peppermints, and on and on. He also has racks stocked with M&M'S, Hershey bars, Skittles, Reese's Pieces, and bubblegum, as if he had walked into a convenience store and bought displays *in toto.*

I am quietly stunned. I know that the restrictive diet my father designed for me was atypical, but still, it is shocking to find, in the home of my team's most decorated player, this monument to everything I couldn't have.

"I call this Sugar Mountain," Jai says, grabbing a pack of Reese's Pieces. "Want anything, just go ahead and take it."

"No thanks," I say, then ask, "You have kids?"

"Two," Jai says. Some might have found that question rude,

considering there is no Mrs. Carson, but Jai treats it as normal conversation. "Boy and a girl. They're great, man. They love this room. When their moms visit, I can't get those kids out of here."

We walk on, through a spacious kitchen with a long dining bar in the middle and a grill and griddle as well as an eight-burner stove against the wall, and into Jai's trophy room. "This is where I keep all the shit they give me," he says nonchalantly. While I inspect the hardware, Jai rips open his pack of Reese's Pieces and pours the candy into this mouth like he is drinking a soda.

I look for, and find, his Defensive Player of the Year Award, which Jai won in his third season in the league. I was still in college back then, and I can remember watching Jai on television and being in awe—the nasty sacks, the open-field takedowns, the strips on running backs, the leaping interceptions. His opponents looked so overmatched that it hardly seemed fair, these ordinary humans having to suffer an assault from this otherworldly terror.

Then I met Jai. Five years before he met me.

We pass through into the next room, which has a flat screen on the wall, fifty inches at least. There are no chairs in this room, just a pair of gigantic mattresses, way beyond king-size. They each look like they could hold six people across, comfortably. The back mattress is elevated a couple feet higher than the front one, and a dozen black pillows line the top of each.

"This is where I hold my movie nights," Jai says, and then he breaks out into a wide smile. "We turn it on in here, you know what I mean?"

"Where do you get mattresses that big?" I ask.

"I have them custom-designed," Jai says. "Same dude who made the mattress for my bedroom."

And with this segue that rolls ever-so-naturally off his tongue, we head up the stairs.

As we hit the landing on the second floor, Jai says, "This is my guys' floor. Cheat Sheet. Milk Man. Todd. They all got their own rooms."

I don't know Milk Man or Todd by name, but I assume that they, like Cheat Sheet, are friends from Memphis.

"What are those guys up to today?" I ask.

"I dunno," he says. "They're off somewhere. Doin' some shit, I guess."

"Good guess," I say.

Jai laughs and continues on up the stairs. "C'mon, let's go. My room's one more up."

As we climb the spiral staircase, I cannot help but feel a rising sense of anticipation for what lies ahead. I wonder how many ladies, or pairs of ladies, or bus-sized tour groups of ladies, have made this same journey with rising curiosity and excitement.

The bedroom is, I have to say, magnificent. First of all, it occupies the entire top floor. You just emerge from the stairs and you are in it, feet sinking into the plush black carpet.

The bed is in the center of the room, circular, low to the floor, and turquoise. It looks like a huge inflatable pool, except that its sides are curved and made of leather.

"Did you design that yourself?" I ask.

"I did," Jai says. "See the way the sides arch like that? You can get some real good angles."

"Angles?"

"I can demonstrate if you like," Jai says, taking a step toward the bed.

"That's fine," I say, and wander toward Jai's dressing area, which is entirely open and in a corner of the room. Racks of suits and dress shirts abut collections of exercise shirts and leisure wear. The shoe rack has to hold at least five dozen pairs.

There is a neon sign on the wall that reads, in scripted red letters, YES.

"You want to see the coup de grâce?" Jai says.

He pulls back the curtains on a door to a terrace that runs nearly the length of the bedroom. The balcony has a kingly white balustrade that is open at the far right end. The opening accommodates a white slide that curls around in a wide loop and drops into the backyard swimming pool. There is no ladder back up.

"You probably know this from the show," Jai says.

"The show?" I ask.

"*Give It Up for JC,*" he says. Of course. This is the name of Jai's reality dating show, which I managed to avoid watching. The show was modeled after *The Bachelor,* except that all of the female contestants competing for Jai's favor were allegedly virgins. After the basic cable series ended, JC and the lucky winner then filmed an NC-17-rated "deflowering" episode that was available only on pay-per-view. I place the word "deflowering" in quotes because those who saw the special—for example, Freddie—questioned whether the woman was a virgin to the porn industry, much less to sex itself.

"I'm afraid I missed it," I say.

Jai has been the jolly tour guide up to this point, but with this remark his smile flatlines. "Time to get our workout on," he says. "The guys are already out by the hill."

I look to the far back of the property, where eight shirtless men are stretched out and talking to one another among a collection of sandbags and weight vests piled on the lawn. In this tony suburban development, they seemed to be doing their best to create the atmosphere of a prison yard. The guys are all linebackers, lean and powerful, some new to the team. The math dictates that two and probably three of the guys here today will not make the final roster.

"Is Too Big showing up?" I ask.

"Nah," Jai says. "If that fat fuck tried to keep up with what we're doing today, he'd have a heart attack."

We gather in the grassy space between Jai's pool and the tree line at the back of his property, and I quickly introduce myself to the guys, a couple of whom are fresh out of college. At six four, I am taller than all of them. At 225 pounds. I am within their range of weight. I could pass for one of them, physically.

Jai begins the workout by marching us back and forth across the lawn in a sequence of increasingly complex lunges. The sun's glare is such that I am sweating two minutes in. After about ten minutes of that we do squats while holding twenty-pound sandbags chest-high. The sandbags are loosely packed, and we have to squeeze in at the elbows to hold them steady. "No sag, punter, no sag!" Jai shouts at me when I let mine dip. Then we place the bags to the side and drop down while Jai leads us through an increasingly difficult series of planks—the last one is a killer, with our arms spread wide and our bodies just a couple inches off the ground. We hold that for a full minute. A couple of the other guys indulge in what I call exercise tourettes, grunting out "son of a bitch" or "motherfucker!"

After the planks we pick up the sandbags again and line up on the ground, facing each other, soles together, for pairs sit-ups—at the top of our raises we pass the sandbag to the player opposite us. My crunch partner is Qadra Ndukwe, a rookie wearing only black nylon shorts and white Jordan basketball shoes. Qadra's eyes are fierce at the top of each lift as he snaps the sandbag to me with a vocal exhale. As we approach fifty reps his breaths become grunts, as do mine. On the last lift I actually moan "Christ!" into the suburban afternoon.

"Liquid time," Jai says. Lying on the lawn is a case of orange Gatorade, the bottles still on a cardboard tray with the plastic ripped open. "Drink up, y'all. We're about to start the real workout."

The real workout is the hill, a fifteen-foot climb at the back of Jai's property, toward the tree line. It is steep and has a dirt path worn up the middle. We are to run up to the top of the hill, curl around to the left, and run down a path that is a little less steep, and then come back and do it again.

As I suck down my Gatorade, I assess the hill with confidence. My home workouts include running seventeen flights of steps up to my Jefferson apartment, usually at least twice per session. I feel confident I can handle this dirt path.

We form a line and begin our ascents. We are to do twenty climbs, in formation. The incline is steep enough to test my balance, but the biggest challenge is coping with Jai's chatter, which is nonstop. He is last in line and ostensibly talking to Qadra about the fraternity brand etched onto his right bicep. But it is closer to the truth to say that Jai is talking and Qadra happens to be nearby.

"You know, I heard some guy the other day talking about developing your own brand, and I am thinking, I might really want to develop my own brand, you know what I mean? One of them irons with a big *JC* on it. How great would that be? After I am done with a woman, I'd take my brand and burn a big ol' *JC* into her ass. Tttssssssss!"

No one responds to this idiocy, as our breath is already being tested by the run, but that doesn't deter Jai, who continues on.

"Shit, this is a great idea for my show. Maybe that's one of the elimination rounds, who is willing to get branded. That would tell you if you're really in control of a woman. I used to think it was whether they let you fuck their ass. But if a woman lets you put your mark on her, you know there ain't nothin' she's saying no to."

After we complete twenty laps, Jai raises the level of difficulty. "Now put on your weight vests," he says. These vests resemble life jackets, except they have iron plates sewn into them and weigh forty-five pounds each.

As soon as we begin running the hill again, with vests weighing us down, Jai resumes his chatter. He is breathing hard, too, but not hard enough to shut him up.

"I got to save that brand idea for the next season. You know there's got to be another season, right? I got, like, a million ideas for episodes. Here's another one. JC got a blindfold on, right, the girls come one-by-one, they put a body part in my mouth, and I have to guess what it is. You know ain't nobody winning that round without putting something good in JC's mouth. And when I say good, I mean real good, you know what I mean . . ."

As I listen to him run on like this—and in these circumstances, with Samuel dead and many people wondering if he is guilty—I think about what Tanner said. If Jai is so self-absorbed and so unaware of anything but his own immediate impulses, he is capable of anything.

"What if a cameraman puts his balls in your mouth?" I say to Jai, in between gasps. "That would be good for the blooper reel, at least."

Qadra chuckles, but the other guys just continue grunting up the hill.

"Okay, bitches, you feeling fresh enough to joke around?" Jai say. "Time to turn it up. Next set, pick up a twenty-pound sandbag, and hold it at chest level the whole time you're going up the hill. Anyone lets that shit drop I'm going to bulldog their ass."

With the sandbag added to the weight vest, the hill becomes genuinely difficult. Before, I had been taking the incline in one burst of energy. Now each step up is a battle and requires its own push, and I am feeling every dig in my thighs. My shoulders are howling as well.

"Keep those bags up, bitches!" Jai exhorts. "We're just starting the fourth quarter. You ain't gonna quit in the fourth quarter, are you? C'mon punter, I see you dragging! Can't you hang? You need me to get you a tampon?"

I am working harder to maintain my pace, but I don't feel like I am dragging. I keep the sandbag high until I have done my required laps, and then I dump it on the ground and greedily retreat to the cardboard tray with the Gatorade.

I am not going to say anything, but I hope we are finished. I am sucking air, my shoulders are fried, and even my legs are feeling worn. The others don't seem to be faring any better. A couple of guys are taking their Gatorade on one knee, while another is leaning back against a tree, eyes wide in disbelief, as if he just escaped some kind of crash.

Jai says, "Okay, y'all, that is some sorry shit I am seeing. Do it again, same reps, except this time you're taking two bags, one on top of the other. If any one of you lets that shit drop, everybody is doing twenty extra laps. Everybody."

It sounds like all too much. Somewhere in my head I hear a whisper that I don't have to do everything Jai tells me to do.

But I stack two bags and press them up to chest level and get in line at the base of the hill. No way am I going to be the first to complain.

After the first lap holding two sandbags I feel like I might die. It is not just the legs and shoulders. My chest is absolutely pounding.

Qadra, who is in front of me, drops to his knees after the third lap and retches orange-pink vomit on the grass. "C'mon, Qadra, keep your ass moving," Jai shouts, jogging in place as he stands over him. "This ain't no college bullshit no more. You working for a living now!"

Qadra stays on his knees, heaving.

"I quit," Qadra wheezes.

"Quit?" Jai drops his sandbags and grabs Qadra by both shoulders and wrenches him back, flinging him to the grass. Jai then gets on top of Qadra and pins the rookie's arms with his knees and grabs his head with both hands. "Quit?" Jai screams, eyes bulging. "Don't use that goddam word. Don't ever use that word." The rest of us have slowed, our heads turned as Jai continues to squeeze, his neck muscles bulging, and Qadra cries in anguish. I fear that Jai will crush Qadra's skull in his hands. "You ain't never allowed to quit!" Jai snarls. "Never!"

"Hey . . ." I say.

Jai whirls around toward me, seething. "Who told you all you could stop!" He lets go of Qadra and yells, "See what happens? One person stops, all these other damn clowns think it's break time."

Jai lifts his bags and we all pick up our paces. Qadra rises, too, and resumes running. The wisp of rest has robbed me of my momentum, and I am battling with every step. My legs are quivering, my arms are shaking, sweat is in my eyes, and my heart is racing so fast it feels like it barely has time to beat. But after Jai's display, I am going to keep running and keep these bags high, no matter what. It's like my dad always used to say to me: *It's just pain.*

After we complete twenty runs, guys are dropping on the grass at the base of the hill. The burn in my shoulders is astounding. My arms are dangling limply at my side. But I remain standing with my chin up, signaling that I am ready for more, if there is more.

"That's it, punter," Jai says, slapping my rear. He looks perfectly calm, as if his outburst against Qadra never happened. "Good run, bro."

Thank God. I go down on one knee, and then to both knees, and I double over with my forearms on my thighs. My pores pump sweat with each heartbeat. I try to breathe deep to slow my heart rate, but it is a struggle to do that, with the way my lungs are heaving. Other guys around me are in a similar state.

Jai is alone in standing upright. He strolls to the crate of Gatorade, picks it up and tosses fresh bottles to each of us. My bottle hits me in the back of the weight vest and bounces off. I reach for it and crack the plastic seal—this feels like a major test now—and drink sitting up on my knees.

"Damn," Jai says in between gasps, sweat pouring from his shaved dome. "That was some good work, y'all. If the Sentinels stink it up this year, it ain't going to be the linebackers' fault."

"Or the punter's," I cough out.

The heads swivel toward me, as if my last thought contains an impudence.

"I almost forgot," Jai says after a moment, walking toward

me. "We got a first-timer here in the yard. You all know how we welcome first-timers."

Before I know it, the guys are on their feet. I feel powerful grips on my arms and legs as I am lifted and carried face-down, with my weary body sinking limply in the middle.

My first thought is that they are taking me toward the house. That is until they stop and I smell the chlorine and hear the whirr of the pool filter.

"Okay, guys," Jai says. "One . . . two . . . three!"

I am flung through the air and hit the cool water face-first, gasping an inhale before I go under. I sink down with alarming rapidity, the weight vest carrying me to the bottom of the pool, which I hit hands first.

I get my legs underneath me and push up toward the surface, but with the weight vest on I barely rise from the floor. I raise my hands up but I don't feel like I come close to cracking the surface. I must be in ten feet of water, at least. I can hear what sounds like laughter through the funhouse filter of the water.

This is scarier than being attacked—being hazed by people who are too oblivious to realize the danger they have put me in.

But I need to settle myself. Panicking will not help.

I am a performer. I can stay calm in the middle of a roaring stadium, with the rush coming at me and 1.3 seconds to get my kick off. I have a good minute here to remove this weight vest.

I right myself and feel the vest's front. It is cinched on with two sets of plastic interlocking clasps. I try the bottom clasp first. It doesn't unlock easily—it requires a firm press on a precise point—but I find that point and it comes apart. I then undo the top clasp. I slide my arms out of the vest. And then I push up to the surface.

I break through the water and inhale deeply and desperately. Kicking toward the pool's edge, I throw my arms over the side, gasping.

Jai is sitting on the pool's diving board, applauding. The others join in. "Goddamn, punter," he hoots. "Goddamn. You a goddamn man." He walks over and grabs my forearms and pulls me out of the pool. I stand on my feet now, feeling both angry and exhilarated. Jai and I stand face-to-face, just a few inches apart, and he regards me with delight—or, dare I say it, pride?

"How'd you become such a motherfucker?" he asks, grinning.

"Born that way," I gasp.

"I bet," he says. He punches me in the gut—not a real punch, a playful one—and then he screams, "Booyah!" and leaps into the pool, arms and legs spread wide, the vision of a free man.

CHAPTER 9

THE OTHER GUYS join Jai in the pool, and I go to my phone and text Vicki for the latest news on Cecil. She says he is doing better. He's been switched from morphine to Toradol—a painkiller I know because it's popular around the locker room. I've never used it, but I've seen plenty of injured teammates rely on it to get through a game day.

I am reassured, somehow, by this speck of familiarity and

join the guys for a half-hour float. I leave Jai's house surprised that he did not once ask me anything about Samuel's shooting. If he had any agenda in inviting me over—and he surely did, since the invitation was unprecedented—my best guess is that it is simply to remind me that I am part of a team.

And it worked. Taking on the hill with the guys made me feel like I am part of a unit. On the team I'm technically grouped as a specialist with the long snapper and kicker, but no other Sentinel does what I do. In reality I'm a position group of one. Today I hung with the linebackers and passed all their tests, and I feel great about it.

Back at the Jefferson, I am hailed down by one of the uniformed young men at the front desk. He has a delivery for me. The police have returned my suit jacket in a plastic cleaner's bag.

At my apartment door, with my suit jacket over my shoulder, I swipe my key card and, after the little light goes green, I turn the handle. As soon as I crack the door I catch a ripe smell and wonder if I left the refrigerator open. I turn on the light and see chaos. A vandal has broken in. Clothes are heaped on the floor and tossed around the living room. Food has been strewn across the walls. Toilet paper is streamed here and there. CDs are broken into shards.

I set down my jacket and go into a state of alert, scanning to see if the intruder is still here. I look to the bedroom door, which is open. I grab a 22-pound weight bar I keep in the entryway closet and, holding this improvised weapon with two hands as if it were a samurai sword, I inch into the bedroom, where the sheets and comforter have been pulled to the floor and the closet doors are flung open. But I find no one in there. I check the bathrooms, and they are empty as well.

I open the top drawer of the desk in my bedroom and see

my passport and checkbook are still in place, as is an envelope with a few thousand dollars in ready cash. The envelope is tucked in the back of the drawer, but it would not be all that hard to find if someone were searching for valuables. If it was robbers who broke in, they were not very skilled ones.

Which makes me wonder if the intruders had another purpose. Jai is the one person who knew that I was going to be out of my apartment this afternoon. And when I was at his place, his second-floor posse has been out "doin' some shit," as he termed it. What if the shit they were doing was right in the middle of my living room? But for what reason—to scare me? I am on their side, and I have not said a word that would harm Jai. I cannot think of an explanation that makes sense.

Unless I was the intended target of the shooting in the first place, and this vandalism is part of the continued assault. But that doesn't jibe either, because the severity of the deeds is decreasing. First you shoot at a man, and then you toss his apartment? What next, a crank phone call?

I return to the living room and begin to pick at the mess. Pomegranate preserves and hummus and tofu have been smeared around among my performance polos and hoodies and compression pants. Kale chips and pumpkin seeds are embedded in the carpet. My superfoods have all been laid low.

Trying to console myself, I remember that I backed up all my CDs on my computer. And most of my athletic wear came to me free, provided by team sponsors. In terms of a financial hit, this is not major. But still, that was my music, my food. These are my clothes.

And this is my place, whatever its shortcomings. However generic and anesthetic the environment of the Jefferson might appear to a visitor, I have spent my entire post-college life here.

It is my home. I feel a sense of calm when I return and hear the door click shut behind me.

It is then that I look to the window overlooking Ritten-house Square and see a message written on the wide pane of glass. I walk closer and see that the writing has been done in what I believe is yacón syrup, judging from the empty bottle on the sill. Yacón syrup is a sweet brown goo that I purchased because it is supposed to have a much higher level of antioxi-dants than anything else you might put on your buckwheat pancakes. The message written on the window:

HERE'S TO YOUR HEALTH

It is a phrase designed to mess with my mind. Here's to your health, so soon after the shooting. Who the hell did this?

CHAPTER 10

I CONSIDER CALLING the police about the break-in, but I do not want to bring Rizotti into this. Judging by the news, his investigation is not making any progress, and I am not going to give him an excuse to focus his attention on my personal life.

But I also need to get out of this apartment tonight.

I call Freddie, who is at his beach house in Longport, New Jersey. Without any explanation, I ask if I can stay there to-night, and he replies "Sure" in a pouty tone that suggests he is not in the best frame of mind himself.

Minutes later, I am in the Jefferson's underground parking

garage, with my eyes on a swivel as I walk to my car. I half hope my attacker will pop out from behind a parked SUV, and then I can at least see his face, after which I can beat on it until my fist is covered in blood. But no such luck, which does not surprise me. If the vandal wanted to ambush me, he could have just waited for me in my apartment, having already taken the trouble to break in.

Although the thing is, no one literally broke in. My door and lock showed no signs of being pried. The perpetrator simply entered—most likely with a swipe card.

I wonder about the guys downstairs. They can make swipe cards in a matter of seconds with a machine at the front desk. At the wages those guys earned, I imagine they can be easily bribed.

I also consider the Tolley clan. They are in the building. They have come all the way from Kansas to support their man. I can imagine them deciding that some low-rent vandalism will get into my head, even more than the shootings already have.

That would be beyond bush league, more juvenile than anything I've encountered in pro football. But the way the last couple of days have gone, I can believe in unexpected lows.

I arrive at Freddie's house toward the eight o'clock hour, with the ocean winds bringing a chill to the evening. Freddie lives right off the protective dunes, in a sleek, modern two-story construction whose white walls blend easily into the beachfront. I enter through the pool deck on the beach side of the house; Freddie always keeps that door unlocked. The home's front has an impressive arched doorway, but I have never seen anyone use it in the three years I have been coming here.

I find Freddie in the living room, in what I recognize as coping mode. He is wearing a black silk full-length kimono and playing Wii bowling on his plasma television. On the coffee table—made from a cross-section of an old-growth tree—sits a half-eaten pizza, still in its delivery box. Freddie's long hair is unkempt, spread haphazardly across his narrow shoulders. The odor of marijuana greets me before he does.

"Hey," I say.

"Hey," he answers distractedly, his eyes trained on the video screen as he lines up his next roll.

It is actually video games that brought Freddie and I together. I don't own a console, but the team lounge at the Sentinels facility is outfitted with both a PlayStation and an Xbox, and I spend a great deal of time in there, as punters often do: while the offense and defense are at work, specialists are left to their own devices. You can only kick so many practice balls and lift so many weights. One afternoon I was playing FIFA soccer with Pablo Garza, the Sentinels kicker, when Freddie strolled into the lounge, took a seat in a recliner, and declared, "I've got next." Thus a beautiful friendship was born. I soon noticed that, despite his vice president's title, Freddie had even less to do around the Sentinels facility than I did.

Tonight Freddie is stoned and in a bad mood, but he isn't letting it affect his game. His score is 191 in the eighth, and he is working off a strike from the last frame. He is on track for a personal high score. He needs two pins for a spare.

"Fuck!" Freddie yells after his roll leaves one pin standing. Then he shakes out his hands, turns to me, and says, "So who was that girl you are getting all cozy with on a park bench yesterday?"

"What?" I am confused. "How do you know?"

"I saw it on Internet, pal," Freddie says. "In case you haven't realized it yet, you've gone from being the fifty-third most famous player on the Sentinels to the second. Which means that if you go snuggling up to some woman out in public, someone is going to snap your picture, and that picture is going to end up online, and every nitwit in the world is going to see it. Exhibit A: me."

Freddie pauses the game and fetches his laptop, a glistening new widescreen Mac that he left sitting on the far corner of the sectional sofa. He clicks a few buttons and turns the screen around to show me a photo of Melody and me in that park with the champagne bottle at our feet. She is leaning in with a devilish grin and holding her whoopie pie inches from my lips. The BUSTIN' LOOSE lettering across her chest gains no more dignity through the medium of still photography. The headline reads: "Punter Parties on Day After Shooting."

I would guess that not even ten people had walked by that little park when Melody and I were there. But all it takes is one person with a smartphone and a misguided sense of what constitutes an opportunity.

"How is this even a story?" I wonder. "Can't a guy just celebrate being alive?"

"Get used to it, buddy," Freddie say. "You're going to be in the news, at least until they have JC behind bars."

Huh. So Freddie is part of Jai's hanging crew, too.

"I bet you ten bucks Jai didn't do it," I say.

"I bet you ten million dollars he did," Freddie says. "Here's some inside information for you, Hangman. Jai Carson is broke. Actually, broke would be a step up for him. He's in debt. Deep. Seven figures, from what I understand."

Amazing. Over his career, Jai must have made more than $100 million in salary and endorsements. Couldn't he have

taken say, two million, and salted it away for when his playing days are done—even if it meant not buying the car from
Hustle & Flow?

"But so what if Jai's broke?" I say. "What does that have
to do with shooting Samuel?"

"It explains his motive, for one," Freddie says. His posture became more erect as he elaborates. "You should have
seen Jai after Samuel's contract terms were announced. He
was in our offices that afternoon, screaming bloody murder—
pardon the expression. Even before Samuel signed, he was
pressing us to renegotiate his deal and get an extension so he
could have a new signing bonus and get that one big check
right away. But no one wants to extend JC at this point in his
career. He's thirty-one. He's got maybe a couple good years
left, and he's already under contract for them. So why should
we sign him to when he's nearly forty and won't be able to do
a damn thing?" Freddie shakes his head. "What does he think
this is—baseball?"

Freddie seems unaware that he is embodying the sort of
managerial coldness that would stoke Jai's rage—or that might
cause offense to me, a fellow player. He swings his arm back
and rolls a virtual strike, sending the video game pins tum-
bling. He reaches over for a high five. I leave him hanging.

"Anyway," Freddie continues, "Jai kept going on and on
about how we are giving all this money to a rookie who hasn't
even put on the uniform yet, but we are fucking over the player
who has been carrying the franchise for a decade. He says he
is going to hold out. And we pretty much dared him to. If he
was being fined for every day of camp he missed, he could
see how much that helped his money troubles.

"Jai was so mad, he was sputtering. He could barely get
his words out. He's barking about how Samuel will never be

worth half as much to the franchise as he is, and that Samuel is taking money that should be his. And think about it: if Jai is saying this to us, can you imagine what he's saying to his buddies when he's out on the town? And of course, his buddies keep telling him that he's right, and so he gets even more pissed off. JC and his crew had it in for Samuel before he ever walked into that restaurant. Then they try to be nice to Samuel, and he goes ahead and acts like he doesn't know who JC is? Disrespects the legend? Come on."

Freddie has the game on pause and he is rubbing his right elbow. It is his recurring Wii injury. When Freddie feels pain, he does not play through it.

"That's interesting, but it's not proof," I say. "Just today Jai was running voluntary linebacker workouts at his house."

"So?" Freddie asks.

"If he's angry about his contract, he's channeling it," I say. "He's getting ready to play his ass off."

"When you talk about something not being proof," Freddie says, "that, my friend, is not proof. And now that I've solved this week's murder of the century, I'm getting back to more important shit."

He takes the bowling game off pause. I look over at the pizza box. Freddie, even though he operates without any dietary restrictions whatsoever, was considerate enough to order a wheat-crust pie with mushroom and spinach toppings— my favorite. I pull off a slice, only realizing as it nears my mouth how hungry I am. I quickly devour that slice, and then a second.

Freddie rolls a strike in the ninth but stumbles in the tenth, getting only a spare and then eight pins with his extra roll. His final score: 243, which earns him the number-six spot on the game's list of high scores. Freddie registers it under his initials: FAG, for Frederick Abraham Gladstone. This was one regard in which Freddie's father had not made his life easy.

FAG holds all the game's high scores except for the number-one position. The top spot belongs to NPG, as in Nicholas Parker Gallow (Parker is my mother's maiden name). Back in February, I spent a long weekend out here, and one snowy day Freddie and I staged an all-day bowling marathon. On what we agreed beforehand would be the final game, I uncorked a perfect 300, which I had never come close to in any of my previous efforts. I then shook Freddie's hand and told him I was retiring from Wii bowling.

Freddie and I played many games—mostly Ping-Pong, pool, and tabletop shuffleboard, all of which he has here in his basement—and the result was almost always the same. That is, I won. Freddie isn't a terrible player, particularly at table tennis, where he can put a mean spin on his serve. But winning is a skill too. I can control my nerves in front of 60,000 people; Freddie chokes when he and I are alone in his game room.

Freddie drops down next to me on the sectional and turns his attention toward his marijuana pipe, a simple wooden piece he bought years ago in Panama. He pulls a plastic bag from his robe pocket and repacks the bowl. His weed smells like pine needles.

"Funny thing is," Freddie says, "with Samuel gone, we're actually better set up to give JC an extension now. Were we so inclined." He laughs. "Drive-by murder. It's a novel way to clear cap space."

Freddie waves a lighter over his pipe and inhales gently, drawing a lazy sizzle from the bowl. I hop up and step to the other side of the room before he exhales, so I don't end up with his smoke in my bloodstream, especially since the team's off-season drug tests hadn't come around yet.

Freddie is well aware that I like to keep my head out of his clouds, too. Usually he makes a point of keeping his distance, often slipping off to the pool deck and blowing his smoke out to the Atlantic. But not tonight.

"Something bothering you, Freddie?" I ask.

He picks up a toothpick and swirls the half-burnt weed around the bowl. "I have to go to Alabama in a couple days," he says grumpily. "For the Samuel Sault funeral. That should be a blast."

"Why you?"

"Orders from Dad," Freddie says with an eye roll, slumping deeper into the sectional. "He's in Macao. So he needs me to go and represent the family."

He flicks his lighter and takes another hit.

"You'll do fine at the funeral," I say. "You'll show up, you'll look good, you'll say the right things, you'll be back here by nightfall. Doing exactly what you're doing right now, if you feel like it."

"Visualization techniques, Hangman?" says Freddie, and curls his upper lip in disapproval. "Really?"

"It's all I've got."

Freddie shakes his head. "So tell me about the girl with the whoopie pie," he says, sitting up a little. "Where did she come from?"

I explain how I met Melody at Stark's. Freddie looks up toward the ceiling. "Melody . . . Melody . . . I wonder if I know her?" Freddie has many women out here—telling them that he is the son of a billionaire and owns a beach house with a hot tub seems to work wonders with the ladies. "I don't remember any Melody."

"Good," I say.

"Though I do lose track sometimes."

"I would, too, in your shoes."

"No, you wouldn't." Freddie grins. "You'd remember every single one—first name, last name, hometown, childhood pet. But anyway. After that whoopie in the park, Hangman, what happened next?"

"Nothing," I say.

"Why not?" he asks, standing up.

"Too soon."

"Too soon after what?"

"The shooting. Remember?"

Freddie shrugs. "Did you go to the bathroom yesterday? I bet it wasn't too soon to perform that physical function."

"C'mon, Freddie," I say. "She was kind of cool."

"Cool?"

"I like her."

"Like her?" Freddie asks, incredulous. "Ms. Bustin' Loose?" He circles the table and stands in front of the television screen. "See, Hangman, this is your problem in a nutshell," he says, pipe in hand. "I bet it means you think you're sophisticated. No, it doesn't. It means you're chickenshit."

"But . . ."

"Don't get me wrong," Freddie says. "I would love to see you in a real relationship. You know how every now and then you will hook up with one of those businesswomen who stay at your residential hotel there?"

"Yes?"

"You should hear yourself tell me about these women, how admiring, how infatuated you sound when you describe them. And after they leave Philadelphia and go back to their regular lives, you're grumpy for a week. You don't even know it, but trust me, you are. And I can tell by the way you keep going back to that housewife artist—what's her name?"

"Jessica."

"Jessica. And it sounds like you've got a great thing going there. That's your move, if you ask me. You should ask her to marry you."

"I think her husband might have a problem with that."

"A-ha!" Freddie says, pipe raised triumphantly.

"A-ha what?"

"That's the first objection you raise, that she has a husband," he says. "It's not anything about her personality."

"So?"

"So if after three years of road testing, that's your only problem, I think you may have found your mate."

"Smoke some more pot, Freddie," I say. "You're seeing everything really clearly."

Freddie puts down the pipe and pulls his hair back, attempting to neaten himself. "She and her husband don't have any kids, right?"

"No kids."

"So this artist woman is basically single, save for some paperwork."

Never mind that he has never even met Jessica. Freddie tends to believe that he can intuit the truth about anything, no matter how few actual facts he is working with. He really would make a fine lawyer.

"Take my word for it, Freddie," I say. "It's just not happening."

"Yuh-huh," Freddie says. "Three years. Something's happening." He gives up neatening his hair and returns to his bowling, starting up a new game. In between my heckles ("Don't blow it here, pal. You wouldn't want to miss this to the left . . . oooh, too bad"), I take Freddie's laptop and click back to the site that has the photo of Melody and me. The story is on the indefatigable news site Footballmania.com, which has a separate blog devoted to the latest developments in the Samuel Sault case.

As I look through the Samuel-related stories, one catches my eye, titled "Carson's Hometown Known for Gang Murders, Retribution." The reporter interviewed characters from where Jai grew up, in a rough part of Memphis, and details a universe of single-parent homes where murder was common and young men gravitated toward gangs to find a sense of family. The story made the case for Jai's guilt, in its way, by offering as an excuse the environment he was raised in. This seemingly sympathetic incrimination-by-poverty was at least balanced out by one quote from a high school assistant coach who knew Jai and wasn't having any of it: "Jai Carson came from here, but when you look around, you see what he's transcended. A gangbanger is exactly what he's worked so hard not to become. And he's not going to throw his life away because some kid didn't know his name."

The man this coach describes is the same one I ran the hill with this afternoon.

I scroll through the other news stories and I begin to understand how my trip to the park became a headline. Reporters are scrambling for any way to get in on the story. I see one preposterous article that evaluates the eleven quarterbacks that Samuel had injured for their potential as murder suspects. The story goes through the players one by one, attempting to account for their whereabouts on the night of the murder. I read the story not because I buy into its premise, but because I am always curious to see what becomes of football players when the game doesn't need them anymore. In this case, though, the ex-quarterbacks hadn't had a chance to become much, as they were all quite young. A few are still in school, while others are going to graduate school or are working pedestrian jobs.

The reporter located nine of the eleven injured quarterbacks. Five guys had strong alibis—"I was at the senior prom—chaperoning," says David Pleasance, whose tibia was snapped by Samuel and who is now a middle school teacher in Shreveport, Louisiana. Four offered weaker accounts of their whereabouts that night, but could be located in places geographically inconvenient to South Philadelphia. "I was at home, on the Internet," said Peter Barbaro, who had his elbow dislocated by Samuel and is now installing drywall part-time in Jacksonville, Florida. "Check with my provider if you want. But don't ask what sites I was on, okay?"

There were two injured quarterbacks the reporter could not immediately locate. One was Herrold McKoy, who played at Mobile State. Samuel ruptured McKoy's spleen, and he needed to be rushed to the hospital for a life-saving operation. He recovered, but he never rejoined his team.

The other was Luke Reckherd, whose last name resonates with dedicated football fans. Luke is the son of Wee Willie Reckherd, who was a great college quarterback and even earned a couple of Heisman votes back in the seventies, despite having gone to a historically black college and standing only five foot nine. But what really distinguished Willie Reckherd was that he played quarterback ambidextrously—that is, he could throw equally well with his right and left hands. He played professionally, too, for Baltimore, though not as a quarterback. They switched him to receiver and punt returner. He performed respectably, but he was never the star he had been in college.

His boy Luke was a five-star quarterback prospect coming out of high school. At six foot five and 232 pounds, he had his choice of major college programs, but chose to attend his dad's alma mater, Langston University. This landed him in the same conference of historically black colleges that included Samuel's school, Western Alabama. Samuel broke Luke's collarbone when Luke was a sophomore, and then tore his MCL when Luke was a senior.

After college Luke signed with a minor-league indoor football team, the Hartsburg Hyenas, but was cut after four games, and the Hyenas couldn't provide the reporter with contact information. After that call, it was time to publish.

My takeaway from this story is that no one has any idea who shot Samuel and Cecil, or why.

Freddie's bowling score drops to 151 in his next game, a sign that the tentacles of cannabis are entangling his mind. Afterward he takes a seat on the sofa—just a breather, he says. He closes his eyes, and soon he is wheezing a light snore. I shake him on the shoulder.

"Hey, buddy," I say. "Maybe you should go up to bed."

"Good idea," Freddie says. His eyes flit open, and he pushes himself up with arms, just a couple of inches, before he drops back down into the softness of the sectional, defeated.

It is a little after eleven. I should go to sleep, too, but my mind is restless. I move Freddie's laptop to the kitchen table and continue to noodle around on it. I don't want to read about the murder anymore, so I look for some distraction. I am curious to see if Melody has a Facebook page. Maybe I can learn the identity of her mystery roommate.

It is then that I realize I do not know Melody's last name.

I search "Melody Stark's," but she does not turn up in any news stories, so that is a dead end. Then I think of soccer. Melody said that as a senior in high school she made it to the Class A state finals in New Hampshire. She is twenty-three now, so she would have been a senior in high school five or six years ago.

I go to New Hampshire's high school athletics site, click around for a while and find the girls' Class A soccer results for those years. I see no Melodys on the rosters. I find Camerons and Brittanys and Tiffanys aplenty, an Antigone and an Abigail and an Alice. But no Melody. I run the same check a year forward and a year back, but I still don't find any Melody. Her story of athletic prowess suddenly looks as dubious as one of Jessica's tall tales, such as the one about the U.S. Mint and the thousand-dollar bills. Except Jessica's lies are just a passing amusement; she wasn't trying to build herself up.

On a long shot, I search for "Melody Winking Oyster." Nothing.

Then just "Winking Oyster Strip Club."

The search doesn't bring up the club's page, as I expect, but it does direct me to a newspaper story: "Providence Strip Club Shut Down." The story, from last summer, says that the Winking Oyster was closed by local law enforcement, and seven employees were arrested because the club had been serving as a base for drug and prostitution rings.

Melody neglected to mention any of this. I close my eyes and breathe deep.

The thing is, I often enjoy the company of people who indulge in what is forbidden to me. Freddie is a prime example. He is so spectacularly *unmaximized*. I will run into him at the end of a long practice, and he will tell me how he slept until

one in the afternoon because he had been up late taking pey-
ote and watching Japanese porn. Being friends with someone
like Freddie reminds me that there is more to me than what I
have been told to become.

I have to say, I got a similar kick when Melody told me
about the network she had set up in the Philadelphia food service industry. Can I really argue to myself that it isn't much
of a leap from snaring free whoopie pies to selling whoopie?

I put the laptop to sleep. My capacity for rationalization is
officially exhausted.

Perhaps Freddie has a point about my instincts with
women.

Still hungry, I go to Freddie's pantry. The lower shelves
are crammed with cookies, crackers, potato chips, pretzels,
jars of peanut butter, boxes of cereal, and flavor units for his
SodaStream. The top shelves are lined with bottles of hard
liquor, mostly Scotch and bourbon, but with enough gin and
vodka to accommodate a guest's preferences. I pull off a bottle
of bourbon that is dimpled and shaped like a hand grenade.

The label announces in elaborate script that this is a bottle
of Blanton's Reserve. I know nothing about the brand, but I
am sure it will do. I grab a glass and head outside to Freddie's
back deck. I sit at the poolside table, which has an umbrella
protruding from the center. I close the umbrella and lash it
tight and settle down for a drink.

I am on my third glass—though it's hard to count precisely,
because I am refilling before I hit bottom—when I think of
my mother, and the way she reached under the table this
morning to take Aaron's hand.

All my life people have told me that I take after my father,
and it's an obvious analysis to make—because of the football,
for starters, and also our competitiveness. But my mother can

be competitive, too. After dinner we used to play hearts to see who would do the dishes, and it was almost always one of the boys who would have to attack the pile in the sink. When she left my dad, after years of having displayed nothing but contentment—to my brother and me, at least—it felt like she was shooting the moon one last time, swooping in unexpectedly for the win. If you can call it a win. But after all those years of apparent subservience when it came to setting the tone of our household, she turned it around with one deed, punctuated by her declaration: "I have a soul, too, you know."

So do we all. I would bet the killer felt the same way, even after he had left a strapping twenty-one-year-old dead by the side of the road.

Samuel and my dad—two lives ending in the street like that. They say it takes three to make a trend, right?

I topped off my glass again, even as I observed, this is the problem with drinking. The drunker you get, the more you want to make all the details cohere into one story. As if my father's car crash had anything to do with why someone killed Samuel.

"Long after tonight is all over, long after tonight is all gone . . ." The chorus of an Irma Thomas song from last night is stuck in my head. Oh, well. I could have worse earworms to live with.

Soon I have drained half the bottle of Blanton's Reserve. I stand up, just to see if I can, and I am perfectly able. I think of the bourbon sloshing around in my belly. I need to rid my body of it as soon as possible, so it won't drag on me tomorrow. I lift the bottle to my mouth and swig straight from it, with the goal of overloading my body's systems.

I walk off Freddie's deck and into the dunes, which is planted with clusters of reeds designed to prevent erosion. The planting is so dense that there is no good place for me to kneel, so I keep walking until I have crossed the dunes and I stumble down onto sand that is wet and soft enough to swallow my feet. The tide is higher than I expected. Blame it on the moon.

A wave climbs the shore and rushes in, soaking the bottom of my pants. I hike them up before they get too wet.

I take a couple of heavy steps toward the ocean and then I drop down to all fours and tell myself that I need to do what I came here to do, and to do it quickly. I slide a finger into my mouth and press down on the back of my tongue, and this ignites the insurgence in my stomach. One heave, two heaves, a third, and then a fourth, as an ocean wave surges in and covers my calves and wrists with chilling water. My hands and knees sink into the wet sand as the wave washes back out, clearing away the vomit. Mostly.

I gather my will and rise to my feet before the next wave comes in. I wipe my mouth and then gasp the cool air. My insides feel wrung out, but quiet.

I turn, leave the water behind, cross the dunes, and walk across the deck, pulling off my dripping pants and flinging them over a deck chair to dry. Then I go into the house and I head up the stairs toward Freddie's guest bedroom. I feel dead, but I keep climbing, one step and then another. Being pantless, I notice the definition in my quadriceps. My legs are the strongest part of me. I hear my dad's voice: *this is why you train.*

CHAPTER 11

WHEN I FINALLY sleep, I am visited by a familiar anxiety dream: I am punting, and I miss the ball when I attempt to kick it. I've had this dream a hundred times. Other people dream about taking a test for which they are unprepared, and I have this.

The unease of the dream wakes me a little after six. The inside of my mouth is fetid, despite having brushed my teeth before I fell into bed. I raise myself up on my arms, and I feel surprisingly fresh, though a little dehydrated. Not that there are many other contenders, but forcing myself to throw up was the smartest thing I did last night.

I swing my legs over the side of the bed, stand up, and look out the window. The beach grass is flapping in the wind gusts. These are ugly conditions, but whenever I have this anxiety dream, my instant remedy is to go kick.

I have a practice ritual I've developed during my previous stays at the beach house. And fortunately, I have the necessary equipment in the trunk of my car—a bag of balls, and a shovel.

The tide is out and the beach is wide and empty, as it would be before seven on a chilly weekday morning in early June. At this point in the season the weather is still too iffy and the ocean too cold for discerning Philadelphians to have decamped to their summer homes full time.

I find a spot on the beach, drop my bag of balls, and begin digging. The shovel I am using is one I rescued from the garage when my father's home was sold. It is old, with a wooden handle and a head of iron, and its heavy head plunges easily into the sand. Within a few minutes I have dug a hole five yards long, and one yard wide and deep—a little coffin corner. Then I walk fifty paces down the beach, pull the drawstring on the red mesh bag of balls, and roll them onto the sand.

Most kickers would hate practicing in the disruptive gusts that come off the ocean. But to me, the difficulty is the point. To nail a coffin corner kick in unpredictable winds is about as hard a thing as a punter can do.

My plan is to hit thirty-five punts, sinking as many as I can into the hole. I have tried this twice before; once I dropped two balls in the hole, the other time zero. But the success does not matter as much as the effort. My true goal is to make thirty-five solid contacts, and the elements can do with them what they will.

In each punt, I mimic my game routine as best I can. Even though no one is centering the ball to me, I get up on my toes, as if waiting to receive a wayward snap. I then call "Hike!"— out loud—and go into my motion as if a rush is coming. I have no timer clocking me, but at this point I would feel an extra tenth of a second as surely as Picasso would have known if he used too much blue.

My first kick, a low liner, amazingly goes in the hole. I imagine I might hit four into the hole today, maybe more. Maybe today is the day I sink all thirty-five.

But thirty-four kicks later, I have still only sunk one ball. Some of it is the wind—with a couple of kicks, the wind gusted just as I dropped the ball, and I considered it an accomplishment just to get my foot on it. But mostly, the problem is me. None of my kicks are horrible, but I can feel my micro-mistakes before the punts leave my foot. I watch the balls in flight as if am a lottery player, hoping a little luck can erase my errors.

When I punt, I inevitably hear my dad's voice in my head. Punting has so few variables that all my mistakes are ones he has seen and tried to correct. *Your first step is slow. You need to plant harder. Your line isn't straight.* I picture him watching me, bent over, hands on his knees, solid in his stance, emitting critiques with the regularity of homing beacon.

"Can you just shut up for once? I'm ten times the man you ever were." That's what I snapped at my dad one spring afternoon, when we were training and he was criticizing my punts with what was, in retrospect, nothing more than his normal severity. But that day, for whatever reason, I fired back, and wildly. I should have told him—if I was going to say anything at all—that I was ten times the *athlete*, but the word that came out was *man*. His answer to me, measured and unfazed: "Not today, bucko. Not even close."

I come back to the house and Freddie is in the kitchen, still wearing his black kimono from last night. He is sitting at the kitchen table, head in his hands, fingers in his long hair, waiting for his coffee to brew. He is not normally up at this hour, even when he goes to bed relatively early, as he did last night. He is one of those people who can sleep for twelve hours at a time, whereas I count half that as a success.

"Did we really need that practice session today?" he asks sourly when he hears me enter. "Every time you kick the ball it sounds like someone is being shot."

He says the word *shot* and I picture Samuel and Cecil, prone on the pavement.

"Sorry, buddy," I say dryly. "Just being selfish, as usual."

"Everybody is these days," he says. "What the fuck is it with people?" He pushes his iPhone across the table to me. "Look at this."

It is an e-mail from his dad.

> Frederick, Everything is set with the family jet. Please be at the charter terminal at 9:30 am tomorrow. Arrange for a car service if you need to. Please express my regrets to the Saults that I couldn't be there in person, and thank you again for representing the family. Love, father.

Freddie pouts balefully, his mouth hanging open. His blue eyes are bloodshot.

"Freddie," I say. "Here's a game that will cheer you up. While you drink your coffee, think of some things you can do today that you would enjoy. Then remember that you have the time and resources to do them all, and go do them."

Freddie lifts his head. "Good point. Maybe I'll get a massage today."

"That's the spirit. Regular massage, or the kind that's illegal?"

"Illegal, of course," Freddie says. "How else am I supposed to relax? And hey, did you see where I left my weed last night?"

"Your robe pocket, I think?"

He slides a hand down into the pocket of his kimono and he smiles.

On my drive home up the expressway, I wonder what I can do to calm myself down. I have to try something.

CHAPTER 12

I STAND IN front of a yellow brick town house on Seventh Street, just north of the bars and restaurants of South Street. This area will be much louder come nightfall, but in the daylight it is quiet and empty. The nametags on the buzzers of this building have been taped over many times, but the one I am looking for is crisp and white and neatly pressed on. Corina Aleksa, 3R.

I press her button, and I am admitted with a drone. Ms. Aleksa has made it here on time, which is encouraging. When I called the ad from the back of the alternative weekly in the Jefferson lobby, she told me in her Eastern European accent that she could see me in an hour and a half, at one o'clock— not because she was booked until then, but because she needed time to get to her office.

I walk up the narrow, creaking stairs of the town house, which looks like it had been a single-family home before it was cut up into smaller units, two per floor. I knock on 3R and the door is opened by a woman who is stunningly beautiful. She is about twenty-five, and five ten, and slim. Her dirty blond hair hangs well below her shoulders and she wears a dark blue-and-green patterned sundress. She holds out a spindly arm to shake my hand.

"Welcome," she says with a warm smile. "I am Corina."

"I'm Nick," I say. "Thank you for seeing me."

"It will be my pleasure, I'm sure." She radiates an inner serenity that I find assuring.

Her office is neatly kept. Her desk, facing the wall, has only a pad and a pen on it. Above the desk is a single shelf dense with books. On the opposite wall is a large black-and-white framed photo of a hummingbird in flight. I see nothing that would offend my sensibilities—no airy aphorisms purporting to explain, in one sentence, the mysteries of the mind.

At Corina's invitation I sit on a wooden square-backed chair, and she shifts the chair at her desk to face me. Then I explain my situation. I attempt to be precise and clinical, but from the first description of the shooting, she reacts as if she is right there on the sidewalk, experiencing the horror with me.

"I read about this, of course," she says, leaning forward, eyes wide with concern. "I am so sorry. How is your agent doing?"

"Looks like he's going to be all right," I say. Before I came here, I checked in with Vicki by text, and she said Cecil is healing well, and there are no signs of infection. The drainage tube is now out of the wound.

"Good," she says, though her brow remains knit.

We stare at each other for a good five seconds. She seems to be studying my face and waiting to see if I might say more.

"So are you ready?" she asks.

"Yes. Absolutely."

"Excellent. We begin with questions. Simple ones. Have you ever been hypnotized before?"

"No." I am expecting her to pick up the pad from her desk, to take notes. She doesn't.

"Not even for entertainment, like in a comedy club?"

"No, never," I say.

"Would you say you are receptive to instructions?"

"I'll do my best," I say, though her question touches on

my greatest concern about coming here. I think of myself as strong-willed, and I expect I will resist by nature. Even if hypnotism works with some, I am skeptical as to whether it will work on me.

"The more you follow my instructions, the better chance there is that I can help you." Corina says this encouragingly, without a hint of preemptive scold.

"I understand. I'll certainly try."

"Excellent. And would you say your childhood was happy or difficult?"

I hesitate. She waits unblinkingly on my answer, as if she was asking a simple question such as my birth date or social security number, and I only needed to reel off the digits. "Why do you need to know that?"

"It helps prepare me for complications. Please answer honestly. The more honest you are, the better chance we have of succeeding."

"The answer is yes," I say. "I had a happy childhood." It is the only response I can give. I was clothed, well-fed, popular, the varsity quarterback. Just about all the boys in my high school would have gladly traded places with me, some desperately so.

But the moment my "yes" comes out of my mouth, I see myself sitting on the back porch of our house in the middle of the night, shivering. I was fourteen years old, and my dad had locked me out because I had been over at a girl's house and missed my ten o'clock curfew by fifteen minutes. I was wearing just a T-shirt and jeans, and this was in October in Upstate New York. The temperature had been about sixty in the early evening, but had dropped into the forties by the time I came home. I tried all the doors and windows, but my dad had locked everything down—even the garden shed, I learned when I sought shelter there. I could have gone to a neighbor, but I was too embarrassed. So I stuck it out all night, shivering. At one point I futilely tried to warm myself by stuffing my shirt with fallen leaves, but after a couple minutes the itch became unbearable.

That night was a quarter moon, now that I think of it. Maybe a little fuller than quarter, more like thirty percent. I certainly had plenty of time to stare at it, sitting back on that lounge chair, never falling asleep, even for a moment. At six o'clock, I heard the lock click on the back door. I opened it and no one was there. I ran upstairs to take a warm shower. When I came downstairs the morning breakfast routine was in full flow. I ate my steel-cut oatmeal and the matter was never spoken of.

"I did have some rough spots, actually," I tell Corina.

"Oh?" she says.

"But overall my childhood was fine. Better than most."

"Good. Now tell me, which from among these is your favorite color?"

She spreads on her desk three pads of square fluorescent Post-it notes—yellow, orange, and pink.

"Orange," I say, just to pick one, though none has any particular appeal.

"Orange it is," she says. She pulls a note off the pad and presses it firmly, at sitting-eye level, on the white wall.

"Adjust your chair, please, so you are looking directly at the Post-it."

I shift around so my eyes are on the orange square.

"Thank you. Now begin counting backward, out loud, from forty. Do it slowly, take a deep breath in between forty and thirty-nine. And a slightly deeper breath between thirty-nine and thirty-eight. And so on."

I begin as she instructed, with her gently reminding me to slow my breath between each count. After I clear thirty she says, "Let your eyelids drop," and we continue. After twenty she says, "Let yourself sleep."

I do not feel like I am sleeping per se, in that I am still aware I am in the room and I can hear her voice perfectly well. If a fire breaks out, I am ready to run. I can feel that I am still lined up with the orange Post-it, even though my eyes are closed. Corina says, "Raise your right arm to shoulder height," and I can feel my arm going up, though I do not exactly feel like I am raising it. Then she asks me to raise my left arm up, and to cross both arms, and I do. I am relaxed, even happy, because I feel like this is working. I feel like I might get what I came for.

"Nick?" Corina says, her voice a notch louder than it had been.

"Yes?" I ask. I feel foggy, half-asleep, but just barely coherent enough to answer.

"We're done."

"Done?" I say, my eyes batting open and feeling stung by the light, though it was no brighter than before.

"Yes, we're finished."

I am confused.

"Did we get it?" I murmur. "Did we get the license plate?"

"No, I'm sorry, we did not," she says. "You told me about the bumper sticker with the quarter moon, but not the plate. We could try again another day if you would like, but I think that would be a waste of your money."

I look at the clock. It reads 1:38, which is at least twenty minutes later than I expected. "What happened, exactly?" I ask. My eyelids are heavy and my nose is congested. "The last thing I remember is crossing my arms."

"You went all the way under," she says. "Most people don't go as far as you did. You are an excellent subject."

An excellent subject. When I had expected to be a tough case.

"I have tissues if you want them," she says, pointing to a floral box on her desk. I am initially confused by the offer, but then I sniffle and drag fingers across my moist cheek and realize that I have been crying.

"I'm okay," I say. "Thank you." I rise and sniffle again and pull four twenties from my wallet and hand them to her. She steps to her desk and tucks the money into a paisley purse. Then she returns her attention to me, looking at me warmly, head tilted.

"You sure you're all right?" she asks.

"I'm disappointed we didn't get the license plate," I say, and then add, "But I know you did your best."

"So did you," she says, and then steps forward and hugs me, the lightness of her limbs accentuating the heaviness of my own. She holds on longer than I would have expected, before letting go and stepping back.

"Take care of yourself, Nick," she says.

"You too, Corina."

"Thank you," she says. "And remember, you have more choices than you think you do."

I walk back down the narrow stairs, speeding up as I descend, and wondering exactly what I might have said while I was under to make her tell me that.

After the session, I return to the Jefferson. I have a task awaiting me there, one that is refreshingly simple: I need to clean up the mess in my apartment. The odors from my splattered food have only become more acrid after a night of neglect. But at least there are no insects. I expected that they might feast on the syrup or the almond butter or the yogurt or the pomegranate preserves, but pestilence hasn't risen up to the seventeenth floor yet. This is one of the benefits of living in a high-rise in which most residents come and go so quickly. While I do my own housecleaning as part of my deal, the building's other units are thoroughly cleaned when tenants turn over.

Revving up Eddie Floyd's album *Rare Stamps* from the digital files on my computer, I begin by sorting through my soiled clothes, with the initial thought that I will create two piles: one for items that can be salvaged and another that will go straight to the garbage. But I soon decide that the right move is to trash everything. I can pilfer new athletic gear from the facility, and my civilian wardrobe is in need of an update anyway.

As I stuff the old mess into garbage bags, I notice that there is a pattern to the vandalism. Everything that has been destroyed—the socks and the CDs and the food—has something in common: it is all mine. Anything provided by the Jefferson had been left alone. None of their plates has been shattered, none of their drinking glasses broken, no stuffing has been ripped from the sofa.

The attack was made exclusively on that which belongs to me.

CHAPTER 13

I spend the rest of the evening at my laptop, studying Footballmania's murder blog. The first stories I read intently, but soon I turn to skimming, and then to clicking the computer's power button and letting the screen go black. The more I read of these stories, the more they distill to one essential fact: Rizotti is getting nowhere. A killer is getting away with it.

My sleep is no more restful than it was the night before. I rise at six, and after a shower and a bowl of steel-cut oatmeal, I power up my laptop and log onto Footballmania again, hoping for some new development, perhaps even an arrest. Again I am disappointed.

A new story, though, catches my eye. Its headline is "Bonus Baby: Woman Carrying Sault's Child Claims Guaranteed Millions." The picture shows a young white woman, pregnant and blond, staring directly at the camera. She is rosy-cheeked, but her blue eyes are expressionless.

Her name is Kaylee Wise, the story says. Kaylee is only nineteen years old, and, like Samuel, she has lived in Vickers, Alabama, her entire life. Unfortunately, she is not quoted in the story. She is spoken for by her attorney, Fred Wilde, who is also credited with taking her photo. It seems like Mr. Wilde has a real full-service operation.

The story leaves me wanting to know more about this young woman hiding behind her lawyer—if she is the girlfriend Tanner mentioned, and what she understood her relationship with him to be. I am also curious to know what Kaylee's family thought of Samuel, and what his family thought of her. If Vickers is as behind-the-times as Cecil described it, I can imagine that an interracial relationship might not have had universal approval.

I pick up my phone and dial Freddie.

"Mmph," Freddie says, answering on the sixth ring.

"Wake up, sunshine," I say.

"Hangman?" he says, his throat thick. "What the shit? It's not even eight o'clock."

"I wanted to catch you before you go."

"Go? Go where?"

"The funeral? You're flying to Alabama today, right?"

After a long silence, Freddie says, "Fuck."

I hear sheets rustling, then a thud, and the sound of a glass breaking. Then a weak fart, and a muttering of curse words.

To think, that before too many hours has passed, this man would be consoling a grieving family.

"My question for you: can I come?"

"What?"

"I'd like to come to the funeral. Is there a seat on the plane for me?"

"It's my fucking plane," Freddie grumbles. "If you want a seat, it's yours."

"Charter terminal at nine thirty, right?"

"If you say so," he says, and hangs up.

I wonder if Freddie can make it on time. The drive from his place to the airport takes more than an hour. If I hadn't thought to call him, he probably would have missed the trip entirely.

* * *

I dress for the funeral in, for lack of other options, the suit jacket and pants from the night of the murder. The pants were pushed to the side of my closet with my collared shirts, and they escaped the attention of the vandal. I have yet to replace the black shoes that became blood-soaked on the night of the shooting, so I wear my brown pair, hoping that no one will be too perturbed at the fashion breach.

When I arrive at the charter terminal, the other members of the traveling party are already assembled. Tanner is there, as well as our team's general manager, Clint Udall. Broad-backed and with a thick neck, Udall was a fullback for Dallas in the 1980s. He is bald and has a bushy brown mustache. Both Udall and Tanner, I notice, have laptop bags slung over their shoulders. Publicists O'Dwyer and Cordero are also on hand, a reminder that Samuel's funeral will draw national media attention. The only person missing: Freddie, of course.

"Gallow," Udall says. "I'm surprised to see you here."

"Freddie mentioned that the team was sending a delegation," I say.

"Glad you're joining in," Udall says. "What's the latest on Cecil?"

"They're hoping that he will be going home tomorrow or the day after." Vicki had reported this morning that Cecil had eaten something close to a meal last night for the first time. It was just a matter of that meal passing through him with flying colors, so to speak.

"I like Cecil a lot," Udall says. "Sometimes I call him just to see what he thinks about a player we're interested in. It's amazing how many small conferences and arena leagues he keeps up with."

Udall begins talking about the talents that you can find these days in arena leagues, and he speculates about how an arena-league champ could probably beat a big-time college team. As he chatters on, I feel like he is doing what so many men do, clinging to sports talk to keep from discussing more difficult subjects.

Meanwhile I notice Tanner, standing off on his own, wearing a trim black suit and a plain black tie, repeatedly looking at his watch. It is now 9:40, ten minutes past the assigned time, and Freddie is still not here. Tanner fines players for showing up even a minute late for a meeting; this has to be verging on a capital offense. We would likely have left Freddie behind if he wasn't the owner's son.

At 9:46, Freddie strolls into the waiting area. The rest of us are in our funeral clothes, but he is wearing tan cargo shorts and a black T-shirt with orange lettering that reads I HATE HIPSTERS. Purple-tinted Oakley sunglasses complete the ensemble. He has a garment bag slung over one shoulder.

"Let's get this bullshit on the road," he declares energetically, as if we have been waiting not for his arrival, but his leadership. As he passes me he looks down at my feet and snickers. "Nice shoes."

We march across the tarmac to the Gladstone family jet. Inside the cabin I settle into a cream-colored leather seat that draws me down and envelops me. Freddie takes the seat next to mine, and immediately pops an Ambien. Tanner and Udall settle into the row in front of me.

After we take off, Tanner pulls out his laptop and begins reviewing video of defensive ends. Across the aisle I can see Udall looking at footage on his laptop, too.

Udall is scouting linebackers. The team is preparing to replace Jai.

Turning my eyes from this aloof piece of personnel management, I look out the window as we fly—it's funny how from high altitude, athletic fields are the most identifiable manmade elements of the landscape—and I think about all the people I might meet today. Not just Kaylee Wise, but also Samuel's parents, his friends and neighbors, coaches and teammates. I wonder what the chances are that the killer will be there, in my sights, maybe even looking me in the eye and shaking my hand.

At my dad's funeral, I learned a defining detail about his death, but that happened simply because I had my eyes open, and I knew the attendees so well. The man who gave my father his fatal nudge, it turned out, had been coming to our house my whole life.

My dad died in a crash on Marker's Hollow Road, not too far from our house. The road winds through an unpopulated valley, and has a posted speed limit of twenty-five miles per hour, reduced to fifteen along its most treacherous curves. Sometimes when we were kids and we had been out to a family dinner, my dad would drive down Marker's Hollow before heading home. He would usually do this in the fall or winter, when the trees were bare. If the moon was full, he might turn off the car's headlights to increase the spook factor. Swooping up and to the left, down and to the right, the drive felt like a roller-coaster ride. Doug and I would accentuate every hard turn with a cry that was a mix of fright and exhilaration. Sometimes my dad would hit the gas as we came over a crest and the car would take a little air, and then we'd really whoop. My mother was the only one who didn't get in on the fun. "Enough!" she would screech. Her yelling would sometimes continue long after we had pulled into the driveway, safe at home.

Looking back now, I could see that my mom's fretful shrieks were as much the point for my dad as our gleeful screams.

There was plenty that my mom was afraid of and my dad wasn't, and he liked to get that on the record.

Even now, knowing how he met his end, those drives did not seem reckless. My dad lived in the area his whole life and knew every curve on Marker's Hollow. None of its bends could take him by surprise. Driving that road was like reciting the ABCs.

On the night he died, he had been drinking at Liston's, a tavern that he had frequented often enough that they kept a mug with his initials on it behind the bar. Posthumous blood alcohol tests indicated he was within the legal limits, corroborating what friends said, which is that he'd had only a couple of light beers. But the other impairment, the one that wouldn't show up in any blood alcohol tests, was the one I learned about at his funeral: my dad had been in a fight at Liston's before storming out. And when my dad became angry, he did not settle down easily. Calming him down was like trying to get lava back in the volcano.

The funeral was on a punishingly cold day, with the temperature in single digits. I remember the browned grass at the cemetery crunching beneath my shoes. Still, the skies were clear and hundreds of people crowded the graveside service. My uncle Rory, my dad's brother, showed up drunk, and in a tie that only went halfway down his belly. Among the mourners were my dad's current crop of high school players. The team arrived together on a school bus, wearing their green-and-white football uniforms over their long underwear. One-by-one they marched to where my mother and Doug and I sat and they all shook our hands. I had met many of these kids before, as my dad liked to bring me around to practice and show me off as an example of what they could achieve, if they only listened to him. At these practices it was plain to see that many of those kids loathed my dad. My dad knew this, too, but he didn't care. His argument was that the players would appreciate his hard ways when they were older and had children of their own.

My dad's point seemed validated at his funeral, because at least a couple hundred of his former players were there, many of them so crestfallen one might imagine it was their own father who had died. The tears were many, the flower arrangements bountiful.

The tribute that caught my eye, though, was sent by a friend of my dad's named George Chamberlain. The assemblage of white blossoms was towering; you would think my father had just won the Triple Crown. And while George had known my father nearly all his life, sometimes coming by on Sundays to watch the games with the neighborhood guys, they were not each other's favorite people. From what I knew of George's finances, the floral display was beyond his means. His son Gary, who was in my class, wore the same winter coat all through high school, even after it became too tight and short on him. Over the years I had heard more than once that George had been laid off from some low-level managerial position. Dad would recount George's career failings, if not with glee exactly, then at least with an absence of sympathy.

So when I saw George's giant wreath, I wondered if I was missing something.

After the service I asked Charlie Wentz about it. Charlie was my dad's offensive coordinator and his closest friend. He is also a bachelor; he had dinner over at the house at least once a week. And he was part of my dad's drinking crew at Liston's, as was George Chamberlain.

"That's some display George sent," I said to Charlie.

"'R.I.P to a true friend,'" Charlie said, reading the words on the sash that went across the wreath.

"What's George up to these days?"

"Um . . . he delivers meals, I think," Charlie said. "Institutional meals. Brings food to the county retirement home, the vocational school, places like that."

"Must pay all right," I say. "Look at the size of that wreath. I didn't think he and Dad were that close."

"Yeah, well . . ." Charlie trailed off.

"Well, what?" I asked.

"Nothing," said Charlie, though not very convincingly. He looked away. "Nothing that matters."

I patted him on the elbow. "Excuse me, Charlie," I said. "I'm going to thank George for the wreath."

George was a bulky and bearded man who wore a dark green winter coat with a big metal zipper over his suit. He was standing with his wife and another couple.

I approached George and placed my hand on his shoulder. The other three, after imparting condolences to me, stepped away.

"So sorry about your dad, Nicky," he said. "So sorry."

"I appreciate that, George," I said. "And thank you for the flowers. Very generous of you."

"It's nothing," he said. "Your dad would have done the same for me."

Not likely.

"Hey, Nicky, I saw you in the playoffs last week," George said. "You were great. Your dad was so proud of you." My dad died the Friday after I had played in my first playoff game with the Sentinels. I had punted well, not that it mattered. The correlation between my performance and the team's success is dispiritingly thin. In my last conversation with my dad, he had ranted about how I would have done a better job at quarterback than the Sentinels' starter, Bo John White.

I forced a smile. "Thank you, George. I appreciate that. I have a question I wanted to ask you."

"Sure, whatever you'd like," George said, though he sounded nervous already.

"Is there anything you can tell me about what happened the night my dad died?" At this point, I had been told that my dad had been at Liston's, and he had a beer buzz going, but not much else.

I said this politely, but I looked intently at George in a way that was meant to be unnerving.

"I don't know, Nicky," he said. "He's probably driven that road a thousand times in his life. I really don't think he was that drunk. . . ."

"That's not what I'm talking about."

"What do you mean?" he said.

"You have a mug behind a counter at Liston's, just like my dad did," I said. "You must have been there. Once the season's over, all you guys are there every Friday night. I just want to know about his last hours. What is the last thing he said to you?"

"Oh, I don't remember, Nicky," George said, and then bit his lip. "I really don't. Again, I'm very sorry for your loss. If there's anything I can do for you, let me know."

He began to walk away, but I grabbed his fleshy upper arm and held on.

"I don't need your politeness, George, and I don't need your flowers. I need you to tell me the truth." I was speaking in a muted tone, my jaw tight. "Pretend we're not at a funeral. We're at a rest stop on the highway. You're going one way, I'm going the other. No matter what you say, we're never going to see each other again. Just tell me the truth. Because I look at those flowers and I think, George Chamberlain feels guilty about something. What is it?"

George bit his lip again. "It's just that telling you, Nicky . . . well, it might give you the wrong idea."

I let go of him and he took a step back. "The wrong idea about what?" I glanced to the side and saw, from a distance, Charlie Wentz talking to another of the Liston's crew, both watching me interrogate George.

"Your dad and me, we both had a few drinks, and we were saying things to each other," George said, his voice quavering. "But you know how people say things, especially when you've been drinking, and it don't mean nothing. You're just saying something to say it."

"I understand that," I said. "This is my dad, George. I know better than anyone on this earth what a hard-ass he could be. Just tell me what happened."

"It was nothing, you have to understand," he said, sounding tired. "We were just giving each other shit."

"About what?"

George slumped. His eyes looked baggy and dark even beyond his age. He took the zipper of his coat and pulled it up high, so just the knot of his blue-and-yellow necktie was showing.

"We were playing darts," he said. "That's how it started. We were playing darts, and he was winning. And he kept calling me Delivery Boy."

"Delivery Boy?"

"Right," he said. "Because of my job. Every time I missed a shot, he'd say something like, 'I don't know, Delivery Boy. That delivery isn't so special.' Some of the other guys were joining in, too, piling on. It just got worse and worse."

I felt like I was listening to a second-grader complain about how the kids at school were teasing him. "So what did you do?" I asked him calmly.

"I started giving back."

"How?"

"You know how it is. You go for a guy's weak spot."

I didn't even need to guess. "So you were teasing him about the divorce. What did you say?"

"I'm not going to repeat it. The words aren't going to come out of my mouth, not at your father's funeral. It wouldn't be right."

He was correct. He did not need to go into the exact wording of his taunts. I could use my imagination—and the less of it I used, the better. Somehow, someway, it would amount to: you couldn't please your woman.

"I'll tell you the last thing he said to me." George now had tears in his eyes. "He told me I was a failure. That I always have been a failure and I always would be a failure."

Funny how George was willing to share that. I was glad I wasn't spending my life in this town. "That's enough, George," I said. "You're right, the details don't matter." I extended my hand. He took it. "Take care," I said.

George shook my hand quickly and walked away, headed toward his wife. Soon Charlie came up from behind me and put his hand on my shoulder.

"Well done, Nick," he said.

"How so?"

"You shaking his hand," Charlie said. "That meant a lot to him. He's had some rough bumps the past few years. I'm glad you were kind to him. The incident can sound worse than it was."

"That's what George said," I answered, quietly noting the

word *incident* that Charlie had used, which sounded a notch stronger than needed for what George had described.

"I mean, really," Charlie said, "it was just one punch."

"Punch?" I looked back at George, who was guiding his wife urgently to the parking lot.

Charlie exhaled, creating a wintry cloud between us, and then he filled me in on the details. George had told me the truth, up to a point, but he had left out the ending. When he started needling my dad about his divorce, my dad shoved him. George came back with a wild right. He hit my dad in the ribs, and the blow sent him stumbling. It wasn't a hard punch, Charlie said—it really just knocked my dad off balance. But he went backward into a table, and he knocked it over along with a couple of chairs. He fell to the ground and a beer from the table spilled onto my dad's lap. He sprang up right away to show he wasn't hurt, but still, it didn't look good, and my dad was left with a big stain on his pants. And then guys jumped in to separate my dad and George, and the fight was over. Which is when my dad really began running down George with every insult he could think of. He wouldn't let up, and finally the guys told my dad to go home.

From a distance I could see George driving away. It was sad, to learn that my dad's life was in such a fragile state that George Chamberlain was capable of provoking him into a fatal froth.

We land in Birmingham just after noon. The temperature is in the upper eighties, and the humidity is magnifying its effect. I can feel the heat on the asphalt through the soles of my shoes as the rest of us stand sweltering on the open tarmac, sweat already beginning to bead, while Freddie changes his clothes on the plane.

When Freddie pops out, he looks fabulous. His suits are all hand-tailored, and they hang on him with an easy elegance. The one he is wearing is charcoal, single-breasted, with a nearly invisible purple stripe.

We have two rental sedans waiting for us. With no discussion as to how we would divide up, the adults climb into one car, leaving the other to Freddie and myself. They pull out first, and we follow.

"So remind me again—what are you doing here?" Freddie says, one hand on the wheel and the other scratching behind his ear, as we exit the airport grounds and merge onto the interstate. "You had dinner with Samuel once, right?"

"Yes," I say. "I just wanted to see a couple things for myself."

"What kind of things?"

I tell Freddie what I read about Kaylee Wise.

"So you've come down here to make some moves on the wealthy widow?" Freddie says with a teasing grin. "I suppose everyone needs a retirement plan."

We ride on in silence.

"I do wonder if she could have had anything to do with the murder," I say after a time.

"Really?"

"Love and money are more classic motivations for killing." I throw this out there as casually as possible.

"I see your point," Freddie says, after considering for a moment. "And she wouldn't even have to be the killer herself. She could have a brother or cousin who's all angry that this big, black football star screwed the blond princess and then abandoned her. So they kill Samuel, they uphold the family pride, and Kaylee gets thirty million while they're at it."

His language is more crass than what I would have chosen, but the logic is close enough.

Freddie, without warning, pulls our car to the side of the road.

"Is something wrong?" I ask.

"No."

"Then why did we pull over?"

"Um . . . hello?" Freddie says. He gestures toward the red roadside shack near where we have stopped, which has a hand-painted wooden sign that reads AUNT LOLA'S BBQ. The dilapidated structure stands on some uninviting acreage, with only a few random weeds popping out of hard-baked soil. No other structures are within sight.

"Are you out of your fucking mind?" I say. Tanner's car is nearly out of view. "Get going before we lose them."

"Look at this place," Freddie says, gazing admiringly at the shack. "We can't pass it by."

"It looks like it's about five minutes from being condemned," I say. I am not even sure it is open, despite a screen door that appears to be unhitched. The only other car in the lot is a dusty red pickup truck.

Freddie turns off the engine. "One day, Hangman, I pray that you actually get on my wavelength, and not just near it," he says, opening the door and letting in a blast of hot outside air. "But here's a basic rule of life. If you're traveling and you see a place like this, you stop, because you're not just getting a meal, you're getting a story about how you were cruising some back road in Assfuck, Alabama, and found this dumpy little shithole and had the best barbecue of your life."

"And missed a funeral because of it," I say. "Which kind of ruins the anecdote."

Freddie mulls this point. "Depends on the audience," he concludes. "Besides, I didn't have any breakfast." He then steps out of the car, as if that clinches the argument, because there can be no greater need than his immediate appetites.

I sit and stew as heat infiltrates the car. Tanner and the others are now out of sight. I somehow doubt that Freddie has directions to the funeral, so I am not sure we will get there at all. This isn't a culinary adventure, it is an act of self-destruction. I wish I had been driving; I could have prevented this.

The air in the lowlands here is even thicker than it was by the airport, and going into Aunt Lola's restaurant provides little relief, either from the heat, or the feeling this is an obvious mistake. The entire restaurant looks like it costs less than Freddie's suit—which, I suspect, is half the fun for him being here.

I find him chatting up a mountainous middle-aged woman in jean shorts and a sleeveless top. The sight of her isn't exactly revving up my saliva glands.

"Nick," he says, looking delighted. "This is Aunt Lola herself."

"Howdy, slim," she says. My first thought is that if this woman has gotten to look the way she did by eating her own cooking, I don't want any of it in my body. Aunt Lola's kitchen consists of one large pot of meat, a plastic bag full of buns, and a jar of pickle slices. Napkins and paper plates rest in torn-open plastic wrappers from the store.

"Pulled-pork sandwich," Freddie says, leaning against the counter. "That's the whole menu. The barbecue is Memphis-style around here. Upstate they do more Carolina-style, with a mustard-based sauce. You like Memphis-style, right, Nick?"

"I only eat Carolina. Can we go now?" One day I am going to knock Freddie's teeth out.

He turns to Aunt Lola. "You'll have to excuse my friend," he says. "We'll have two sandwiches."

"You're gonna love it," Aunt Lola says to me with a discomfiting wink.

We then watch Aunt Lola prepare the order, which she manages to turn into an endurance event. I swear I've seen guys run the length of a football field and back in less time than it takes for her to undo the twist-tie on a bag of buns. Eventually she gets down to the ladling of the meat, and we are handed our pulled-pork sandwiches on paper plates. The buns are so flimsy that eating as we drive is out of the question, unless we want the food to end up in our laps.

So Freddie and I sit outside at a table. One bite of the sandwich is all I need. The sauce is sickeningly sweet, as if Aunt Lola decided that the best way to make it tangy was to add Tang. Add in the toughness of the meat, and I feel like I am biting into candied tire.

Freddie chews away happily though. I wonder if I have just lost my taste for this kind of food. Jessica once told me that the danger of prioritizing function over pleasure in my diet was that I might be reprogramming my taste buds; that the area of my brain wired to enjoy decadent foods could atrophy. She told me this after I had refused to try the deep-fried bacon that she had brought home from some allegedly gourmet food shop. "If the part of your brain that craves fatty foods withers, think about what happens next," she said. "Right next to it is the part that enjoys sex. Your brain is like your mouth— if one tooth starts rotting, those next to it will follow. Pretty soon, the only things you'll enjoy in this life will be kicking footballs and thinking that you're better than everyone else."

But no part of me wants to eat this mess from Aunt Lola's. I take my paper plate and fold it around the remains of the sandwich.

"Don't tell me you don't like it," Freddie says, mouth half full. He swallows and then adds, "This is a great sandwich. Great fucking sandwich."

By way of registering my dissent, I squeeze my plate extra-tight around the sandwich. Then I stand up, hold the bundle aloft, take a step-step-step, and kick the sandwich across the road.

As my leg rises up I feel a sharp twinge up the back of my thigh. My hamstring. Shit.

"You can be such a bitch," Freddie says.

I now do not care anymore about the sandwich, or the funeral, or Freddie, or anything else except the pain running up the back of my leg. With minicamp starting in two days, and Woodward Tolley on the hunt. This is horrible.

It is my fault, too. I know better than to make a full kicking motion with no warm-up, especially after sitting for hours on that damn plane and then in the car. I shouldn't have come here to Alabama in the first place. I should have stayed behind in Philadelphia, taking care of myself and sticking to my routines.

This could well be the precise moment when my life begins to fall apart. I could lose my job to Woodward Tolley, I would have to leave Philadelphia and fight for a roster spot somewhere else, assuming I could even get an invitation to camp. All because of this mistake.

I walk around gingerly, trying to keep myself loose.

Freddie, oblivious, continues eating—his chewing is becoming slower and more strenuous as he nears the end of his sandwich. His joy seems to have worn off. After the last bite, he looks at his wrist to check the time, even though he is not wearing a watch. I have seen him do this, oh, about a thousand times. The gag never gets old.

I continue pacing, and the shock in the hamstring seems to be subsiding. This might be okay, I tell myself. I would have to stretch at the first opportunity, but this might not be that bad.

"Do you have directions to the funeral?" I ask Freddie.

"No, not really," Freddie says. "But it can't be that hard to find. The town probably has three streets in it, right?"

I go to the driver's side of the car to take over command of the expedition, and Freddie tosses me the keys without argument. We drive up the highway about five miles and pass a small sign that reads WELCOME TO VICKERS, POP. 580. We also pass a small brick post office, a Quonset-hut agricultural supply shop, and a gas station.

And then nothing. We don't realize that we just passed through downtown Vickers until we are back in the countryside.

I make a sharp and bumpy U-turn on the hardpan, circling partway off the road and then back on again. Freddie puts a hand on his stomach.

"That barbecue not sitting too well?" I ask without sympathy.

"Sitting beautifully, friend," Freddie says through a grimace.

I pull into the gas station and ask the attendant for directions. He is a young man with the name ELVIS stitched in red letters on his pale blue work shirt. Leaning down to the level of the open car window and resting a hand on my door, he gives instruction that includes such phrases as "take the first left after the soybean field" and "take a right at this really big tree." We can't miss it, Elvis says.

"I'd be at the funeral myself, if we didn't have to stay open," he says. "I hear the team paid for the whole spread. Hey, you're the Sentinels' punter, aren't you? Nick Gallow?"

"Yes," I say. To be recognized in public—this is a first. And out of town, even.

"That fucking JC," Elvis says bitterly. "I hope they hang the bastard."

"We'll see," I say. "A man's innocent until proven guilty, right?"

"If that JC ain't guilty, I'll eat my own shit," he says.

Nice to see a man standing behind his convictions. I thank Elvis for the directions and go.

We turn off the main road and after a quarter mile we are driving over loose gravel. The landscape offers only intermittent farmland and occasional clusters of modest houses. "What do people here do at night?" Freddie wonders out loud.

These are the roads that Samuel must have pushed his mother's Chevy Malibu along when he was a teenager. I imagine Samuel doing that on a scorching day like this one, where the sun castigates anyone who ventures out of the shade. If Samuel played defensive end with that same stubborn determination, he would have been worth his $64 million.

After five minutes of driving, I feel lost. My leg is not in great pain but my hamstring is tweaked enough that I am aware of it, and that awareness is adding to my cumulative anxiety.

Then I see lines of cars and trucks bumper-to-bumper along the roadside. All of a sudden the parking is as tight as it is on Broad Street in South Philly. As I drive along, I scan the bumper stickers, but see only flags, fish, and sports team logos—many, many sports team logos, mostly from colleges and high schools.

We continue on the road and see the church itself, which looks like an old barn that has been painted white and had a cross hammered to its side. The service, we can see, is being held outside. At least five hundred people are here, many more than the church can hold. And I can see that the service is already in progress. We drive a couple hundred yards past and finally find a parking space on the roadside.

Television cameras capture Freddie and me walking up late to the ceremony. With the chairs all occupied, a business-like teenager in a black suit and a skinny red tie directs us to stand in the back. He hands Freddie and me white paper fans with which to cool ourselves. Tanner, sitting with the others a few rows from the back, turns and notes our late arrival with an angry flash from those blue eyes. Great. Whatever Woodward Tolley is doing right now, he is gaining on me.

We join the back row and I put the heel of my injured leg forward and lean slightly back, trying to stretch my hamstring as much as I can without being ostentatious.

The service is being led by a heavyset older man in sunglasses and a flamboyant purple-and-orange robe. He has no podium or dais; he is on the grass, speaking into a handhold microphone he has removed from its stand, stalking back and forth, speaking in call-and-response style to the audience.

"God gave Samuel a gift!" the preacher says.

"Yes!" comes the congregation's response.

"God made Samuel fast and strong!"

"Yes!"

"People called Samuel the next big thing."

"Yes!"

The congregation grows progressively more boisterous with each response, though I can see Tanner sitting stonily, frowning, eyes shifting, while others clap and shout around him. I am not aware of Tanner's religious beliefs, but whatever they are, it is apparently not this.

"Some say he is the next evolution of man."

"Yes!" Freddie yells idiotically, hand cupped to mouth, as he joins the call and response—ironically, of course. I nudge him with my elbow and glare.

"But we all know Samuel's real strength!"

"Yes!"

"It is his love of Jesus!"

"Yes!"

"Samuel is with Jesus right now!"

"Yes!"

"Jesus doesn't care if he's fast or strong!"

"Yes!"

"There's only one measure that matters in heaven!"

"Yes!"

"It's how much love you have in your heart!"

"Yes!"

And so on and so forth. I don't especially care for the lyrics of his speech, but I enjoy the music of it, and latch on to the one idea in there I can appreciate, which is the hope that somewhere and some way, goodness is eventually rewarded.

After the righteous reverend finishes, he calls up the next speaker: DaFrank Burns, who is sitting in the front row. The two men hug as they pass.

DaFrank, wearing a black suit, places the microphone back in its stand. Since I saw him at the hospital he has touched up his already short haircut with fresh tapering on the side. He looks nervous as he fiddles with the mic stand to raise it up to his height.

"Welcome, my brothers and sisters," DaFrank begins in a Southern accent more pronounced than I had heard from him in our previous encounters. "I'm happy to see so many people here to honor such a wonderful man. It shows how much love there is in this town and in this world for my brother Samuel. I see Samuel's mother and father and his sister, Selia. I see aunts and uncles and cousins. I see many friends here from Western Alabama. That's Puma pride right there. I even see some people here from the Sentinels. And then there are the television cameras, and I am glad they are here because they represent people all around the world who have only come to know Samuel in death."

At this last note people's heads turn to the cameras. One cameraman is kneeling in the center aisle for a straight-on shot of DaFrank, while another is to the side, his camera trained on the front-row mourners.

"I have been thinking and thinking," DaFrank says, "how do I tell people all about my brother. And I decided that the best way to do this is to use Samuel's own words. Words that come from his heart. I'm going to read an e-mail that Samuel sent me. He wrote this ten days ago, not long before he signed the contract that made him a Sentinel."

DaFrank reaches into his jacket pocket and removes from it a folded sheet of paper.

"Before reading this, I want you all to know that Samuel is a private man, and he didn't like to say much in public. I think the only thing in this world he was afraid of was a microphone." He looks up. "So if you are watching, Samuel, I am sorry, but I have to do this."

DaFrank unfolds the piece of paper and reads:

I need help, DaFrank. I don't know what to do. I'm so confused. All anyone talks about is how much money I'm going to make, how big a star I'm going to be, how I can have anything I

*want. I listen and I nod my head and all the time I'm thinking,
why?*

*The more people talk, the more I think I should stay right
here in Vickers. Is that insane? I like playing football. But why
does it have to be such a big deal? Why do I have to leave home?
I feel like if I sign that contact I'm also agreeing to all these things
that I don't want and don't need. Even the money. It's too much
for me.*

*But if I say I want to just stay home, everyone would be mad
at me. The team would be mad at me. Fans would be mad.
Cecil would be mad. Everyone in Vickers, they'd all make jokes
about how stupid I am to turn down all that money. They'd say
I'm a mama's boy. Or that I'm whipped. But I want to spend
my life right here. I think I'd be happier if I wasn't a Sentinel.
Tell me, is that crazy?*

DaFrank lowers the paper and slips a thumb and forefinger underneath his glasses to daub the tears.

"Samuel, here's my answer. You wouldn't be crazy, brother.
You wouldn't be crazy at all. You knew what you loved and
what mattered to you, and there is nothing crazy about that.
I wish everyone on Earth was that crazy."

DaFrank lowers his head and holds his fist to his lips. He
appears to be on the brink of full-on weeping. He rushes out
his last words: "I just wish that's what I had told you then."

In the front row, I see a woman with blond hair, her shoulders shaking. I can't tell for sure from behind, but I am guessing this is Kaylee Wise. Strangely, she has a couple of seats to
herself; no one is by her side.

After hearing Samuel's letter, I wonder afresh about Samuel's contract with the Sentinels, and how Cecil agreed to it
so early, rather than waiting until closer to training camp like

most rookies do. If Cecil knew Samuel had been wavering in his desire to play, he would have wanted Samuel to sign when he was in a mood to do so, whether it was the best offer or not. Cecil couldn't risk Samuel changing his mind later in the summer. If Samuel had quit on the Sentinels, Cecil's reputation would have never recovered.

After the service, I walk forward, toward Kaylee Wise. I expected that she might be a difficult person to get an audience with—pregnant, sort-of widowed, possibly about to be rich, and in her hometown. But no. As mourners stream from the service area toward a buffet set up on folding tables behind the church, she moves slowly and alone. Wearing a sleeveless dark-blue maternity dress, she is struggling with her pronounced baby bump on this sweltering day.

"Excuse me," I say. "Ms. Wise?"

"Afraid so," she says with a soft Dixie accent. Up close, she looks even younger than she did in her photo. Her cheeks are puffed and her eyes are bloodshot, and she grips a white handkerchief with her long, unpainted fingers.

"Hello," I say. "I'm Nick Gallow, the punter with the Sentinels. I was with Samuel . . ."

"I know," she says, cutting me off but then smiling. "I know." She is covered with a film of sweat. She squints toward the food line, already at least a hundred deep.

"Look at all those people," she says tiredly, crossing her arms.

"I'm sure everyone would let you go right to the front . . ."

"Forget it, I don't like owing anyone anything," she says. "I'm just going to sit for a minute."

Before I can say anything she turns and retreats to the folding chairs, grabbing the nearest seat. They are empty now, except for a young man in a crisp white suit sitting toward the back. He has a shaved head and is bent in what appears to be intense prayer. He is broad-shouldered and lean, and I would not be surprised if he was a teammate of Samuel's from high school or college.

"Do you know who that is?" I ask Kaylee quietly as I sit down beside her and tilt my head in the direction of the praying figure.

"Never seen him before," Kaylee says. "But that's a Southern funeral for you, it brings everyone out of their tree stumps. You ever been to one before?"

"No."

"These things go all day, all night," she says, and then she squeezes her hands and knocks her knees together. "I just want to go home. My mom's all by herself. She had a stroke two years ago, she can't hardly get around anywhere."

"I'm sorry," I say.

"It happens," she says with a faint smile. "If it wasn't for my mama's stroke, I wouldn't have been with Sam. When she came home from the hospital, she couldn't get up the stairs by herself. I'm friends with Sam's sister, Selia—at least I was— and Selia asked Sam to come by each morning and carry my mom down the stairs. At night he'd return and carry my mom back up."

Kaylee fiddles with a ring on her finger. It is a simple and inexpensive ring without any stone, just a metal heart at its center.

"What did you think of the e-mail DaFrank Burns read at the service?" I ask her. "I had no idea Samuel has such mixed feelings about coming to Philadelphia."

She turns her eyes to me with pity, for my ignorance.

"Wasn't anything mixed about it," she says. "Two weeks ago he flat-out told his agent he wasn't going to Philadelphia. I was in the room when he made the call. But that, Cecil Wilson talked him out of it." She was turning bitter now. "Cecil said to him, 'Just give it a chance. If you don't like it, home will always be there for you.'"

Her face remains expressionless, but tears flow down her cheeks.

"Did you think about following Samuel to Philadelphia?" I ask.

"I would have loved to go," she says. "I'm so sick of all the dimwits in this town. But I couldn't abandon my mama. I'm not that kind of daughter.

"If Sam had been drafted by Atlanta, everything would have been fine. We could have come up and back all the time. Atlanta was trying to trade up for him, too. But I guess you all up in Philadelphia just had to have him." She raised her handkerchief and daubed at her eyes. "I just don't get why a burger flipper can choose between Burger King and McDonald's, but a player worth $64 million has no say at all in where he goes."

Kaylee obviously did not appreciate the rigidity of the league's drafting system, or its goal of equitable distribution of talent. She just cared about her ailing mother, her unborn child, and the man she loved.

"I really wish I could get out of town," she says. "My last year or so all my cousins have been treating me like I'm a bucket of pig slop because I was dating a black man. Like they're anything special. Then last night they come by the house like everything is all fine and dandy between us, all because they think I'm going to be rich. Where were they when I needed them?

"And Sam's family, they used to like me, but now they're mad at me, all because I went along with that lawyer, this jerk from Birmingham with a silk necktie who told me I was entitled to a bunch of money and he could get it for me and I wouldn't have to do anything except sign a piece of paper. That's what the devil does, right—just asks you to sign a piece of paper."

She slumps in her chair, which makes her dress ride up on her thighs. I look over to the food line, which has doubled in length since we sat down.

"Let me get you something to eat," I ask.

"Sure," she says, folding her hands on her belly. "I won't move a muscle."

I do not believe my instincts are infallible, and I have only spoken to Kaylee Wise for five minutes. But if it turns out that she had anything to do with Samuel's shooting, then I should give up ever trying to figure out anything about anything.

I walk gingerly to the buffet area, coddling my hamstring. My leg is better than it was, but it isn't feeling right, either. Tomorrow I will go to the Sentinels' facility and get a massage from a trainer.

The food line is a long one. The guests who have already filled their plates are reassembling the chairs from the service and sitting down to eat and talk and laugh. It is as if the buffet is a magic tunnel, removing the funereal mood from all who pass.

I notice Tanner and Udall speaking with an older man and woman, both over six feet tall, who have a girl alongside them, nearly six feet herself. Cameras are trained on the group as O'Dwyer and Cordero hover nearby. This must be Samuel's family—which means the girl is Samuel's sister, Selia. She is a slim girl with high, regal cheekbones and long, thin braids.

As her parents talk to Tanner and Udall she leans on her father's meaty shoulders, her slender arm threaded through his, and her head is turned away. I remember how Samuel wasn't one for making nice with strangers, and his sister seems to share his aversion.

I look back to the seating area and Kaylee is still alone, head now propped on one hand, looking overwhelmed. The young man in the white suit is still sitting several rows behind her, head bent. He, at least, is not here for the food.

I scan the crowd and the line ahead for Freddie, but I don't see him anywhere.

I finally arrive at the food tables, my stomach yawning, and see that the buffet is a cardiologist's nightmare: fried chicken, fried fish, fried pork chops, fried okra, sliced ham, macaroni and cheese, deviled eggs, French fries, sweet potato pie, banana pudding, yellow cake, and chocolate cake. There are mustard greens and collard greens, but they have thick chunks of ham in them.

The entire menu is outside my diet, but I am hungry. I take pieces of fish and chicken. Plus the mustard greens, and the mac and cheese. This is for Kaylee and me to share, I tell myself. So I take a couple of more pieces of chicken and fish, and some more greens, too, trying to avoid the bigger hunks of ham.

My plate full, I walk back to the chairs. Kaylee is now gone. So, for that matter, is the young man in the white suit. I peer around but I do not see Kaylee anywhere. I wonder if she had enough and went home to her mother.

I sit alone with my full plate of food and start in on the fried chicken. Which is crunchy and juicy, and even though I suspect that the "juice" is lard, the chicken is about the best thing I have eaten since I don't know when. I take another bite and then another.

I am on my second piece when I am joined by Freddie.

"Have you tried this chicken, buddy?" I ask. "Forget that barbecue stand. This is the meal you'll be telling stories about."

"We have to get out of here," he says, standing over me and tugging anxiously on my sleeve.

"Why?" I ask.

"I have a very urgent need," he whispers. Then, in case his meaning is not clear, he adds, "I have to take a shit. *Really bad.*"

"Just go inside," I say. "The church must have a bathroom."

"It does," he says. "It's the locked door with the sign that says OUT OF ORDER."

"No Porta Pottys?"

"No!" he says. "I looked everywhere."

Freddie pogoes gingerly from one foot to another. Denying him is not an option.

Or is it? He wanted a great anecdote to tell.

"Fine," I say, and I stand up. "Let me just figure out where to put my plate . . ."

Freddie snatches the plate from my hand and marches it to a nearby garbage barrel and dumps it, along with my food, and then continues urgently toward the car.

I catch up to Freddie, whose strides are narrowing as he squeezes himself tight.

Soon we are in the car and on our way.

"Where are we going?" Freddie says. The sweat is beading on his forehead.

"The gas station." Which is a good seven minutes away, and Freddie does not seem confident he will last that long. "Unless you have any better ideas."

"How about one of these houses," Freddie says, looking

out the window. "Southerners are famous for their hospitality, right?"

"Everyone's at the funeral," I say. "I don't think we want
to go door to door, hoping to find someone who's home."

Freddie frowns.

"I wonder if this is one of those small towns where everyone trusts everyone else, and so no one locks their doors?"

I keep on driving. I have no interest in being part of a
break-in, especially one with the most embarrassing motivation ever.

We arrive at the gas station with Freddie about to squirm
himself in half.

"Can I have the men's room key?" I ask our pal Elvis.

He is watching a baseball game. Without taking his eyes
off the television, he opens a desk drawer and begins feeling
around inside. After about ten seconds of clatter—he would
have found it in one second if he stopped watching the game—
he fishes out a key, attached to a wooden ruler, and hands it
to me.

Freddie is stationed by the entrance to the bathroom,
his feet crossed. I quickly walk over and hand him the key. He
uncrosses his feet and takes a half step toward the restroom,
then freezes.

"Goddammit," he says.

"What?"

"I'm stuck."

"What do you mean?"

"I can't move," Freddie mutters through clenched teeth.
Sweat is beading on his forehead. "If I take a step, I'm going
to lose it."

Oh, hell. I grab the key from his hand and open the bathroom door for him. And what a bathroom it is. It looks more like a storage closet that happens to have a toilet and sink in it. The cement floor is foul and stained. Elvis should have been in here cleaning instead of watching the game.

"You can do this, buddy," I say to Freddie. I pace out the walk for him. "Three steps. Three steps and I'll close the door behind you. You can do this."

"I can't," he says. He scrunches his face. "I won't make it."

For lack of any better ideas, I place my hands on Freddie's hips and lift him up—"Gentle, gentle!" he shouts—and deposit him in the bathroom. Then I close the door behind him.

That should do it. Now all Freddie has to do is turn and drop his pants. . . .

Then I heard a big *whoosh* and a splat. Like oatmeal shot out of a spray gun onto cement.

"Fuck! Fuck! Fuck!"

Oh, Freddie. So close. So close.

Elvis approaches, having been drawn outside by the shouting. He and I exchange uncomfortable glances.

"If I was in the market for a clean pair of pants," I say, "which way would I be headed?"

Elvis's face goes grim. "There's a Walmart a few miles up the highway," he mumbles.

I go to the bathroom door.

"Freddie, I'm going to head up the road, get you a change of clothes," I call. "You just hang out."

"Oh, great," Freddie says bitterly, as if I am the person responsible for this mess, rather than the one helping him out of it.

A quick trip up the road and there I am, in a Walmart. It occurs to me this is the same Walmart where Samuel's mother's car broke down, and the thought of him pushing her Malibu that same distance I just drove, in the middle of summer, is now positively astounding.

I grab the first pair of khakis I see, then a blue button-down shirt, and boxers. And some socks, and sandals, because I don't want to guess on shoe size, and I return to the gas station. Freddie is still in the bathroom. I knock on the door and he opens it wide enough for me to hand him the bag of clothes.

Elvis emerges from his office, hands on hips, glaring at me. I pull out my wallet and hand him $200.

"For your trouble," I say.

He grabs quickly at the bills. "Thanks," he says, surprised, folding my cash into his chest pocket. "If you're going to pay like this, you can crap on the floor any time you like."

Now that is true hospitality.

I text Cordero to see where the rest of our crew is. They are still at the funeral, she says, and they are wondering where we are. I write that Freddie has "stomach troubles."

She texts back: *Nice euphemism.*

Freddie emerges from the bathroom, looking about as bad as I have ever seen him—both spiritually and sartorially. My guesses on his clothes sizes were off, especially with the pants, which are so billowy he has to cinch them by hand at the waist. Instead of hiding his shame, my purchases are accentuating it.

"If I ever hire a personal shopper," he says, "don't bother applying."

"You're welcome."

My phone rings. It is Cordero.

"Tanner's clock has hit zero," she says. "We're headed to the airport."

"Okay," I say. "We'll meet you at the charter terminal."

I take the wheel for the drive back. Freddie slumps in the passenger seat and distracts himself with his iPhone.

As we retrace our route back to the airport, I am frustrated. I talked to Kaylee Wise, but that has only served to close one avenue of suspicion. I never had a chance to speak to anyone else, to learn anything more about Samuel, all because Freddie had to stop for barbecue. This trip was a waste. I should never have let Freddie go into that restaurant.

To make this car ride even more uncomfortable, the fecal odor has not been entirely left behind in the gas station bathroom. Freddie has thrown away his soiled clothes and washed himself as best he could. Still, the smell lingers.

The thing about Freddie is, he wasn't always like this. He would drink, of course, and get high, and every now and then he would dabble in the party drugs, and he always had women coming and going. But it never felt out of control. He didn't used to have "incidents" like this one at the gas station. He wouldn't have reacted so immaturely to a simple request from his father to attend a funeral in his place. It strikes me that Freddie, hopping continuously from one diversion to another, is as lost a soul as I've known.

"Hey, listen to this tweet," he says, holding his phone up to reading position. *"Police source says charges against Carson 'a matter of time.'"*

"Who tweeted it?"

"A reporter," he says. "Who is actually retweeting it from some other reporter, it looks like."

"Is there a story link?"

"I don't see one."

However muddied the sourcing, this is discouraging. It suggests that Rizotti has locked in on his target.

Meanwhile, Rizotti didn't bother to come to Samuel's funeral. He is too busy running in the wrong direction. Not that I saw anything down here worth seeing. But then, I really didn't have a chance to look. I feel like I often do on the sidelines during games, watching bad throws and missed tackles, and wishing I could run out onto the field and make the damn plays myself.

"So where are you going to get my ten million dollars?" Freddie says. "You better line up some seriously high-paying skills clinics. Maybe the sultan of Brunei wants to learn the coffin corner."

"If the police actually had evidence on Jai," I say, "they would have arrested him already."

"Oh, it's coming, Hangman, it's coming," he says.

"Freddie, why do you seem happy about this? Jai plays for our team. Your team, actually. You kind of own it. Remember?"

"Yeah, well," Freddie answers sullenly, "who gives a fuck?"

"About what?"

"About any of it," he says. He shoves himself upright in his seat. "You know, everywhere I go, all anyone gives a shit about is the goddamn Sentinels. Who you drafting? How's the team look? Here's all anyone needs to know: every year we put a bunch of guys out there and they play somebody else's guys and somebody wins and somebody loses and the next year we do it all again. That's it. It's all a giant pile of bullshit." Freddie picks something out of his teeth with his pinkie fingernail. I hope he washed those hands well. "And no one even cares who wins," he continues. "No one. The players are just here to make money, and the fans are just pretending to care so they don't have to think about their lives. It's like this huge Ponzi scheme of caring, of people pretending that something is extremely important when we all know that it doesn't matter one bit. I'd love it if the whole damn structure just collapsed. So if it turns out that Jai killed Samuel, and people have to think about that for a while, what kind of heads are underneath those helmets, what craven hearts beat underneath the uniforms they salivate at the sight of, maybe it would break the illusion, let everyone see what a big pile of crap it is they've been building their lives around." He presses some buttons on his iPhone, toggling over from Twitter to a video game. I roll down the windows, but the heat only amplifies the odor.

"There's a shower on the plane, right?" I ask.

"Yup," he says.

"Thank the lord."

"You said it."

We arrive at the charter terminal ahead of Tanner's party. Credit that to our head start, and my heavy foot, because I was not going to have an impatient Tanner waiting on me again. The terminal is a humble space with only a few banks of seats and a drugstore and a sandwich shop. Freddie and I take seats on the contoured plastic chairs.

"Wanna see some pictures?" Freddie says, holding out his iPhone. "From the funeral. Pretty good stuff."

Before his bowels betrayed him, he had been collecting images of eye-catching characters. He has a few pictures of older women in ostentatious formal wear, complete with feathered hats and loud costume jewelry. He has a shot of a little boy in cornrows and a bright green tie. Then he shows me a sequence of pictures of a particularly rotund man: the first shot is a close-up of the back of his shaved head—specifically the collected rolls of fat, which look like a pack of hot dogs. Then come photos of the same guy as he turns around and smiles eagerly, his gold front tooth glinting in the sun.

"I really just wanted the neck-roll shot," Freddie says. "But the guy heard the *click* sound effect on the camera and turned around. For a second, I thought he was going to pop me, but it turned out he was happy to pose."

The poor guy had no idea he was a prop in Freddie's condescension. Maybe he was better off not knowing.

My hamstring, which had been quiet for the drive, is panging again.

Before too long, a swift-moving Tanner leads his crew into the terminal.

"Where the fuck did you disappear to?" Tanner snaps at me, with surprising anger.

"Helping out Freddie," I say. "He wasn't feeling well."

Tanner glares at me for a moment and then says, "I need to buy some antacid. Wait right here." He heads for the terminal store, while O'Dwyer, Cordero, and Udall, in uncomfortable silence, quietly register Freddie's change of wardrobe, probably notice the smell, and try to act like everything is normal. No one, of course, says a disparaging word. Such are the privileges of ownership.

"Wanna see my pictures from the reception?" Freddie says to Udall, changing a subject that wasn't ever raised. "They're kind of funny."

Udall takes the phone and thumbs through the pictures. "This is really unbelievable," he says, shaking his head. He tilts the phone in my direction. "Do you know who this is?"

He is showing me a photo of the neck-roll guy who posed for Freddie. "Should I?"

"Not really," Udall says. "But I scouted him. A couple years ago he was a quarterback. Now look at him."

A quarterback? I am not surprised to learn that Freddie's objet d'art is a former player, but with his girth I would have guessed he was a nose tackle. "What the hell happened to him?" I ask.

"Samuel happened to him," Udall says. "He's one of the infamous eleven. Samuel ruptured his spleen—in the last game of his senior season, too."

"Really?" I say. "What's his name?"

"Herrold McKoy," Udall says.

Herrold McKoy. I remember the name from that story that tried to track down the players Samuel had injured. McKoy was one of the two who couldn't be found.

"Was McKoy any good?"

"As a college player he was actually outstanding," Udall said. "He put up some huge stats, made big plays, won a bunch of games. But I didn't see him as a prospect. His throwing motion was too long by half, and he took way too many chances. In the pros he would have been picked apart." He shakes his head. "It's funny," he says. "I counted five of Samuel's victims at the funeral today."

"Five? Who were the others?"

He rattles off the names. The one that jumps out to me is Luke Reckherd—the other missing player from that story, the son of the great Wee Willie.

"Which one was Reckherd?" I ask.

"I bet you saw him, he was hard to miss," Udall says. "Tall guy, white suit, shaved head. He was sitting and praying while everyone else was hitting the chow line."

So that's who that was.

"Didn't he go to Langston?" I ask. Up in Maryland.

"Yup," Udall says. "Just like his dad."

"So he would have had to travel a ways to get here?"

"I guess so," Udall says. "If he's still in Maryland."

That strikes me as odd. Kaylee hadn't recognized Luke, which suggested he hadn't visited Vickers during the time when she and Samuel were together. And Samuel spent nearly every night of his life up until a few weeks ago sleeping under his mother's roof, so it was difficult to figure out how a relationship between he and Luke would have developed. There might be a simple explanation. Perhaps Luke and Samuel met in some setting that Kaylee wouldn't have known the details of—a photo shoot for conference stars, or something like that. I wish I had had time to ask Luke about it, so I wouldn't have to stand here and wonder.

"Were people still hanging at the church when you took off?" I ask Udall. "I was told the funeral could last into the night."

"The reception was still going strong," he says. "But Jerry wanted to leave. So we left."

Tanner returns from the airport shop holding a roll of Tums. "You all didn't have to stand here and wait for me," he says. "You could have been on the plane already. Let's go! Time to move out."

Even if the funeral is supposed to go into the night, there is no guarantee Luke Reckherd and Herrold McKoy are still there. And there is a one-tenth-of-one-percent chance they would have anything useful to tell me. The easy choice for me is to climb into this private jet and go home. Tomorrow morning I could be at the team facility, having a trainer massage my panging hamstring.

Still, I linger as the others cross the tarmac.

"Gallow!" Tanner barks from midway up the plane's steps. "Let's go!"

Freddie, O'Dwyer, and Cordero all turn their heads, looking back at me, waiting.

"Actually," I say, "you all go on ahead without me. I'll get home on my own."

CHAPTER 14

I RENT A car and begin the drive back to Vickers. As I traverse these flat and featureless roads for the second time today, I immediately begin to question my choice—not just about staying in Alabama, but also about expecting to learn anything of value from talking to Herrold McKoy or Luke Reckherd. My justification for staying is: it is a starting place. They are two among the many people I can talk to, to learn more about Samuel and his life, and what might have really happened the night of the shooting.

Herrold and Luke and I also have something in common. Our quarterback careers ended with a hit. In my case, at least, it was a blow that indisputably changed my life.

I was a junior at Hudson Valley State, and it was our season opener, and I was starting my first game after having sat on the bench as a freshman. We were playing on national television, on a Friday night, against a school from one of college football's power conferences. We knew we were in for a beating—on the scoreboard, and physically. I had been making cracks around practice all week that the players should be getting a chunk of the athletic department's paycheck for this game—$400,000, according to the school paper—given that we were the ones who were going to be bruised and broken the next week.

Before the game our coach, Vernon Dorie, called me into his office. Dorie had coached at Hudson Valley State for thirty-two years after having played center there. The joke was that his parents dropped him off as a freshman and he never left. He was not what you would call a man of expansive interests, but he knew football, and how to handle young men.

I sat in Dorie's office, with its white cinder block walls, studying the Coach of the Year awards behind him—he had been winning them long enough that the certificates had gone from plain black-and-white lettering to color with hologram insignias. He was a potbellied man with thin black hair and age spots from decades of afternoon practices. He wore his authority lightly, but he was decisive in his pronouncements. If your effort at practice was sluggish, he would stand over you and, in a calm but firm voice, ask: *You're wasting my time, and even worse than that, you're wasting yours. Why are you here, if you're not giving your best? Seriously, why?*

"This is going to be a tough one tonight, Gallow," he said gravely from across his desk. "Ten minutes into this game we could be losing by three touchdowns."

"We won't be," I said. His eyelids lowered with my answer.

"I've heard the jokes you've been making around practice, Nick," he said dispassionately. "Jokes have their place. But in the game tonight I want to see you lead. On every play, no matter what the score. I want to see you getting guys in the huddle, making sure they're lined up right, keeping everyone on task. You do that, and no matter what the final score is, I'll know I have my quarterback for the rest of the year."

For the rest of the year. Which implied that if I failed, he would give the ball to the next man in line. We had a freshman quarterback named Travon Turner, a kid from the Bronx who could run like a track star and sling it through a brick wall. Dorie historically did not play freshmen, but he was letting me know that if I gave him reason to, he would.

Cut to late in the fourth quarter. We were on the road, and playing in a stadium that held about eighty thousand people—as opposed to our home field, which accommodated less than a third that. And we were losing 53–0. We hadn't scored a touchdown, and I had twice been tackled for safeties. The stands, nearly full at the beginning of the game, were now half vacant. Many of those who remained were heckling to keep themselves entertained. And the stadium was empty enough that I could hear each lame taunt.

Hey, Gallow, I can see your vagina from here.

But I was doing what Coach demanded of me, rising above circumstance and situation. I was relentless in my command, even if that relentlessness had gotten us nowhere. With time for one drive remaining, I was determined to take our guys to the end zone. I strung together a few medium-length completions and first-down runs, and we had the ball down to the twenty-one-yard line with six seconds left in the game. We had no timeouts. I had one more chance.

I took the snap from the shotgun position and I looked to the right, where a flanker was running a corner route, but the defense had him bracketed. Then I looked to the tight end over the middle, but he was sandwiched between a linebacker and a safety. Another flanker was crossing underneath toward the left sideline—which was the wrong route. That wasn't the pattern I gave him. He was open, but if I threw to him, he would be tackled short of the goal. Dipshit.

But I saw that the tight end had gone to his secondary route, and he was breaking open along the back of the end zone and . . .

That's when it all went dark.

I know, only from having seen the film, what happened. A freshman linebacker, excited to be making his first sack, launched himself, and his helmet slammed me underneath my jaw. My head snapped back. I was unconscious before I hit the ground. I lay on the field for a good five minutes while the stadium emptied, the game over. When I eventually came to, I could not identify the man standing over me, who turned out to be Coach Dorie.

I stayed in the hospital for three agonizing days. Because of the concussion, any light felt like a high beam shining in my face. I had no energy at all. What solid food I ate that first day I vomited right back up. I felt like a newborn, unsuited to a harsh new world.

My parents, then divorced just a few months, couldn't be in the same room together, so they divided up my visiting hours. My mother would come first, and she would sit by my bed and tearfully plead for me to quit football. Then my dad would take his turn and act as if my condition was no more serious than a paper cut. On his second visit, he brought me a squeeze ball so I could exercise from my bed.

When I left the hospital, I returned to practice right away. In fact I returned too quickly, not wanting to cede my starter's role for even a week. I vomited in the locker room beforehand and tried to pass it off as nerves, but during warm-ups, when the trainer saw me shielding my eyes despite overcast weather, he pulled me from practice. After that Coach Dorie told me that he didn't want to see me near the field until I was fully healed, and he assured me that no one in his program lost his spot because of an injury.

But Travon Turner took over at quarterback, and the kid played great. Before long people were all abuzz about "The Bronx Bomber." Within a couple of weeks the lights didn't bother me, I could inhale chicken burritos without upchucking, and my thoughts were running clear as a high mountain stream. I was acing my human origins 101 midterm and I could read *The Crying of Lot 49* and recognize that it was Thomas Pynchon, and not my brain, who had scrambled the letters in the word *potsage*. But no display of mental acuity mattered. The team won eight of the ten games Turner started, and Hudson Valley made the post-season for the first time in four years, and I was done.

I sat on the bench my junior year, watching Turner light up the scoreboard from the sidelines while my college eligibility faded away.

Then during winter break my dad and I were at the house—my mother left it for him to haunt—and we were eating turkey chili and watching some forgettable college bowl game on television when he asked me, "How badly do you want to get back on the field?" He said this casually, not taking his eyes off the TV set. But his proposal clearly had some thought behind it.

My dad's plan was that I convert from quarterback to punter. I would come to spring practice and win the job from our regular punter, who seemed to botch at least one kick every game. On weekends I would make the hour-long drive home from college and spend my Sundays drilling with my dad at my old high school stadium.

The transformation was not a pleasurable one. Punting

drills can be insultingly mundane, especially when you have been a quarterback and your job requires understanding what every player on offense and defense will be doing on every play. The first session with my dad I spent an hour doing nothing but drop the ball repeatedly to the ground, without ever kicking it.

During our long training sessions I sometimes wondered about my dad's motivations. He had not dated anyone since my mother left, and he never would. The one guaranteed result of his plan was that he and I would spend every weekend together. I thought that might be the point as much as getting me back on the field.

One day our practice was particularly trying. It was spring break and most of my teammates had gone to Cancun. But with spring practice not far off, I decided to spend the entire week training in Waverly.

It was maybe forty-two degrees out that day, and there was a light rain. We were doing an accuracy drill. I lined up on the sideline while my dad positioned himself thirty yards down field and told me to kick the ball directly to him.

We had done this before and it had gone fine, but that day I just couldn't place the ball in his hands. First my kicks were going off to the left. Then I overcompensated, and everything went right. If I hit one good punt, the next time I would chunk a low-liner. The goal had been for me to hit five good kicks in a row, but after a while my dad lowered the mark to three. Still, it was too much.

Finally I hit two in a row straight to my dad. "Okay, this is it, Nicky," he said, clapping his hands and then sniffling. "Nail this one and we can go home." I took my step-step-step, dropped the ball and shanked it colossally to the right. The ball hammered the metal bleachers with a mordant clang.

The echo seemed to reverberate for an unusually long time. Instead of picking up another ball, I walked forward to my dad.

"I think I'm getting sick," I said. "Can we go home?"

"No," he said, immediately and without hesitation, even though his eyes betrayed weariness.

"But if I'm sick . . ."

"Not until you get it right. Go back to your spot."

"Maybe this isn't the best idea," I said. "Me becoming a punter."

We stood silent, eyes locked, as those words hung in the air longer than any ball I would ever kick. Because we both knew their import. If I wasn't punting, my football career was done. And we had been building my football career ever since I could grip a Nerf. It was what we did together.

My dad was not the tallest or the stoutest man, but he was wiry and had outstanding posture. He entered a room chest- and chin-first. With his narrow eyes, thin eyebrows, and pointed nose coming at you, you looked down expecting his fists to be balled. Every morning he would begin the day with push-ups, sit-ups, knee bends, and jumping jacks by the side of the bed.

Perhaps it wasn't the biggest surprise that my mother needed to get out of the house.

My dad came to me and pulled back the hood on his yellow rain slicker. I was a good six inches taller than him. His thin gray hair was matted down, his skin was raw, and he was looking older than I had ever seen him. He sniffled deeply before speaking.

"You wish you were with your friends down in Mexico, don't you?"

"Yes, I do." That afternoon I had received a picture from Cancun showing our team's tight end judging a hot legs contest; the woman in the photo was allowing him to conduct an investigation that went to the highest levels of her government.

"You think those guys are having the time of their life, and you're missing out."

"Yes," I say.

"You still don't get it, after all these years," my dad said, more sad than disgusted. "If you quit tonight, it will be the biggest mistake of your life. You'll look back ten, twenty, thirty years from now, and you'll wish you could come back here to this moment and keep on working. I know it. I absolutely know it."

He sniffled again, and turned to the empty stands, as if he was looking for someone he expected to be sitting there. "But it's up to you, kiddo." He folded his arms, trying to warm himself. "You're twenty-one years old, you're not mine anymore. The choice is yours. And if you really want to quit, you'll never hear me say another word about it. You'll still be my boy."

I stayed. And my dad's plan worked, better than he imagined. I won the punting job that spring, I worked even harder that summer, and I went out as a senior and I made All-Conference. Among the people who noticed was Cecil Wilson. He put together a DVD highlight reel and sent it to every personnel man in the league, and one of them actually invited me to camp. That chance turned out to be all I needed. I went to Philadelphia and I killed it.

I still remember when Coach Huff called me into his office and told me I had made the Sentinels. My expectations coming into camp had been low. The team's incumbent punter, Cory Veal, had been in the league eleven years. I was sure Huff was calling me in to cut me. But he said, "Congratulations, Nick, you're a Sentinel. Don't let me down."

After I gushed the appropriate thanks, I went out to my car, still in my uniform, away from the locker room where several freshly cut players were packing away their possessions into garbage bags, and I called my dad. My hand was shaking so much, I had to prop my elbow against the car door to keep the phone steady as I told him I had made the team. I was a pro. "I knew it!" my dad said, his voice rising. "I knew they'd have to keep you! You gave them no choice. You're too damn good."

He went on and on, nearly babbling. We both recognized the grand joke of it all. If I hadn't been concussed, if I hadn't lost my quarterbacking job, if I had never become a punter, I wouldn't be a Sentinel. It's the rare quarterback who goes from a small school like Hudson Valley State to the pros. But we punters perform our tasks in relative isolation, which means the level of competition we faced in college doesn't matter. We can come from any damn place.

My dad and I talked until my phone battery died. I'd never heard him happier. It was the greatest day of my life.

CHAPTER 15

THE AIR CONDITIONING in the rental car dies about halfway to Vickers. Even with the windows open, the ride is a steamy one, but I don't care. The closer I come to the church, the more my heart rises. I am happy to be doing this. Or if not happy, at least excited. It is a long shot, it might not make sense, but at least I am doing something. When I was talking to Kaylee Wise back at the funeral, when I was scanning the bumpers for quarter-moon stickers, when I climbed onto that plane this morning, I felt like I was taking control, instead of waiting for someone else to solve my problem.

If you are trying to categorize people, you can do a lot worse than to sort them into two groups—those who enjoy responsibility and those who avoid it. Some people want to be presidents and CEOs and star players. Others hope that someone else will make good decisions for them, give them a job, and lead their team to victory.

Which one do you want to be? This is the last line of the "first practice" speech that my dad gave every August to his players at Waverly High.

I arrive back at the church almost three hours after I left, with the daylight tempered in late afternoon, and I am encouraged to see plenty of cars lining the road.

About two-thirds of the people are still at the funeral. Most sit in folding chairs in makeshift circles on the grass. Some men are actually tossing a football in a clearing across the road—among them, I notice, Herrold McKoy. I watch Herrold drop back to pass, his belly jiggling under his mustard-colored dress shirt. I see Udall's point about Herrold's windup being too long, but he still throws a beautiful spiral.

I also notice, propped against the far wall of the church, a set of four Port-O-Lets. The ones for which Freddie had "looked everywhere."

Unbelievable.

I scan the crowd, looking for Luke Reckherd, but I don't see his white suit. I am standing among circles of seated mourners, my hands on my hips, when an older woman, walking with a four-pronged cane, stops and asks me, "You looking for someone?" She wears thick glasses and a black polka-dotted dress and peers up from under a wide-brimmed white straw hat with a black ribbon on it.

"Luke Reckherd," I say.

"I'm afraid I don't even know who that is," she murmurs. "But then I guess I don't know who you are either."

"My name is Nick Gallow," I say. "I was a teammate of Samuel's."

"I'm Mrs. Louis Malone," the woman says with a nod.

"Are you close to the Sault family?"

She smiles, revealing what look like store-bought teeth. "I've been living two doors down from the Saults for half a century."

"Wow, that's amazing," I say. "The place I live in, my neighbors don't last fifty days."

She looks confused, as if I am explaining a concept out of science fiction. "Samuel's parents were actually about to leave me. They were going to move up to Philadelphia with their son." She sighs. "Now they're not going anywhere. Maybe you can ask them about that boy you're looking for."

She raises her cane and gestures to a man and woman seated together at the head of a circle of chairs. It is the people Tanner and Udall were talking to earlier. The father, whose name I remembered as Morris, wears a simple black suit. He has a broad nose and sunken eyes, and a wide physique that must have filled the cab of the trucks he drove cross-country. The mother, Eugenia, shares her son's light skin. She is engaging in give-and-take with the people near her, while Morris sits stonily, looking exhausted and dispirited. The mother is clasping hands with her daughter, Selia, and wiping a tear from the young's girl's eyes—which are broad-set and, viewed from this angle, remind me of her brother's. Whereas

Samuel—when he smiled, at least—had a sort of hangdog handsomeness, Selia has the severe beauty of a couture model.

While Samuel's parents are composed, Selia is nakedly distraught, making no effort to mask her anguish.

I walk toward their circle and heads turn as I near, and Morris's eyes lock onto me with a glare. "No more interviews," he barks.

"Easy, Morris, easy," says Eugenia Sault, standing up and letting go of her daughter's hand.

Samuel's mother is nearly as tall as I am. Her black dress hangs loosely on her, as if she'd just lost ten pounds. Her eyes are streaked with red. She places her free hand on my elbow. "Maybe one or two questions. It's been a hard day."

"I'm not a reporter, actually," I say. "My name is Nick Gallow, I'm . . ."

"You're the punter!" she says, hand to her heart, and with a smile that frightens me, so jarringly does it contrast with her bloodshot eyes. "Selia, this is the Sentinels punter." Selia looks up at her mother hollowly. "So what?"

Samuel's mother places her hand on my arm and we move a couple of steps from the circle. I offer her nervous condolences and she politely inquires about the health of Cecil. I want to ask her if she has any idea what might have happened to Samuel, but of course if she had even a hint, she would not be standing here with me.

"Do you know Luke Reckherd?" I ask.

"Luke Reckherd?" she says, puzzled. "Is he with the Sentinels?"

"No, no," I say. "I saw him at the service. Was he a friend of Samuel's?"

"Not one I ever heard of," she says. "And I was with that

boy every day he was on this earth." Her eyes fill with tears, and she adds, "At least until the last few."

Her jaw begins to quiver and she turns away. I place my hand on her shoulder, which is startlingly bony. "Thank you," I say. "And again, I am so sorry." Without a further word she returns to her seat and buries her face in her hands.

I walk away, feeling stricken, and also disgusted. I sit down for a moment to collect myself and think this through.

After a while my eyes are drawn to the football flying across the road, and so I drape my jacket over a folding chair and walk across the road with the intention of speaking to the game's quarterback, Herrold McKoy. But before joining the action, and without making too much of a show of it, I stop behind a car and dig my heel forward and lean back in a hamstring stretch. My leg feels, if not perfect, at least passable. I have certainly played through worse. Tomorrow afternoon, with some luck, I will be back in Philadelphia and I can have a massage from the team trainer to get me ready for minicamp. I soon join the group of guys milling about, waiting for a pass from Herrold.

Herrold, noticing a new arrival, throws me an easy floater. The throw is a little short so I have to trot a few steps to catch it, and then I just let my momentum carry me until I am standing near Herrold.

Herrold claps his hands for me to toss him the ball back, but I turn and zing a low spiral to a lanky young man in a white shirt and black tie. He catches the ball without moving, and then sets it down for a second as he shakes the sting off his hands.

"Not bad," Herrold says to me. He claps his hands and the ball comes back to him.

"Go out," Herrold says to me. "Deep route."

I glide straight and easy for seven steps and then veer to the left. Herrold throws a pass sharper and tighter than what I had seen from him before, as if he were responding to my pass, reestablishing himself as the big arm in this game. But he throws wide and low. The ball smacks the ground, kicking up dust. I collect the ball and trot back toward the group. Herrold claps his hands for the ball again.

"You go out," I say to Herrold. "Give me a pattern."

"What?" he says.

"C'mon, you've got some moves, right?"

Herrold shakes his head but then runs straight upfield, makes a comically exaggerated fake to the left and then breaks right. I throw the ball high, aiming it deeper than where Herrold has been running. Herrold accelerates and makes an impressive one-handed catch. The core of a natural athlete still lives under that Rabelaisian shell. He spikes the ball triumphantly, but then he bends over gasping, belly on his thighs. He looks like he might retch, just from a few seconds of sprinting.

"Goddamn," announces Herrold, righting himself and wiping his brow. "Time for a pie break. Herrold will be back in a minute, y'all."

Herrold slowly walks across the road and heads toward the buffet. I jog up alongside him.

"Mind if I join you?" I say. "I haven't had dessert yet."

"Sweet potato pie, man," says Herrold with a friendly wheeze. "Got to have it. It is outstanding!" Another wheeze. "Banana pudding ain't bad either." Wheeze. "I think I'm going sweet potato this time."

I briefly consider the idea that Herrold might have killed Samuel just to hit this buffet.

"Someone told me that you're Herrold McKoy," I say. "Is that right?"

"Most definitely," he says happily, extending a sweaty hand for a shake. "You want an autograph, I got a Sharpie in my suit jacket."

"That's okay," I say. "But thanks for asking."

We hit the dessert table. I rarely eat sweet potatoes in pie form, but they are loaded with vitamins and a staple of my diet, so I take a small slice. Herrold takes sweet potato pie also, as well as a big dollop of banana pudding and a slice of frosted yellow cake.

"Should we have a seat?" I say.

"Sure."

We walk over to an empty circle of folding chairs and sit down. The metal creaks dubiously beneath Herrold's weight.

"How did you know Samuel?" I ask.

"Just from playin'," he says.

"Were you guys on a team together?"

"Oh, nothing like that," he say. "But down here, it's all one big community. We look out for one another. You a reporter?"

He asks that last question with too much eagerness.

"Not a reporter," I say. "Just a friend."

"That's cool, that's cool," he says, making fast work of his desserts, the plastic fork disappearing into his meaty hand.

We eat in silence. It strikes me that Herrold isn't showing much curiosity about me—how I knew Samuel, how I came to throw a football so well.

"So what are you up to these days?" I say.

"Oh, a little of this, a little of that," he says. "A couple months ago, I was in a charity bass-fishing tournament. Anything Herrold can do to help kids."

A charity bass-fishing tournament. So that accounts for one day.

"Anything else?" I say. "Do you work?"

"Got a cousin who owns a sports bar," he says quickly. "It's called Newsome's. He likes to have me hang out there. It draws in some folks, you know. People who want an autograph, or just want to talk football. So I do that a few nights a week."

So his job is to eat burgers and drink beer and talk about himself. I wondered if his pay extended beyond his bar tab.

"Nice work if you can get it," I say.

"People like to see me," Herrold says. He gives his belly an agreeable pat. "And there sure is a lot of me to see."

"What's up with that, if you don't mind my asking?"

"I eat a lot," Herrold says with a laugh. "If it ain't the bar food, man, it's my mom. She's the best cook in Alabama. I come down to breakfast and there's biscuits and gravy and sausage and eggs, and then after I get my fill of that, it's like, whoa, I've got to go back to bed."

"Were you working at Newsome's last week?" I ask.

He hesitates for a moment before mumbling, "Uh . . . yeah, yeah, sure." It is the first time in our conversation he has paused before answering. And on the money question.

"Where is Newsome's, anyway?" I ask. "In case I'm ever in the neighborhood and want to drop by."

"Down in Mobile," he says.

"Newsome's in Mobile," I say. Perhaps I would visit after the funeral, to verify where he was on the night of the shooting, although that feels like a lot of effort to pursue an awfully long shot.

"Gots to get back in the game," Herrold says, standing up and slurping the last bit of pie off his plate. "You coming?"

"Maybe later," I say. "I'm just going to sit for a moment."

Herrold goes back to the game while I remain seated, but I am not alone for long. A husky and broad-shouldered man with a neatly trimmed beard and mustache approaches me. He looks to be around my age, and he wears a heavy gold wedding band on his left hand. "Hey, you're the Sentinels punter, aren't you," he says with a curious smile. "Nick Gallup?"

"Gallow," I say. "Nick Gallow." I bet Jai is never mistakenly addressed as Jai Carseat. "But yes, I'm the Sentinels punter."

I stand and we shake hands. He squeezes hard enough to communicate a serious workout regimen.

"I'm Marcel LeSeur," he says. "I'm the D-line coach at Western Alabama. Samuel was one of my boys."

"I'm sorry for your loss," I say. "Would you like to have a seat?"

"Yes, thank you." He sits. He too is a larger person than the chair was meant for. He leans forward, forearms resting on his thick thighs. "I saw you were talking to Herrold McKoy."

"Yes. Do you know him?"

"Watched plenty of his film, if that counts."

"Did Samuel know him?" I ask.

LeSeur laughs. "About as well as a truck knows a deer it runs over."

"There were a lot of Samuel's victims here today," I say. "I saw Luke Reckherd around, too."

LeSeur taps my arm. "I saw him, too. What is that all about?" he says, looking mystified. "That white suit and all that nodding."

"I was hoping you could tell me," I say. "Did Samuel know him?"

"Not that he ever told me about," LeSeur says. "Shame about Luke Reckherd. He could have been the best quarterback this conference has ever seen, if his knee hadn't been torn up." LeSeur says this without any acknowledgment that it was his pupil who did the damage.

"You have any idea who could have wanted to take a shot at Samuel?"

"Besides JC?" he says, raising his eyebrows.

"Yes," I say, with enough firmness, I hope, to discourage further intimations about Jai.

"Absolutely no idea," he says. "No one does. That's what I came over to ask about, to be honest with you. You were actually there."

I picture the shooter's car driving away, my eyes on that stupid quarter moon instead of the license plate. *You fucked up, punter.*

"I wish I knew what happened," I say. "I have no idea."

LeSeur nods, and then we sit in silence, avoiding each other's eyes.

"Your coach still around?" he asks.

"Tanner? He's long gone."

His mouth sags. "Dang. I wish I could have talked to him today," he says. "He and I got to know each other a little bit when he was doing background work on Samuel. He told me maybe he'd help me with a job after the draft. But after he picked Samuel I called him a couple times and I never heard back."

"Coach Tanner is a man who loves his schedules," I say. "I doubt his leaving today had anything to do with you."

"Oh, I'm sure he wasn't avoiding *me*," LeSeur says, with an odd emphasis on the last word.

"Who was he avoiding then?"

LeSeur looks around to see if anyone is within earshot. Then he pulls his chair close and says in a low voice, "Before the draft, Coach Tanner came down here to Vickers twice to meet with Samuel, okay? Does two trips sound like standard procedure to you?"

It doesn't. One visit to a hometown, or even none, would be the norm. Teams have plenty of other opportunities to talk to prospects—combines, pro days, or visits to their facilities.

"Tanner's career was riding on this pick, so I can imagine him wanting to double-check everything." I say this as if I believe it, though I can hear myself rationalizing. "You can't underestimate how anal Tanner is," I add.

"Who are you telling? Tanner's first trip down here, he and I watched game film of Samuel for six hours," he say. "Six goddamn hours. Every play, he asked me what Samuel's assignment was, and checked it against what Samuel actually did. And he took notes on each play we watched."

"Yeah. He's a fun guy."

"He takes care of business, to be sure. At least, he did that first time around. But then he comes for a second trip, and all he does is stop by the office for five minutes," LeSeur says. "He asks for some statistical reports that I could have e-mailed him. Then he says, I gotta go. He wouldn't tell me where. He didn't talk to any of the other coaches, or anyone else at Western Alabama. You tell me why he made that second trip."

I sift through possible explanations, but come up wanting. I wonder if Tanner might have been researching something about Samuel's personal life, but that doesn't make sense. Teams have investigators to do that sort of digging.

After I have been silent for a while, LeSeur says, with an insinuating lift of the eyebrows, "Remember. He's a man."

"Tanner has a woman down here?" I ask.

LeSeur nods. "That's what I hear."

"Was she at the funeral?" I ask. That would explain Tanner's hurry to leave, possibly even his grumpy mood at the airport.

"She was here, absolutely." LeSeur leans his head in close and whispers, "No girl is going to miss her brother's funeral."

CHAPTER 16

AFTER MARCEL LESEUR moves on to mingle with the other mourners, I sit on that folding chair for a good long time by myself.

I try not to stare at Selia Sault, who is now talking to some friends. She is the tallest among them by a good six inches, and she looks dour as they chat with her, her bloodshot eyes occasionally drifting off into the distance. I now wonder if all her sadness is the result of her brother's death, or if seeing Tanner come and go wasn't a second stab to the heart.

Selia is beautiful—and I can see how she could be spectacular if she were carrying herself with confidence—but her looks are beside the point. She could be the Sistine Chapel and it would not begin to justify Tanner's choice. He is married, he is fifty-one years old, he is the highly paid leader of our team. Selia is a college sophomore, and the sister of his top draft pick. And this is a man who barks at players if their uniform shirts are untucked. I can't ascribe any relations between them to love or even lust. It is self-destruction, pure and simple. It is as if Tanner looked at Selia and said to himself, hey, here's an opportunity to undermine my career, my family, my authority, and my reputation with one ejaculation.

I stand up and talk to a couple of more folks, and I pick up some nuggets about Selia. She is attending her brother's school, Western Alabama, on a basketball scholarship, and she is majoring in education. Simple questions about what kind of girl she is return comments like "sweet" and "nice." I ask if she had been planning on moving to Philadelphia along with her parents. A college teammate of Samuel's says he heard something about Selia transferring, but he wasn't sure if it was actually happening.

I imagine this young girl on her way up to a big scary city up North, where she would know only one person in town outside her family: Jerry Tanner.

The Saults leave the funeral when the sunlight fades, and so do I. I drive back to Birmingham, where I book a room in the first motel I can find. Then I cross the highway to a convenience store, where I buy a toothbrush and toothpaste, and also a can of coffee, because I need something cylindrical and firm to help stretch my hamstring.

In my room, sitting on the edge of the bed, I look up the phone number for Newsome's in Mobile. I realize when I get the manager on the line how much I am hoping he will say something that incriminates Herrold. Instead he grumbles, "That freeloader was here every day last week."

If Herrold had been unaccounted for that would, at least, have given me a possibility to consider, something to think about besides Tanner and Selia and their couplings. If the two of them did have sex, where would they have gone? I hadn't seen any hotels around Vickers. Did they do it in her room while her parents were out? In the back of his rental car?

The thing is, it wasn't all that hard to imagine Selia being attracted to Tanner. He presents himself as strong and authoritative, and more seasoned knees than hers have buckled when a judgmental figure shines a smile on them. I know that I've glowed all through the night after a simple "Good work" from Tanner, and I can't stand the guy.

What I really don't consider, though, is the idea that Selia might have become infatuated enough with ol' Jerry that she decided she was going to leave Alabama for Philadelphia. If she was moving to be near her love—with or without an invitation, under the guise of being near her family—then the married Tanner had a motive to see Samuel done away with.

I remember how Tanner called me into his office the morning after the shooting. I assumed he was concerned about Jai being the killer. But now I wonder if he had a more personal motive for questioning the standing eyewitness to the crime.

I set the coffee can on the hotel room's tan carpet and remove my suit. Then, in my white T-shirt and boxer shorts, I take a towel from the bathroom and wrap it around the coffee can. Using my hands to propel myself, I roll my leg back and forth over the can, using my body weight to massage the hamstring. Then I lie down, the carpet's rough weave itching my back, and I pull my leg back over my head.

I let my leg drop and stare up at the ceiling, and I count the dead bugs in the light fixture overhead. Nine. How many times, I wonder, has the employee assigned to clean this room looked up at those insect carcasses in the fixture, thought about getting a ladder, and then decided, "Ah, what's the point?"

CHAPTER 17

MY PLANE TICKET from Birmingham to Philadelphia cost $1299, which somehow did not meet the legal definition of robbery. I have to connect through Charlotte, and the second leg of my flight home is delayed because the airline discovers, moments before I am to board, that they have not assigned a crew to the airplane. So I spend three extra hours in the Charlotte airport on top of my scheduled four-hour layover, and lose whatever shot I had of getting the hamstring massage I need from a team trainer. I go to a gate that isn't being used and I stretch as best I can on the floor. For my one meal at the airport I find a Chinese restaurant and order rice and vegetables, which I can eat only after I stand by a garbage receptacle and drain off as much of their heavy sauce as I can.

My taxi delivers me to the Jefferson just before midnight.

The opening day of minicamp is also the first team gathering since Samuel's murder, and judging from the number of news trucks in the parking lot, our practice is the most important thing happening on the planet. When I disembark from my Audi, the lenses all turn toward me.

Tanner, that master of control, has not yet informed his players of the work schedule for the first day of camp; he will only do so following a team meeting at nine. I am in my stall at 8:40, halfway into my uniform, securing my wallet and phone into my lockbox, when Jai strides in. He is the last player to arrive, and he is carrying a large cardboard box in both arms.

"Santa is real, y'all, Santa is real," Jai booms. He yanks open the lid of the box and lifts out two fistfuls of T-shirts, black in one hand and white in the other, with lettering on each that reads THE JC INNOCENCE PROJECT. He is modeling the black T-shirt with white lettering. "I brought enough for everyone, even you guys whose asses are going to be cut in a few days. I got white-on-black and black-on-white. Choose your crime."

Players stream toward Jai, lining up for T-shirts. If much of the outside world is assuming that Jai is guilty, in the Sentinels locker room the reverse is true. Jai is our teammate, so players are on his side, and it is as simple as that.

The mass display of uncritical thought makes me uncomfortable, even if I agree that Jai is innocent. And if we are all to wear matching T-shirts, I would prefer a message that commemorates Samuel.

Woodward Tolley, a couple of lockers down from me, joins the rush. He returns with two T-shirts, one in each color.

"Souvenirs," Woodward explains with an apologetic shrug as he returns to his locker and sees me standing, arms folded, watching the scene with disdain.

As the crowd dissipates Jai notices me. He pulls a black T-shirt from the box and marches toward me.

"Hey, punter, come out tonight," he says, tapping me on the chest with the shirt, which I do not grab. "Me and some of the guys are celebrating the first night of camp."

I keep my arms folded, and Jai pulls the shirt back, holding it at his side.

"I usually celebrate the first night of camp by resting up for the second day of camp," I say.

"Oh, come on now," Jai says. "You can't act all butt-hurt about me not knowing who you are and then when I invite you out, you're all like, I need my beauty rest. Don't be murky."

"Fine. I'm in," I say, giving in to an urgency—dare I say, a neediness—behind Jai's jolly eyes. I really would prefer to get a good night's sleep. But once I declare that I am in, I am committed. I will try to keep my appearance to under an hour.

Jai throws the T-shirt at my chest and I catch it.

"Here's something to wear. It's at seven or eight or something like that," Jai says. "At Stark's. I know you know where that is."

I drop the T-shirt on my lockbox and leave it resting there, unfolded, as I finish dressing.

I report to the team's main meeting room, which is a throwback to my college lecture halls, except that it is freezing. Tanner keeps the room chilled to 54 degrees, so meetings move quickly. When players started wearing hoodies to keep warm, he banned those, too. All around the room I see goose bumps on muscled forearms as guys settle into their chairs.

"We have a lot to accomplish in these three days," Tanner says, standing at a lectern. Just looking at him, so confident in his authority, my stomach acid rises. "But before we get down to business I thought one of the coaches should say a few words about what's been happening the last few days. Here's Coach Huff."

Huff, who has been leaning against a side wall, limps toward the lectern, but not all the way to it. He is only centering himself in front of his audience, as he does not use a microphone. His crisp barks needed no amplification. Tanner often called on Huff when he needed to get the guys' engines going. Tanner and his top coordinators are tacticians first.

They are the CEOs. Huff is the only one of our commanders with a soul of brimstone.

Today, our special teams coach appears somber, but purposeful.

"Four days ago, we lost a teammate," Huff begins. He clasps his hands together and holds them under his chin. I look over at Tanner, who stands at the side of the room, arms folded, one leg crossed in front of the other, as if he were modeling for a JCPenney catalog. "Samuel Sault was shot and killed. He was twenty-one years old. He was standing outside the stadium that he never got to play in.

"And you know what? It's an awful thing, but it happens. People die too young all the time, even football players. Especially football players, it seems. Sean Taylor. Darrent Williams. Thomas Herrion. Korey Stringer. I could go on and on. On opening day there will be nearly seventeen hundred players on a league roster. I can guarantee you at least a dozen of them will die before they're forty. It could be murder, it could be cardiac arrest, it could be who knows what. But it will happen. Maybe to someone in this room. Maybe two of you, maybe more. There are no quotas, there is no plan. The San Diego Chargers went to the Super Bowl in 1994. Six men from that team never lived to see forty. One died in a car crash, another in a plane crash. One was struck by lightning."

Huff unclasps his hands and holds his right fist at chest level as he takes a step forward.

"Now, if you've been watching the television these last couple days, you hear these commentators, they talk about how a death like Samuel's puts everything in perspective, reminds you of what's really important. To which I say, Bullshit. That's only true if you don't know what's important to begin with. I have been playing organized football since before I had hair on my nuts. I know exactly how important this game is, and I can tell you, if I was told that I had one more day to live, I'd spend it like I'm going to spend it today, out on that practice field, competing every second, telling you to get your asses off the ground and run hard and hit harder and do what you love to the best of your abilities."

Huff's volume rises, as does a darkness in his eyes.

"There is only one way to play this game: like you have a hellhound on your trail. And make no mistake: there *is* a hellhound on your trail. He is after you. The hellhound may be me. It may be Coach Tanner, or some other coach who doesn't like the way you do things. It may be the man sitting next to you, who plays your position better than you do. It may be age, it may be injury, it may be your own weakness of purpose. It may be a madman who shoots a rifle and drives off into the night. The hellhound can shift into many forms, and you may not always recognize him. But it's after you.

"And you need to play like it. Because sooner or later, the hellhound will get you. And when it does, you are going to want to know that you did your best when you had the chance." Huff raises his hand and makes a fist. "I want to see you doing your best with every minute you have been granted on that field. While it lasts. Because it doesn't, ever, for anyone. It never, ever lasts."

Huff's speech is received with absolute quiet; most players aren't even looking at him. They stare at their desks, off to the side, anywhere but forward. Some undoubtedly are listening and startled by the morbidity of Huff's theme; most are likely confused because they came into this room expecting to be told to keep their pads low and drive through their legs, not to gather ye rosebuds while ye may.

After Huff hobbles off to the side, Tanner steps to the

podium again. He has listened inexpressively to Huff's speech, and now he moves onto Sentinels business items. The first is to inform us that he has closed our locker room to the press; usually reporters are allowed to come in following the afternoon practice, but at this camp no one will be cornered at their lockers. Tanner also asks us not to speak to reporters if they contact us elsewhere. Only Tanner and our quarterback, Bo John White, will speak to the assembled media—the two of them have had as much media training as your average senator—and then camera crews will be allowed to grab video from the first ten minutes of practice, after which they must leave. "We have enough challenges ahead of us. We can't do anything that makes our work more difficult."

Like having an affair with Selia Sault?

Tanner then releases our schedule for the day. In the morning session, offense and defense will work separately, and in the afternoon, we will work on a punting phase. I am pleased with this, because on any given day it is not guaranteed that we will be scheduled to punt at all.

Practice begins with the players assembled on Field 1. Our strength coach, Kurt Sauer, a young man with a shaved head and the most pronounced trapezius muscles I have even seen, leads all eighty players through fifteen minutes of warm-up, as he has dozens of times before. Even as disgusted as I am with Tanner, it feels good to be out on the grass with the guys, in our brown-and-gray colors, assuming the formations we have in years past, in better times. I am in my usual spot toward the back right, and I hear the grunts and moans and juvenile jokes. Too Big is situated directly in front of Jai, and when Too Big leans forward into a calf stretch, his pants slide down revealingly. "Easy, bro, last time I saw that many pounds of crack I was watching *Cops,*" Jai says, and guys laugh much more than is warranted. Everyone is happy to be home.

The horn sounds and players disperse into their groups. The thirty-eight offensive players work on Field 1. The thirty-eight defensive players are on Field 2. And on Field 3, you have the pure specialists, all four of us—me, Woodward, Pablo, and his camp competition, a thirty-year-old kicker named Rodger Hulce, who has bounced around the league, never lasting with one team for more than a season. Hulce is a little guy, only five foot seven. Pablo isn't much taller. Woodward and I look more like regular position players, but still: if this was grade school, you would assume that Field 3 is where they put the kids who hadn't been picked for the game.

I begin my cycle of warm-up punts. My pace is relaxed and methodical as I take my time between kicks, which leaves me plenty of opportunity to study young Woodward.

It doesn't take me long to see that Woodward is a formidable competitor. Long and with a youthful bounce in his step, his stroke is confident and consistent, smooth and clean. I also notice, when he works on his targeted kicks, that he is a skilled practitioner of the drop punt, where you hold the ball pointed downward instead of flat, and when it lands it bounces straight up. This technique gives coverage guys a better chance to down the ball where it's landed.

I prefer the coffin corner to the drop kick. The coffin corner has long been out of fashion around the league because of the risk involved—if you aim out of bounds and mishit the ball, you can end up with a seven-yard punt. But I trust my own consistency; I have never shanked a punt in competition. And the coffin kick gives me complete control. I am taking the other team's return man out of the play, and also eliminating my dependency on my team's coverage guys, who can be dishearteningly inept; they have accidentally knocked my drop kicks into the end zone more than once.

"How you doing, Nick?" This is Huff. He has sidled up to me on the practice field. He is wearing wraparound shades and a brimmed outback hat with a cord dangling underneath his chin.

"Feeling good," I say. "All things considered."

"I heard you went down to Alabama for Samuel's funeral," he says.

"That I did."

Huff nudges me with a conspiratorial smile. "How was the food?"

"Awesome, now that you mention it," I say. "The fried chicken was amazing."

"I'll bet," Huff says. "I grew up in Clarksdale, Mississippi, so I've been to a few funerals like that myself. Too many, in fact. But thank God for that food. Helps you remember that it's good to be alive."

"Yup," I say.

Huff nods. "Tanner told me you stayed down there an extra day, didn't come back on the Gladstone family jet. What was that about?"

I stiffen at the mention of Tanner's name, and I wonder if Huff is being inquisitive on his own behalf, or that of his boss. "When we left, I hadn't had a chance to talk to Samuel's family," I say. "I wanted to go back."

Huff seems to be studying me—though it is hard to tell exactly what he is thinking behind those wraparound shades. Then he says, "You're good people," and punches me in the shoulder. "Stay strong, Nick. I'm looking to see what you got today."

"You've been watching me for half a decade, Coach," I say. "You already know what I've got."

Huff grins. "It's like my daughter says to me, Nick. You're only as funky as your last cut."

"Don't I know it." Huff punches me in the shoulder again and limps away.

The punting unit's segment is scheduled for fifteen minutes. Woodward and I should kick maybe five or six times each, with each of those plays being filmed for review by the coaches. Not that the coaches will focus on just Woodward and me. The choice of punter is, from their perspective, one of the simpler questions to resolve. The trickier problem is evaluating the guys who are going to fill out the rest of the special teams units. These players are usually the most marginal guys on the roster and the turnover is heavy. Some players make a career of special teams coverage, but not many. It's like sharing a $99-a-night hotel room in Panama Beach with six of your buddies: it's fine when you are just out of college, but the older you get, the less right it feels.

In that analogy I am the hotel manager, watching these young men come and go, and hoping they don't make too much trouble for me.

"Gallow," Huff shouts. "Let's go. You're up."

I trot onto the field. We are beginning with punts from the offense's twenty-five-yard line.

It is a pleasant and comfortable day with little wind. I set myself, feeling calm, receive a perfectly centered snap from John Backlund, my long snapper, and hit the ball well, although a little chunky, just a smidge high on my foot. It turns out to be a forty-six-yarder, a decent enough distance, and with good elevation and hang. The returner can only bring the ball forward a few yards before he is tapped down by the coverage unit.

We run the play again from the same spot on the field, and my swing is more in tune.

"Yeah, Nick!" Woodward shouts, clapping, as my kick sailed upward. "Nailed it!" Like I needed to hear it from him. And what, my first attempt isn't worth cheering? The ball flies fifty-seven yards. My only regret is that I didn't cut entirely loose and send the ball even further.

On my third kick, Backlund snaps the ball high—I have to jump for it to keep it from going over my head. I come down and quickly collect myself, getting the kick off before the rush reaches me, but because I am hurried I do not get a strong lift from my plant foot. The kick goes forty-five yards, but it travels low and fast and reaches the returner before the coverage can get downfield. The punt is brought back seventeen yards before the returner is tapped.

As soon as the whistle blows, Backlund turns and finds me. Backlund, a bearded and burly Minnesotan who also plays defensive tackle, is an eleven-year veteran and has played in Philadelphia for three years. He has a wife and six children at home. He is truly a man doing a job, which is why I am surprised by any lapse in professional execution.

"Snap got away from me, Nick," he says.

"I noticed, John." I rap my knuckles against his helmet. Every one of these kicks matters, and I need him on his game. "At least I showed them the old man still has his reflexes."

And I am an old man, at twenty-eight. That's how I feel, anyway, competing against a twenty-two-year-old.

Huff blows his whistle and waves me off the field. It is

Woodward's turn. As I cross paths with him while running, I reach out and we slap hands in encouragement.

Woodward kicks high and hard, showing as much power and accuracy as he had on the practice field. His first kick goes fifty-two yards, and his second goes forty-eight and really hangs up there. For each, only a minimal return is possible. And Woodward really creams the last kick. He hits a sixty-three-yarder that has the returner backpedaling and turning to make an over-the-shoulder catch.

"Hoo-wee!" comes the exclamation from one of the players. "'Scuse me while I kiss the sky!"

The shouter is Jai, of course. Who else? He is on the sidelines with his helmet off, one of the group of established veterans who can slip into full spectator mode during special teams work.

Huff blows his whistle and moves the line of scrimmage up to the opponent's forty-eight-yard line. We are moving on to short kicks, where we will try to drop the ball close to the goal line.

"Gallow," Huff calls. "Back to you."

I am eager to get to this segment of the drills, because this is the part of the game where I excel. Kicking for distance matters, but the ability to pin an opponent deep is the punter's most important skill. It's the closest we come to a big play.

With the first kick, I go for the coffin corner, and I hit a pretty good one, placing the ball out at the nine-yard line.

"Okay, number eleven, we're all very impressed," Huff shouts. "Let the coverage guys get in some work." At least for our practices, this is the problem with the coffin corner; it leaves the coverage guys with nothing to do, and thus nothing for the coaches to evaluate.

For my second kick, I employ the pooch—I just have the feeling from warm-ups that my pooch will work better than my drop today, and so I go with it. I hit my kick a shade early, which means the ball's arc of flight is more vertical than I wanted it to be. The ball is fair-caught at the sixteen-yard line. Which is an acceptable result, but I can do better.

And so can Woodward.

Huff blows his whistle and gives me the wave. I had been hoping for one more punt, but I am done.

No hand slap from Woodward this time as he and I pass each other. This is his chance, and he knows it. The Super Bowl is pressure, but this may be worse. At least in the Super Bowl, you know you've made it that far down the road, but moments like this are the difference between making the team and watching your career die.

I watch from the sidelines, arms folded. If Woodward is feeling the stress of the situation, he doesn't show it. He looks relaxed and even happy as he awaits the snap.

Woodward beckons and Backlund delivers the ball directly to his waiting hands. Woodward catches the ball and turns it point-down and kicks, and it goes up and up and up. And as the ball begins its descent, I can see that he nailed it. His kick might as well have been to my stomach.

The returner lets the ball drop. It hits at the three-yard line and bounces almost straight up. It actually moves a shade backward on the hop. A gunner fields the ball easily at the four, and players who have run downfield bump shoulders in celebration. Meanwhile Woodward, who had drifted halfway downfield, claps with satisfaction.

Shit.

Everyone runs back and Woodward lines up for his second kick. He can just play it safe now; if he drops the ball anywhere inside the fifteen, he will win the day. And in our two-man race, the chances are few.

Woodward fields another clean snap from Backlund—dammit, why wasn't that bearded fuck as accurate with me, is there a conspiracy between these two Midwestern boys?—and Woodward gives the ball another one of his long, clean strokes.

From the moment the ball comes off his foot, I see that Woodward has overhit it. Severely. His punt flies so far beyond the field of play that a front-office guy in a straw hat and a golf shirt, idly spectating several yards behind the end zone, attempts to catch the ball with one hand while holding onto his coffee. He drops both the ball and his coffee cup, his bungling underlining the extent to which Woodward's kick is a complete botch.

I stand stoically on the sideline, just as I had for Woodward's previous kick. But I would be lying if I did not admit to a Schadenfreude-fueled rush of adrenaline. As good as Woodward's first kick has been, the second is a disaster, a complete mental lapse. Woodward looks crushed, as if he has pulled out of the driveway without looking and accidentally run over the family dog.

Woodward has two things to prove in this camp. One is his physical ability. The other is that he has the mental firmness to withstand the pressure of the job. Woodward clearly has the leg—he might even have an edge on me in that regard—but this gaffe, this obvious miscommunication between his brain and his body, will plant doubts. Sweet, sweet doubts.

The air horn sounds. Practice is continuing, but the special teams phase is done. What a perfect note to end on.

CHAPTER 18

AFTER PRACTICE ENDS, I see Eleanor Cordero standing by the door that leads from the fields to the locker room. She is wearing a navy jacket and a skirt that shows a little tanned leg, and she is holding a pink message slip in her hand.

"How'd we do out there today?"

"I'll take it," I say. "What's going on?"

"Interview request," she says, with an apologetic smile.

"Can't you just refer them to my statement?" Which I still have not read.

"I thought you might want to hear about this one," Cordero says. "This reporter is asking about a very specific . . . allegation."

She weights that last word with particular grimness.

"It's about Cecil Wilson," she says. "The reporter claims he has gambling debts. With a bookie from Cleveland."

Gambling debts? I had never heard Cecil discuss betting at all, except for the occasional stray reference to a point spread for an upcoming game. But that's about as common as discussing the weather.

"Who is this reporter?"

"His name is Scott Nellie, he writes for CBS Sports," she says. "He is young, but he's broken some news, mostly about contract signings and player moves."

Which means that Scott Nellie has developed relationships with agents. Saavy agents can manipulate reporters with the promise of exclusives the same way a veteran quarterback can move around a safety with his eyes.

"Nick, is there anything the team needs to know about?" Cordero asks.

"I hope not," I say.

"If there is, please tell me," she says. "It's my job to help in these situations. No matter what the story turns out to be, it's best if we tell it first."

I take the message slip from her hand. "I don't have any story to tell just yet," I say. "But thank you, Eleanor."

I shower quickly and drive to the hospital. I find Vicki and her daughters huddled around Cecil, watching *Toy Story 2* on an iPad that Violet is holding at a lazy tilt. The looks on their faces suggest they have seen this one many times before. Cecil is sitting up in bed, drumming his fingers lazily on his belly, and his eyes lift eagerly from the screen when he sees me come in.

"You're looking better," I say.

"I feel better," Cecil says. "No signs of infection, they've even been dialing down my painkillers."

"They say we should be leaving tomorrow morning," Vicki says.

"Congratulations," I say to Cecil. "You made it through." I want to place my hand on his, but I see the many bruises from where IVs had been inserted and I refrain.

"Do you mind if I talk to Cecil alone for a moment?" I ask Vicki.

"Sure," she says. "Violet, pause the movie. We'll take a little walk. We could all use some exercise."

Violet pokes at the iPad screen and leads the reluctant parade out the door.

When they are gone, I ask Cecil, "Do you have your phone in here?"

"Vick's been keeping it from me," says Cecil with an affectionate smile. "Have you been trying to reach me?"

"I haven't," I say. "But someone else may have been. I had an interview request from a reporter. His name is Scott Nellie."

"Nellie?" Cecil says, confused. "That kid?"

"You know him?"

"I've never met him, but I've talked to him," Cecil says. "He's polite but persistent. After I signed Samuel he called twice a week, every week, asking how negotiations were going. What does he want with you?"

"I'm told that he's chasing down a rumor," I say. "About gambling debts."

"Gambling debts?" says Cecil. His eyes drain of their vigor. He reverts to looking like he has just been shot.

"Yes, gambling debts," I say. "Yours."

Cecil tucks his chin into his chest and closes his eyes. It is true. Good lord.

"Were you betting on football?" I ask with false equanimity.

He opens his eyes and looks up, directly at me. "Yes."

Unbelievable. What an idiot. Cecil will lose his agent's license if the league ever finds out. In sports, it's the deadliest sin. This is because all major leagues realized around, oh, say, 1919 that their businesses wouldn't survive if the average fan believed that gamblers were influencing results.

I began reviewing past conversations with Cecil and wondering if he had been subtly pumping me for information. I particularly thought of the calls we would have the mornings before my games—the ones I used to have with my dad until he died, and then Cecil stepped in. We would invariably discuss how practices had been that week, which players were injured, what the game plan was. I had found his weekly check-ins reassuring and parental, but now I wonder if the real point of those calls was to make himself a more informed bettor.

And if I am wondering this, so will league officials. So will everyone, if this news gets out.

I had admired Cecil, not just because of the work he did for me, but because of the way he committed himself to a dream of becoming an agent and made it come true. That admiration is dying in this hospital room.

"I only bet college," Cecil says, reacting to the disgust on my face. "Never the Sentinels, never the pros at all. It is just . . ."

"It is just what?" I snap. If he only bet college games, it wouldn't do him much good, because any kind of indebtedness to bookies is a problem. But that could offer me a thin layer of distance. If that is really true; if I can believe anything Cecil says.

"I watch so many games," Cecil says. "I figured I could pick teams the same way I can pick players. And I needed the money. The way my deals worked with you guys, it isn't easy on me."

When Cecil was getting started, he attracted clients like myself and DaFrank by doing our first contracts for free. He said he would wait until our second deals to take the standard three percent, and in the meantime he would only take a percentage from whatever side work he could get for us making appearances at skills camps and sporting goods stores and the like. But the arrangement was his idea, not ours. And he had been taking his three percent from my Sentinels paychecks since my second season.

"You realize everything you've risked, right?" I say.

"I know. But think about it, Nick," says Cecil, his voice firmer, and meeting my eyes for the first time since I raised the subject. "Taking risks got me where I am. If I didn't take chances, I would still be that hardware store manager wishing he could do more with his life. I wouldn't be here—and you probably wouldn't be here either."

I remember how Cecil hustled on my behalf when I was a no-profile free agent. "You make it sound as though I owe my life to you chasing after a bad bet, trying to make it good."

Cecil nods. "Don't you?" I momentarily want to rip open his wounds.

"How deep in are you?" I ask.

"That's the other thing—I'm not in deep at all," Cecil says. "I'm completely out. I paid what I owed the day before the shooting, right after I got the check for Samuel's signing bonus."

"Really?" I say.

"Yes, really," Cecil says. He places his IV-scarred hand on his heart. The gesture irks me with its hamminess.

"Is this why you had Samuel sign so quickly?"

"No, no," Cecil says. "I could have held Samuel out until mid-August, it wouldn't have mattered. Once I had Samuel locked in as a client, these guys knew they'd be getting paid eventually. They're businessmen, they didn't mind letting the vig pile up. The money was coming sooner or later."

"But what if Samuel never signed his contract?" I say. "DaFrank read an e-mail at the funeral. . . ."

"I know, I heard all about his speech. God bless DaFrank, but that is baloney. Samuel was just having a moment of cold feet because of Kaylee. Remember, Samuel came out after his junior season. He chose to go pro. He wanted this."

"He made that choice back in January, though," I say. "Back then he wouldn't have known Kaylee was pregnant."

"That's true," Cecil says. "But they were going to work something out. Everything works out when you have sixty-four million headed your way. And he was going to have his whole family up here with him."

"His whole family?" I ask. "Was his sister coming?"

Cecil looks confused as to why I would care. "I don't know," he says. "I heard she was looking into transferring to Temple, but I don't know if that was actually happening."

So she might have been in the city.

"Christ." Cecil grimaces. "This is going to ruin me."

"No shit," I say.

But I wonder if the ruination of Cecil is the very reason this rumor was fed to a reporter.

"Hello, this is Scott Nellie."

"Nick Gallow," I say. I am calling from my car in the hospital parking lot, which is beginning to feel like my unofficial office. Nellie sounds young, but his tone is confident and polished.

"Ah, thanks for getting back to me," he says. "And I just want to express my sympathies. . . ."

"Thank you," I say. "I understand you're calling about my agent, Cecil Wilson. Is that correct?"

"Yes, it is, unfortunately," he says. "I've heard some things, and I haven't been able to reach him for comment, but I at least wanted to . . ."

"What have you heard?"

"Um, well . . . it's gambling," he says cautiously. "I've heard he owed some serious money to some shady folks."

"Listen, Mr. Nellie," I say. "I'm not going to talk to you on the record, I'm not going to talk to you on background, or whatever terms you guys are using these days for when you print all the information but don't put anyone's name on it. I'm just talking to you one-hundred-percent off the record. Or I can hang up."

"I guess," Nellie says without enthusiasm. "But if you're not on the record . . ."

"The point is this, Mr. Nellie," I say. "You're getting the story wrong. At the time of the shooting, Cecil had no gambling debts whatsoever. None. I don't know exactly what he might have done in the past, but it has nothing to do with what happened to Samuel. And I'd hate to see you get the story wrong because you're being manipulated by agents who just want to trash the reputation of one of their competitors."

"I'm not being manipulated by anyone," Nellie says hotly. "And I don't want to get anything wrong, either. But if you feel so strongly about this, you should go on the record."

"The tip is bad. I know it."

"My sources are good," Nellie says. "Their information has always been solid."

"What kinds of scoops have these sources given you—that their clients want more money?"

Nellie pauses before saying, with intentional cool, "This shooting is white hot. No one wants to read about anything else. If I can get in on it, I'm going to. I still have some reporting to do, but when I'm ready, I'm going with what I have."

"Please check with me before you print anything," I say.

"Whatever anyone says on the record, I want a chance to rebut. And if no one says anything on the record, you shouldn't run your story."

"I appreciate the professional advice," he says with a tincture of sarcasm. "And as a professional, I wouldn't be doing my job if I didn't ask you a couple questions about yourself. Because I've noticed you haven't denied that your agent bet on games. So I need to know: Did you ever supply Cecil Wilson with inside information about the Sentinels? Or anything that he might have used when he was placing bets?"

"Absolutely not," I say. "That you can print. Good-bye."

From the hospital I drive to Boyd's in Center City. I need to replenish my wardrobe before I return to Stark's tonight. I find myself looking forward to dinner with Jai and the guys, to stupid chatter and the clinking of glasses.

I enter the venerable Boyd's department store with the modest ambition of buying shoes, a pair of pants, and a shirt. But once inside, everything looks like something I want. In a half hour I walk out with seven new shirts, five pairs of pants, six pairs of socks, and new black dress shoes. This will fill the closet a little.

I am back at Stark's, and looking better than ever, in dark blue Irish linen pants and a pale gray collared shirt. The restaurant is buzzing, with tables full and young patrons, mostly men, clustered three-deep around the bar. The Samuel Sault saga has apparently been good for business.

In the entryway, I scan the Stark's wall of fame, and I notice an eight-by-ten of Wee Willie Reckherd, father of Luke

Reckherd, from when he played for Baltimore. The photo shows off his fabled ambidexterity: both hands are holding footballs and are cocked back to throw. This strikes me as sad, because Willie Reckherd never played quarterback in the pros; at the time he signed this picture, he wasn't throwing with either hand. The old quarterback's signature skill had been reduced to a publicity photo gimmick.

I see Jai and friends at the same table as the other night: upper level, right corner. I also look around for Melody, who I have not spoken to since we shared that bottle of champagne five days ago, and I see her. She is waiting on three men in suits who seem to be living by the motto of: *older, balder, heavier.* One man, whose remaining hair is white, tells a joke and Melody laughs heartily and places her hand on his shoulder. I tuck away whatever thought I had of saying hello to her and walk to our table.

Jai's dining party includes Cheat Sheet, Too Big to Fail, the rookie Qadra, and a couple of other defensive players. The guys seem to have been here awhile. The table is covered with plates of meat and half-consumed beers. Given that we are in the middle of minicamp, I find this scale of consumption astonishing, especially the drinking. I would never load myself down with a depressant while I was competing for my job. Jai has, over the years, shown no such need for moderation. Which only proves that just as some of us are faster and some of us leap higher, some metabolize alcohol better than others. The problem is, for every man like Jai, who processes booze as if it is Gatorade, there are a dozen players who torpedo their careers trying to keep pace.

Jai is wearing a silver sports jacket and black T-shirt. He notices I am approaching, claps his hands and then counts off with his fingers, one-two-three.

"Gallow!" they all shout in unison. Sometimes you just want to go where everyone knows your name.

"Nick Gallow," Jai says as I sit down. He and everyone else seem to be feeling their drinks already. "N-I-C-K motherfuckin' G-A-L-L-O-W. Here at last."

I greet Jai with a fist bump.

"Wow," I say. "You not only know my name now, you can spell it."

"Oh, come on, bitch," Jai says with a giddy smile, elbowing me playfully as I pull in a seat next to him. "You got to stop crying about that. Don't act like me not knowing your name isn't your fault to begin with."

I raise my eyebrows at this.

"What did you ever do to make me notice you?" Jai says. "You're good and all, but come on, man. Here's my advice to you, Nick Gallow. You want people to know your name, you have to play with your cock."

I am glad I did not yet have a drink of my own, because I might well have spit it out.

"I was telling some of these guys here before, when you're out there on the field, your energy, it's got to come from your cock," Jai says, instantly slipping from conversation into lecture mode, with head tilted, hand raised, and brow knit, as if he is a physics professor explaining an arcane but critical aspect of string theory. "You see some guys, they play with their heart, they're all heart. Then there's other guys, they play with their head. That's you, Nick Gallow. I can tell. You play with your head. All businesslike, never fucking up too bad. But me, when I'm out on the field, I'm playing with my cock. All day long."

Qadra, who has been chewing on a rib, laughs convulsively, half-chewed meat visible in his open mouth. Jai turns toward the laughter with a face of serious disappointment.

"Shit, man, you think this is a joke. I'm giving you the key here," say Jai. "This is major. This is my cause, my message to young men everywhere. Women, too. Hey, Cheat. Do you think we could do a T-shirt that says, 'PLAY WITH YOUR COCK'?"

"I can't think of a single reason why we wouldn't," says the pastor, holding out a fist, which Jai bumps. Cheat Sheet is wearing yellow-rimmed glasses that match his sports jacket. "I'll make a note to myself right now." He pulls a pen from his jacket pocket and jots the inspirational phrase on his palm.

I hope that he remembers why he wrote the note when he wakes up tomorrow.

"The point is," Jai says, "there's a game going on, Nick Gallow, and you're not in it. I'm not talking about the game on the field. I'm talking about the whole bullshit all around us. The fans, the media, everything. It's all a game, and there's a lot of ways to win. You don't even have a nickname, do you? How can you be in the game if you don't have a nickname? Cheat Sheet, what should we call this motherfucker?"

"Hmm," Cheat Sheet says. "How about 'Ass Kicker'?"

I shake my head. "That would make me sound like a kicker who's an ass."

"I got one," says Qadra, his voice slurring. I would peg the rookie as the most inebriated guy at the table. "Legs Diamond. You know, like the musical." He giggles as his suggestion is met with confused silence.

"How about something with the word 'boot' in it?" Jai says.

"'Booty Call'?" Too Big chimes in from across the table. "That way, whenever we needed to punt, we could say, 'Time for Booty Call!'"

"That's it, man!" Cheat Sheet says, clapping his hands and then pointing at me. "You're Booty Call!"

"How about Hangman," I say, before a consensus forms among this star chamber that I must, absolutely, for all eternity, be known as Booty Call. I explain about how punts have hang time, and hangmen work in gallows. And my last name is Gallow, as Jai has recently learned.

"That's no fun, man," cries Cheat Sheet, holding his empty glass. "Booty Call!"

"I like Hangman," I say.

Jai rubs his chin. "You really think you're badass enough to pull off Hangman?"

"You think I'm closer to pulling off Booty Call?" I ask drily.

"It should be Booty Call," Jai says. "But we'll try Hangman, see how it handles." He holds out his fist, and I bump it.

Jai has a porterhouse steak in front of him, which has been cut into chunks for family-style dining. The meat is already halfway gone. Jai sets the plate in front of me. The steak, cooked rare, is seeping blood.

"Eat up, Hangman," Jai says.

"I don't eat red meat," I say. "I'll order some fish."

"You want to be a hangman and you don't eat meat?" Jai says, laughing.

"I read this health tip a few years ago," I say. "The fewer legs an animal has, the better it is for you."

Jai motioned for Qadra to swing a plate of smoked bratwurst our way.

"Here you go, Hangman," Jai says. "Sausage don't have no legs." He lets the line hang there a good couple of seconds before he follows it up with a wink. Thank goodness.

And here is Melody joining the party, in her snug pink top and black skirt, greeting me with a salacious smile and playfully bumping my shoulder with her hip. I had liked her in part because she seemed so uncomplicated, as easy to read as the name on a candy wrapper. Now I look at her and wonder what she really used to be in her Winking Oyster days— prostitute, drug dealer, pimp?

"Well, well," she says. "Look who's back. Camp over?"

"Two more days," I say.

"Let me guess," she says. "You'd like a tonic water. Lemon, right?"

"Lime this time," I say.

"I like that you're so unpredictable," she says. "And can I assume all these steaks and sausages on the table are not part of your diet?"

I glance quickly at the menu. "I'll have a Caesar salad with lobster claws. Dressing on the side. Light dressing, if you have it."

"Natch," she says. And she is off.

"Now hold on a second, Hangman, I got a question for you," Jai says. "You been talking about this diet rule, the fewer legs the better. Don't lobsters have more legs than . . ."

"Oh, shit," says Cheat Sheet.

The pastor is looking toward the restaurant entrance, where Rizotti has just walked in, wearing a particularly ugly and ill-fitting brown suit. He is flanked by another man in a suit, and six uniformed officers.

The unit marches directly to our table.

"Hello, Gallow," Rizotti says as they assemble before us. "Surprised to see you and JC here out together. You told me that you and this piece of shit here weren't exactly pals."

His phrasing implies that I am the one who has called Jai a piece of shit. I wonder if he has learned that maneuver in a finishing school for pricks.

"The past few days," I say, "have brought my teammates and I together."

"You're either one of the most forgiving souls I've come across in ages," Rizotti say, "or one of the dumbest."

The detective turns to Jai. "You are under arrest for the murder of Samuel Sault," he says. He then reads the Miranda warning, keeping on with his recitation even as Jai shoots up from his chair.

Two officers come behind to place Jai in handcuffs. Jai complies, even as his eyes burn. "I'm being framed," he shouts, neck muscles straining, as he is marched out of the restaurant. "These bitches are framing me."

The officers also cuff Cheat Sheet, who goes more peaceably, as befitting a man of God.

I stand up from the table and Rizotti steps close enough to me that I can smell the smoke on his breath. "Is this really your first time out to dinner with Carson?" he asks.

"Yes," I say.

"I bet he invited you, right?" he asks smugly.

"He did," I say uneasily. I am discomforted that any assumption of Rizotti's might prove correct.

"Not that you'll ever thank me for it, punter," Rizotti says, with a sickening grin. "But I bet I just saved your life."

CHAPTER 19

IT IS SUNRISE on the second day of minicamp. I would normally be up by now, preparing to win the day. Instead, I pick my phone off my nightstand, sink back under my comforter, and set about reading the bad news.

The police searched Jai's car in the Stark's parking lot and found a rifle in the back. The serial number had been filed off, but preliminary ballistics tests showed that it was the same rifle that was fired at Samuel and Cecil. The police have it now: the damning physical object on which all their suspicions can be hung.

When Rizotti said that he had "saved my life," he was implying that Jai had brought the rifle to Stark's because he intended to use it on me—which made no sense. I have been trying to protect Jai rather than incriminate him. Still, I think back to the workout at his house, and how Jai had the guys throw me into the pool with that weight vest on, and wonder if it was more than just pure dopiness. I imagine a headline: "Punter Dies in Freak Hazing Accident." Subhead: "Carson: 'I Never Even Touched Him!'"

But I remain convinced that Jai is being railroaded—if not by the police, then by someone else. That rifle had to have been planted, because if it is the murder weapon, then Jai would have to be an insane idiot to drive around with the central piece of evidence against him shoved in the trunk of his car.

The problem for Jai is that "insane idiot" is pretty much the jury pool's perception of him.

Cheat Sheet had been charged, too. According to an anonymous police source, the hope is that he or Jai will turn on the other in exchange for a plea deal. "Sooner or later, one of these two pieces of s— is going to wise up," the source said.

The stories about Jai's arrest, I could not help but notice, do not mention my name at all.

I suppose that Jai's arrest is going to keep Cecil's name out of the news as well. A story speculating that he was the intended shooting target is now effectively obsolete.

Especially since, judging from the comments I am seeing online, any sense that Jai is innocent until proven guilty has disappeared from the conversation, and people are spewing forth with gleeful hatred. They are enjoying this too damn much.

It is nearly seven o'clock. I would usually be making oatmeal right now, but I just stare up at the whiteness of the Jefferson ceiling. The more I think about it, the more I realize that someone at Stark's has to be involved in this somehow. The shooting took place after we left the restaurant. The gun must have been planted while Jai and I were dining there. That feels like more than a coincidence.

I would bet Melody knows something, too. She is an operator. She's been in Philadelphia a year, and already she walks into shops and is handed things for free as if she's the Godfather. I told her we would get together after camp, but now I wonder if I should wait that long.

But for now, off to work, where Jai's arrest has surprisingly little effect on the Sentinels. Or at least, that's what Jerry Tanner, our masterful commander, wants the world to believe. At six o'clock he had sent out a team-wide text:

Reminder: Camp today at 9 a.m. sharp! No comments to media about non-football matters. No distractions!

The clown didn't even deign to mention Jai's name in his message.

Many of the guys show up at the facility wearing their JC INNOCENCE PROJECT T-shirts, a scene that is duly recorded by the television cameras. But players ignore the questions shouted across the parking lot fence, and once they're inside the facility, those shirts are put away, as is the topic of the arrest. A group of offensive linemen talk with loud and sarcastic enthusiasm about the weather, as if there were nothing more important going on. *Sunshine, no wind, what a perfect day for a practice! Great opportunity to get better!* The guys put on their pads—pissed, but ready to work as instructed.

Usually if Tanner breezes through the locker room at this time of day, he says little more than *Let's work hard today!* or some other vacuous exhortation. Today, though, he steps to the center and calls for attention. He has told us not to talk about Jai, but from the somberness of his eyes he looks ready to break his own command.

"I know there's a lot of reasons to be distracted today," he says, posture crisp but his voice a little hoarse, and his eyes not meeting anyone's in particular. "But we need to keep going about our business. All of us have worked too hard to get here. If we fall behind this week, we will pay for it when the season begins. And then we'll be in an even worse place than we are now. We'll be failures, and no one will care about our excuses. You know why so many people fail? It's because it's so easy to do. It's so damn easy." He says that last line a notch quieter on the dial. "There's only one way for us to get through this, and that's together."

Unless you get cut. Then you're on your own, and good luck with that.

To cap off his speech, Tanner announces the schedule for the day, and it includes no punting whatsoever. In the A.M. session the kickoff units are practicing, and in the afternoon the only special teams phase getting work is the field goal unit—and Tanner prefers to use his quarterbacks as holders, so I will have nothing to do with that.

I do not even need to be here today.

I am able to make myself useful, at least, in the morning drills. While Woodward heads out to Field 3 to kick more practice balls, I offer myself up as an extra arm, to throw to tight ends or running backs or even linebackers when the quarterbacks are off doing their own drills. I have served in this function before, and I know the coaches appreciate it. Also, I don't mind showing that I still have quarterback skills, on the off chance that one of these days they might notice that, hey, the punter throws a pretty good ball, doesn't he?

Beyond that, working with the position players this morning has another upside. If Woodward is punting by himself while I am working with the rest of the team, that will only accentuate his feeling that he is an outsider and that maybe he doesn't belong here.

After the morning session, Woodward and I are at our locker room stalls, just a few feet apart. He is sitting on a stool, head down, mouth tight, forearms resting on his legs. He wanted to kick today even more than I did, to erase the memory of that mental gaffe on his last punt. He could feel his three days slipping away.

"C'mon, Woodman," I say, throwing a scrap of athletic tape at his sullen mug. "Let me buy you some lunch."

"Sure," he says. "Thanks." He comes along quietly. We eat in the cafeteria, which looks a lot like a standard college dining hall, except that all the diners are large males in shorts and T-shirts, and most are millionaires.

I load my plate with grilled chicken and steamed broccoli. Woodward selects a few slices of roast beef and a baked potato. Roast beef and potatoes happened to be my mother's standard Sunday night dinner, before I took my father's dietary restrictions a step further and cut out red meat.

We find a quiet spot at the end of a long table. There Woodward lets it all pour out.

"I don't know what happened yesterday," he begins. "My focus was good all morning. Every practice kick, I was hitting all my marks. And then that last kick, I just spaced out for half a second. Spaced out? How does that happen, that you prepare for months and months, and then the moment comes and your brain takes a shit?"

His eyes show red in the corners. He has lost sleep over this. In his anguish he seems more genuine.

"The human mind," I say. "It's a tricky thing."

"Mine isn't," he says. "At least, it didn't used to be."

"Sometimes it's funny," I say. "People do the absolute thing they should not do. Look at all the people who still smoke cigarettes, for instance." Other examples: an agent who bets on football, or a coach who sleeps with the nineteen-year-old sister of one of his players. Or, for that matter, a father who has a couple of drinks and speeds his car down a winding road. Or a drive-by shooter who kills a twenty-one-year-old and becomes a murderer, when there had to have been a better way. "You ever figure out why, you should let them know."

"I'll tell them about it when we're all down at the unemployment office together," Woodward says with a forced laugh.

"I don't know how it works in Kansas, Woodward," I say jokingly. "But around here, if you want to collect unemployment, you have to have a job first." Woodward's eyes flash hurt. "Don't sweat it," I add quickly. "I've been to enough camps to tell you this: you've got the goods, and you're doing just fine."

Woodward looks unconvinced as he gazes out the cafeteria window toward the practice fields. "Tomorrow," he says, "I'm going to do better than fine."

After lunch, it is back out onto the field. I watch the offense and defense go at each other in eleven-on-eleven drills. The guys are practicing goal-line situations, the offensive and defensive players crash into each other in close-quarters combat. The hits are thunderous.

After fifteen minutes of this, a horn sounds, and then the offense and defense switch positions. Now the offense has the ball on its own one-yard line, needing to advance the ball out to avoid a safety and, at the very least, get some room for the punter.

But this is a drill, so whether the offense moves the ball off the goal or not, I watch. I suppose if I really wanted to, I could practice waiting to come into the game. Not that I need such practice. In my years as a punter, I have become an expert on waiting—which is, in its way, the most challenging part of my work.

I have a metaphor that I often employ to calm myself on the sidelines. I tell myself that my mind is the sky, and my thoughts merely clouds drifting by, here one minute, gone the next, just passing things, always ready to blow by.

It's all a little wispy and delicate, I know, but I need something to help me detach from the situation, because I am constantly readying myself to do something that I do not get to do. On first down, I'm feeling the anticipation of running out there to punt. Then second down comes and the threat level increases. On third down I can feel the excitement in my legs as I get set to take the field the moment the next play ends.

So I get all psyched to do that. I visualize getting set, receiving the snap and having a successful step-step-step-kick. And then, more often than not, nothing happens. The offense makes a first down. Or commits a turnover. Or the coach just decides to go for it on fourth, as has been happening more and more in recent years. (All because some economics professor wrote a paper on the efficacy of teams going for it on fourth down, and one coach read it and talked about it in an interview, and now everyone does it. Thus the conspiracy to keep me off the field grows ever wider.)

The bottom line is, you mentally prepare to punt dozens of times during a game, but you actually get to kick far less than that. Imagine being a sprinter where most of the time when you get in the blocks, the words you hear are: "On your mark . . . get set . . . stop!"

It's maddening, honestly. After a certain point in the game I no longer give a goddamn about whether we're winning or what's best for the team. I want our offense to stall out because I am just dying to get on the field. Dying to do something other than stand on the sidelines and watch the clouds go by.

With about fifteen minutes to go in the afternoon session, Freddie ambles out onto the field. He is wearing a brimmed hat—as are most of the coaches—but the rest of his outfit is more befitting a man of leisure. He wears a mauve Oxford shirt, untucked, baggy white cargo pants, and his Oakley shades.

He shuffles along and stands next to me.

"You got that ten million you owe me?"

"I don't pay out on arrests," I say.

"So you're waiting for Jai to be convicted?"

"I need a confession," I say. "Without that, I won't believe it."

"You are one cheating bastard," Freddie says airily, head tilted back, as if he is trying to balance a Ping-Pong ball on his upper lip. "How goes your quest to find the real killer?"

"What?"

"I did a little Googling," Freddie says. "I figured out why you stayed in Alabama. Those quarterbacks that Samuel injured, did you get them to spill?"

"No one spilled a damn thing," I say, thinking of Herrold hoovering down every crumb of his pie.

Freddie turns his gaze toward me. "Is something wrong with you, Nick?" It is hard to tell with his Oakleys, but I think he is concerned.

"What do you mean?"

"Is your head right?" Freddie asks. "I wonder if you don't have some kind of post-traumatic stress disorder. From the shooting, I mean. You were essentially in a combat situation for a few seconds."

Longer than a few seconds, if you count the time I waited for the ambulance to arrive while Samuel and Cecil were bleeding torrents.

"That's not it," I say. "I don't think so, anyway."

"If you need help, I can recommend a wonderful therapist,"

Freddie says. He waits the requisite beat before adding, "The massage therapist I saw the other day. She has an unbelievable ass."

"You're an unbelievable ass," I say. "Maybe your worries can be rubbed out that easily, but not mine."

Freddie sullenly kicks at the turf with his white Converse low-tops. The shoes are new, so he is trying his best to pick up a grass stain.

"Someone at the funeral told me that Tanner went down to Alabama twice to visit Samuel before the draft," I say. "Is that right?"

"Yes," he says. "He took the family plane both times. Wanted to be all cloak-and-dagger about it, so no one would see him in the airport."

I scan the field, searching for Tanner. He is a good fifty yards away, monitoring the quarterbacks.

I decide to reveal to Freddie what I heard about Tanner and Selia Sault. I have been wanting to tell someone.

Freddie blinks his eyes in disbelief and says, "Wow." After a further pause: "Good for him. Is she hot?"

I am confiding in an idiot. "She's nineteen," I say.

"So . . . yes? Are there pictures of her online, you think?" He is already reaching for his iPhone.

I shake my head and walk away a few steps, even though I have nowhere to go.

"Holy shit!" Freddie shouts, one hand pointing at me, the other hand over his mouth. "You think Tanner did it!"

I whirl around and look about to see if anyone has heard this cry, but no heads are turned. I walk back to Freddie, if only to lower the volume of his babbling. "What's your theory, Hangman?" he says. "She was going to move up here with Samuel and get up in Tanner's business, so he commits drive-by murder to keep her down in Alabama. Do you actually believe that?"

"No," I snarl. "And shut up." I am actually feeling guilty, now, for having ratted Tanner out. Not that he doesn't deserve grief, but I would hate for the story to come back to me. "Don't tell anyone I told you this," I say. "Please."

"I don't know, Hangman," Freddie teases. "You seem to be asking an awful lot. What do you ever do for me?"

"Just don't say anything."

Freddie shrugs his shoulders, smirks at me, and walks away. He strolls up the sideline and settles next to Clint Udall, who is watching the drills attentively. Freddie begins talking animatedly at our general manager, and Udall nods, occasionally saying a few words in response, all the while keeping his eyes on the action. Freddie glances back at me and grins. He knows I am watching him, and he is messing with me. At least, that is what I hope he is doing.

CHAPTER 20

IT IS THE night before the last day of minicamp, the night before my last chance to demonstrate to the Sentinels that I am the calm, centered, businesslike veteran they want as their punter.

It is the veteran's voice that whispers to me, telling me to stay home and rest. It tells me not to pick up that phone.

"Hello. Melody?"

"Nick?" she says.

"Yup, it's me. I know I said I would call when minicamp was over, but I feel like doing something tonight. You free?"

"I am," she says brightly. "Just here at home."

"Perfect," I say. "Can I swing by?"

"Umm . . . sure," she says. "Are we going out somewhere?"

"That would be the civil thing to do, I suppose."

In the early dusk of one of the longest nights of the year, I climb into my Audi and drive north. One nice thing about Melody's grimly quiet neighborhood—no shortage of street parking. On her block it's just my car and the same new red F-150 that was there before. I press her doorbell, a pale orange circle, and don't hear any sound, so I knock my knuckles against the door's worn metal frame.

Melody answers quickly, as if she was waiting by the door. Her smile broadens when she sees me. She has a band in her hair, made from a glittery dark green thread that accentuates the color of her eyes. She is dressed in jeans and a dark blue top with a ruffled neckline that plunges deeply, exposing enough curvature to immediately give the evening a PG-13 rating.

"You look nice," I say. I wonder if I should shelve my questions and make this the kind of date Melody thinks it is.

"Come inside for a moment," she says. "I have someone who wants to meet you."

In the narrow space that is their living room, a scrawny man in his forties sits on the worn arm of a floral-pattern sofa. He has unkempt long brown hair with streaks of gray, and he is wearing a Sentinels T-shirt whose shade of brown is slightly off, suggesting the shirt is an unlicensed knockoff. He has the same pale coloring as Melody, and he shares her green eyes as well.

"This is my uncle," Melody says. "Vaughn."

Uncle—good. Though Vaughn's smile is unsettling, both for its nervous enthusiasm and because his teeth remind me of a poorly hammered garden fence. His bloodshot gaze corroborates the scent of marijuana about him.

"I'm a big fan, man," he says, his voice both raspy and boyish.

He comes forward to shake my hand. I squeeze firmly and find that Vaughn has the grip of an old rag doll.

"That hit you put on Dez Wheeler in the Atlanta game last year, that was awesome," he says with a breathless smile. "That has to be the coolest punter highlight ever."

"Thank you so much," I say. "That's very kind of you."

"Look at you, Nick," Melody says, playfully tapping my elbow. "Mr. Superstar."

"Have a good time, you two," Vaughn says, seeing us to the door.

I drive out of Melody's neighborhood, back toward the Interstate. Melody rolls down her window and lets the breeze tousle her hair. "So where we going?"

"How about the Winking Oyster?" I ask.

She clucks her tongue a few times. "If you want to go to a strip club," she says, "I know a couple in town that are pretty good."

Really? I have never done that on a date before. I have a hunch Melody would be the right girl to try it with.

"Let's just go to Penn's Landing," I say.

"Sure," she says. She sounds cheery, expectant. "Is there a bar down there or something?"

"We could just go for a walk by the river."

"A walk by the river," she repeats delightedly, in a soft singsong voice. "I knew you were the romantic type."

Soon we are there. The Penn's Landing waterfront has a maritime museum and a few historical sailing ships that visitors can tour during the day. During the winter, the city sets up a skating rink here, and in the summer it hosts concerts and ethnic festivals on the weekends. Tonight, though, the only noise is coming from the one restaurant in this stretch, which is on a retrofitted historic boat. From its large outdoor deck, I hear the boisterous sounds of young people enjoying the night. I would bet half those people haven't even figured out what they want to do with their lives. I feel a generation older than they are.

I lead Melody along a brick walkway that juts out into the Delaware River and then turns right and runs parallel to the shoreline. The walkway goes a couple hundred yards down the river until it dead ends. The view ahead is of a large condominium, built on the water, whose shape is supposed to resemble a clipper ship. A large banner with a phone number advertises vacancies.

We reach the end of the walkway. I push myself up to sit on the low concrete railing, and Melody pushes herself up, too, sitting alongside me, her bare arm flush against mine. In the glow of the walkway lights, her lips look particularly pillowy.

She places her hand on my left thigh.

"Wow," she says, sounding genuinely surprised. "I don't think I've ever said this to a man before, but nice legs."

"Thanks," I say. "I've done a few thousand squats a week for the past half decade. I'm glad I have something to show for it."

Her hand is now massaging my thigh—after we have been here for all of one minute.

"I suppose you heard about Jai being arrested?" I ask.

"I did," Melody says, without any enthusiasm for the topic. "Crazy, huh?"

"Very crazy," I say. "Especially since he didn't do it."

"You still think he's innocent?" she says, her massage slowing. "Even with the rifle they found?"

"I think he's being framed," I say. "What do you think?"

She purrs and raises her hand to my chest. "Do we really have to talk about this?"

I remove her hand. She sits upright.

"Here's another subject to talk about," I say. "What exactly did you do at the Winking Oyster?"

"I was a bartender," she says sourly. "I told you that the other day. What's up with you?"

"I ran a search on the Winking Oyster and I came across this story about how it had been closed down by the police," I say. "I was just wondering, were you part of the drug business there? Or the prostitution?"

She pushes herself off the rail and straightens her shirt.

"I don't like you looking into me," she says, her back to me. "Maybe you should just take me home."

I don't move and after a couple of seconds of silence she stomps down the brick walkway, without looking back. I slip off the rail and catch up to her.

"If you think you're better than me, I've got news for you," Melody says, quickening her pace. "You're not."

"I don't care about the Winking Oyster," I say. "That's your business. But you need to tell me what you know about the shooting."

"I don't know anything about it," she snaps, glaring at me. But she also stops walking.

"Samuel was killed after leaving Stark's. Jai was framed while he was eating there. You were there both nights. You're telling me you can run your little misdemeanor ring or whatever you called it, but you're in the dark about this big thing that happened in your own shop?"

"I only know what I read in the papers," she says acidly, folding her arms and looking off to the side.

She's holding something back. I can feel it.

"Please, Melody," I say. "My agent was shot, one of my teammates is dead, another is in jail. I don't want to make trouble for you. I'm just trying to figure out what happened."

She places her hands on her hips and bites her lip. "You made $970,000 last year, right?"

So while I was reading about her strip club, she was looking up my salary. What a modern romance.

"You have it right," I say. "To the dollar."

"If I tell you something that helps you, I want money. A lot of it."

Money, of course. It's disappointing to hear her say it, but I don't really care. Because if she has information that she thinks is worth selling, then the police have indeed arrested the wrong man.

"I'll take care of you," I say. "If what you have to say is worth it."

"And you have to promise you won't make me go to the police," she says, eyes brimming with anger.

"Why no police?"

"Because I don't like the police, and I don't trust them," she says firmly.

"But a man's life . . ."

"No," she says. "No, no, no."

She glares at me, arms folded.

"Okay, I get it," I say. "Just tell me what you know."

She breathes in deeply. "I don't think JC did it either."

I feel a rush of excitement. "Who did?"

"I don't know," she says. "But I don't think it's JC."

"Why?" I ask quickly.

"The night Samuel was killed, early in the shift, this guy comes into the restaurant, and he's hanging around the bar," Melody says. "He calls me over and when I try to take his order, he offers me five dollars to call him if Samuel Sault comes into the bar. I tell him it's going to cost him fifty, just to throw a number out there, try to get him to up his offer. But he agrees to fifty. I called him before I even put in your order. But he didn't come back the whole night, not even after you all left. I would bet if someone followed you from the restaurant and it wasn't JC, it was him."

"What was his name?"

She pulls her green band from her hair and studies it, as if something is wrong with it. "He never gave it to me. He was kind of weird looking. He was older, and black. He was wearing a sports jacket, but it was frayed at the collar. If I had to bet, I would guess he was a bum that someone paid to be his front man. But whoever this bum is working for, I would bet that's the killer."

My initial excitement dissipates. With Philadelphia's shamefully large street population, the man that Melody is describing would be impossible to find. And what she is saying, even if true, doesn't provide me with any proof. It's just a story, vague and secondhand.

"What about the night Jai was arrested?" I ask. "Did the guy ask you to call him again?"

Melody searches for a moment before answering, "No, but everyone knows when JC is coming in. He always tweets it, in exchange for a forty percent discount off his tab."

I would have to review the bill from the night of Jai's arrest.

After he and Cheat were dragged out, I ended up paying, and I don't remember seeing any discount.

"Do you have the guy's phone number?"

Melody fished around in her bag, but then stopped and shook her head.

"I have it on my phone, but I just remembered, it wouldn't do you any good," she says. "I tried calling the night after the shooting, but the number was already dead. It must have been one of those prepaid burner phones. You know what those are?"

Yes, I did, from having watched *The Wire*. And last year a member of the league's players association, advocating for health benefits for retired players, actually made a comparison between football players and burner phones—how both are used for a while and then tossed aside—in an interview that was widely read among people who care about such things. My mother had forwarded me the story.

Now that Melody has shared her information, I am befuddled. She has confirmed my instincts and suggested an alternate theory, but she hasn't given me anything I can use—no decisive piece of evidence I can hand over to Rizotti to let him know there's another track to explore.

"Please, you have to go to the police," I tell her. "If you have some charge hanging over your head because of the Winking Oyster, I'm sure they will let it go if you help them with this."

"Oh, really?" she says, an eyebrow dubiously cocked. "First of all, the police have their guy. I don't think they'll be all that eager to reopen the case. Second of all, I don't think punters have the power to speak for the district attorney. And third of all, JC can afford a good lawyer. I'm not going to go to prison so I can save that loudmouth some money on attorney's fees."

I am regretting my promise to Melody about not taking her to the police. But I said what I said, and I keep my promises. And furthermore, I cannot guarantee that her arguments are off base.

But what is interesting is that when I suggested that Melody might be avoiding the police because of what she did at the Winking Oyster, she rolled with that suggestion in a way that implies I was right. Perhaps she is a parole violator, or maybe even a felon on the run.

I pull out my wallet and hand her all the hundreds I have on me.

"Is that all I get?" she says, thumbing through the bills. I have given her about a thousand bucks, maybe a little less.

"Yup," I say. "Be happy with that."

We walk back to the car. Every time we pass a happy couple holding hands or giggling, we sink deeper into an uneasy silence. On the ride home, to break the quiet, I ask Melody why she lives with her uncle.

She doesn't answer for about ten seconds, but then grudgingly allows, "Vaughn's the closest thing I have to a father these days."

"What happened to your parents?"

She folds her arms. "Really wanna know? You're not going to use it against me?"

"Yes."

She sighs, and begins. "First, there's my mom. She skipped out when I was two. Then there's my dad. He's in prison."

"For what?"

She hesitates.

"The thing you need to understand about my dad is," she says, "he's the sweetest man I've ever known. He taught me guitar. When I was a little kid we'd spend our Saturday nights practicing in the den. One year we won a red ribbon at the county fair for best duet."

She sounds genuinely warmed when she talks about this memory, but my stomach can't help but knot, waiting to hear what her doting father did to be locked up.

"One day he and I were coming home from the supermarket," she says. "The market was only a couple miles away, so we'd walk. It gave us something to do, and we'd save on gas money. So we are walking and this kid drives by. He's talking on his cell phone, and his side mirror hits me in the elbow. I fall to the ground, groceries are everywhere, I'm screaming. And the kid gets out of the car to see if I'm okay. He still has his cell phone in his hand. And my dad snaps. He didn't get that it was just the mirror that hit me. He chops the kid in the throat. And the kid dies."

"He dies?" I say, aghast. "From one hit?"

"It landed in exactly the wrong place, and crushed the kid's throat," she says. "Just plain bad luck. I'd never seen my dad hit anyone, ever. But he throws one chop and the whole world changes. It's like he is struck by lightning. It's like we all were."

"That's unbelievable," I say.

"The worst part was," Melody says softly, "my dad was given a public defender who was so dumb he couldn't even beat me in checkers. My dad ended up getting fifteen years."

"Did your mom ever hear about what happened?"

Melody looks away. "I don't know," she says. "Wherever my mom ended up, she must have forgot to send postcards. That's okay, people say that Daddy always knew better how to handle me anyway. Although they also tell me I'm a lot like her. I don't know what that means."

I think I do.

* * *

When we pull up to the house, I tell her I'm sorry.

"I'll be fine," she says. "You take care of yourself. Eat a whoopie pie every now and then." And she leaned forward and kisses me on the mouth, and I let the kiss hang for a while. It's an escape to an alternate reality where neither of us have the problems we have and this was just a plain old date.

Soon she pushes her tongue into my mouth, and I place my hand on her back. She raises one knee up on her seat, and then another, and she grabs on to my shoulders with both hands and leans her body into mine.

But I am wedged behind the steering wheel and we have the gear shift between us. Our mouths locked, we adjust our bodies, struggling to find a comfortable position.

And yet I do not want to move to the backseat—or, even worse, into her house, where we might have to chat with Vaughn for a few moments—because I know that in the process of separating and moving, the spell will break.

And so we twist within our confines, me working a hand underneath her shirt, forcing its way onto the lace of her bra, but with the back of my hand, so my feel is more of a flattened squish. She places her hand in the crotch of my jeans, but her arm is bent such that she can only press down. She attempts to twist her body around, looking for a more manageable angle, but her contortions push her up and over the seat, so she tumbles slow motion, headfirst, in the back of the car.

The fatal separation has happened. She rights herself in the backseat and pats the fabric, inviting me to join her. But already I can feel my buzz disappearing.

"I have to be going," I say. "And so do you. Good luck, Melody."

She shakes her head in disappointment, but it is an act.

She knows, too. "Hope your camp goes well tomorrow, I'll be rooting for you," she says, and then she lets herself out from the back. I watch her walk to the door of her house and I feel oddly gratified when she shuts it behind her.

As I drive home, my mood only elevates. The clock on the dashboard shows it is a shade past midnight, but I am not concerned at all about coming in weary for tomorrow's mini-camp. I am ready to beat Woodward, and then to go on from there. I feel like I can save Jai. I am going to win.

CHAPTER 21

BY THE TIME I arrive back at the Jefferson, however, my enthusiasm is subdued, because I still have no idea what that next move should be. I consider going to the police on my own, but if I talk to them, then they will want to talk to Melody. I will have led them to her doorstep, which I said I wouldn't do.

I feel like a Cub Scout with one stick. I know I can start a fire, if only I can find something to rub against.

I cannot sleep. My lack of rest will make tomorrow's camp a battle. But I've had plenty of sleepless nights before games and I've always found energy when the ball hits my hands.

It is one of my rules that if I am still awake in bed after fifteen minutes, I get up so that I do not create an association between my bed and sleeplessness. At 1:05 A.M. I am on the sofa, watching the fourth season of *Weeds,* when I receive a text from Freddie.

You up?

I pause the show and dial his phone.

"What's going on?"

"My father called this afternoon," Freddie says, voice slurred.

"And?"

"He's talked to Jai's defense lawyers," Freddie mumbles. "He's arranged it so I can go to their offices tomorrow. Work with them on the case. Perry Mason, Jr., that sort of thing."

"Why did he do that?"

"I guess he still hasn't given up on the idea of his son becoming a lawyer," Freddie says.

I hear him breathing heavily into the telephone and hear the echo of his breath as well. The reverb is so pronounced that I wonder if he is calling me from a bathroom.

"So go to their law offices," I say. "What's the big deal?"

He grunts and then groans. He does not sound well.

"Being an unpaid intern at thirty-three," he mutters, "is not a good look."

"Try it," I say. "Just go for one day. If you hate it, don't go back. All your amusements will still be waiting for you when you get home."

It is silent on the other end, until I hear a violent heave. Then a clatter and a crash, and the line goes dead.

At 4:00 A.M. I am still pounding episodes of *Weeds*. I wish for a do-over of my conversation with Melody, a chance to persuade her to go to the police.

I need a new argument, I realize. I need to make this as beneficial to her as it is to me.

I need to find out just what is hanging over her head from the Winking Oyster.

As the dawn nears I decide to ask Aaron for help. He said he knows people in police departments all over the East Coast. And he would know the most efficient way to procure what I need.

My only hesitation is that I have never asked Aaron to help me with anything before.

But at 6:14 A.M. I send Aaron a note.

> Hello, Aaron. It's Nick. I know this is going to sound strange, but can you get me the police report from Providence, Rhode Island, for the closure of a club called the Winking Oyster about a year ago?

A minute later, my phone rings. It is Aaron, up already. Of course he can't just answer by e-mail, he has to call. Open the door a crack and he comes bursting through.

"Hey, Aaron," I say pleasantly. "Good morning."

"Morning, Nick," he says. "How are you?"

"Fine, fine."

"Your mother and I are in Elmira," he says. "After last week, she's a little jumpy about the idea of being cut off from the world."

"Sorry to hear that, Aaron," I say. "I know you like that cabin very much."

"I do. I'm curious about this request you made. What's the Winking Oyster?"

"It's a strip club."

"Hmm," he says. "Why do you want to know about it?"

"I just need the report," I say.

"For what?" Aaron asks, his tone businesslike.

"I'm friends with a woman who used to work there," I say. "The other day I came across a news story that said the club was closed because it was a front for drugs and prostitution. I'm trying to find out how much she was involved."

"Don't get too close," Aaron says. "You don't need a police report to tell you that."

"I know, I know," I say. "I just want to see how far away I should stay."

"What's happening here, exactly? I think . . ."

"Can you get the report?"

He pauses at being cut off. "I'll try," he says hesitantly. "It should be doable."

"How soon can you get it to me?"

He pauses again. I am too eager. "We'll see," he sighs. "It's a yes-or-no request that can be fulfilled with a few clicks, so with a little luck, I could get it to you today or tomorrow."

"Good," I say. "Very good. Thank you, Aaron."

"You're welcome."

I feel a roiling in my stomach. I could imagine what my dad would say if he heard Aaron and I cooperating with each other, building bonds. *So now you're on his side, too?*

"Say, Aaron. You ever been to Peekskill?"

"Once, many years ago," Aaron says. "With your mother, actually . . ." His voice trails off. He has just let slip that he was there on the book group trip for T. C. Boyle's *World's End*. They were together my senior year of high school. I was living in that house, and I had no idea at all.

CHAPTER 22

FOR THE MORNING of the final day of minicamp, Tanner has not scheduled any special teams work. I will have nothing to do, but that is fine. In the afternoon session everyone will play in a simulated game. We will go four quarters. Time will be kept, referees will call penalties. If all proceeds normally, Woodward and I will punt four or five times each, probably more.

I have been hoping for this. I have played in simulated games before, and they can be fun. They also place extra pressure on players whose jobs are in jeopardy. As far as I was concerned, the more pressure, the better. I knew I would be ready to perform. Whereas Woodward had already shown a propensity to gack.

The day is cool and overcast, with only the faintest of breezes. Ideal weather. No sun to get in your eyes, no heat to strain your endurance, no gusts to knock down your kicks, nothing extraneous to factor in.

In the morning Woodward and I each take to Field 3 to practice. Woodward is quiet and methodical, chin down and eyes on the ball. When I first met him, he seemed happy just to be here; now he looks like it will kill him to leave.

Afterward, he and I have a peaceable lunch—eat with a guy once in the cafeteria, it's hard to get rid of him. I ask him what he has done with his down time in the city. He says he has gone jogging along the Schuylkill River, on Kelly Drive. I don't jog because I don't think endurance runs help with a punter's short-burst tasks, but if Woodward wants to pound his knees for miles at a stretch, *vaya con Dios.*

"I really liked all those old boathouses down there," he says. "With the college logos on them. Cool to find that in the middle of a big city."

"Philadelphia has a long-standing crew tradition," I say.

"I saw a bunch of kids out there in their school colors, coming in from a practice," he says. "They looked like they were having fun." He sounds a little wistful.

"Yeah, those days are gone for you, buddy," I say. "You're working for a living now."

"For a few more hours, anyway." He shrugs.

"Ah, come on. You're going to make it in this league, Woodward," I say. "Sooner or later." After a pause I add, "I would prefer later, of course."

"And I'd prefer now," Woodward says, looking down.

We share an awkward laugh.

Then Woodward says, waving his fork aimlessly, "You know what I don't get? It seems like at least a third of the guys here don't even like football."

I do the mental math. "That sounds about right."

"So why are they here?"

"The money," I say. I think of Jai, an extreme but not atypical example of players who build a lifestyle that demands piles of cash be thrown continually into the furnace.

"I guess that's a reason," Woodward says. "But I don't see how you can push through all the work, day after day, if you don't really like it."

"It's a lot of money," I say. "And for most people, this is the only identity they know or want to know."

"Do you like playing football?" Woodward asks. "You don't seem to, really."

I am surprised by this. "I would enjoy it more—and so would everyone around here—if Tanner wasn't such a prick. And the business end can be brutal. But I love playing. Always have, always will. Snap me a ball and I'm happy."

Woodward smiles in recognition. "Same for me," he says. "Too bad there's not more balls to go around."

For the game we are divided into two teams, the Brown and the Gray. The Brown is made up of the first-team offense and second-team defense. The Gray side consists of first-team defense and second-team offense. Each side has third- and fourth-stringers scattered among them. The special teamers wear hairnet-like webbing over their helmets—some blue, some red—so guys from each team can sort themselves out quickly when they have to be on a punt or coverage unit. Woodward and I can punt for either Brown or Gray, and we will be called into the game at Huff's discretion.

These camp games are historically intense because jobs are on the line, but it is also a time to let loose. Guys on the sideline cheer good plays and heckle bad ones as if they are fans in the 700-level who have just cracked their fifth beers. Early in today's game, a receiver stumbles and falls in the open field without having been touched, and one of the players on the sideline yells, "You should see a doctor about that narcolepsy!"

The heckle comes from Seth Kuhnert, a six-five, 345-pound left tackle who wears his long blond hair in a ponytail. Kuhnert is two seasons into a five-year, $41-million deal, and he is one of the team's most irreplaceable assets, so he can relax and enjoy the day. Most of the guys making catcalls are established players who are all but guaranteed to be here in the fall. You could say the camp has eighty people competing for fifty-three roster spots, but in reality it is closer to forty people competing for the fifteen or so jobs that are genuinely up for grabs—the fifth wide receiver, or the ninth offensive lineman, or the dime back, or the third quarterback. Or the punter.

As I stand and watch today's game, I feel myself going slowly mad. The problem is this: no one is punting. The Gray offense, under the direction of Bo John White, is moving the ball well. That you might expect. But the Brown team offense, led by backup quarterback Marty Yount, is carving up the defense as well. Every third down, I strap on my helmet and prepare to run onto the field. But I never get off the sidelines because the offenses just kept going. The defense just can't make a stop. I am missing Samuel and Jai in a new way.

The first quarter ends without a single punt. The second quarter goes the same way, with the offenses strolling up and down the field. I wait and wait and wait, biting deeper into the insides of my lower lip.

Finally, a couple of minutes before halftime, a third-down pass by Bo John White sails over a receiver's head out of bounds. It is time for the first punt of the game.

"Ten!" barks Huff. "Go!"

Ten is Woodward's uniform number. He is getting the first kick.

That is fine. It doesn't necessarily mean he has leaped ahead of me on our two-man depth chart.

The ball is on the offense's thirty-three-yard line, which will give Woodward a chance to put some leg into it.

And he does. He takes the snap and rockets the ball high

and deep, giving the coverage unit plenty of time to get down-field. The returner catches the punt on the fourteen-yard line, but he can bring it back just four yards. So Woodward's kick is fifty-three yards, with a net of forty-nine.

Very well done. Shit.

The first half ends without me getting a chance to answer. Halftime, thankfully, doesn't last any longer than the horn blow. No ceremony, no bands, no panel discussions in the TV studio. We go straight to the third-quarter kickoff, which is good, as I am dying to have a turn. On its first possession the offense stumbles to a quick three-and-out. Time for another punt.

"Ten!" Huff calls.

Woodward again? I look at my position coach and wonder if his brain is working right. He took plenty of knocks as a player back in the '80s. Are the aftershocks setting in now, this very afternoon? Did he forget that I haven't had a punt yet? Or is it that Huff already knows what I can do, and he wants see as much of Woodward in a game situation as he can?

I think back to that first time I saw Huff after the shooting, back in the locker room. He was talking at length to Woodward, and then brushed me off with a few awkward words. I wonder if Huff knew even then that he was planning to cut me.

Woodward takes the field on the twenty-two-yard line and lets loose another boomer, fifty-one yards, high enough that the returner signals fair catch, not even bothering to attempt a runback with the coverage guys already in his face.

Fuck me.

After that, the offenses resume motoring up and down the field as I watch helplessly, waiting for a stall-out so I can finally kick. But every third-down screen pass or slant pattern seems to pick up just enough yardage to keep me on the side-lines.

By the fourth quarter White and Yount have ceded the quarterbacking to greener players. Our rookie fourth-string quarterback, Onderay Marshall, is in the game and he decides to try a deep ball instead of going to the check-down receiver for the easy gain, and he overthrows his target. Thank God for his incompetence. It is time for another punt.

"Ten!" Huff shouts.

What? Woodward again?

The team wants to make the switch, of this there is no doubt. I can't even argue with their logic. Woodward is perfectly fine, it is plain to see. Why devote a $350,000 bonus plus a few hundred grand of extra salary for a position of secondary importance, when this team has so many other areas in which it needs to improve?

He sets up on the offense's forty-eight-yard line, giving him a chance to kill the ball inside the twenty. If Woodward hits this, he will correct his mistake from two days ago, and erase all doubt from their minds.

This could really be it for me.

I begin to sort through the other teams around the league that aren't firm at punter. I might have to send Cecil begging again to secure me an invitation to a training camp, just like he did when I was a rookie. Of course, Cecil is still weakened by his gunshot wound. Which means I will be doubly fucked. I imagine another team's punter getting injured and their G.M. being flooded with calls from other agents while Cecil sits on his backyard deck examining his scar.

Thus will my career go down the toilet. What a mess.

Breathe. Breathe. Breathe.

I watch Woodward count the ten men in front of him,

carefully pointing at each. He is taking care to get every detail right.

Then Backlund delivers the snap—and it comes out wide to Woodward's left. Woodward reaches out and knocks down the ball with his hand, but he isn't able to control it. He dives on the loose ball, but it squirts out from underneath him and is collected by a defender.

At which point I stop panicking about my job long enough to worry about Backlund's. He has snapped eleven balls on film in this camp, and he has missed his target twice. The Sentinels have no replacement for him at long snapper on the roster, but they can fix that quite easily between now and the season's opener.

This isn't like Backlund. Before today, he had two bad snaps in all the years I'd worked with him. I hope he hasn't developed some ghastly mental hiccup. It's happened to plenty of athletes: the mind suddenly sabotages the body, and the career. In one season, former Colt Mike Vanderjagt went from the most accurate field-goal kicker in history to a guy who couldn't make a chip shot. In baseball, All-Star second baseman Chuck Knoblauch suddenly couldn't throw the ball to first. In golf, Ian Baker-Finch went from winning the British Open to spraying balls into the wrong fairways.

But this is Backlund's problem. At this juncture I don't need to be thinking about him or Mike Vanderjagt or Chuck Knoblauch or Ian Baker-Finch. I need positive images in my head. I could very well be standing at the precipice of my career. When my chance comes to punt—if it ever does—I have to be ready to nail one. I have to let these clouds roll by.

I close my eyes and visualize my punt routine. Limber stance. Easy catch. Flat drop. The top of my foot meeting the wide bottom of the ball. Up, up, and away.

I just need a chance. Onderay Marshall is back on the field and leading the offense again. I have to root for him to throw inaccurately, but not so inaccurately as to be intercepted. I call up a precisely calibrated hex, and it works. On a third-and-four, Onderay throws a short pass out in the flat a good five yards over the head of his intended receiver. It is time for another punt.

"Eleven!" Huff shouts.

Finally. My number has been called. I have a shot.

I trot onto the field and take my position, standing up on my toes, loose, hands to my side. I stand at our forty-nine-yard line, which means that I can go for my coffin corner. Put it out of bounds inside the five. I can remind them just what a weapon I am.

Of course, if I go for the corner and miss, I am fucked. I slept horribly last night, and the night before. But I have practiced this too many times not to go for it when I need it most. I have spent practice session after practice session in an unvarying and monotonous routine, all in order to build muscle memory, and I need it now. The left corner. I can drive that ball straight into the left corner and end this competition now.

I give the signal, and Backlund snaps me the ball. It comes out to the right. The far right. I cannot field it cleanly. Fucking Backlund.

I lunge and snag the ball with both hands before it hits the ground. But now I am bent over and turned to the side, and the rush is coming quick. If I try to right myself and punt, my kick will be blocked. That is the last thing I need.

So I run farther to the right, sidestepping the defenders who are charging up the middle and also evading a rusher who has made a clean break coming from around the left side. He is closing in on me quick.

I keep running to the right and, looking upfield, I see a #80 with that goofy webbing on his helmet. I have no idea who #80 is, but God bless him, he is doing exactly what he has been instructed to do when the play breaks down, which is to run a short out pattern. A defender is shadowing #80, a half-step behind.

I rise up and throw an adrenaline-powered dart that hits the receiver in the chest. He makes the catch and turns, taking a step upfield before he is tackled.

The pass gains eight yards. We have a first down.

I can hear the vets holler and applaud. If I am not mistaken, I even hear Bo John White call out, "Oh, shit! Gallow's after my job!"

Someday, Bo John. Someday.

As I run off the field, I veer toward Backlund.

"Nice one, Nick," he says, giving me a hard pat on the rear end as I pull up alongside. He seems unconcerned about his two blown snaps.

"What's going on, John?" I ask. "You okay?"

"I'm fine," Backlund says with an easy smile as we settle on the sideline next to each other and take off our helmets. "It was Tanner. He told Huff to have me give you and Woodward each a bad snap. Wanted to see how you'd handle it."

Great. As if this week hasn't been stressful enough, Tanner has to increase the level of difficulty. What a cock. But if he's giving me a test, it means he hasn't decided to cut me.

And now Tanner knows that when a play breaks down, he would rather have me back there than Woodward.

The public will never see my pass to #80, never know about it, never care about it. But right now it feels like my Bradshaw-to-Swann, my Montana-to-Clark, my Manning-to-Tyree. It is too soon to say that I have beaten Woodward. I suspect they will continue to look at us through the first cuts of regular training camp, at least. But with that play, Tanner's uptightness will become my friend. Every time he thinks about replacing me, he will see the image of the ball squishing out from underneath Woodward, and he will know that if Woodward turns the ball over like that during a regular season game, he will wish he had paid me that $350,000.

And if I survive till training camp, and the team pays me that bonus, it will blunt the Sentinels' financial incentive to switch punters. Once behind me, the $350,000 will work in my favor, because if they've sunk that much money into me already, they might as well hold on to me.

Nothing is settled, but my math just became a whole lot better. I feel like I will remain a Sentinel for a while longer. I should survive through to August.

CHAPTER 23

As I JOG in from the field, I see Cordero waiting by the entrance to the locker room area. She smiles broadly when she sees me. She is such a sweet, upbeat gal; it pains me that I am coming to dread the sight of her, all because of the job she does.

"I talked to Scott Nellie," she says with a sly smile. "Sounds like you handled him quite well."

"Who were you checking up on, me or him?" I ask.

"A little of both," she says. "Have to keep my children safe. Speaking of which, Freddie Gladstone texted me. He says he needs you to call him right away." She says this with her customary good cheer, as if she didn't have anything better to do than pass me messages.

"Thanks, Eleanor," I say. "You're the greatest."

I trot into the locker room and, still in full pads, retrieve my BlackBerry from my lockbox and go outside to return the call in privacy.

"I did it," Freddie says, sounding a little breathless. "I am coming to you live from a real working law office. This might not be that bad, actually. Everyone is very friendly, well-dressed. A couple of the secretaries are hot. The only dickish moment so far was when one of JC's lawyers told me not to speak to the press at all."

"So his lawyers are competent, is what you're telling me."

"Pretty much."

"What are they planning?"

"I don't know. I'm still trying to figure out how the coffee machine works. They have all these flavor packs, but I can't figure out where they go."

"You can survive without the flavor. Just read up on the case." I pause before adding, "Call me later. Let me know how the day goes."

By the time I emerge from the showers, Woodward is already gone. Which disappoints me. Back in college I read *The Iliad*; one of my favorite details from that book is how the great warriors, before fighting, would dine with each other and exchange gifts as a sign of respect. I like that tradition; it recognizes that those men, despite battling for opposing armies, are a brotherhood. I have no gift to offer Woodward, but I want to at least give him a proper farewell.

Back at the Jefferson, I drop in on the Tolleys. When I

knock, it is Woodward who opens the door. He is in a plain white T-shirt and jeans, looking particularly young.

He has a hangdog sourness on his face, but he clears it quickly when he sees me. "Nick, this is a surprise."

He holds a garbage bag in his hand.

"I hope I didn't catch you in the middle of something," I say.

"No, no, I am just helping to pick up a little before we check out tomorrow," Woodward says. "Come on in."

I enter and see four sleeping bags on the floor, and clothes in various piles alongside them. Plus empty bags of pretzels and corn chips, and cans of beer. Many empty cans of beer. The room is fetid and airless. Woodward said he was helping, but I see no one else here.

"Everyone's out getting cheesesteaks," Woodward says. "Can't go to Philadelphia without eating a cheesesteak, right?"

"Afraid not," I say. "How come you're not with them?"

"To tell you the truth," Woodward says, with a forced smile, "after today, I don't have much of an appetite."

"C'mon," I say, though I feel a guilty rush of hope that he has been cut already. Has Udall pulled Woodward aside after practice and told him it is all over? "You had a great camp, Woodward. I was very impressed."

"Really?" he says darkly, bending over to pick up a can of Coors Light and chucking it into his bag. "How about that bad snap? You caught yours and threw for a first down. I dropped mine and then I didn't even cover the ball."

At that point the toilet flushes, and a young woman emerges from the bathroom. She is in her middle or late teens, and is wearing blue-jean shorts and a black sleeveless T-shirt, and her dirty blond hair hangs down below her shoulders.

"This is my cousin Annie," Woodward says, smiling at her warmly. "She's keeping me company."

Annie slinks over to shake my hand.

"Hi, Annie," I say. "I'm Nick."

"Nick Gallow?" she says. Her smile disappears and her handshake loses what little force it had.

"Yes," I say.

She turns to Woodward. "What's he doing here?"

"He's a teammate," Woodward says, with emphasis.

She shakes her head. "If you say so." Then she flops down on the sofa and turns on the television.

"Do you have another garbage bag?" I ask. "If we work together, we can have this place clean in five minutes."

"No need, Nick," he says. "I'll take care of it."

"You're still the rookie around here, right?" I say. "Go get me a trash bag, now."

Woodward smiles and fetches me a bag from the utility closet. I begin to clean while Annie remains perched on the sofa watching television. After clicking past a few shows, she settles on the reality program *Celebrity Fit Club*. As I fill my bag, I listen to the contestants on the show. One exclaims, *I look like a pregnant man!*

I am impressed with the quantity of Coors Light the Tolleys have gone through. Every time I look under a dirty shirt or giveaway paper from the lobby, I find a few more. They must have gone through five cases of beer this week.

Near one sleeping bag I come across a small black cardboard box, with red lettering that reads WINCHESTER VARMINT X. I open it and find three bullets inside. I study the outside of the packaging and see that the box originally contained twenty bullets, for a .270-caliber rifle.

"Those are Uncle Frank's," Woodward says. He is suddenly standing behind me.

"Quite the hunter, is he?" I ask.

"He likes to eat what he's killed," Woodward says. "He hasn't been to the meat section of a supermarket in five years. Remember how I invited you over for fried turkey the other day? He bagged that turkey himself. He had to drive a few hours out of town to find a place to hunt, but he did it."

"Frank's a real genius," Annie mutters. "Spent sixty dollars on gas to kill a twenty-dollar bird."

"Sounds like a remarkable fellow," I say. "Did he take his rifle with him to stalk the wild cheesesteak?" In my cleaning I had not seen a gun to go with these bullets.

"He wouldn't leave it lying around," Woodward says. "It must be in the truck."

"Smart man," I say. "You wouldn't want a rifle to get in the wrong hands."

Standing there, with this box of bullets between us, I let the silence linger—just like that officer did to me at the scene of the shooting, hoping I would blurt out something, just to fill the quiet.

"How's your agent doing?" Woodward asks.

"Better," I say. "He's home." Vicki had texted me upon their arrival in Ohio.

"That's great," Woodward says. "Tell him I wish him well."

"I will," I say. "Thank you for that."

Then we resume cleaning, as *Celebrity Fit Club* babbles on in the background. The instructor is now barking at a recalcitrant dieter. *"You can't do this on your terms! It's not your game anymore!"*

I look at the mess Woodward's family has left behind, and

I wonder how much help it actually was for Woodward to have the whole clan in town this week. From what I can see, Woodward's support system could be a real drain.

In my cleaning, I hit a cluster of snack-food packaging—an empty box of Tastykakes, some empty Fritos bags, a couple ice-cream sandwich wrappers that have been licked clean. I hope this isn't what Woodward's per-diem check was used for.

And then I find the tatters of a gray Sentinels T-shirt, one that Woodward must have brought home from the locker room. It has been slashed sideways repeatedly.

"Oh, that's nothing," Woodward says, reaching out an arm. "Let me get that . . ."

In holding up the shirt I see the name GALLOW handwritten across its back in black Magic Marker, along with my number eleven.

Whoa.

I look at Woodward, who gazes down and away, in the general direction of his cousin. I turn to Annie just in time to see her looking back toward the TV, and snickering as she shakes her head.

"Any comment?" I ask him calmly.

"You know how it is," he says, hands in pockets, head tilted askance. "Everyone wants me to make the team so badly. They were just letting off some steam the other night. No one meant anything by it."

The shirt has been attacked with such enthusiasm that it is barely in one piece.

"No hard feelings?" Woodward asks pleadingly.

"No," I say. And I mean it. Because I'm not a complete hypocrite, and I can't say that I haven't wished failure upon my young friend.

Though now I really wouldn't have put it past his family

to have trashed my apartment a few nights ago, as if they were a pack of bratty kids on Mischief Night.

I throw the shirt in the garbage and within minutes Woodward and I finish our work. The place is, if not clean, at least presentable. We set our bags near the door.

"Good-bye, Nick," he says, extending his hand.

"See you at training camp in a few weeks," I say. "Let the competition continue."

"Let's hope so," Woodward says.

"I'd bet on it," I say. Then I turn to Annie. "Good-bye," I call to her. "Nice meeting you."

"You leaving already?" she sneers, without taking her eyes off the television. "Got what you came for, did ya?"

More than I expected, actually.

When I return to my apartment, I open up Footballmania .com and scour their news stories about the shooting, but I cannot find the detail I am looking for. This is the problem when football beat writers have to flip a switch and become police reporters. Not a single article mentions the caliber of the bullets that hit Cecil and Samuel.

I text Freddie, asking him to look into that detail. It is an unlikely scenario, to be sure, but I need to check in the name of thoroughness. I want to know if it was a .270, on the off chance that Uncle Frank's rifle is missing because it has been planted in the back of Jai Carson's car.

CHAPTER 24

FREDDIE RESPONDS TO my query by saying that he's left the office already but he will look into the matter tomorrow, if he remembers.

I don't believe it likely that the Tolleys are behind the shooting, with me as their target. Nor do I regard it as impossible. Three years ago, in 2006, the punter for Northern Colorado State was stabbed in the leg in a parking lot, and the culprit turned out to be a player he had beaten out for the job. And Northern Colorado State is a small school, with a weak football program. But one man was willing to commit felony assault so he could punt there. Obsessions don't always make sense. It is the rare Romeo who chooses wisely the Juliet he would die for.

Minicamp is done and we are off for more than a month, until full camp begins at the end of July. But I wake up the next morning feeling like I need to work out. Between the trip to Alabama and then minicamp itself, my muscles feel antsy. They are telling me that I have fallen off my fitness routine.

I begin in my apartment, doing two hundred squats with my twenty-two-pound weight bar yoked across my shoulders for added resistance. Then I do two hundred push-ups and another three hundred squats, and then go down to the lobby and run up seventeen flights of Jefferson stairwell.

I finish in just under an hour. I shower and poach myself

an egg, and then I check my phone to see if Freddie has gotten back to me. It's coming up on 9:00 A.M., and he is surely not even in the office yet.

I think of what else I might do today. My agenda is suddenly empty. I could visit my mother, as I had promised, but I don't want to leave town. My loose plan for these days had been to spend them at Freddie's beach house. But Freddie is working, so that is out.

After these camps are over, or especially after a season is over, I often go through a down period that I would compare to postpartum depression, except that I don't want to analogize between bringing a new life into the world and a three-day minicamp.

The red light on my phone blinks. A message, from Aaron.

> Take a look. I'm sure there have been more embarrassing police investigations but I can't think of one.

The document is too big to download on my phone, so I boot up my laptop and open the report on the Winking Oyster. I scan for Melody's name, but I do not see it anywhere. If the report doesn't mention her at all, this is going to blow my theory about her criminal past, and it certainly won't arm with any piece of information that I can use to get her to talk.

I go back to the top and read more thoroughly, and I soon find the reason for Aaron's disdain. Vice police worked the strip club for ten months before they moved in for what seemed like a small number of arrests.

The police did nab five dancers for offering sex services and two bouncers for dealing in ecstasy, amphetamines, and marijuana, but no bosses were arrested. The operation must have gone on for so long that its main targets got wind of what was happening and beat their way out of town. Then the cops realized the big fish had gotten away, collected whatever they could, and shut down the club, just so they would have something to show for all their drooling recon. A single sentence tucked meekly at the bottom of the report told the story: "The club's co-owner, VAUGHN PENDERS, and a bartender, ALICE PENDERS, disappeared on December 9. They are believed to have been key figures in these operations and are actively being sought."

Vaughn. If Melody's uncle worked at the Winking Oyster, that would explain how she ended up there. But who was Alice and how did she fit in?

And then it clicks. I search the New Hampshire Class A semifinalist soccer rosters, the ones I had examined days ago looking for Melody. There I find her, on the roster of Bonner High: Alice Penders. With a little Googling, I find a brief story on their semifinal win, mentioning that Alice scored the winning goal.

She wasn't lying about her athletic exploits. She was lying about her name.

I shut down the computer and throw on jeans and a T-shirt and I drive to Melody's—Alice's—home.

When I pull up the first thing I notice is that the F-150 is gone. I knock on the door. No answer. I pull open the screen door and turn the handle. The place is unlocked. I step in and call out "Melody?" but hear only a slow drip from the kitchen.

In the kitchen the cabinets are open, and nearly empty. I see a quarter-full box of pasta, a jar of peanut butter with a few scrapings left, and an open bag of marshmallows with ants crawling through. The refrigerator is equally barren, with just a jar of Hellman's and a drained bottle of Heinz ketchup in the door.

I climb upstairs and find two uncarpeted bedrooms, furnished only with mattresses on the floor, each stained with its own brown watermarks. One room smells overwhelmingly of smoke. The other has, in the corner, a white candle mounted in the top of a bottle of champagne, with wax drippings running down the side. I pick up the bottle and examine it by the window. The champagne is Cristal, and I can see my phone number on the label, partially obscured by the drippings. I open the closet of that room—just a dozen wire hangers, all pushed off to one side.

Melody has become Alice, and she has disappeared.

I drive back home with my radio off. I am in no mood to listen to anything. Back at the Jefferson, I breathe deeply and dial her number. Maybe if I tell Melody I know everything, that will put the fear of capture into her, and she will do the right thing.

Beep-beep-beep. This number is no longer in service.

I hold the phone straight out with my right arm, and I take a step-step-step across my living room and drop it, ready to boot the phone up into the ceiling in frustration. But I stop myself in mid-kick, letting the phone fall harmlessly onto the beige carpet.

When I apply the brakes, I feel pain rifle up the back of my right leg. The hamstring again. The hamstring was fine all through camp, but now it is back again, reminding me it is still my master. Tend to me, or suffer.

I slowly unbutton my jeans and slide them off, preparing

to stretch yet again. Unbelievable. I will spend much of my summer on my back, nursing this stupid tendon.

It is a disheartening prospect. Before I begin, I decide to watch the *SportsCenter* highlight clip of my hit on Dez Wheeler, which I haven't looked at in a few weeks. I grab the remote and with a couple of boings I am in my DVR's memory banks.

But the clip is gone. I find no *SportsCenter* in the archives at all. I turn the DVR on and off again and begin the search anew, but it doesn't help. My greatest moment as a competitive athlete is gone.

And I had that clip protected every way I could to make sure the machine didn't erase it by accident. That digital file is my greatest treasure.

It couldn't have just vanished.

Right then I knew who broke into my apartment, because I have told only one person about the clip. Only one person was ever invited to sit with me and worship at the shrine. She didn't worship, actually, she entered the church and then scoffed. It didn't matter than I replayed the clip again and again for Jessica, attempting to convince her of the moment's perfection, pointing out my aggressive approach on the tackle, the way my hit sent Wheeler flying in one direction and the ball in the other. I explained to her how you couldn't cast a better villain than Dez Wheeler, a showboating egomaniac. . . .

"'Egomaniac'?" Jessica cackled. "Can you really call someone else an egomaniac after you've just shown me this clip for the eleventh time? You bow down to a false idol, Nick, and it's called You Winning."

I think back to the day after the shooting. Jessica had invited me over, and I told her I wanted to be alone. And then

Melody invited me on a champagne picnic and I went. Jessica must have seen the photo of Melody and me in the news and figured that she had been lied to. So she came in here and trashed my treasure. Here's to my health indeed.

For some reason, I laugh.

CHAPTER 25

AT LEAST FREDDIE is happy. So I learn when he finally calls in the late afternoon.

"They've given me my own office!" he exclaims. "We're on the twenty-third floor. I can see the statue of William Penn from my window. And I discovered where they keep all the pastries."

That is nice.

"Tell me, Freddie, after you finished sucking the filling out of the jelly doughnuts, did you find out anything about the case?"

"Now that you mention it, I have," Freddie says. "I had a secretary print me out my own copy of the case file. First off, your little detail. The gun used in the shooting was a .308, not a .270." So Uncle Frank and his rifle are in the clear. Which is good. "Also, if you're interested, I saw reports from Alabama police about the alibis of Kaylee Wise and her brothers and cousins. They were all accounted for on the night of the shooting."

That crossed more dark-horse candidates off the list. Although the Wises could know people in Philadelphia who could have acted by proxy, especially with the prospect of Samuel's money in front of them.

"Do you have any idea what Jai's defense strategy is going to be?"

"From what they tell me, until any better ideas come along, their plan is to go after Rizotti. They're going to try to prove that the rifle isn't Jai's and make it seem like Rizotti planted the evidence. You aren't the only one he's told about his admiration for Mark Fuhrman, apparently. They'll try to do to Rizotti what O.J.'s guys did to him."

The plan sounds perfectly ugly. I have known about it for ten seconds, and already I am sick from it. Not that I wouldn't put the worst of human impulses past Rizotti, but it doesn't track as the answer. It seems like the greater motive for planting the rifle in Jai's car belongs to the actual shooter.

I ask Freddie, "Do his lawyers have some list of people who might have a grudge against Jai?"

As I utter the words, I realize that compiling a list of Jai's enemies might take weeks, if not months or years. His personality is such that he can outrage hundreds of people casually, and without knowing it.

For instance, ever since Jai was taken in by police, the cable channel that aired his reality dating show *Give It Up for JC* has been running its eleven hour-long episodes on a never-ending loop. I watched some of it, and the show is even more tasteless than I might have guessed. The topper was the elimination sequence at the end of each episode. The remaining "virgins" competing for Jai's affection—and I agree with Freddie's analysis that the women seemed far more experienced than they claimed to be—all gather in Jai's bedroom, where, clad in bikinis, they await their fate. Jai then selects one of the girls and leads her out onto the balcony. He tells her how beautiful and special she is, and that one day she is going to make some man—perhaps many men—very happy. But not Jai. Not tonight, anyway.

Then Jai ushers the woman to the far side of the balcony and sends her down the waterslide. With a *whoosh* and a splash, her TV moment comes to a close.

I wonder if a woman could get so upset over such humiliation that she would seek revenge. Or maybe an angry dad would—that feels more right. But still, murdering Samuel for the sole purpose of setting up Jai is too extreme to make sense. If you're going to kill someone, why not just go directly after Jai?

And these women knew what they were getting into when they agreed to be on Jai's reality show. Although it's true that most people, when they enter a contest, only imagine themselves winning; the pain of losing can be a complete surprise.

My phone buzzes. I have a new message—from Jessica's husband Dan, of all people. Even though I never answered his first e-mail from days ago.

> Nick, I've been reading about what happened, and I hope you are doing OK. I am still abroad but I will be home soon. I understand this might not be a great time to have dinner, but if there is anything Jessica and I can do to help you in this difficult time, please let us know. Dan.

There is a guy who has a finger on the pulse of his marriage.

I walk to the window, which offers a view of Center City's office buildings at dusk, and try with my fingernail to pick at the residue of *HERE'S TO YOUR HEALTH*. The words, spelled in syrup, have congealed to the point of intransigence. They seem to have grafted completely onto the glass.

Maybe I should just find someplace else to live. Maybe it is time for me to move out of the Jefferson, superstition be damned.

As soon as I think of moving out, I know I should do it. I will wait until after I have beaten back Woodward and my next season is secure. But then I will go. I imagine seeing apartments with a real estate agent, buying my own furniture, and I know that I should have done all that a long time ago.

Speaking of things I should have done a long time ago: I need to pay Jessica a visit.

CHAPTER 26

THE STEAGALLS LIVE in Society Hill, a section of the city well-preserved from the days when Philadelphia was the center of a young and growing country. Many of the brick-facade homes date to the 1800s or even the 1700s and feature signs in their windows boasting of their historical lineage, noting that the original owner was a sailmaker or a merchant or a signer of the Constitution or the engraver of the first U.S. currency.

Jessica's place, which stands on a corner, is a three-story town house with a checkerboard pattern of red and black bricks. It is wider than the other homes on its block, occupying a double plot. Near the curb stands an iron post once used to hitch horses, and rooted by the front steps is a metal wedge for scraping mud from the soles of your boots.

On my first visit here, years ago, Jessica told me that her home had its own storied past. During the Revolutionary era, she said, it was the residence of an early feminist named Joyce DeWitt, who competed with Betsy Ross to create the first American flag. DeWitt's design, a field of bright green surrounded by pink fringe, was rejected by the founding fathers in favor of Ross's stars and stripes. DeWitt was so angry that in her pique she attempted to form an opposition government to carry her flag. In her government, only women would be allowed to vote, hold political office, own property, captain ships, and consume alcohol. DeWitt called her political movement Green Day, Jessica said, which is where the rock band took its name from.

A quick Google search that night at home confirmed what I suspected, which was that Joyce DeWitt is actually the name of an actress on the '70s sitcom *Three's Company*, which now reruns daily on basic cable. In the show, DeWitt's character was the dark-haired "smart one," and her most rebellious act was to trick Mr. Roper into letting two girls have a male roommate, by telling the landlord that he was gay. Green Day's name is in fact a reference to a fondness for marijuana.

It is nearly 10:00 P.M., and Jessica's house is glowing with electricity, a sure sign that her husband Dan hasn't returned from his trip. Jessica likes to keep every light in her house turned on while she is awake. Her husband, as befits an ambitious Fed official moving in a socially aware universe, favors a more environmentally conscious policy toward energy use; when he is home he dims as many lights as he can. Then he goes away and Jessica returns to draining the power grid.

I ring the bell.

"Who is it?" I hear Jessica call from what sounds like a couple of rooms away.

"Norman Fell," I answer, as lightheartedly as I can while shouting through a door. "I've come about the rent."

I hear footsteps approaching, and Jessica opens the door with a dramatic swing. Which is in itself a surprise, because when I visit she usually pulls the door back slowly, shielding herself behind it, lest we be seen together by her neighbors for even a second. She imagines someone might be taking pictures.

But tonight she stands unabashed in the doorway, wearing a loose white tank top that shows off the lean musculature of her arms, and billowy paisley pants. Her black hair is pinned up in a way that accentuates the sleekness of her features—the dark narrow eyes, the high cheeks, the thin aquiline nose that she swore to me had never been worked on.

"Now why in the world would Norman Fell see Joyce De-Witt about the rent?" she sneers. "Mr. Roper would see Janet about the rent. I would call that a subtle difference, but it isn't really that subtle, is it?"

The banter seems light enough in its content, but the energy behind the words is decidedly sharper.

"You're right," I say. "This really isn't about the rent."

She narrows her eyes.

"Did you come here to let me have it?" she says. "This should be *soooo* good." She turns her back to me and walks through an arched foyer into the high-ceilinged living room. I follow her, closing the door behind me. She settles into the corner of a red-and-white-patterned sofa with high armrests. The sofa is flanked by two purple slip-covered chairs. On a wooden end table sits a glass of port, a crystal dish filled with walnuts, and a copy of *InStyle* magazine.

Also on the table is a framed photo of her husband, Dan. In the photo he is wearing a suit and sitting at a table, speaking into a microphone. Dan has a slight build, and is pale and completely bald. "Now I know what Moby would have looked like if he had gone to business school," I joked when I first saw the photo a few years ago. "He is testifying before Congress in that picture," Jessica responded. "Believe it or not, some people might find that more impressive than kicking a football." She could cheat on Dan, but she would not let me run him down in her presence.

"Can I get you something to drink?" Jessica says, though she is deeply nestled into her seat and making no gesture toward moving. "Maybe some white wine? I have a half-open bottle of barely adequate Sancerre in the fridge. You would probably like it. Though it seems that lately you prefer champagne. Or is that only in the afternoon?"

So she did see the photo of Melody and me.

"I should have come by sooner," I say.

"It's fine." Jessica yawns. "I know how busy you've been."

Her line echoes a running joke between us, born from our indolent afternoons together. When one of us proposes a future rendezvous, and the other seems to wonder if that time would work, the other quickly inserts, "I know how busy you are." The joke being that, especially out of football season, neither of us is ever all that busy.

"It seems like you found the time to buy yourself some new clothes," Jessica continues dryly. I am wearing a thin light blue sweater, part of my Boyd's haul. "I suppose it does force you to upgrade your wardrobe, when you know the paparazzi are going to be taking your picture."

I feel like she is baiting me to bring up what she did to my apartment. She wants me to raise the heat.

I cross my legs, spread my arms and lean back in my chair.

"Funny how long we lasted, isn't it," I say. "Three years. It's not something I ever expected."

"I certainly didn't," Jessica says. "Not with the way you talked."

"Talked—about what?" We have never discussed our future, beyond the next date, as far as I can recall.

"You are always going on about how punters don't have any job security," she says. "You make it sound like you could get cut after one bad game."

"I could," I said. Punters and kickers are the easiest players to replace. Take one out, plug in another, and you're ready to go. It's not like we have an entire offense to learn.

"That first summer of our little dalliance, your team signed another punter to compete with you in training camp, that guy, Mallard Fillmore. . . ."

"Phil Mallamore," I correct.

"I know what his name was," she says. "But we called him Mallard Fillmore. You made it sound like he was going to take your job. But he didn't. And then last year it was the Australian . . . What was his name?"

"Liam Menzies."

"Right. You went on for weeks about how appalling it would be to lose out to a man named Liam."

"That was a joke. For your amusement."

"And I'm sure there's some other punter this year that you're all worried about. What's the name this time?"

"Woodward Tolley," I say. "He's the best one yet, actually."

"I'm sure. And I bet you've been obsessing about how the Sentinels will cut you any second now. Am I right?"

"It happens," I say. "All the time."

"But you made it sound like it would happen to you. We've had good-bye sex more times than I can count, but you've never had the courtesy to actually leave."

This conversation isn't getting us anywhere, but at least she is speaking with directness and honesty.

"I want to ask you one question," I say. "And I want you to promise me you'll give an actual answer. No zingers, no deflections, no crazy stories."

The wineglass in one hand, she reaches back with the other and tugs down on her shirt, which has been slipping revealingly in front. "Fine," she says, shoulders square. "One question. Go ahead."

"Thank you," I say. "Ready?"

"Out with it," she says with a taunting swirl of her index finger.

"How come you and Dan haven't had any kids?"

She starts a little and her throat tenses, as if she is choking, and then puts down her wine. Then she stands up and walks out of the room. I hear a door closing, and then no more movement. Ten seconds pass. Twenty seconds. A minute.

She is not coming back. I wonder about leaving, but then decide to wait her out.

I study the painting on the wall opposite my chair. It is one of Jessica's, and it is, by her design, impossible to describe. It looks like there might be a wooden table in the foreground. Below the "table" is what I believe to be a human arm—but I am just guessing, and that is the point. Jessica wants her paintings to instill uncertainty. You can see that some sort of figurative action going on, but it is impossible to identify, because she has made the point of view so close. You would need to zoom out by a few factors to take in the full scene. "That's how most people live their lives," she once explained, tiredly, when I pressed her. "They can't see what's right in front of their faces. Because they're too close to it." At the time I took her answer as a jibe at her husband; now I wonder if she hadn't been talking about me as well.

I hear a flush, and then Jessica returns, striding swiftly. She repositions herself from the sofa to the purple chair opposite mine, and she sits straight up, legs crossed in those billowy paisley pants, retrenched and ready for battle.

"So this is how it is," she says. "For three years, we never talk about anything more personal than the ingredients in your smoothies. And now you want to unearth the secrets of Jessica's cold, dark soul?"

She is talking about herself in the third person. Never a good sign.

"That doesn't answer my question," I say.

"You're not thinking that it's because of you, are you?" she says. "That I haven't had a child with Dan because I'm holding out hope that we can have little baby punters? Is that what you want to hear?"

"No," I say. "It's the last thing I want to hear, actually."

"Fine," she says. She places her hands on her knees, and holds her head high. "Here's the truth. I don't want to have children because I want to put an end to it all. I just don't want things to continue. This is my gift to the world. I am putting an end to it all, or at least I am clipping off my personal branch of the tree. Think globally, act locally . . ."

"What are you talking about?" I say. "What is it that you don't want to continue?"

She shakes her head. "I promised to answer one question," she says. "That's a second, and a third. Please, Nick, for the sake of all that is good and holy, in the name of God and football, let's respect the rules of the game."

She picks up her wine again and resumes drinking, all the while staring me down.

Either Jessica's reason is a dark and difficult one, or she is just being melodramatic and she knows it: she doesn't want to say out loud whatever she is thinking and hear how self-pitying she sounds. She does not want to find out that what she really lacks is not a solution, but courage.

This, after all, is a woman who never attempts to sell her paintings, lest she subject herself to the indignities of the marketplace.

"When is Dan coming home?" I ask, changing tack. Yet another question, but this one she answers.

"Not for a couple days," she says. "He sent me an iPhone photo last night of himself with some minister from Portugal. Want to see?"

She offers the phone but I decline with a wave.

"My idiot husband, he's figuring out a way to save the European economy," she says with a forced smile. "Meanwhile, he doesn't have a clue that I've been taking birth control pills for the past four years."

"He sent me another message today," I say. "I think he's figured out about us."

Jessica shakes her head in disgust. "He hasn't figured anything out, trust me." She unfolds her legs and sips her wine.

"Can we talk about my apartment?" I ask, with almost academic detachment.

"Oh, the apartment," she answers. "I hope you didn't mind." She adds a naughty smirk, as if all she has done is play a prank on me.

"How did you get in?" I say. "I bet it is those damn swipe cards, isn't it?"

She nods. "What else would it have been?" she says. "I'm not the crowbar type. I had an old Jefferson card in my handbag."

"So you go to the front desk . . ."

". . . in a low-cut top with no bra and tell them that my card has been demagnetized. I've been in and out enough. . . ."

". . . that they just assume I gave you one. Very smart."

"Thank you," Jessica says triumphantly. "If you lived in a regular apartment with a lock and key, this never would have happened." I imagine her in my apartment, tossing my clothes, rooting through my refrigerator for bottles to overturn. I wonder if she let her anger show on her face then, if her eyes were aflame, if her movements were suddenly spastic and haphazard rather than graceful and assured.

"How about another favor?" I say.

"What'd you have in mind, Troy?" she says, raising her eyebrows.

In her inviting eyes I see that in spite of what she has done, and all the tension of this evening, we can pick up again right there, just as if nothing has changed, and her vandalism would be shoved away into its compartment, and our clothes would be off in seconds. This episode wouldn't matter at all, except to give fresh confirmation of how little anything matters.

Which sounds good, now that I mention it.

I rise from my chair, walk over to Jessica, remove the wineglass from her hand, and set it on the table. Then I lean down over her chair, slide my index finger gently under her chin, prompting her head to tilt her head back, and I kiss her. Before long I slide my left arm underneath her legs and my right arm around her waist. When I have her secured, I squat down and lift her up. She throws her arms around my neck, and it feels as if the whole of her body is curled into my chest.

I carry her upstairs. It feels like this was my purpose for coming here tonight, I just didn't know it. We arrive at the bedroom and I set her down on top of her crimson comforter. For the first time all night, Jessica's dark eyes relax.

I pull her top off, and then she and I race to remove her bottoms. We remove them together, the pants and her pink cotton panties coming off in one bunch. She falls backward, nude, throwing her arms overhead, waiting for me to settle in on top of her. But I stand up and close the bedroom door. Then I go to the wall switch and flick off the bedroom lights.

From that distance I take in the sight of her lean and shadowy figure. She is lying on her side, the lines of her thin hips and shoulders caught in the dim illumination of the light from the hall seeping under the doorway.

"Get over here," she breathes. "Now."

It is nearly 2:00 A.M. and we are still awake. Jessica lies on her stomach, head turned and resting on her hands, as I sit beside her and run my index and middle fingers slowly up and down her spine. My touch begins as a caress but turns into more of a massage as Jessica urges me to press harder. I groove more deeply with each pass from the top of her neck to the softness of her bottom. Jessica once declared to me, "I want my ass to be as tight as a Coen brothers' movie. Not one of their comedies either. My ass is going to be like *No Country for Old Men*." Jessica goes to the gym at least five times a week, taking yoga, Pilates, kickboxing, Zumba, and whatever else the teachers roll out. And while her bottom is shapely and firm as a result, it is not quite *No Country for Old Men*. Only in a movie can you actually edit out all the looseness.

She closes her eyes. "Have I ever told you about my grand-mother?" she asks quietly.

"I don't think so."

"I don't even know why I asked you that," she says. "Of course I haven't. You would remember if I told you about her. Or at least, I would remember."

"Tell me now," I say. "If you'd like."

Her eyes pop open for a moment and then close again. "Her name is Grace. She's in a home."

"How old is she?"

"Eighty-three. But it's not an old folks' home, it's an insti-tution. She's been in this place for nearly half a century."

"How come?" I stop with the rubbing.

"Don't stop, keep going," she says, and I begin with my fingers again, pressing hard as I trace her vertebrae. "She at-tempted suicide when she was younger. Several times. She would swallow things—detergents, ointments, paints—and then she'd have to be rushed to the hospital. She needed to be watched, and she couldn't be responsible for taking care of a child. My mom was six years old at the time. She had to go live with her aunt and uncle."

She says this quietly, without any great emotion, as if she is telling me that she has a dentist appointment tomorrow.

"She's getting the best care. New England's finest families send all their crazies there. I go up every year with my mom and dad for Christmas, and on Grace's birthday in April. It's in western Massachusetts, on a beautiful piece of real estate— seventy acres, and with a wooded walking path and a stream. For her birthday, if the weather's right, we'll do a picnic and pass around bread and jams and cheeses. If you saw a picture of it, you'd have no idea anything is wrong with any of us."

"Sounds like a nice place," I say. "If you're going to be somewhere like that."

"You've seen it, sort of. That cluster of paintings in the downstairs hallway, they were all done on the property."

Jessica is referring to four small paintings that hang together in a grid. The paintings depict the same view of a path leading into the woods, in the four seasons of the year, all with wild and intense color. The winter view uses vivid whites and blues and blacks to impart a feeling of violent chill. In spring, the budding trees are cut through with a harsh sunrise. Summer is an overripe, suffocating green. In the fall, the leaves have gone red and orange and yellow; the forest looks as if it is on fire.

"You did those?" I ask with surprise. The paintings are very good, but not in her style. I wonder if she painted them when she was younger and didn't have such an aversion to straightforward representation.

"They're not mine. Grace did those," Jessica says, and lifts her head up briefly to turn to the other side. "She's a painter, too."

Right then I see it—not just what Jessica wanted to put an end to, but why Jessica and I have been together so long, why we fit so well together. We are more than just two underutilized people with plenty of free time.

I have told Jessica that my father has died in a car crash, but I never told her that I believe, to some degree at least, he died by choice.

I let a good five minutes pass in silence, trying to select a place to begin, before I realize that Jessica has fallen asleep.

I slowly lift my left knee across her body and ease myself down on the other side of the bed. In three years we have never actually spent an overnight together. Most often we see each other in the afternoon. But if it is at night, one of us always goes home.

Tonight I slide under the sheets, turn on my side, facing away from her, and I pass out within minutes.

CHAPTER 27

THE NEXT MORNING, there we are. Jessica and I sit at an antique wooden breakfast table stationed by a window looking out on her small but densely planted backyard flower garden. We eat bowls of bran flakes with slices of banana, like we are the most normal couple in the world. Still, though, I have not said anything to Jessica about what I began thinking of before I fell asleep. My hesitation now, in the cool light of day, is that if I explain to her exactly how much we have in common, it might deepen our relationship in a way that will lead to trouble. Because if she and I take a giant step forward together, we will bump into her husband. And what then?

"Can I tell you something funny?" Jessica says, setting her spoon down in her bowl.

"You've done it before."

"A couple days ago I was visited by a police detective—this tawdry lump of a man . . ."

"Rizotti?"

"Yes!"

I wipe a dribble of soy milk from the corner of my mouth. "He's the clod who questioned me the night of the shooting."

"Isn't he something?" she says, spooning honey into her tea. "I still think you can see the stains on the carpet from where he drooled when he was pretending not to ogle me. Anyway, he has printouts of all your text messages. . . ."

"Fuck," I say.

"Fuck indeed," Jessica says. "So naturally he wanted to know all about our relationship."

"What did you tell him?"

"That I met you a few years ago, and that you pose for me as a model every now and then," she says. This is true. "I even showed him the drawings. I have to tell you, Nick . . ."

"Yes?"

"He looked at them rather longingly." She smiles, delighted, as she cradles her mug.

"Oh my," I say. "I'm surprised this hasn't ended up in the papers."

"I told the good detective what my dear old hubby does for a living, how closely he works with the Treasury Department—which includes the FBI," Jessica says. "I suggested to him that his discretion would be appreciated. And his indiscretion would most certainly not be."

"I wonder how many people have seen those messages," I say. Even if Rizotti hasn't leaked them to the press, they are surely floating around the police department. And the district attorney's office.

And Jai's defense team would have access to them as well. Which means Freddie is seeing them. I can imagine him sitting at a desk, mouth full of cruller, calling in anyone who passes by his door to come check out my texts. *Hey, I know this guy!*

Of course, if Freddie has access to my phone records, he would also have access to everyone else's involved in the case.

I shoot Freddie a note.

> Do you guys have the same phone records the police have?

> We do. Reams of them.

> Can you e-mail them to me?

"Who are you texting?" Jessica says.

"Freddie," I tell her.

"The drug addict?" Jessica says. Apparently the stories I've told her about Freddie haven't left a great impression. "What's he up to now?"

"Did I ever tell you he has a law degree? He's working with the Jai Carson defense team."

"That's weird," she says. She rises and takes her bowl to the sink, her bare feet scuffling along the floor tile.

Freddie replies.

> Check your e-mail. 512 pages of phone records. Enjoy your vacation.

"So I think I'm going to go to the gym," Jessica says as my prompt to leave.

"Do you mind if I hang out here and use your computer?" I ask.

She turns, looking as if I'd just asked her to do long division in her head.

"Dan's still away, right?" I ask.

"Sure," she says, a small smile forming. "Hang out as long as you like." She walks up behind me, places her thin hands on my shoulders and kisses my ear. "I'll probably go to Whole Foods after the gym. Text me if there's anything you want."

Jessica sets me up in the bedroom and logs me into her laptop. She leaves for the gym and I poke around the documents Freddie has sent.

My first thought at reviewing these phone records is that it's frightening how deeply law enforcement can delve into people's lives. My call and text records are there, as are Jai's, as are Cheat Sheet's and Too Big's. They have also collected the phone and text records of several Stark's employees—including "Melody," aka Alice.

I can't help but start with Alice's records. I look at the date of the shootings, beginning at around 8:15 P.M., the time that Samuel and Cecil and I arrived at Stark's. She sent a text to a number with an area code 240 that she hadn't called at any time prior to that. *Here now.* This must be the text she has told me about, the one that alerted that homeless-looking man about Samuel's arrival at Stark's.

She called the same 240 number the next morning. According to her story, this was when she tried to reach him and his number wasn't working.

Except they talked for eleven minutes.

Then she called the 240 number again later that afternoon, for three minutes. I take out my phone and pull up my call log and see that Alice dialed that number just before she texted me to set up our champagne picnic. She called the 240 number again early that same evening, after I dropped her off at home. That call lasted six minutes.

She called again the day Jai was arrested, at around 3:30 in the afternoon. I go onto Jai's Twitter account and trail back in the posts. Her last call to the number was just after Jai tweeted his dinner plans. Just in case the killer hadn't seen already.

I dial the mystery 240 number.

Beep-beep-beeeeep. This number is no longer in service.

I Google the 240 area code and find that it serves central and western Maryland. I find another page that lists the towns covered by the area code. One of the towns is Hartsburg, which clicks with a tab in my memory. I have seen the name Hartsburg recently, I am sure of it.

I search for "Hartsburg" and scan the results. Hartsburg Chamber of Commerce, Hartsburg High School, Hartsburg Historical District, Hartsburg Police Department, Hartsburg Airport, State Farm Insurance of Hartsburg, Hartsburg Hyenas.

The Hartsburg Hyenas. Luke Reckherd's last team.

I click on the Hyenas link and up comes their Web page.

At the top of the page is the team logo: a small hyena, howling up at the moon. A giant, grinning quarter moon.

CHAPTER 28

FROM THE GRINNING moon, the same one I saw on the bumper sticker on the back of the shooter's car, my mind bounces to another image: Luke Reckherd at Samuel's funeral, in his white suit and shaved head, bobbing in prayer.

I text Aaron, asking him to run a search on Luke Reckherd to see if he has any criminal history. He answers my text with a phone call.

"So you don't think Jai Carson is the killer," Aaron says.

"What do you mean?"

"I can Google, too," he says. "I saw that Luke Reckherd was one of the guys injured by Samuel Sault. And that his whereabouts on the night of the killing were unaccounted for, at least according to one hastily written news story. What are you up to, Nick? Forget that question—I know what you're up to. Tell me, if you discover anything about the shooter, what are you going to do about it?"

"Give the information to Jai's lawyers," I say. I am sure I will get around to telling Freddie about this sooner or later.

"I doubt Jai's lawyers need your help," he says.

"Aaron, one teammate of mine is dead, and another is being falsely accused. And my agent just had his guts shot up. You remember what it is like to be part of a team, don't you?"

The line goes quiet and then I hear Aaron exhale heavily. "This is the last request I'm helping you with."

"Thank you."

Twenty minutes later, he calls me back.

"Luke Reckherd has three arrests on his record," Aaron said. "Two for possession of marijuana, misdemeanor level. The other is for aggravated assault, but the charge was dropped."

"What is the aggravated assault charge about?"

"Aggravated assault means he attacked someone with a weapon," Aaron says. "In this case, the weapon was a giant inflatable banana."

"A what?"

"Inflatable banana. He was messing around at a party. Somehow he managed to swing an inflatable banana hard enough to break some kid's nose."

I chuckle, and then regret it. "Anything else?"

"Luke doesn't have a permit for a weapon," Aaron says. "But his dad does. Willie Reckherd has a permit for a hunting rifle." Hmm. So Aaron has gone beyond the scope of his assignment, rather than just doing the minimum requested. And he has discovered that proud papa has a gun. Which means that if Luke Reckherd was living at home, he could easily grab a weapon and run out the door.

"Thanks, Aaron," I say. "I appreciate it."

"Promise me you're not going to put yourself in a dangerous situation," Aaron says. "You need to be careful when there are guns involved. Trust me on this."

"Don't worry," I say. "I'm not going to take any unnecessary risks." I choose that last phrase carefully. Because who knows what I might decide is necessary before this is all over.

"Has your mother ever told you why I quit the police force?"

"No," I say. "She hasn't."

He inhales deeply. "I shot someone. Shot him dead. He was nineteen years old." He pauses. "He had a gun, and he shot my partner with it, and he was aiming at me next.

"It was a justified killing. Couldn't have been more justified. Still, this shooter just was a kid with mental health problems—turned out he wasn't taking his meds, and he wanted to die, but he didn't have it in him to shoot himself. So I had to fire a bullet into his head." I hear a sniffle on his end. "I handed in my badge when I realized I didn't ever want to be in that position again."

"Wow," I say. "I'm sorry you had to go through that."

"Me, too," Aaron says. "But the point is, sometimes you can't know what you're getting into until after you're already in it. You don't want to learn that one the hard way."

* * *

By the time Jessica returns from the gym and Whole Foods, I have formed, if not exactly a plan, at least the outline of one.

"Want to go on a trip together?" I ask after I help put away the groceries.

"Where did you have in mind?"

"Maryland," I say.

"Baltimore? That could be fun. Crabs are in season."

"I was thinking more toward the western part of the state. There's a town called Hartsburg I want to go to."

"How wonderful," she says with false cheer, setting a package of pita bread on the counter. "Hartsburg is on my bucket list. After Cape Town and Angkor Wat, of course."

"I have to go there, tonight," I say. "If you want to stay here, I understand. I mean . . . I know how busy you are."

CHAPTER 29

As WE DRIVE west on the Interstate, Jessica takes control of the car radio, dialing in soft rock from the eighties. She "ooohs" when she lands on REO Speedwagon's "Can't Fight This Feelin'."

"What are the odds of me ever improving your musical tastes?" I ask.

"About the same as me ever improving yours."

We roll on, locked into this station, and soon Hall and Oates remind us that private eyes (clap-clap) are watching you (clap-clap), watching your every move (ooh baby).

"Eighties music is what brought Dan and I together," Jessica says, curled down in the seat, her bare feet crossed and resting on the dash. "I was at Smith, he was getting his MBA at Harvard, and he showed up at a party at my house. My roommates put me in charge of the stereo, and he came over to compliment me on playing the greatest song ever."

"Which was . . . ?"

"Madonna," she says. " 'Crazy for You.' "

Fair enough. At least it wasn't the Smiths.

"Now, here's the bigger question," I say. "Did he really like the song? Or was he just complimenting you because he saw you from across a crowded room. . . ."

"Crowded room," Jessica says decisively. "Why else would a Harvard MBA student come to a Smith party? On the other hand, he still does listen to eighties music. If he's going out, his getting-dressed song is 'Don't Stop Believin'.' "

"Did he get that from the last episode of *The Sopranos*?"

"From *Glee*, actually," Jessica says with a small laugh.

Cool.

"Speaking of Dan," I say. "Why is he inviting me to dinner? Are you sure he doesn't know about us?"

Jessica sighs. "Yes, one hundred percent," she says, sounding mildly disappointed. "He was looking through one of my sketchbooks, which is how your name came up. But I told him you're just a model, same as I told that detective. Dan made a brief show of acting jealous, but then he let it go. It's not like I don't draw other models, male and female. I'm pretty sure he picked up the sketchbook because he was hoping to see a naked woman."

She pauses, and then adds, "He was actually very impressed that I knew a real live Philadelphia Sentinel. Hence the dinner invitation. He's a football fan, unfortunately."

Our first stop in Hartsburg is a Rite Aid, where I buy Jessica the props she will need—a pad and a pen. Then we drive on to the Hartsburg War Memorial Coliseum, a classically styled five-thousand-seat arena that looks like it was built in the 1950s, when the city of about a hundred thousand people expected that the circus would always be coming to town. Tonight the parking lot is a third full, for a game at the end of the Hyenas' season.

"I'll wait out here," I say to Jessica. "Someone may recognize me if I go in with you."

"Recognize you?" Jessica says, eyebrows raised. "We're full of ourselves lately, aren't we?"

"After the game just try to talk to the Hyenas' coach. His name is Randy Hillock." Not that the name would mean anything to Jessica, but Randy Hillock played safety on a couple of championship teams in the early nineties. "Tell him you're a reporter doing a story on the players Samuel Sault injured, and you need help finding Luke Reckherd."

"Can I tell them I'm with *GQ*?" she says, excited by the notion. "I see sports stories in there sometimes."

"Knock yourself out."

"It'll be perfect. If I'm from *GQ* it will explain why I don't seem like a typical sports reporter."

"Brilliant choice. You're wonderful. Now go."

She gets out of the car, studiously checks her appearance in the reflection of the passenger side window, straightens her skirt, and walks confidently, pad and pen in hand. My stomach does a flip as she disappears inside the arena.

The game had started at 7:00 P.M., and it is now nine. These arena games are designed not to test a fan's attention span. I imagine the crowd will be spilling out before too long.

Sitting alone in a parking lot, I search the local radio stations. I bounce from country to pop to talk before giving up and turning the radio off. I think back to Luke Reckherd at the funeral, in that white suit, praying long after the service was over. I wonder if this tall and strange athlete, confronted with his misdeeds, would see the virtue of peaceful surrender.

I am beginning to sweat just sitting here. I step out of the car, hoping some fresh air will settle me down. But almost immediately I kneel down and vomit half-digested pita and baba ghanoush onto the cement stanchion of the light pole. The first heave is tentative, the next two thunderous.

My throat burning and my eyes watering, I stand up and look around, but no one is there to notice, which is good. I don't need anyone coming over to help, and this is not a big deal. I have thrown up before a game more than once—I did it before my one playoff game, actually, and that went fine. I tell myself it is good that I have gotten this out of the way. Better now than later, wherever this night goes.

Sweat drying on my face, I look up in the sky. The moon is a couple days past full, on its way back down again.

Soon a large goateed man emerges from the arena's loading ramp, with a collie close at his heel. The man carries a black shoulder bag with the words K9 SHOWTIME on it in neon yellow. I am guessing that the bag contained Frisbees, and that this man's job is to run onto the field with his dog and hold the fans' interest during play stoppages. If his night is done, this means the game will soon be over.

And it is. Minutes later the masses, such as they are, begin streaming from the arena's wide banks of doors and down the steps to the parking lot. The crowd includes many boys in pee-wee league uniforms and shoulder pads, carrying helmets and walking with their parents. My guess: these kids played on the field as the half-time entertainment. This would be smart community relations for the Hyenas, and a way to fill the seats with these kids' parents and siblings.

A half hour later, after the parking lot has emptied, Jessica comes up the same ramp as the dog act. She looks around for my car, finds it, and waves enthusiastically. She has something, I can see it in her step.

"It's amazing how people just start telling you things when you have a notepad in your hand," Jessica says after she gets in the car. "The coach hasn't talked to Luke since he cut him, but he heard something about him going to work at his dad's restaurant. In a town called Berry, which is just down the road."

"Good," I say. I have already read about the restaurant and I have the address.

"If Luke is there," Jessica asks, clutching her pad, "do I keep up my reporter disguise and ask him where he was on the night of the shooting? That's too blunt, right?"

"Probably," I say. "For now, let's just go there, have something to eat, and see what happens."

"What if we learn something important? Is that when we call someone else in?"

I start the engine. "We'll figure that out as we go."

"But what if we're face-to-face with this killer, and we know it and he knows it? What happens then?" She sounds more curious than concerned.

"I'll perform," I say. "It's what I do." Even as the words escape my mouth, I wish I could pull them back. They feel like an invitation to bad luck.

She clucks her tongue and says, "You do realize this performance won't involve punting a football, right?"

To drive to Berry we have to backtrack east a couple exits on the Interstate. The restaurant is called Wee Willie's Rib Revue, and the food is supposed to be good. In my research on Luke I came across a "Where Are They Now?" story from a few years ago about the place. The story claimed that Willie not only owned the place but worked several days a week as a manager. A photo showed him bald-headed and resplendent among a sea of patrons.

The story also included a video clip, filmed at the restaurant, which showed Willie's legendary ambidexterity in action. A slab of ribs was laid before the former quarterback, a broad-shouldered man with slits for eyes and a cherubic smile. Holding a meat cleaver in each hand, Willie chopped away at the ribs rapid-fire until they were transformed into a pile of dismembered meat and bone. The patrons in the background cheered the display as Willie raised the sauce-soaked cleavers triumphantly into the air.

The restaurant is down the road from a string of shopping centers just outside Berry's modest downtown. The story I read boasted of a surging business in which patrons were waiting for tables; tonight, the parking lot is maybe a quarter full, and this is a Friday night.

"Quite the happening spot," Jessica says dryly.

"It's okay. We're not here for the baby backs."

Wee Willie's Rib Revue has, if nothing else, a distinctive sign. Above the Wee Willie name is an image of a quarterback with both arms raised and a football alternately lighting up in his right or left hand. To be an ambidextrous quarterback is truly impressive. I remembered all the time I spent in high school, training my right arm to make every throw on the field. Willie would have had to put in twice the work I did.

The entry area of the restaurant is decorated with five framed Wee Willie jerseys—one each from high school and college and then three from the pros. Which surprised me. I knew Willie played for Baltimore, but according to the placards underneath the jerseys, after five seasons there he spent a year each in Kansas City and Detroit.

The college jersey of Luke Reckherd also hangs on the wall. According to the placard, Willie's #6 was unretired by Langston University so his son could wear it, too. Willie's old Langston jersey is plain dark blue with an orange number, while his son's modern #6 features orange piping on the sleeves and shoulders. No one can leave well enough alone.

The restaurant is brightly lit, and its red-and-white-checked tablecloths glisten with reflected light, as does the brass rail on the bar. It is as if they were tipped off a couple of days ago to a visit from the health inspector.

So much preparation for so few customers. The nausea returning, I look around for Luke or Willie, but I don't see either.

"Two for the bar," Jessica says to the hostess, a young woman with a dour smile.

"No problem," she says, grabbing two menus. "Follow me."

She walks us to the bar and, after we sit, places the menus precisely in front of Jessica and I, as if centering menus is an art in which she has been carefully trained.

"A server will be right with you," she says. "Enjoy your meal."

The bartender, a middle-aged woman with blown-out dark hair and blush generously applied to her cheeks, peels her attention away from the basketball game on the television and ambles our way.

"Welcome," she says. This is Brenda, according to her name tag. "Can I get you anything?"

"Just some wings for now," Jessica says.

"Anything to drink?"

"I'll have a Stella," Jessica says.

"Club soda for me," I say. "With lime."

The waitress pours our drinks and punches the food order into the bar computer. Then she has nothing else to do. The lack of customers is going to be our friend.

"Excuse me, Brenda," I say, calling her back.

She returns, with an uneven gait that suggests a chronic hip injury. "Something else I can help you with?"

"Just a question," I say. "Do you know if Wee Willie is going to be in tonight?"

"I'm not sure," she says, her smile sagging. "He'll stop by every now and then, but his business partner handles most of the operations."

That story I read claimed that Willie was here most nights. But then, it surely isn't the first time a reporter has been misled in the quest for free publicity.

"So what does Willie do with himself these days?" I ask.

"What do you mean?" she asks.

"How does he spend his time," I say, "if he's not here?"

"Why do you want to know that?" she says, drawing back. I haven't even gotten to inquiring about Luke yet.

"My boyfriend here used to play quarterback in high school," Jessica interjects. "But he couldn't cut it in college. Broke his heart."

Brenda manages to smile sympathetically, as if this is a real problem. "What do you do now?" she asks.

"He's a fitness instructor," Jessica answers. "But he pines for the old days. He wonders what his life would be like if he had actually made it as a quarterback."

Brenda shrugs her broad shoulders. "If you're a fitness instructor," she says, "I say, thank God and don't look back. You can do that for years. Football, you have to pray for your health. Look at Willie's boy Luke. Back in high school, they said he had a million-dollar arm, and then he got hurt and he's done at age twenty-three."

Under the bar I give Jessica's thigh a grateful squeeze.

"What's Luke up to these days?" I say.

Brenda shrugs again. "Beats me."

"This is a beautiful restaurant," Jessica says. "He should be working here."

Brenda shakes her head. "Not his thing. Willie thought Luke might join the business, and even brought him by about a month ago for dinner. But Luke wouldn't eat anything on the menu. He ended up having a bowl of rice without any gravy in it, and plain steamed carrots."

"Luke is a vegetarian?" Jessica asks, as if she finds the notion hilarious.

"He's a vegan, I think," Brenda says. "Whatever he is, it was news to his dad."

I notice a mid-thirtyish African American man with a shaved head approach the bar. He is wearing a navy-blue shirt and a black vest with black pants that distinguishes his uniform from the regular staff, and his name tag is gold, whereas the others are black. He is stocking the bar's cooler with fresh beer bottles, but he also appears to be monitoring our conversation.

"So is Luke still kicking around Berry?" Jessica asks.

"Brenda!" the man says. "Could you bring some Bud Light from the stockroom, please? I'll cover the bar."

Brenda hobbles into the back. The man, whose name tag reads Gordon, stands before Jessica and me.

"I'm the manager here," Gordon says. "Can I help you folks with anything tonight?"

"Nope," I say. "Think we're good."

"I bet you all are from out of town," he says.

"That we are," I say.

"Whereabouts?"

I hesitate. Philadelphia seems like too revealing an answer.

"Philadelphia," Jessica says.

"Really?" Gordon stiffens a little. "Our ribs are good, but that's a long way to come."

He wears a plastic smile now, and he is studying my face.

"We're just road-tripping," I say. "I'm a big football fan. This is our first stop on a pigskin odyssey."

"Going to Canton?" Gordon asks.

"Oh, yes," I say. "That's our end destination. This'll be my second time there." I have in fact visited the Hall of Fame once, with Cecil. It's only a half-hour drive from his home. "Let's face it, Nick," Cecil kidded me that day. "The only way you're getting into the Hall of Fame is if you buy a ticket." As of 2009, no punter has ever been elected to the Hall of Fame; it is the only position in football without a single player enshrined.

"It's a great experience," Gordon says. "All that history."

"Eleven businessmen get together in 1920 in an auto showroom and decide to form a professional football league," I say. "And now every fall . . ."

". . . a nation of men becomes completely boring," say Jessica with a cheeky smile. She rests her hand on my bicep. "But I indulge him. It's funny what love will make you do."

"Enjoy your trip," Gordon says with a slap on the bar. "And let me know if I can help you with anything."

"Will do," I say.

As soon as Gordon walks away, I pinch Jessica hard on the arm for the Philadelphia slip-up.

"Ouch!" she says. "What's that for—saying I loved you? Easy, Nick. I'm just playing a part."

I want to explain, but Brenda is back with our wings, which are arrayed like flower petals around the edges of a yellow plate, with evenly cut strips of celery and carrots placed between them.

"Let me know if you need anything else," she says. And she quickly moves to the other end of the bar.

Jessica and I each pick up a wing, and I eat, despite some lingering nausea. The sauce is light but has a kick. I rarely eat wings because they are deep-fried, but tonight I have a second. And a third.

"You know what the most interesting thing we've learned so far is?" Jessica asks, whispering conspiratorially.

"What's that?"

"Luke is a vegan. Here, in Berry. We're pretty much in Appalachia, right?"

I see her point. "I wonder where he might go to feel catered to," I say. "There can't be too many options."

"I'll ask those ladies over there," she says.

Jessica picks up her Stella and heads toward two tanned bottle-blondes in jean shorts and white T-shirts. They look as if they are still drawing their fashion cues from early Britney Spears.

I hope Jessica will be quick with these women. I feel like we are inching closer to something, but I worry about the smallness of this town in which we are asking questions. It is about the size of where I grew up, and I know how news can sprint from one end of town to the other.

The women seem initially confused by Jessica's visit to their table, but within seconds they invite her to sit down. Soon they are all looking at me and suppressing giggles. Even with their laughter partially stifled, they are making enough noise to stand out among the dining room's thin population. I can see that Gordon, who has now positioned himself near the door, is taking notice.

Soon Jessica is back with me.

"Mike's Lube," she says. "According to Brianna and Madison over there, it's where all the alternative types congregate, and its menu is all, as they put it, weird vegan shit."

"How'd you win them over?"

"Once I explained to them that you are my fitness instructor cousin who recently realized he was gay and wanted to go on a road trip to experiment with his sexuality outside his hometown, they were more than ready to pitch in."

I am annoyed, and not because of the gay reference. Jessica's explanation is inconsistent with what we told manager Gordon, should he decide to ask those girls what Jessica talked to them about.

"Mike's Lube," I say. "Let's go. Now." I toss a twenty-dollar bill on the bar and quickly strip one last chicken wing of its flesh, even though I can already feel the grease from those first three wings roiling up in my digestive tract.

Mike's Lube is maybe ten minutes from Wee Willie's, on an old two-lane state road leading out to the countryside. It is a former quickie oil-change place that has been transformed into a coffeehouse and lounge. The big sign still says MIKE'S LUBE, but the marquee lettering underneath—which once might have carried a message such as PENNZOIL $19.99—now simply reads MIKE'S GONE.

The lighting scheme is orange and purple and the former lube shop's garage doors are rolled all the way up, giving the club a tropical, open-air vibe. Couches and chairs are set up both inside and along the building's perimeter. It feels like an alternate reality from the rest of Hartsburg. As Jessica and I walk toward the entrance on this warm night, she clasps my hand, her fingers cool as they interlace with mine.

Inside, the pit where mechanics once worked on cars from underneath has been converted into a subterranean DJ booth; a wiry, pale, and shirtless man with a tattooed chest spins low-key electronica. In the lube shop's former waiting room is a café.

I look at the crowd, such as it is. Maybe eighteen people. Most are young. I see two fortyish women and a man who are together, but everyone else looks under thirty, probably under twenty-five. They wear T-shirts and plaid flannels and ripped jeans; if this group took its collective wardrobe to a secondhand shop, they'd be lucky to get twenty bucks for it.

It's funny. In the locker room, I can imagine myself to be a fringe figure, the alternative. Then I walk into a place like this and I feel like G.I. Joe.

"This is surprising, at least," Jessica says.

"Don't say I never take you anywhere," I say. "Find us a seat. I'll get us some food."

I head back to the café counter. The menu, written on an old whiteboard in green marker, includes vegetarian sand-wiches, tabbouleh salad, bean salad, cookies, and popcorn topped with nutritional yeast. For beverages they sell coffee, tea, juice smoothies, and natural sodas, but no booze. Leaflets pinned to the wall advertise crystal healing, massage, guitar lessons, and hand-crafted jewelry.

The counter is attended by a muscular young woman with pug-like features and black hair with a thin blond streak. She is wearing the T-shirt of a band called Ariel Pink's Haunted Graffiti.

"It's my first time here," I say to her. "What do you recommend?"

"The kava tea is one of our most popular items," she says. "We blend it ourselves."

"I'll have that, then," I say. "And to eat . . ." I re-scan their menu. "How about two peanut butter and jelly sandwiches?"

"Great choice," she says. "Those come with our homemade raw-food carrot cookies."

"What's a raw-food cookie?"

"It's made through dehydration," she says. "It never goes in an oven."

Hmm. So they are ridding the world of the scourge of oven-baked cookies.

As the woman makes the sandwiches I ask, as casually as possible: "Say, does Luke Reckherd ever drop in? Someone over at his dad's place told me he hangs out here."

She pauses, her knife in the jelly jar.

"Who wants to know?" she says.

"I'm a football fan," I say.

"Ugh," she says. "I hate football. What do you like most about it—the violence or the boredom?"

"The boredom," I say.

"I once read this book, by a very good female athlete," she says, putting down her knife. "The book was called *The Stronger Women Get, the More Men Love Football*. The author said that men are so into football nowadays because it's their last refuge. A woman can do pretty much every job a man can, and they can play every sport a man does—except football. So men cling to it because it's the last place where quote-unquote manliness still matters."

"Women actually can play football professionally," I say. "If you count lingerie leagues."

Her dark eyes bore in on me.

"But the book sounds interesting," I say. "I'll check it out."

She finishes her construction of two thin sandwiches and deposits a dehydrated cookie onto each plate. The brownish-orange disks land with a thud.

"Enjoy," she says curtly. "Peace."

I carry the teapot and our plates to Jessica, who has located us on a set of facing armchairs with a checkerboard tile table between them. Jessica's face is lit with a purple glow, her eyes cast to the distance. She looks both impatient and Wiccan.

"Any luck?" Jessica asks as I sit. The seat of my armchair is lumpy, and I would guess this piece of furniture spent a couple of decades in someone's basement before making its way here.

"I think Luke does come here," I say. I look back at the counter, where the woman who made our sandwiches is now eyeing me through the glass. "But only because of the way the counter woman clammed up when I mentioned his name."

I scope the club. Despite the languid beats of the electronica and the slouched postures of the tea-drinking customers, I feel like the people here will not be easy to chat up. We have inadvertently infiltrated a closed society, and such societies tend to guard against outsiders. It would be as if a friend of the team accountant sauntered into the Sentinels' locker room, and asked me if I could tell him, just between us, which players are on human growth hormone.

But we are here, and we came to try. I look around the room for a promising candidate. The DJ has a small placard announcing that we are listening to the sound styles of MC Lovelife.

"How about him?" I say to Jessica.

She pulls out her iPhone and does a search on Mr. Lovelife. She scrolls through a couple screens and says, "I can work with this."

Jessica saunters over to the DJ, a little sway in her hips, and she waves and smiles at him as she approaches. The scrawny young man looks confused but still welcomes this woman in the tight skirt and sleeveless top as she kneels down to speak to him. At first I see only one-word answers but Jessica keeps at him, touches his bony elbow, and before long his words begin to flow.

His mind is only half on her, though, and half on the music. Every now and then, his attention shifts to his laptop and Jessica has to wait while he fiddles with his beat files. From out of the darkness, I see another car pull into the parking lot, a dark sedan, and I watch to see who gets out. It is two women in their early twenties, with lean builds and hair not much longer than your average Marine. Meanwhile, Jessica continues to wait. This is all taking too long, I can feel it.

I taste the kava tea. It is dull and bitter. I bite into the raw vegan cookie. It is hard against my incisor, and I put the cookie down. I do not need to chip a tooth eating something I never wanted in the first place. I wish this place had Oreos. I wish I could eat an Oreo without feeling like the fate of the universe was at stake.

I consider the customers at Mike's Lube. It is tempting to slap the "weirdo" label on many of these people but they seem, if nothing else, relaxed. I would guess that many, if not all, of them survived horrible upbringings and difficult childhoods. But they made it here, and they seem happy about it. I could use a place like this for myself, back in Philadelphia. The closest I have to that right now is my workplace—which is the reverse of how it should be. Maybe I needed to join a rowing club.

Or find a bar and take up drinking.

Jessica returns to me. "Just to warn you," she says as she sits down, "we may be hit with some autograph requests."

"Why?" I say. "Did you tell him who I was?"

"Like that would lead to autograph requests?" She smirks. "I told our DJ friend that I am the bass player for the Cherry Bangers. I reminded him that he and I met at the Ocean Grove New Music Festival last year."

It is my cue to ask her if she found out anything about Luke Reckherd. But I say nothing.

"You were right," Jessica volunteers. "Luke Reckherd does come here. But the DJ hasn't seen him in at least a couple weeks."

I breathe deeply and process this information. "So, Luke hasn't been here since Samuel was shot."

"The DJ also said that he thinks Luke is living with his dad," Jessica says.

"Sounds like this guy really opened up to you," I say.

"I think it's the first time in ages he's seen a woman wearing makeup."

"You are a wonder," I say. "We should get out of here."

"Where are we going—to Luke's father's house?"

I don't answer. I don't know.

"Or do you mean we're going back to Philadelphia?" Jessica asks, leaning back in her chair. Her body language suggests she is not quite ready for this to end.

Though now that Jessica has mentioned going home, the thought is inviting. I could share what I've learned with Jai's legal team, and let them take it from here. We are getting close to something here in Berry, and it isn't like me to leave a job partway done. But maybe I should try quitting and see what it feels like.

My phone tells me it's 10:09. Just past my old high school curfew.

"Let's go to one of those hotels by the Interstate," I say. We may end up going home tomorrow morning, but I want to see how I feel when I wake up. More than once I have lost motivation at night only to find it afresh the next morning.

"What are these, anyway?" Jessica asks, taking the cookie from my hand.

"A bad idea," I say. "Let's go."

Jessica picks the peanut butter and jelly sandwich off the plate and takes a bite as we walk to the car. The sound of the drumbeat fades enough for me to notice a faint but persistent chorus of crickets from the countryside. I stand by my car for a few seconds—the drum and the crickets seem to be making music with each other in a cheeky call and response—but then MC Lovelife ups the tempo and the moment is over. I get in the car and Jessica follows.

"At some point," I say to Jessica, "we need to talk about us."

"Us?" Jessica asks, her mouth gummed up with peanut butter.

"Yes," I say. "We're not going to get all the way into it at this point in the evening, but the basic topic of discussion will be this: I don't think we should go on as we have been."

Jessica studies me with a furrowed brow. "Do you want to break up?" she asks, sounding like she is more curious than offended.

"I'm not saying that."

"Do you want me to leave my husband?" The words come out of her mouth with surprising ease.

"I'm not saying that either," I say, and then I add, "But it should be one or the other. That's what we should figure out together."

Jessica considers this for a moment, swallowing down the last remnants of sandwich from her mouth before asking, "Can we make a game of it?"

"A game?"

"Let's each write what we want to do on a piece of paper. If they match, we'll just go from there, and we won't have to say another word about it." She is sitting straight up, her eyes alive. "We'll do it tomorrow morning, over our complimentary continental breakfast. You slide your paper across the table, I'll slide mine. Let's have whatever this is between us come down to one moment. Good?"

"Good," I say. "No matter what happens, let's not spend hours and hours talking about our relationship and the future and what's going to become of us."

"Absolutely. I couldn't agree more."

After pulling out from Mike's Lube, I notice the headlights of a car behind us, hanging close on an otherwise empty road. It follows us through a turn.

After the car follows us through a second turn, I point it out to Jessica.

"The driver is probably headed toward the Interstate, just like we are," she says, though she swivels and looks. "I imagine the road out of town is a popular one."

But I take another turn, and the trailing car does the same.

"See," I say to Jessica. "He's staying right behind us."

She yawns.

"Well, Magnum P.I., I guess you better try to lose him."

I turn left, deviating off our path toward the Interstate, and the car behind us follows. Then I go right on the first street I come to, planning to take another right to reconnect with our original route. But the road curls left and carries us away from civilization, as it narrows and heads into the woods.

I don't know where I am going, and the car is still behind me.

We disappear into the tall trees, and I have no place to turn around. Now the headlights aren't just following; they are closing in. Meanwhile, the road is one curve after another.

"Jeez, he's really on your tail," Jessica says, sitting up.

"Thanks for the update," I say.

The trailing car now veers across the double-yellow lines and speeds up so it is alongside me. He noses ahead of my Audi and swerves hard right, cutting me off. As he does this, I catch a glimpse of the driver: it is a man, he is bald, his mouth wide open in delight.

I brake hard and swerve. So does he.

My Audi screeches sideways. Jessica screams, and I brace for impact as we go off the road.

Instead, we skid into a leafy clearing just off the road and brush up against some low bushes, cushioning us from the trees beyond. The other driver comes to a stop alongside us, blocking our access to the road.

"Don't move," I say to Jessica. She reaches for the door handle anyway. "Stay inside!" I shout as I jump from the car.

The other driver has emerged as well. Our cars' headlights illuminate our arena.

Before I see the man's face, I notice the glints of metal. He holds a meat cleaver in his right hand and an ax in his left. Then I see the narrow eyes, the thick neck, the broad shoulders bared in his tank-top shirt.

Wee Willie Reckherd.

I also see that he is not wearing any pants. Just boxer shorts and running shoes. As if he was woken from sleep and grabbed what he could and ran out the door.

He looks menacing and unbalanced. I would bet that he was the weird-looking "homeless" man who approached Alice at Stark's. She would have recognized the guy who offered her five dollars for information on Samuel if she had just looked up at their wall of fame.

Willie's breath is a controlled pant; I can see the tension in his muscled forearms. From the car Jessica screams "I'm calling the police," but he shows no sign of caring. He crouches as he moves in, taking small but steady steps, keeping himself low.

"You or me," Willie murmurs in a high and soft voice. "You or me."

Then he lunges forward and swings the ax. I dodge to my right, and his other arm comes forward with the meat cleaver. I grab his arm in mid-blow and quickly shove him hard to the side. I can feel from the firmness of Willie's shoulders that his body is in better shape than his mind. He stumbles back but remains on his feet. I dart to the side to create space between us.

Willie's display of balance is unnerving. More than two decades removed from the game, he still has his reflexes and athletic instincts. And two bladed weapons firmly in his grip.

Then I see some sort of book fly through the air and hit Willie harmlessly in the shoulder. He turns toward my car. "Leave us alone, you crazy asshole," Jessica shouts.

The book, I see, is my Audi owner's manual, apparently the best weapon Jessica could find inside my car.

"Pop the trunk!" I call to Jessica. "Pop the trunk!"

The trunk door rises as Willie makes a hard run at me. I dodge to the right again—I remind myself to go left the next time, in case he is scouting my tendencies. After again side-stepping to open up some distance between us, I run for the trunk and grab the shovel I have stowed in there with my bag of practice balls.

Now I have a weapon, too. I raise the shovel, gripping hard on its handle with both hands, my heart pounding, every muscle awake. Willie and I face each other, and for a moment he stops in his crouch and assesses how this metal shovel might change the dynamics of our combat.

I calculate, too. And I realize that by making it harder for Willie to attack me up close, I've invited the former quarter-back to drop back and throw.

A second later Willie rears back his left hand and hurls the ax at me. It spins through the air and I jump to the left. The axe hits my car, clanking hard against it before it drops to the ground.

Willie charges me directly, the meat cleaver raised. I swing the shovel and hit him flush in the hand, knocking the cleaver to the ground.

He is without weapons. Now Jessica jumps out of the car. She circles around and presents herself legs wide, skinny arms up. She must have picked up this pose from a kickboxing class at the gym.

I move around, trying to place myself in between them, but before I can she attacks Willie with a roundhouse kick. He blocks it with a forearm, then swiftly grabs her by the neck and slams her face against the side window of his car, before she can even scream. Jessica drops limply to the ground.

I cannot check to see how hurt she is, because I have to

keep my eyes on the madman, but I do not hear any sound or movement coming from where she lies.

I swing my shovel again at the empty-handed Willie. My shot is angry and wild, and glances off his shoulder. He drives into my body, pushing me back against the hood of my car.

Then he punches me in the face. Which startles me, because despite working in a world of hard hits, I have never been punched in the face in my entire life.

And then Willie grabs my head and plunges his teeth into my neck. He is gnashing around, searching for my carotid artery.

I drop the shovel and stick my thumbs in Willie's eyes— not enough to gouge them out, just enough to force Willie to loosen his grip. He pulls back, and then I grab him by the shoulders and push him, driving hard with my legs, and this time he tumbles to the ground.

As Willie falls, I sneak a glance at Jessica and see that she is not moving.

I look at Willie and see a new problem. I accidentally shoved Willie toward where his ax was resting on the ground.

He picks it up. I back off, and he takes a couple of steps and throws wildly, with a near-sidearm motion. The ax sails high and wide. I hear it crash into the thicket of the woods.

Now Willie and I both scan the ground, trying to locate his remaining weapon, the meat cleaver. I see its blade catching the gleam of the headlights. Willie's eyes are on it, too. The cleaver is equidistant between us—about five yards in front of me and five yards to his left.

I visualize my next move as clearly as if a coach has drawn it out for me on a chalkboard with Xs and Os.

Willie lurches for the cleaver.

As he does, I let my muscle memory take over:

Step. Step. Step.

Kick.

I catch Willie just as he is bending down, and I punt him right in the jaw.

And I feel a pain more violent than I have never known. Lightning rockets up my leg and shoots straight through the top of my head. I feel like I have been split apart.

I stumble backward, helpless. I have kicked something I shouldn't have kicked—an object that is hard and fixed, rather than buoyant and untethered. Reeling, I make the merest attempt to put my right leg underneath me, only to feel it scream out. The leg is broken, ruined. And so am I.

I fall to the ground and howl in agony.

I am mere feet away from a man who is trying to kill me and who, as soon as he collects himself, will have a meat cleaver at his disposal and an immobilized prey before him. I am done. As a punter, as a living being on this Earth. I have been taken down by, of all people, Wee Willie Reckherd. Another wannabe quarterback who couldn't get his way.

I let my head fall to the ground and close my eyes. So this is where I have been leading myself all along. I exhale a cold breath and think of my dad, dying on his own poorly chosen road through the woods. Here I am, one last time, acting just like him.

CHAPTER 30

TANNER STANDS OVER me, his blue eyes relaxed. He likes to present himself as a man who knows it all, but at this moment he allows some surprise.

"There's no way around it, Nick," he says. "You saved our season. You're our MVP."

"Thanks, coach," I say. He has been here for a little more than ten minutes, but I am still adjusting to the weirdness of having Tanner standing in my living room, his hand resting on my armchair as I recline on the sofa. Not even the side effects of the Vicodin were this disorienting.

Tanner arrived alone at my door at precisely 10:00 A.M., per the appointment arranged by his secretary, and I know that he is slated to leave at 10:15. I glance at my phone, resting on my coffee table, and see it is now 10:14.

"I've got to get going," Tanner says. "Listen to the doctors, Nick, do your work, and you'll be back before you know it."

One minute left. Not an ideal amount of time, but I need to bring this up.

"Before you leave, coach," I say. "I have one question for you."

"Sure," he says, though he keeps his body half turned toward the door.

"It's about Selia Sault," I say.

Tanner's jaw tightens.

"What about her?" Tanner says, his voice quieter than usual.

"You didn't get her pregnant, did you?"

He looks down, head hanging. "I did not get her pregnant," he mutters. Then he turns and meets my gaze. "She told me she could handle it, but she couldn't. It was a mistake."

"She's nineteen," I say. "How could you think she has any idea what she can handle?"

Tanner glares. "It was a mistake," he repeats, biting off each word. "I will learn from it, and she will, too. I believe that. This is what life is, making mistakes and learning from them."

He glances at his phone.

"Good-bye, Nick. Get well soon." He turns his back to me and walks out, right on schedule.

I walk nowhere these days. I fractured my right fibula and sprained my right medial collateral ligament as a result of my kick to the head of Willie Reckherd. Jessica's nose was broken, though not too severely, and the bruising heals more every time I see her. Meanwhile, the doctors project that I will be dancing the tango—or at least, I will be physically capable of dancing the tango—by mid-September, a couple of weeks after the season begins. In the meantime, Woodward Tolley will be taking my place as the Sentinels' punter. I try not to go crazy at the thought of him running onto the field for our opening game while I sit and watch.

But for the most part I am enjoying my enforced downtime. My mother and Aaron have rented an apartment in the Jefferson for the month, and they bought a small outdoor barbecue and set it up on my balcony. She grills lunch here almost every afternoon—turkey burgers or chicken sausage or fish. Some days, I smell the charcoal and I ride the sense memories back to the summers of my childhood, when my mom would grill at the house we would rent for a couple of weeks on the shores of Lake Cayuga.

Then I see Aaron sitting on my sofa, reading *The Atlantic* magazine while absent-mindedly scratching his inner thigh, and I jolt back to the present.

I have been receiving people just about every day—Freddie, Jessica, and at least half the Sentinels roster have dirtied my rugs over the last few weeks. My teammates freely describe me with a word I have come to loathe—*hero*. It fits so poorly with what I have learned about what happened out in the woods, on what Freddie now likes to refer to as the Night of the Punter.

In Willie Reckherd I know that I confronted not a man gone bad, but a mind gone wrong. I could see it his eyes that night, when he came at me in his underwear, swinging his blades, biting my throat. Science has since confirmed it.

My kick snapped the neck of Willie Reckherd. He died instantly. The autopsy afterward revealed extensive brain damage, believed to be the result of having sustained multiple head injuries while playing the game. His thoughts had darkened, and he had lost his impulse control. I could not celebrate what I had done to Wee Willie because the man wasn't evil. He was injured.

And how did he receive this injury? By living by the same creed that I and so many other players did, that you play through the hurt. *It's just pain.*

With many former players, brain damage leads to suicide. In the case of Willie Reckherd, he turned his violence outward—with his choice of target becoming more inevitable, the more I learned about his final months.

Rabidly competitive all his life, Willie has been a demanding restaurant boss in the best of times. But in the past couple of years at the Rib Revue, he had made the transition from hard-ass to asshole. If a table wasn't cleared promptly, or if he saw thumbprints on a brass rail, Willie would dress down his employees in front of his customers. Among the locals, Wee Willie's quickly became known as a place to witness an unpleasant scene.

After a point, Willie's partner—Gordon, who I met at the Rib Revue that night—convinced the marquee attraction to stay away from the restaurant. But still, Willie was living his life in Berry and getting into yelling matches with bank tellers and supermarket checkout girls. You tell enough locals to fuck off and there goes the profits.

So Willie became a disreputable figure in the town where he was once adored, and his restaurant was falling into unprofitability. Then there was Luke, who went to Willie's old school, who wore his number, and who was going to become the quarterback Willie never had the chance to be. Until Samuel Sault came along and sent his boy to the hospital not once, but twice. It would have been hard enough for him to see Luke get cut by the Hartsburg Hyenas, but Luke made it even worse by telling Willie he was going away to live in an ashram in the Kentucky hills and study meditation and healing—which, to Willie's old-school ears, was about one step short of Luke saying he was going to Sweden to begin treatments for gender reassignment surgery.

Then Willie turned on the TV and saw a press conference trumpeting Samuel's arrival in Philadelphia, and his $64 million contract. He grabbed his rifle and drove to Philadelphia and visited, among other places, Stark's, which he knew from his playing days, and enlisted a waitress as his sentry.

After the shooting, Gordon figured out what had happened. He confronted his childhood friend and business partner, and Willie confessed every detail. Gordon took Willie's gun from him, mostly out of fear that Willie would kill himself. He stayed by Willie's side, on a suicide watch. Then Alice called Willie's phone, threatening blackmail; Gordon spoke to her and offered her money in exchange not just for silence but reports. Our champagne picnic, it seems, was part of Alice's reconnaissance work, a chance to debrief an eyewitness. And when it was clear that I had seen nothing and the police were focusing their attention on Jai, Gordon realized he had an opportunity to throw suspicion off Willie permanently. He executed the frame-up to save his friend and his business.

The importance of Samuel in Willie's imagination—the extent to which he had made Samuel the scapegoat for all his son's shortcomings—became clearer when I received a letter from Luke Reckherd. Although "received" is the wrong word, because the letter was not delivered to me. Luke wrote me an open letter—which, like an open relationship, can leave you wondering exactly whom the openness is supposed to benefit, besides the person who suggested it. He posted his message on his Facebook page. Actually, it was on the Facebook page of his ashram.

But its tone, at least, was welcome.

> *Dear Nick Gallow,*
>
> *I write to you from a place of peace and understanding, a place in which people use their strength not to conquer and hurt, but to help and heal. I believe this is a needed antidote, the yin to the yang of the life I have led.*
>
> *The first time Samuel Sault injured me in college, my father guided my rehabilitation, and he motivated me with hate. He placed pictures of Samuel on my mirror and told me that Samuel symbolized all that I must overcome. Then Samuel hurt me again, and his message became more intense, more unhealthy. I was supposed to be angry at Samuel, but by this time, I was really angry*

at my father for this mission he was forcing on me. So I tried to ruin his plans indirectly. I would smoke pot on the library steps and get busted, but the school would keep giving me second chances, and my father would push me harder still.

Even after I was cut by the Hyenas, my dad wouldn't let it go. So I let him go. I told him his demons were his, not mine. I said this without realizing how many demons he had.

I want nothing more than to heal. I am still learning how much I have to overcome. My dad had wounds that couldn't be let go of, but I believe I can let go of mine. Nick, I hope you can as well. I want you to know that I bear you no ill will.

Namaste, Luke Reckherd

Jessica comes by regularly enough that I am able to monitor the slow fading of the darkness that Willie's blow left around her eyes. On her first visit, she came in the company of her husband, Dan. She and I never did get to exchange notes about our wishes for the future, but showing up with Dan was message enough. He was wearing a sports coat, despite it being a warm Saturday when he visited.

"It's so nice to finally meet you," he said. "Even though all we did is exchange e-mails, can I tell people that I knew you when?"

To see Jessica together with her husband that day disturbed me more than I thought it might. He was wispy and physically weak, as I had seen in pictures, but in person he radiated a confidence and ease that was its own kind of strength. Jessica had talked about Dan so dismissively, for the most part, that I had come to picture them as two predatory animals at opposite sides of a cage. But seeing them side-by-side, occupying the same space so easily, he unthinkingly placing his hand on her arm when he asks her a question, and she not minding at all—they bore an uncomfortably close resemblance to a happy couple. Their marriage was missing something, obviously. But not everything.

"Sure," I told Dan. "Drop my name. Why not?"

"I feel embarrassed about those e-mails I sent you," Dan said, smiling sheepishly. "Invitations for dinner and all. As if I didn't have some ulterior motive. I should have just come out and asked you what I wanted to ask. You probably guessed it from the very first."

I looked at Dan expectantly, waiting for him to fill in the blank.

"Tickets," Dan said. "I wanted to see if you could get me a block of tickets to the Washington game in October. I had this idea that I was going to invite the Open Market Committee staff up here. You wouldn't believe how crazy the guys down in DC get about football."

"Oh, I'd believe it," I said, almost disappointed it was all so simple. "Here's what I'll do for you, Dan. I promise that if I play for the Sentinels this season, I'll round up every ticket for you I can." His eyes lit up. And this is a guy who helps manage the largest economy in the world. I would have been able to really make Dan's day by hooking him up with DaFrank Burns, but unfortunately DaFrank is no longer in Washington. He was cut after his team's minicamp. He's now hoping to hook on in Miami.

"But you have to be back with the team, right?" Dan said, concerned. "The Sentinels can't cut you. After all you've done, that would be a PR disaster for them. They wouldn't do that just to get a little bit better a punter, would they?"

A little bit better a punter. Such an insignificant position. This, in the middle of asking me for a favor.

"I wouldn't put anything past anyone at this point," I said.

Dan leaned in close, but not too close.

"They don't know, do they?" he whispered. No one else was in the room besides he and Jessica, but he seemed to think what he was saying was just too scandalous to say in full voice.

That darn Jessica. She had definitely been watching too many *Three's Company* reruns. But I guess telling her husband I was gay is, at this point, the entirely predictable explanation she would offer up to explain her jaunt to Maryland with another man.

"You'd be surprised how blind people can be," I told Dan, "to what's going on right in front of them."

"True dat," Dan said, and then grinned at Jessica, like the phrase was part of some long-running in-joke between them. "True dat."

Jessica has come back several times since then, and without Dan. We haven't so much as touched each other in these visits, and she seems afraid to even sit next to me on the sofa. But that's okay.

I've heard athletes say what they love about sports is the certainty it offers: you know the rules, you know who the winner is, and you know when the game is over. The best thing about life, I think, is that there are no rules and, as long you have your breath, you still have a shot. The game never ends.

I receive come-ons from agents who want me as a client. I ignore them all, even though I do need new representation. When Cecil came to visit me, I fired him.

"I will always be thankful for what you've done for me," I told him as he stood at my bedside. "But your betting could have ruined both of us, and you knew it, and you did it anyway."

Cecil put up the facade, at least, of a man who knew how to take a loss.

"It's funny that you're letting me go now," he said, with an effort at a smile. "So soon before your $350,000 bonus is due."

I am going to collect that bonus, too. Udall has assured me of this, even though I am currently on the team's physically-unable-to-perform list.

"When you get your percentage," I told Cecil, "please put it in the bank."

The offers I have coming from the other agents are entirely credible—I now have the attention of the biggest sharks in the ocean. But for now, at least, I am toying with the idea of representing myself.

I receive a postcard from Alice. The front reads GREET-INGS FROM INDIANA, and it has no return address; the postmark I trace to a town chiefly of note for being on Inter-state 70. She congratulates me, apologizes for her lies, and says, "I wish I knew a better way to make money."

I have received plenty of gifts, the strangest of which was from Jai. He delivered it personally, with the help of his min-ions.

"Hangman, you are about to see how JC takes care of people who take care of him," Jai said, standing in the door-way, a day after I came home.

I heard a ruckus from outside and leaned forward on my crutches and looked down the hallway. There I saw Too Big to Fail and Cheat Sheet—the latter struggling considerably—carrying what looked like a coffin, except its exterior was fab-ric, and purple. As they brought it near, I saw that it was decorated with a painting of Jai, nude, aping the pose of Da

Vinci's *Vitruvian Man*, but with starbursts all around him. One starburst was strategically placed between his legs.

"Do I even want to know?" I asked.

"This, Mr. Gallow," Jai said, with a beatific gleam, "is your new best friend. This is JC's personal hyperbaric chamber."

I had heard of players using these chambers, which are supposed to spur cell development and speed the healing process. The science behind them isn't completely verified, but many players swear by them.

"This baby is the whole key to JC being JC," Jai explained. "I spend an hour in here every day. You pop out of one of these, you're all ready to get your game on. Even if there ain't no game, if you know what I mean. It helps every inch of you recover. You get me, right?"

"I believe so, yes," I said.

"And the best part about this baby is, it's got speakers inside, too," Jai said. "Top-of-the-line shit. It's rigged so that the second the lid closes, *Sack Dance* is coming at you in quadraphonic stereo."

Sack Dance is Jai's R&B album, a collection of soporific screw songs he released a couple of years back. The single was called, regrettably, "Puttin' in the Dime Package."

"Spend an hour a day in here, and you will cut your recovery time by thirty percent," Jai said.

The chamber was the ghastliest and most tasteless gift with which I have ever been presented. But I accepted it, because the math was irresistible. If it really cut my recovery time by as much as Jai said, I could be back for Week One. I have been using it daily, ever since my noise-canceling headphones arrived in the mail.

After the drop-off I invited the guys to stay for lunch, and they did. My mom grilled for the whole crew.

As we ate together that day, I couldn't help but think of my dad. Even though he didn't care much for Jai's antics, he was openly in awe of him as a linebacker. He would have loved to share burgers and beer with the former Defensive Player of the Year. Instead, it was Aaron who ate with us. He actually asked Jai which position he played.

But it's like the coaches say. No use thinking about the guys who aren't here. Play with the ones who are.

It is the day before training camp, and I am feeling more restless than I have in my entire recuperation. I know that tomorrow the news will be overrun with images of my teammates running around without me. Freddie comes by at two in the afternoon, as he has more or less every day. On these visits he brings an old Xbox with him and hooks it up to my television, and then he takes the console with him when he goes, at my insistence.

"I think maybe I should let you keep this baby from here on out," Freddie says as he connects it into the back of my television. He is wearing white cargo shorts and a green Presidente beer T-shirt.

"Nah," I say. "I'd rather only play it when you're around."

"Thank you, Nick, for walking directly into my segue," Freddie says as he joins me on the sofa. "Because I'm not going to be around. I'm leaving for a while."

He hadn't mentioned anything like this. I search Freddie's eyes for a coming punch line, but I see none. "What's up?" I ask.

"Being in that law office, Hangman, made me realize I would be happier if I was doing work of my own." He does not seem embarrassed to have realized this for the first time in his early thirties.

"You going to take the bar exam again?"

"No, no, no," he says with a dismissive wave of the hand. "Fuck the bar exam, fuck the legal profession, fuck all that. For now, anyway. But I want to do something different. I have a book idea. Travel guides. I want to write a whole series of them. Here's my title: *If I Were a Pervert*: *A Guide to Going Away and Getting Away with It*. The books will be for straitlaced people who go on vacation and do nutty things they would never do at home. And I'll tell them how to do it. I'll direct them to the wildest party scenes in Cabo, the best bath houses of Japan, identify the European brothels that feature women who are, in fact, women. Or not, whatever the readers prefer.

"I came up with the idea in the pantry at the law office. I was telling some of my travel stories and the lawyers were just amazed. They couldn't stop asking me questions."

"Way to impress the partners, buddy." If Freddie ever did pass the bar, there was one place he would never be hired.

"If nothing else, I'll enjoy the research," Freddie says. "Anyway, I'm leaving tomorrow for Morocco, and I don't know when I'll be back."

The start screen is up for the game Freddie has chosen—ice hockey—and it idles there as our controllers rest on our laps.

"Why Morocco?" I ask.

"For one, it's supposed to have an amazing hash scene," he says. "And it's beautiful, allegedly. But the main reason is, I've never been there. So even if I don't end up actually writing the books . . ."

"Freddie," I say. "Don't tell me you're envisioning quitting before you even get on the plane."

"It's not so much that I'm considering quitting," Freddie says coolly, "as that I'm factoring in a realistic possibility. I am, after all, me."

"You have a point there."

Freddie laughs. "You should join me," he says, nudging my elbow.

By way of answer I pick up a crutch from beside the sofa and tap at the baby blue soft cast in which my leg is encased.

"I'm healing," I say. "I actually think Jai's hyperbaric chamber is working."

Freddie smiles but shakes his head. "I have long since given up telling you what to do," he says. "But one day, when you're locked in your health coffin over there, trying not to listen to music that you hate, and you think of me on the beach, just know you can join me any time you want." Freddie cocks an eyebrow. "You and me, Hangman. Morocco. It could be an all-time classic."

"I'll think about it," I say. And I will consider it, this lark, because I've said I would, even though joining him in Morocco would require me torpedoing my career, putting my obsessions in cold storage, letting go of all that I have spent my life building. It's a change that's almost impossible to imagine, except that there's no reason I can't actually do it.

Who, exactly, would I be disappointing?

But even in thinking about it for these few seconds I already know that I won't be going anywhere, because I have a better dream: being back for Week One.

My leg is healing quickly, I can feel it, and that "health coffin," as Freddie terms it, is helping. When I am in there I close my eyes and I can visualize my future. I will be on that field, ten yards back, counting the men in front of me. That first snap will arrive in my outstretched hands. I will punt the ball, and everything will be perfect.

ACKNOWLEDGMENTS

In expressing gratitude to the people who helped bring *Hangman's Game* to life, I must begin with Jennifer Weiner. Without her encouragement, I would have never undertaken this project in earnest. She's the best.

Joanna Pulcini has been a tremendous agent, teacher, and friend. In Joanna's office, Katherine Hennes was a shining star. Thanks to Rosemary Ahern and Ken Salikoff, for their readings and counsel.

At Thomas Dunne Books, Toni Kirkpatrick edited *Hangman's Game* with great care and insight. Jennifer Letwack has been a pleasure to work with. Thanks to Jane Liddle, for her sterling copyediting, and also to David Rotstein, Kenneth J. Silver, Shailyn Tavella, Cathy Turiano, Kelsey Lawrence, Melissa Hastings, and Paul Hochman.

Doctors David Patchefsky and Elizabeth Hexner helped with medical matters. I learned much about punting from a phone conversation with the great Sean Landeta. I must thank my friends at the best sports publication the world has ever known, *Sports Illustrated*. It was on an assignment for the magazine several years ago that I attended a Colts practice, noticed Hunter Smith throwing to linebackers during an interception drill, and thought, "Wow, punters really do have a lot of free time."

For years Joe Vinciguerra and I have talked about story

ideas, usually his, and we continued that hallowed tradition with *Hangman's Game*. Though the details are hazy, I believe Joe was also one of the guys in the room, along with Steve, Will, Jack, Rollo, Tubbe, and possibly others, when we were watching a game all those years ago, and we joked about how the Jets' punter, Nick Gallery, had a name that sounded like it should belong to a private detective. That was a good time.